TALULAH'S PIE

A novel

ERIC REDMON

FELICIA GROS

Karie,
Continue to spread good ripples
wherever you go!
Felicia & Eric

First published in the United States of America in 2020 by Eric Redmon & Felicia Gros.

Paperback first published in 2020 by Eric Redmon & Felicia Gros.

ISBN: 978-0-5787-2039-5

This special book, we dedicate to five
wonderful human beings
who have made our lives so meaningful.
They are our legacy and our hearts live on through them.

~Our Children~
~Bret Andrew Redmon~
~Carrie Elizabeth Herbaugh~
~Caitlin Elise Cowen~
~Evelyn Catherine Cowen~
~Maxwell Ridley Cowen~

Having you all in our lives is a light
that can never be extinguished!

With eternal love.

ACKNOWLEDGMENTS

First and foremost, we thank God almighty for this amazing world filled with endless stories. We humans can be a mess at times, but I believe we're all getting better. We just need a little more time. Each of us, though, is a source of a great story.

This book would not be what it is without the input of my wife and co-author, Felicia Gros. She mellows my words and softens my outlook on life. Working together with me from the inception of *Talulah's Pie,* Felicia graced our cover with her beautiful artwork. Her art depicts what the character, Marie, painted, as an interpretation of what Talulah's bakery could be.

Special thanks to Felicia's mother and my mother-in-law, Kathleen Gros for evaluation of the original script. Also, Susan Jones, our faithful friend, and neighbor provided her input. Both helped forge a rough manuscript into a polished novel, with valuable critique.

Thanks to Carrie Herbaugh, who used her magical eye to capture the cover art and back cover photo in digital form. Carrie is my treasured daughter, now grown into an awesome mother, wife, and career woman.

Talulah's Pie is the third book that Laura Read helped us to transform. An author herself, as well as an editor and freelance designer, Laura turned Felicia's art and Carrie's photo of it into the cover for this book. Laura also formatted the book for digital release and publication. Thank you so much.

Finally, a hearty thanks to our readers and your search for a story worthy of your valuable time. We have written characters who will come alive as you read. Our greatest wish is for you to enjoy them as much as we have. Reading about them might also reveal little parts of our hearts.

Eric Redmon
Winchester, Virginia
2020

"Let today be a day where you take nothing for granted. For life is fleeting, fragile and precious and can change on a whim. Say all the things you really want to say to your loved ones today, say the things you would regret should they pass on and your words remain unspoken. Rejoice, for you and they are alive today – and should you or them pass on to unknown shores, rejoice even more for you have a wonderful love story to tell."

~Jackson Kiddard~

TALULAH'S PIE

PROLOGUE

Could it be a myth that conscious awareness originates in the brain alone? Is it naïve to believe the possibility that our heart, a muscle the size of two fists, might hold the key to unlock the infinite array of human emotion? Some believe that our brains work with our body, especially the heart, to influence perception, cognition, and emotional processing.

Did you know that your heart starts working long before you are born, with each beat sending life-sustaining nourishment to every cell? Each compression supplies every organ, including the brain, through a complicated series of blood vessels. One heartbeat is strong enough to send blood along a course of sixty-two thousand miles, a fantastic feat repeated one-hundred-thousand times a day.

The heart is in control of our destiny, and when it stops… our physical body is no more.

Eyes can see, noses can smell, ears can hear, and our skin can sense pain and protect us, but our hearts are so much more: they aren't just symbolic; they tell the world who we are.

Speaking of the heart, are you familiar with the origin of Valentine's Day? Saint Valentine wasn't fictional. He was a real person who opened his heart and shared his beliefs with all people he encountered. Even in prison, awaiting his execution for refusing to convert to Roman paganism, they say that he healed Julia, the blind daughter of his jailor. Then, on the night before his execution, he wrote the first "Valentine card", addressed to her. She was no longer blind, and he signed it as "Your Valentine".

So, it was, that from a mere man who would later become a Saint, Valentine's Day was born, and every year on February 14th, many hearts become filled with optimism. New love, hopes of continued or rekindled love; all offer wishes for hearts to merge. It is a day like no other and began as a tribute to one who loved people he met unconditionally.

Sometimes, the harder we look for a mate, the more elusive they become. But just bide your time. Someday, when you least expect it, someone will cross paths with you. It could happen anywhere at any time. At school or work, or you might find yourself at a party, alone and lonely. Then, suddenly, someone who realizes you are by yourself walks up and makes you feel welcome. Love, our most cherished and powerful emotion, begins with a small spark sent from one heart to another. You never know when that spark will happen, but remain patient with the belief that God works in mysterious ways.

Marie and Paul lived for eighteen years without each other. As they began their first year of college, both were unaware that love might cross their path. At first, it was the furthest thing from their minds. But, they were powerless to stop what their hearts were lacking. The heart has no problem convincing the mind of its desire. Like many relationships, Paul and Marie's began by chance… or did it?

I

FALL SEMESTER - 1978

Savannah was one week into her first year at Tulane Law when her brother, Paul, and their parents arrived in New Orleans. Paul was ready to begin his freshman year at Tulane. Their parents had graduated from this esteemed school years before, as did Savannah this past spring.

Paul was ready to fly on his own. He packed sparingly, knowing he'd be sharing his dorm room with another student. When they arrived, the other student wasn't there yet, and seeing the size of this room; Paul was happy to have traveled light. He hoped his roommate was easy to get along with because they would soon be falling over each other in this small space.

Paul loved his family and was thankful to be attending this school. He didn't take for granted how privileged he was to be here. His father had worked hard and was a successful physician in their hometown of New Roads, Louisiana.

He was unusually close to his entire family but was ready to usher his parents back to their car after they finished unloading. As he told them goodbye, only tears of joy and thankfulness appeared. The path moving forward thrilled him. He quickly returned to his room to unpack.

Education is multifaceted. It involves learning about the world around you, as well as about yourself. While placing his clothes in the dresser, he was unaware that his horizon was about to be broadened in ways he'd never imagined. Someone else was arriving today, also as an incoming freshman: a person that would forever change his life.

Marie, an only child, was also dropped off today. She and her parents arrived from Morgan City, Louisiana. Solidly bonded to her mother; they would miss each other tremendously. Affection for her father was more related to him being a good provider. She would not miss him personally. Although very successful as a shrimping company owner, he had become increasingly possessive of his daughter. For that reason alone, she was ecstatic to be here for a fresh start.

It wasn't until the week before the deadline to register that her father agreed that she could enroll and move away from home. One of his stipulations for her was a private room. He wasn't sure about her, as he said, "rooming with some girl I've never met".

Marie was thrilled with the thought of a place to herself. In her mind, having no roommate meant she would have more space, so she packed anything and everything she might need. It was a lot. Her art supplies were a priority. Then, clothes for all seasons were needed, casual and formal. Make-up and accessories… let's just say that their car was packed full. Her father, already upset with his little girl leaving home, had threatened to pull his small fishing boat behind the car to transport all her things. Humiliated by the thought of arriving at school with a fishing boat in tow, Marie painfully tempered her needs. Still, she utilized every spare inch of her father's sedan to transport her necessities.

It was quite a shock when she turned the key and pushed the door open to her dorm room. Marie was horrified: it was as small as a closet. As her father flipped on the light, it was the first time in months she'd heard him laugh.

As he stepped inside, he said, "I told you not to pack so many things!"

Marie wanted to cry but refused. Her mother patted her on the shoulders from behind.

❧

Across campus, Paul didn't know Marie existed, nor would he have cared, for the moment. Finding a mate was the furthest thing from both of their minds. They arrived today with a similar focus on their futures. Neither had the slightest urge to find someone to date, much less become a soulmate. But love has no concern with any person's timeline. It is everywhere and requires no formal place to happen. Amore calls the shots. It wouldn't be long until these two young people felt something they had never felt before in this experiment called love.

Falling in love is no different than any science experiment. Like any trial, it begins with only the *potential* for success: not a guarantee. Relationships, like chemical reactions, can, and do, end abruptly. The first requirement of any successful test is the combination of the right ingredients. Only time would tell for these two young people. First, they had to come together.

Monday morning came at last. These two young souls prepared themselves for the first class of their college careers, and at 8 am, events would begin that would rock their world. Most people meet hundreds, perhaps thousands of others in their lifetime. The majority of those we meet linger only briefly in our lives. With eighteen other students, the odds remained remote that Marie and Paul would share anything more than awkward glances. But *love* had other ideas.

❧

At the beginning of the first day, their teacher, Ms. Oglethorpe, introduced her students to procedural information and their obligations. Marie, arriving late, and having missed that part, didn't notice that her teacher stopped talking until she was seated. After plopping her notebook down on the desk, Marie continued to stand as she noisily rummaged her hands around her purse, searching for a pen. Finally, she sat, only to find Ms. O. and the rest of the class staring at her. Then, Ms. O. continued from where she was interrupted, informing all that this would be a fast-moving course.

Paul, in his element, was anxious to move past this required course to pursue the advanced literature classes his English major offered. His last class as a senior in high school was much more challenging than this. The ease of this transition allowed him time to adjust to university life.

Marie viewed the same class differently. For her, this was Hell. This course had nothing to do with Art, and she saw it as a required waste of time. The last thing in the world that interested her was having to suffer through reading and interpreting "the hard to read and impossible to understand writings of dead people". Later in the evening, that is what she told her parents during a phone call home. She saw no possible usefulness that might come from this "painful ordeal". Her father bit his tongue while her mother patiently listened as she said, "I swear Mom, our professor looks like one of the people in the stories she is forcing us to read! She is pale as a ghost herself, and seems completely unsympathetic about her students!" Before hanging up, she reiterated, "I can't wait to do something in my major!"

Her father, when he did speak, always provided a blunt perspective, saying, "You can't get to your major if you don't pass this class, Marie. And don't forget, if you flunk out of there, you're going to have to come work with me. I can't keep a secretary in my office."

Problem was, he also had a way of running secretaries off. He seemed to expect too much from everyone. But Marie knew he meant what he said, and those words would not be forgotten.

Like a child that signs the dotted line at a military recruiting station, Marie would soon learn that she would have to handle this on her own. Although she could call them to unload, her parents couldn't solve this problem for her.

Wednesday, was the second day of their shared course. Marie was late again. This class reminded her of receiving a "time out" as a child. Even a minute of this punishment seemed like a year. *This is torture,* she thought.

At the end of this class, all sat quietly as Ms. Oglethorpe posted the first project on the blackboard. It read:

It is 1851. A highly respected newspaper employs you and assigned you the task of critically reviewing the short story that was written by an exciting new writer, T.S. Arthur, "An Angel in Disguise." Provide a comprehensive critique and the rationale for your view in a style fitting of the time.

Length: 300 words. Due after Labor Day on Wednesday morning, Sept. 6, on arrival.

After writing this on the blackboard, Ms. O. wiped the chalk from her hands on a towel, then turned toward her students and said, "Beyond our cursory discussion here today, there will be no further explanation given for this first assignment. I know it is a tough one, but I want to get a feel for the aptitude of this class."

Paul folded his arms together and sat back in his desk, smiling as he thought, *piece of cake.* This assignment was an easy one for him. He glanced around the room, taking note of the other student's reactions. Most appeared resigned to the request. Then, his eyes settled on a girl on the other side of the room. She looked panicked as she scribbled the details in a notebook hurriedly.

He had noticed her the first day for more than one reason, her long blonde hair always in a ponytail; her entrance, always late. Most people, including him, sat in the same spot in each class. She did too, but only because it was the only unoccupied seat when she arrived. So far, she maintained a perfect record: late both times.

The girl was pretty, and she seemed to know it. She also made it evident to all that she couldn't give a rat's ass about this class. Her entrance, no earlier than five minutes after class began, caused Ms. O.

to stop talking with the interruption. The girl was oblivious to the sudden silence from the podium when she arrived, as well as the scowl offered by Ms. Oglethorpe. As the rest of the class turned to gawk, she waltzed in, loudly dropped her books on the desk, then sat. She was brash, no doubt.

Now, what she saw on the board appeared to have caught her attention. Paul couldn't help but notice the eyes of "Little Miss Always Late". They were bugged out and unblinking as she gawked at the blackboard with obvious horror.

He chuckled to himself. It was quite a show, and he was happy he'd looked in her direction to see it. He imagined what he'd write if given the assignment to describe her eyes at this moment. It would read something like: "*Suddenly, the requested task shoved her off 'I don't give a shit peak' and plopped her firmly into 'Oh shit valley.'*"

As Ms. O. finished her encouraging words, the wide-eyed girl suddenly commanded collective heads to turn as she began a coughing-sneezing fit. Everyone stared at this disruptive student sitting in the last seat of the back row. Nobody knew what to do. Even the teacher was at a loss of words, as everyone wondered what was happening.

Embarrassed, the girl rose from her seat and ran from the class, leaving her belongings on the desk.

Something had triggered her response, and Paul wondered what it was. *Was it stress? Could that have set her off?* She intrigued him. His mixed feelings made it unclear if he should feel sorry for her or happy that she, and her distractions, were gone.

Just before dismissal, she slipped quietly back through the door, collected her things, and left.

❧

Essays were turned in the next Wednesday as requested. Paul flourished with the ease of this class and was ready for Ms. O. to step up the pace. Grades for the first assignment were expected today.

Paul knew he had done well before turning in his paper and was not surprised when Ms. O. returned it with an "A+. Well done!"

He watched as the teacher passed down each aisle, wordlessly handing out the papers to each student. "Little Miss," his new personal nickname for her, sat in her usual seat. No sooner had Ms. O. placed her essay on the desk, that the girl began another coughing-sneezing fit. Like before, it sent her scurrying from the room. Again, she left without grabbing the paper or her books from her spot. Seconds later, the bell rang outside, signaling the end of the class.

Paul was in no hurry to leave, and within a few moments, he was the only person remaining. He was curious if what the teacher placed in front of her was the cause of her visceral reaction. Hesitantly standing, Paul grabbed his knapsack and walked directly to her desk. He thought, *this assignment had been so easy, surely the girl had done well.*

Curiosity overpowered his usual shyness and hesitation to snoop. His feet led him directly to her desk, where he stood gawking at her essay. On it, he read, "D-minus. Please apply yourself with greater zeal on the next assignment."

Paul was shocked. This poor girl was off to a terrible start.

Suddenly, he heard the classroom door open. Before he could look up, he knew who had just caught him violating her personal space.

He backed up a step, raised his head, and saw her standing just inside the door, glaring at him. Paul braced himself for the worst.

Shocked by what she had seen, Marie indignantly blurted, "Excuse me? I don't believe anyone gave you permission to look, much less stare at my paper."

Paul's voice cracked with embarrassment, "Please forgive me. I had no right. You left so quickly." He felt the urge to run but resisted. Embarrassed, he shrugged his shoulders and said, "You left your things behind… I was concerned."

She didn't respond. Feeling unsteady on her feet, she collapsed into the desk closest to the door and proceeded to shove her face into the palms of her hands.

Paul stood by, motionless, as she began to cry obnoxiously. Although it wasn't often that he heard someone cry like this, it hadn't been long enough since the last time.

One of his sister's friends referred to this as a "nasty cry". Her wailing was so loud that if a fire alarm had gone off in the hall, they couldn't have heard it.

Growing up with a sister had been an eye-opening experience for Paul. Each time he thought he had his sister figured out, she morphed into some unknown person. The roller coaster gyrations especially took root during the teen years when boys and the first pimple arrived. To him, women were a kaleidoscope of emotions that no man would ever be intelligent or powerful enough to understand. At a young age, he had come to the belief that there were certain things in the universe that he would never comprehend, and he was okay with it.

In his brief experience, nasty crying was loud, "I don't care whose ears I hurt," inconsolable crying. Without a chauvinistic or judgmental bone in his body, he found this term relevant to his prior experiences with the female species. He also found himself woefully unprepared for what he faced now as this bereaved woman gave nasty crying a whole new meaning.

After a minute, the sobbing slowed as she caught her breath and haltingly said, "I was an honor student in my high school class. I've never even made a 'C' in my entire life."

The wailing resumed with added vigor. She looked up at him for only a moment, possibly checking to see if he was still there, then threw her face back into her hands. Tears and other secretions mixed into a mess on the desktop.

Paul, feeling beyond helpless, looked around and spotted a box of tissues on the teacher's podium. He moved quickly toward them. Fumbling his way through the gauntlet of desks, he bumped one, causing it to teeter over, banging into the floor. It surprised him that this sudden crash didn't faze nasty cry land. He reached the tissues and extracted a handful.

As he approached her, the crying began to ease. She raised her reddened face to see him holding a paper cloth carefully in her direction, from arm's length.

She lowered her guard only enough to snatch this inadequate

apology from him. Then, she demanded, "I need more." Paul, remaining at a safe distance, extended the rest of the tissues to her.

She proceeded to blow her nose in a very unflattering way. *What did it matter*, she thought, *this guy is cute, but he'll probably never speak to me again.*

It took a little while, but when her breathing slowed, the silence allowed him time to consider what to say. Through stiff lips, he offered, "It's just the first paper, and for someone who's not an English major, I'm sure it was intimidating."

There was no response.

Paul waited a moment, fearing he had added insult to injury, then added, "You're not an English major, *are you?*"

The silence continued as Marie looked at the desk with a wet top in front of her. Using the tissues to wipe up the mess, she cast an eye to the other desk where her paper and books remained. A feeling of humiliation washed over her. Not only had this guy seen her terrible grade, but she had just shown him her worst side too. Humble pie seemed warranted, and that feeling surprised her. She'd never felt this way before, thinking, *he seems genuinely concerned.*

"I guess this was my welcome to college. I hate this class, and it was so embarrassing to receive that grade. I'm sorry you had to see me act this way. My name is Marie. Marie Landry."

"I'm Paul Morel."

What happened next surprised him. This girl, who was hysterical only moments before, stood and extended her hand to him. She wanted to shake his.

Recalling the large volume of nasal secretions that he'd witnessed only moments prior, he hesitated before bravely grasping her hand as he said, "Nice to meet you, Marie."

"Are you an English major, Paul?"

"Yes."

"I assume you made a better grade than I did?"

"Yes."

"Like the best?"

"Yes."

"Could I pay you to tutor me on this next assignment?"

"No."

Without responding, Marie turned away and walked to her desk. On arrival, she scooped up her things. As she turned around, Paul could see tears again.

He needed to say something quickly. "I didn't mean I wouldn't tutor you. I was just saying you couldn't pay me. It'd be an honor to help you, Marie."

Immediately, the tears dried up. Marie turned abruptly to walk away as Paul stood watching in disbelief. As she reached the door, she spun around with a massive smile on her face to say, "I'm going to read this next assignment first, then when we see each other Monday, I'll give you my number so we can meet. Maybe you'd at least let me buy you dinner?"

The door closed behind her, allowing Paul to take a breath finally. He closed his eyes and thought, *Lord, get me the number of that Mack truck...*

2

LEARNING AND YEARNING

Marie couldn't believe how much of her time this English class was tying up. Luckily, her other courses of French, Algebra, and European History came more naturally to her.

After finishing her classes on Thursday of the next week, she devoted her entire evening to this latest assignment from her "friend," Ms. O.

She pulled out her notebook and turned to the scribbled text:

Read: "A Haunted House," by Virginia Woolf. By Monday, September 18th, submit a 250-word synopsis comparing the two families inhabiting the house.

Marie shook her head. Her first thought was, *who comes up with crap like this? Life is too short!*

Procrastinating, she placed the opened notebook on the table with the library book she'd checked out from the library. *I can't believe I have to do this,* she thought, turning toward her small refrigerator to pour a glass of unsweetened tea. After a sip, Marie reluctantly sat to read.

The book checked out from the library was *Monday or Tuesday,* written by Virginia Woolf. It was a collection of eight short stories, including the assignment. Marie began the most straightforward part of the task ahead, reading the 700-word short story.

Luckily, only a glass of tea long, Marie closed the book and considered herself mentally done with Virginia Woolf for the evening. She came to the quick decision that her time would be spent more wisely in the French lab, which would be open for about another hour.

Not being a person who admitted defeat readily, Marie rationalized that she was nowhere near the point of allowing this one class to conquer her, despite her dislike of it. She would just put it off a while longer. Grabbing her French book and keys, Marie walked away from the evil notebook, headed to parlez vous some Français.

As she walked out of the dorm, personal reflection caused an admission; winning this battle with Ms. O. and English Lit would require her to sacrifice more bodies at the front lines. Paul immediately came to mind.

❧

Friday was the last class before the assignment was due. Faithfully late, Marie endured the awkward silence always provided for her entrance and sat in her usual place. Still avoiding eye contact with the teacher, she glanced at the left side of the class and found Paul in his spot. Breathing a sigh of relief that he was there, she heard Ms. O. proceed with the lecture, which didn't sound at all helpful in regards to the assignment. Some nonsense about metaphors and similes.

The hour-long class seemed to last a week today. As soon as Ms. O. finished talking and turned to leave, Marie dashed over to where Paul was collecting his things.

As he looked up to greet her, he smiled and said, "Hello Marie. So, what is your verdict? I'm assuming you've read the assignment; do you still need help?"

Mocking the lecture today with her attempt at a "simile," Marie replied, *"Does green mean go?* Yes, I'm in deep trouble with this stuff."

"Okay then, my weekend is wide open. Where do you want to meet?"

Marie replied, "I thought maybe a restaurant would work. The library wouldn't allow us to talk much. And remember, I'm paying!"

Paul hesitated for a moment while he considered, then said, "I know this area fairly well. My sister graduated from here last year, and she showed me some good restaurants not far from the school. How about the Camellia Grill, have you been there?"

"No. But that sounds fine."

"Great. Meet me at the streetcar stop outside the university at 5 pm, and it's a short ride. Bring your notebook and story with you."

"Okay, but I'm dying to know, did *you* like this short story? I was bored to tears!"

A slight smile appeared on his mouth, but he didn't respond. This story had not been his favorite, but he didn't want to say anything that would make her even less interested in getting the job done.

Marie, mustered patience as she waited for his response. *Surely, he heard me?*

Paul hesitantly began to walk away, but after a few steps, he turned back and said, "I'll reserve my opinion until we finish your paper."

Promptly at 5 pm, Paul waited on Marie and the streetcar. He was hungry. *Where is she?*

Five minutes later, just seconds after a trolley passed, she arrived. Watching her waltz in his direction, dressed in a casual, yet beautiful way and sporting a sweet smile, she magically satisfied his hunger. She created a much different and unexpected reaction: a more profound desire. She was gorgeous—her beautiful, long hair, free and unleashed from the ponytail in the light breeze. Tight blue jeans accentuated her curves, and a loose-fitting, crisp white shirt created a mental snap-shot that he hoped he would never lose. As the air passed over her, it washed her scent over him. He imagined her perfume was from some heavenly flower found only in an exotic rain forest.

He stood motionless, almost trance-like, as she approached, wondering, *Am I dreaming? Is this the same person from class?*

Approaching him, she said, "Hi Paul, thanks for coming!"

Paul extended his hand as she moved closer, casting her arm over his shoulder to hug him tightly. He was unprepared for her absence of inhibition as she pressed her body against him in a way that defied unfamiliarity.

Surprised and blushing, he said, "It's nice to see you. You look great!"

She looked so good; he regretted not having clean clothes at his dorm to wear. Like most boys, his mother had spoiled him for years, and the adjustment to washing clothes for himself hadn't been easy. He existed in a new state he referred to as "detergent conservation mode."

Marie's eyes were locked only on his face and his flushed cheeks as she replied, "You look great too! Are you hungry?"

"Yes, I'm starving."

"Well, here comes a streetcar, guess this one's for us!"

It was a short ride down to the corner where St. Charles Avenue meets South Carrollton and the Camellia Grill. Serving customers since 1946, it remained a staple of great Southern atmosphere and cooking.

After a few minutes, they were seated, then it wasn't long before their waiter appeared.

He walked up and eyed them both with mocked suspicion, then smiled and said, "If y'all have been here before, it's been too long since I've seen you! Clarence is my name, and great food is my game,"

Their waiter presented in a white shirt, black bowtie, and pants. He sported a smile as wide as his face, as he continued, "Waiter, tour-guide, match-maker, or spiritual adviser, whatever you desire, I can help you!"

"Nice to meet you, Clarence," said Paul, "I've been here before, but my friend hasn't. She might need a minute to decide."

"This is your castle while you are here. Please take your time and enjoy it. I'll be back with some ice water, for y'all!" Despite how busy this restaurant was, Clarence appeared to have all the time in the world for his patrons.

Marie was impressed. "Wow, Paul, this place is great, a perfect choice! Thank you. What do you normally eat here?"

"Well, sometimes, I get the red beans and rice with andouille sausage… that is unless I'm in the mood for red beans and rice with andouille sausage!"

Marie giggled at his comment as she looked at the menu and asked, "Have you ever had the catfish? I love it back home and think I'll try it here."

"I've heard its good, but you'll only catch me eating…"

Marie interrupted, "Red beans and rice with andouille sausage!"

They both laughed.

Clarence returned with the water and took their order. Before he left, he said, "You should both save room for dessert."

Marie excitedly chimed in, "Oh yeah? What do y'all have tonight, Clarence? Something delicious?"

Clarence leaned over and spoke lower, as he said, "Ya'll are in luck this evening. My Aunt Talulah has a bakeshop just down the way on River Road. It's not far from here. They tell me that Kings and Queens come from thousands of miles away to taste her baked pies. If I threw a rock from here, I could land it on Aunt Talulah's tin roof. It's that close! She usually sells out just after three in the afternoon, but I heard she is opening late this evening so you might be in luck. If you want a ride, I can call my cousin, Antoine, and he could drive you there for dessert and wait till you're ready and drive you back here. I can tell you one thing, for certain, I've never met anyone who went, that didn't go again. Y'all think it over and don't stuff yourself silly here. As good as our food is, I'm telling you, you'll regret it if you don't taste one of Talulah's pies! I'll have your dinners right up."

Paul looked at Marie, who appeared to be having the time of her life, and said, "We're not getting much done on your English assignment."

Marie didn't miss a beat as the procrastinator in her spoke, "It's not Monday morning yet. I think, when we finish, we should take a walk for some of that delicious pie!"

3

TALULAH'S PIE

Clarence's directions were perfect. Four blocks away on River Road was a small house whose clapboard had lost its paint years before. Under the eve of the roof of this shotgun house was a sign. It was hanging by chains, and on it was the shape of a golden-brown pie. The lettering said, Talulah's Pie. The sign moved back and forth in the gentle evening breeze, beckoning them closer.

Under a narrow porch was a Dutch door that was open on the top half. Over the door, was a sign that said:

Order Here – Pick up Here
Eat Anywhere Else
And Enjoy

On the left side of the door was another sign, indicating selections:

Apple
Cherry
Strawberry
Raspberry
Blackberry

Blueberry
And For Peoples that don't like Fruit,
Chocolate

As they stepped up on the porch, the most delicious smells wafted through the door from the kitchen within. They could hear someone singing in the back, and whoever it was could have been a famous gospel singer by the tone.

With satisfied stomachs from the Camellia Grill and plenty of daylight left, they waited patiently. Time seemed to stand still as they sniffed the heavenly smells and listened to the beautiful singing from inside. After a few minutes, people started lining up behind them, probably locals who were privy to the timing of hot pies from this magical place.

From behind, they heard someone say, "That Talulah shore can sing gospel!"

They both turned around, nodding in agreement while feeling guilty for being in front of people who knew Talulah better than they did.

Then, in the blink of an eye, Talulah, still humming, entered the front room from the kitchen, carrying a metal tray filled with steaming pies. Placing them on a table close to the door, she grabbed a metal shaker filled with powdered sugar and generously sprinkled the golden pies. Then, she flipped on a warming light before approaching the door.

While humming, she looked out the door over the heads of people waiting in line. Then, as if the sky was her auditorium, Talulah began to sing a song that everyone in line behind them knew, as they sang with her. It was her trademark song that heralded the start of another evening selling her pies. She bellowed:

"Come and see Talulah,
In the evening every night!
Come and see Talulah,
You can't only take one bite!

Oh, come and get a warm pie,
Till your belly says, 'No more!'
Oh, come and see Talulah,
As my pies, come cross, the door!"

With that done, Talulah suddenly became very business-like and focused. With a booming voice, she called, "*NEXT!*"

Talulah stared at Marie, who was first in line, prompting her to say, nervously, "Miss Talulah, I'm not a fruit hater, but could I have one chocolate for here, please, and one to go?"

Turning to Paul, she said, "How 'bout you, honey?"

"Since she's paying, Miss Talulah, I'd like a Strawberry for here and an Apple *and* a Peach to go."

Suddenly, from the back of the line, they heard, "Talulah ain't got no peach, son, it ain't on the sign!"

Talulah leaned over with her elbows on the top of the door and said, "The man be right, Mister, if Peach was on Talulah's sign, I'd get you one, real quick. You is obviously new here, how 'bout you pick something else."

Paul, somewhat embarrassed, said, "Cherry. Yes, could I have a cherry instead, please."

From the back, "Good choice, son. Cherry be on the sign!"

In a heartbeat, Talulah returned, handing each a bag. She looked at Marie and said, "That be five dollars, Missy, tax included."

Paul felt compelled to put in a good word for their waiter, as he said, "In case you were wondering how we found you, Miss Talulah, Clarence sent us."

She snapped back, "That boy got a mouth on him! I spec he ought 'a be keeping his mind on his job. I don't want him 'a lose it cause 'o me! Him and Antoine ain't too big be placed over Aunt Talulah's knee!"

Marie extended the money as Talulah snapped it away, only to yell, "NEXT!"

They walked away, guarding their warm bags as though they contained the Hope diamond.

4
CRITICAL ASSIGNMENT

Darkness greeted their ride back to school on the streetcar. The operator, possibly near the end of his shift, sounded his bell at any car in an intersection on the way back to school. Paul and Marie laughed and carried on like best friends as they replayed their shared afternoon and dinner experience. It came out slowly that neither of them had looked forward to this encounter. Marie dreaded working on the assignment, and Paul admitted he had never been so intimidated by someone he didn't know. They laughed together at these revelations.

For them, what began as a request for help, had in short-order taken on a new life. What remained unspoken was that each had planted a seed in fertile soil.

No work had been done on the class project tonight, so they made plans to meet at the entrance to Audubon Park, close to school, tomorrow at 10 am. They parted awkwardly at her dorm, this time with a brief, awkward hug and a smile. Marie agreed to bring a blanket so they could sit under one of the famous Live Oak trees Paul had mentioned.

Paul was on cloud nine. "Little Miss" was actually nice to be around.

❧

For Paul, Saturday couldn't come fast enough. Unlike Marie, he hadn't read the assignment by Virginia Woolf, and it wasn't easy to concentrate on it after he arrived back at his dorm room.

His roommate wasn't the problem. He wasn't there, as usual. They hadn't found a way to connect, and Paul realized it might not ever happen. Nathaniel was from New York and seemed to have no interest in being friends with him. His parents had both gone to Tulane, and he had little or no love for college: except the nightlife. A partier, he was rarely home before midnight.

It didn't take long to finish reading this unusually short, short story, and he wasn't sure if he could honestly answer Marie's question about whether he liked it. He reread it, then decided it would be best to consider it more seriously tomorrow. His focus tonight was elsewhere. His mind, as he turned out the light, was not at all concerned with a ghost story. A different kind of ghost was haunting him and her name was Marie.

❧

Two amazing things happened at ten o'clock the next morning. Marie was at the park entrance, waiting on him for a change. Her welcoming smile greeted him from a distance. With her things in a neat pile on the pavement, she had two arms to place around his neck this time to extend an incredible hug. *They just kept getting better,* he noticed. She lingered in his arms, and both felt an intensity that neither expected.

Backing away, she said, "I just wanted to see if I could make you blush again. That was so cute yesterday."

Paul's whole body was blushing, and he needed a distraction. As they released, he reached for her pile and said, "Here, I'll help you carry your things."

He picked up the blanket, her library book, and her notebook, and they walked into Audubon Park, a jewel of open space nestled in the heart of the Garden District.

They walked along the meandering road in the direction of the river. As they walked, Marie inquired, "Have you spent much time here in this park?"

"Not as much as I'd like," he replied, "but my sister has. I called her last night to tell her what we were doing today. Savannah told me I should keep my eyes open for signs leading to the 'Tree of Life', an ancient and famous Live Oak Tree that's here."

Pointing at a tree not far away, Marie said, "Is it like that one, over there?"

"That's a younger one. It's probably just a hundred years old. My sister said that the 'Tree of Life' is almost 250 years old. Etienne de Boré planted it and he was the first person to grow sugar cane in Louisiana. This park is on his property."

"Wow, Paul. We are walking through history! They're gorgeous. Look how long those huge branches are! It looks like even the branches can sprout more roots!"

"Yes, the branches get so long and heavy that they touch the earth, which helps support their weight and gives them water and nutrients when new roots shoot into the ground."

Paul stopped for a moment to survey the area. After looking around, he pointed and said, "Let's walk to that Live Oak over there. It's away from the road and away from other people. We can hopefully get some work done there."

"Okay," she said, "but while we are walking, why don't you tell me why you couldn't sleep last night."

"It was Virginia Woolf's fault," Paul said, as he crossed two fingers, "you know, the spooky story."

It was a cool and beautiful fall day with a light breeze. They moved just under the canopy of the tree to limit the direct sunlight and spread Marie's blanket on the ground.

As they settled into opposite corners, Marie laid the book down between them, opening it to the first page of "A Haunted House". She blurted, "I've got to say, the only thing haunted here lately is me; I'm so worried about this assignment. You know, Paul, I can't afford to make another bad grade on this. With another poor mark,

I'm not sure I'd be able to pull up my average by the end of the semester."

Paul picked up the textbook and pretended to read. He didn't respond to Marie's comment.

After a minute of silence, Marie had to ask, "Cat got your tongue, sir?"

Since the surprise hug yesterday, and the even better one this morning, fears were mounting for him that this was all too good to be true. Maybe this was just all business between two new friends. And that would be okay, but the other possibility would have been more to his liking. Now, he wasn't sure, but he knew his delay in response was making things awkward.

His father always told him, *"The best defense is a good offense."* He needed to change the subject and see what happened. Until today, Paul had always held back from saying things that might seem overly affectionate, especially with someone he'd just met. His next words took an effort for his voice to produce as he replied, "I'm sorry it's taken me so long to tell you how pretty you are."

Marie's mouth turned up at the corner, and her eyes twinkled. Now, she was the one with the delayed response. Her mind raced. She hadn't expected him to say anything like this today. Most guys were lamely incapable of expressing any semblance of emotion, and he had just given her the sweetest compliment. Although it was true, at least at first, that she had only been interested in completing the assignment with a high grade, something had quickly changed. It hadn't taken long to see there was something incredibly endearing about him that promptly reached out and touched her heart. But, the mere thought of how easily she might fall into a relationship with him, made her nervous. Silently, she reminded herself that all she needed was help on this assignment. Looking down at her book, she said, "Thanks, that was so nice of you to say." Marie picked up her notebook and started paging through it, before saying, "So, I guess it's time to get started!"

Not the reply Paul hoped for; it also didn't surprise him. He smiled graciously and said, "I think we should start by having you read the story out loud, then we'll go from there."

Marie, not expecting to be called on to read out loud, rolled her eyes. Then, she hesitantly picked up the book and began to read, "'Whatever hour you woke, there was a door shunting.' What the hell does 'shunting' mean, Paul?"

Paul couldn't help but notice this sudden change in her demeanor. She seemed irritated with him. *I should never have said what I did. Now everything is awkward.*

Realizing they just needed to get through with this, and hoping it was only the assignment that had flipped her switch, he said, "It's an old term, used in this context to mean 'shutting,' he said.

"Well, that is my main problem with these assignments. Why can't Ms. Oglehorns pick something for us to read that isn't freakin' ancient?"

He said, "She's the teacher and the one responsible for your grade, so I suggest you read on."

Marie had gotten her "harrumph" out of her system, at least temporarily, so she continued to read the rest of the story out loud without pause.

After she finished, Paul asked, "So, what did you think?"

Without hesitation, Marie's tongue started wagging, "This so-called author, Ms. InkBlot Woolf had to be on some exotic hallucinogenic concoction to come up with a cockamamie story like this. If I'd been the 'alive' couple living in this house, I would have enlisted the chain draggers to help me fabricate a 'For Sale' sign!"

Paul rolled over and started howling. There was one unique thing about Marie. She was real. He laughed so hard he began to cry. Wiping his eyes with both hands, he pulled them away to find that she had laid down with her face close to his.

Marie had suddenly found Paul irresistible. *It's his fault,* she thought.

She began to whisper with her mouth close to his, and as she did, he could feel the air from her words touch his lips. She said, "You flattered me earlier. In a way, I wasn't expecting when you told me I was pretty. I loved that."

Then, it happened. The universe, heaven, and all God's angels circled these two young hearts and placed their lips together.

He was afraid to breathe or move in any way. Her lips were so soft and moist, and as they kissed, he could smell her hair.

What happened removed any uncertainty from his thoughts. This kiss was not just a peck on the lips from someone wanting to use him for a class project. It was *passion,* and it felt so good.

Some things have such power that it cannot be quantified. A kiss that makes time stand still is one of those. Paul wasn't sure how long this kiss with Marie lasted, but when their lips separated, he believed that they each took part of the other with them.

Opening his eyes, he found hers gleaming at him, almost begging him to say something.

She wouldn't be disappointed this time, either. "That was incredible," he said.

Marie coyly brushed her hair back and asked, "Now, would you like me to read the story to you again?"

Quickly he responded, "Please don't, but can we do whatever just happened again soon?"

"I don't know… does this mean I have to buy you dinner again?"

"Oh, hell no. But now those pies from Talulah… I'll expect you to spring for some of those."

Marie reached out to tickle him, then moved her arm over his chest, hugging him and nuzzling his neck. He was not disappointed when their lips met again.

It wasn't long before they rolled under the blanket beneath the shade of a watchful evergreen guardian and a beautiful southern sky.

5

MONDAY LOOMS

Paul squinted into the early afternoon sun as he pulled the blanket away from his face. Marie, tightly nestled against his chest, chirped, "I'm not ready to leave our cocoon yet, Paul. Do we have to?"

His hair and clothes akimbo, he said, "Marie, we should get out from under here. Someone might think something else is going on under this blanket and get us arrested!"

Marie responded by tickling him in the same vulnerable spot, causing him to squirm and laugh as he rolled himself into broad daylight.

Standing quickly, he glanced around as he walked further under the tree and sat on one of the large draping branches that kissed the ground.

"Where are you, Paul?" Marie's head popped out of the blanket, her hair a full mess, asking dramatically, "You're not going to put me back to work, are you?"

Hearing no response, in a flash, Marie was up, straightening her clothes as she smiled at him and added, "It's a shame that Ms. Ohmagosh has to get in the way of such incredible snuggle time!"

"Speaking of Ms. Ohmagosh, we really should get some other

work done today," Paul used emphasis by pointing at the library book lying unattended on the ground next to Marie's purse.

Marie, appearing compliant, walked over, but instead of picking up the book, she reached into her purse.

Pulling out a brown paper bag, she turned to face Paul, saying, "Okay, if we must, but first I have a surprise."

Marie almost ran to where Paul sat and plopped herself down on the branch next to him. From the bag, she retrieved one of Talulah's pies, the other chocolate one from last night.

"Here you go, my favorite teacher," Marie split the pie in half and handed Paul his share, "we shouldn't have to suffer this assignment on an empty stomach!"

"Thank you, Marie! I am surprised you didn't eat this already, mine are long gone."

"Maybe we could go there again, like really soon!" she said.

As they quietly finished their pies, Paul reminded Marie what their English teacher required in the assignment. "The good news is that this story is not very long and not very involved. Like any story written by an author, people speculate about what the writer meant. But, that's also the neat thing about writing; every person is free to interpret what they read in their own way."

Marie appeared to be listening while licking the chocolate filling from her fingers. After a moment, she responded, "Well, what if Ms. Oh-that's-not-right, doesn't like *my* interpretation of her little assignment?"

Paul laughed at the latest version of their teacher's name and replied, "Well, that's where it gets interesting. You are the author of your paper, and your teacher has the right to let you know what she thinks, kind of like a 'review.'"

"Well, her first 'review' of my work was pretty bad..."

"Then make this one better! She wants you to tell her in your own words how the living couple is like the dead couple, as well as how they are different. That's all there is to it."

"You make it sound so easy, Paul. These kinds of things don't come easy to me. I can look out around us and apply paint to a canvas and make you wonder whether the view or my painting is reality. But this English stuff and I are like mixing oil and water."

"I look forward to seeing your paintings, but in the meantime, try to plow that same passion into this assignment. Instead of using oil, use words to paint a picture for Ms. O."

Marie kissed him on the cheek and said, "Thank you for helping me, Paul. Keeping in mind what you just said, I'd like to try this again, but on my own. Would you walk me back to my dorm? I need to get away from you for a while so I can concentrate on something else!"

"I sure will!" Paul walked over and picked up her notebook and started to write. "Here's my phone number. I'll be in my room doing the same thing unless my roommate is there. In that case, I'll be unreachable in the library."

Marie wrote her number on a torn-off piece of Talulah's pie bag and stood to hand it to him. She pulled him in close for another one of her famous hugs and whispered, "Thanks, Paul, I really enjoy doing schoolwork with you!"

"School work?" Paul asked. "It felt more like a date!"

She released him as quickly as she'd grabbed him and turned to pick up her things, saying, "Okay, call it a date. But then *you* get to pay next time!"

❧

When he returned to his room, Nathaniel was still sleeping off the night before. Paul grabbed his things quietly and left for the library. Marie had one copy of the book containing the short story and hoped he hadn't waited too long to get his hands on another copy.

All three copies of *Monday or Tuesday* were checked out. The librarian suggested that he access the story on microfiche. That took a while, but after finding it, he was able to complete the assignment in less than an hour.

For Paul, the library was like a candy store. With nothing left on his schedule for the day, he enjoyed going row by row through the books. He couldn't imagine writing a book himself and admired those who did. He walked through his favorite section, Fiction, seeing there the names of famous writers, living and not: Agatha Christie, Charles Dickens, Stephen King, Edgar Allan Poe, and his favorite, Ernest Hemingway. As he walked along, he realized what it was he liked best about fiction: the fact that imagination has no limits. Poetry was his second favorite, and he had dabbled in a little of that himself.

Little did he realize as he lost himself in the stacks, that someone special was doing her best to reach him. A short while ago, Marie tried to call him, only to wake Nathaniel on the tenth ring. When his unfamiliar voice responded, "Yeah, who is this?" she replied, "Sorry, wrong number!" then hung up, grabbed her paper, and headed for the library.

The Howard-Tilton Memorial Library is one of the nation's most extensive. Marie's second visit there was for one reason only, that being to find Paul. She had no idea where he might be, but was anxious for him to read what she had written.

Not finding him in any of the study areas, Marie went up and down the aisles. Almost about to give up, she spotted him sitting on the floor, appearing immersed in a book at the end of a long row. As she walked up to him, he raised his head from Hemingway's, *The Old Man and the Sea.*

"Fancy meeting you here," he said, "can I help you, ma'am?"

Trying to whisper amid her excitement, "Either put that book up or check it out, we need to go outside where we can talk. *I've finished the assignment!"*

Marie was dancing in her spot as though she needed a restroom in the next second.

Paul didn't understand her rush, and knew he shouldn't quickly trust his foot which had fallen asleep.

"Can't you move a little faster?" she said, "I can't wait to show you what I've done!"

Unsteadily, he stood to place his book back in its resting place. Then, holding his finger to his lips, urging quiet, he pointed with his other hand toward the exit. Marie nodded approval.

Paul whispered, "I didn't expect you would finish so quickly. Are you sure you're ready for me to read it? Don't you want to take a little more time?"

Marie proudly stated, "I took your advice. I started hating it less and loving it more. I value your opinion, Paul, and I'm ready for you to read it. So, keep that skinny ass of yours moving in the direction of that door!"

She's noticed my ass, he thought with pride.

6

WORDS

Marie held onto his hand tightly as she ran from the library. She didn't stop until she reached a bench not far from the entrance. Turning to face him, she held Paul's shoulders and forced him to sit, then sat next to him.

In her hand was a single sheet of paper that she proudly held before him, stating, "I hope you like what I've written."

Paul, still trying to catch his breath from the mad dash, slowly and carefully grasped the page held before him and began to read out loud. "Virginia Woolf, like an artist, used words to paint a magnificent picture of life transcending death in her short story, 'A Haunted House.' The assignment requested that I compare the two couples occupying this old home: the living and the dead. For me to do that, it is necessary to interpret another picture; one that the deceased husband left, through words in his diary."

Paul stopped momentarily and glanced toward Marie with a look she interpreted as either shock or surprise. *Or was it both,* she wondered?

He focused again on her paper and continued to read silently.

When he finished, he looked over at Marie, who was waiting as patiently as a pregnant lady three days past term.

His face was without expression, obviously still considering what he'd just read.

"Well?" she asked. Paul's blank stare moved to the sidewalk in front of them and began to freak her out.

She felt compelled to fill the verbal dead space with something, almost anything, so she blurted, "I dug deep into my art background, as you instructed me, Paul... please, dear LORD, can't you say something?"

Finally, he turned to face her and placed his arm on her shoulder.

What is this? A consolation? She wondered.

"Marie..." he began cautiously, "you've written a great paper, but..."

"Paul, I can't take this. I'm going to cry. What do you mean, 'But?'"

"But... I counted the words, and it is two words under the minimum. Don't worry, though! All you need to do is sign your name! I believe Ms. O. will love it."

She lunged at him so fast it scared him. Marie squeezed his neck without regard for his next breath. Barely able to breathe, he grabbed her arms and gently pulled himself free.

"Paul, I can't thank you enough for helping me! What you told me in the park turned my attitude around, and made such a difference."

There were tears in her eyes as she backed away from him, and as she calmed down, he returned the paper to her.

With the weight of the world released, Marie's demeanor changed again as she sprang from her seat. She leaned over and kissed Paul on the lips before stating, "I am so tired, I'm going to go back to my room and sleep for a week!"

"Well, if I were you, I'd set my alarm for Monday morning. You've come too far to be late." Paul stood and smiled at her as she walked off.

"Hey!" He called after her, "I'm going to go back in and give Mr. Hemingway some deserved attention. If you happen to wake up by tomorrow, give me a call. Maybe we could go to the park again and look for that old de Boré tree? Then afterward, we could hop a streetcar and go see Talulah!"

Over her shoulder, came her response, "Not just yes, but HELL YES!"

❧

Paul was thankful that he had checked out several other books. He'd had a peaceful Saturday evening finishing his essay for Monday's class, as well as reading more Hemmingway.

He was fast asleep at 1:36 in the morning when the door banged open, and Nathaniel returned, flipping on the lights before undressing and pouring himself into bed. It was mere seconds until his roommate was asleep. By playing the part himself, he had avoided unwanted, painful, drunken verbal nonsense, a trap he hadn't escaped last time. When the coast was clear, he slipped out of bed and turned the lights off himself.

By the next morning, he waited in a chair under the phone for her call while reading, *For Whom the Bell Tolls*. It was 9 am, and he hoped she would call soon. Nathaniel's snoring was giving him a headache.

❧

It was Sunday, and Marie would typically have been in church with her family if she was at home. Having slept hard last night, she was up early and had already called home to speak to her mother and father before they left for mass. Sunday was the only day her father's shrimp boats didn't run. Still, it was a rare morning that he wasn't at the boatyard tending to some need. Today, when she needed to hear their voices, she was fortunate to be able to speak to them both.

After talking to her mother for a while, her father picked up and said, "Your mom tells me you've met a young man?"

"Yes, Dad. I can't wait for y'all to meet him."

"An English major, is he?"

"Yes, sir…"

"Not much of an income from a profession like that!"

"Daddy, we have only been on two dates, this is not a serious thing at all!"

"I'll go on record to say, that's not what your mother's saying…"

"What?"

"Your mother's never been wrong, Sweetie… at least that's what she tells me. Here's your mother back."

Marie and her mom spoke for at least another half hour until her father threatened to pull the cord. She missed her mom tremendously, and it was good catching up. Marie had never been away from home this long. She hung up the phone and tried to imagine what she had said to her mother about Paul to give her these ideas. Was it the tone of her voice? Or that all the new things happening to her also involved Paul? She too felt something that she hadn't before, and it scared her. She had never fallen in love with any boy and was not anywhere near being ready now.

Shortly after 10 am, Paul's phone rang, and Marie was relieved when he picked right up.

"Paul?"

"Just a second, Marie. I'm trying not to wake my roommate up."

Nathaniel snorted a few times, then rolled over, falling soundly back to sleep.

He stretched the cord into the bathroom and closed the door as best he could, saying, "Hello, Sunshine."

Marie said, "Hello, my favorite teacher! I hope you've finally quit procrastinating and managed to get your assignment done, Paul Morel!"

"I did, and I hope you got some rest."

"More than enough," she said, "I slept almost as well as those dead inhabitants of Ms. Inkblot's haunted house! It's such a good feeling to be ahead of the game for a change. Are you still interested in the park?"

"If it leads to you and Talulah, I'd have to say a resounding 'yes!'"

"I need 30 minutes, and I'll meet you at the park entrance."

"See you soon," Paul said.

❧

It was a gorgeous day, and not only did they find the Tree of Life, but they also toured the Audubon Zoo, seeing all its wondrous and exotic animals, a place they vowed to return.

By 4 pm, it was a long walk back to St. Charles Avenue to pick up a streetcar toward Talulah's. Each was unconcerned about actual dinner, and could almost taste the warm, heavenly crust of their choice.

Marie sat next to the open window, and as they approached the turn onto South Carrollton Avenue, she pulled the thick wire cord over their seat, requesting the next stop. The car came to a sudden standstill in front of the Camellia Grill, and as they stepped off, they heard the familiar sound of the air brakes pumping up in advance of the next need.

They'd only been there once but could have closed their eyes and found the way. They hoped that the line wouldn't be too long when they arrived.

Paul viewed the gravel lot ahead, saying, "I think we lucked out, Marie, we're going to be first in line again!

It felt strange to stand before this iconic ray of confectionary heaven without anyone else there. *But something wasn't right.* Something was different. The top portion of the Dutch door was closed, and no singing emanated from inside.

They shared a glance, then proceeded closer. The time was right, but not only was there no incredible smell, but there was no smoke coming from Miss Talulah's chimney.

"Marie, it doesn't appear she's open today."

Marie immediately sank to her knees on one of the steps, held her hands as if praying, and looked at him to say, "No, Paul, please, please, don't say that! I've waited too long!"

Pulling her up, he responded, "Come on, Marie, it's only been 48 hours! She's probably closed on Sundays, and we just didn't know it."

"I think we should sue!" Marie defiantly stated.

"Don't be ridiculous. If you did, you'd never get what you truly want!"

Marie turned away, kicked a piece of gravel with the toe of her shoe, placed her hands into her pants and said, "Well, it's your turn to pay, Paul Morel, and I'm past hungry now. You need to carry me back to the streetcar. I'm feeling weak..."

Marie placed her wrist to her forehead, dramatically acting as if she might faint at any moment.

Ignoring the ploy, Paul walked past her and said, "Let's take a ride on the streetcar and get a poboy down in the French Quarter."

"Go all that way there? What if the French Quarter is closed too?"

"It's not that far, and it will be a beautiful ride there and back. The only time the Quarter closes is when the Earth stops turning."

"Lord, Paul Morel, I hope that never happens, at least before we eat tonight!"

7
MONDAY

The Acme Oyster House had it all. Only a short walk into the Quarter from where the streetcar let them off on Canal Street, the Acme filled them up in short order. Marie had an oyster poboy, and Paul had one with roast beef and "debris," shredded beef simmered extra-long so that it picks up more seasonings and gravy. Full, satisfied bellies rode back with them to school.

Due to the late hour, Paul walked Marie to her dorm entrance. Before going in, Marie showed him the window to her downstairs corner room and said, "I don't want to be late in the morning, so as you pass by here on the way to class, please don't just tap, I want you to bang on my window to make sure I'm up. Okay?"

Her dorm wasn't on his usual way to class. In fact, it was quite a bit out of the way. Despite this, and without hesitation, he said, "Sure, I'd be happy to do that. I had another wonderful day with you today. Thank you."

Her hands grabbed his face, pulling him to her lips. Then, still holding him, she withdrew just enough to look into his eyes and say, "See you soon, Paul Morel."

Monday morning brought rain. Waking early, as usual, Paul made himself ready for class. His roommate, Nathaniel, rolled over, pulling his pillow over his head to avoid the light from Paul's lamp, as he put his assignment and books into his backpack. Next, he grabbed his poncho, left the room as quietly as possible, and arrived at the cafeteria when they opened at 7 am.

After finishing two eggs over easy, toast, and a second cup of coffee, he planned to arrive at Marie's window by 8 am. When Paul looked out the window, it was even darker than when he arrived, and the rain had intensified. Despite that, it was time to go. He knew that some parts of him were going to get wet this morning despite being mostly covered. He hoped he wouldn't have to stand outside her window for long. Campus police would frown on a guy snooping around an easily accessible window outside the girl's dorm.

What he saw when he arrived at her dorm caused him to laugh. Taped to the inside of her window was a hand-painted sign. It displayed a realistic depiction of Marie, sitting in a desk chair next to another one. It was their English class. It showed her turned around, facing the rear of the classroom, with a look of concern on her face. One of her arms held on to the empty chair as if she was guarding it. Beneath it was the words: You better get moving, Paul Morel, I'm saving your seat.

He smiled all over himself as he walked away. Just the thought of her beating him to class was laughable. She had set him up for a good chuckle this morning. Marie had a gift for knowing how to start his day.

By the time he arrived, the rain had soaked his pant legs and his shoes. Just inside the door, he removed his poncho. It had done an excellent job keeping his head, backpack, and upper body dry. He rolled the poncho up and left it by the entrance.

After a short hike up the stairway to the 2nd-floor classroom, he saw a large blue umbrella outside the closed doors, standing in a small pool of water on the marble floor. The heavy wooden door opened quietly on its well-oiled hinges revealing Marie, sitting in a desk next to where he usually sat. She was the only one there.

She'd been watching the door, waiting for him to arrive. Just like her painting, her arm was resting on his chair. Marie greeted him with, "It's about time you got here, I've been doing my best to save your seat! Been catching up on your sleep, have you? It looks like you got here just in the nick of time!"

Paul, ready to play along, walked to the desk that Marie usually sat in at the end of the last row. He placed his hand on it as if he was about to sit there.

Marie was only going to allow this game to go so far as she called out, almost yelling, "Don't you dare, Paul Morel. I didn't get up this early to sit back there again!"

Feeling confident that he had her full attention, Paul smiled as he strolled toward the front of the room from the opposite side, circling toward the podium, where he stopped. Maintaining a blank expression, he extended his arms to grab the front edges of the podium as if *he* were the professor. Leaning forward, appearing to squint over imaginary glasses, the mock professor glanced side-to-side at the empty desks in front of him, coming to a stop when his eyes fell on Marie. Using a falsetto voice, he said, "Well, Ms. Landry, so nice that you would grace us all with your prompt presence for a change. Perhaps you could come up to the front of the class and tell us more about the career-changing epiphany you experienced that may have caused this?"

Marie could play with the best of them. She cleared her voice as she rose from her seat and waltzed up to the side of the podium. Using accentuated hand gestures, she began, "Good morning, classmates. In answer to Ms. Oglethorne's unusually nosey request, I will tell you all, being here early for this class was not easy for me. You see, I've met this guy who normally sits over there." Marie pointed at Paul's usual seat.

Paul could hardly contain himself. She was quite the actress, and it appeared that she was just getting revved up.

"Since meeting him, I've developed a completely different attitude about this class, one that I had initially dreaded attending." Marie accentuated this last statement by raising her wrist to her forehead with closed eyes as if she was about to faint. Then, looking at Paul, she said, "You see, Ms. Okeydokey, I'm an artist, not a writer. But my special, obviously late male friend, has taught me a new appreciation for literature, and at the same time, I've grown unusually fond of him."

A distant voice said, "Thank you, Ms. Landry. I'm so thrilled about your change of heart. We'll see how far you've come when you turn in your assignment. Now, is there room for me at *my* podium?"

Marie's eyes remained frozen on Paul, whose lips were not moving. Paul slowly removed his hands from the podium and turned to face the voice. Ms. Oglethorpe had also arrived quite early, entering silently from a door on the side of the blackboard. They had no idea how much of this she heard but assumed the worst.

Several other students arrived just then, and Ms. O. took this opportunity to cast the two flounder back into the sea as she called out to the new students, saying, "Good morning to everyone, and welcome back to English Lit! I hope you all brought your completed assignments!"

Marie remained in place, unable to move, as Ms. O. began to arrange her notes on the podium. When the shock faded enough for Marie to consider moving, it amazed her to see that Paul was already sitting at his desk. She forced her feet to move as she focused on her co-conspirator, thinking, *traitor!* As promptly as her legs allowed, she took her seat, continuing to fear the worst.

As Ms. O. busied herself writing on the blackboard, Marie leaned over to whisper, "I think we're in trouble."

Paul started to chuckle and, under his breath, said, "It's a good thing you're a great artist. At least you won't starve!"

"You saw my painting in the window?"

"Yes, it made me laugh while I stood there like a peeping Tom, looking in your window during a monsoon! Luckily, I'm not in jail! Oh, and your picture is incredible!"

"I couldn't wait to tell you good morning!"

Promptly at 8:30 am, Ms. O. walked past each student to collect the assignments. Paul noticed that Marie's body posture stiffened when Ms. O. walked past and remained for the rest of the class. She was already worried about her grade, and being caught goofing around this morning hadn't helped.

As they walked away from class, Marie admitted, "It's going to be a long time until Wednesday."

"You have nothing to worry about," he said. "Your paper is excellent."

"Even if it is, she caught me mocking her and her name as she walked in! We could both be toast now!"

"Well, as they say, 'what's done, is done.' What I'm not sure of is what I'm going to do after school today."

"Why is that?"

"I have a tough decision to make. I can eat at the cafeteria this evening, or I can get pie from Miss Talulah. If I choose pie, would you like to come with me?"

"Marie slapped his arm as she said, "Wild Oglethorpes couldn't keep me away from Miss Talulah's this evening!"

Marie could make him smile without even trying. She was blessed with physical beauty too, but that alone was nothing without her fun-loving personality. She was spunk on steroids. They walked together to her next class.

8

TALULAH'S

The rain stopped around noon. Paul arrived at her window that afternoon to tap and let her know he was there. Through the pane, he saw another incredible new painting. This one showed the front of Talulah's establishment, painted so well it could have been a photo. Standing close to the Dutch door was a couple holding hands, and the top part was open as smoke billowed from the chimney.

He was in awe. It was them in the picture. He stood there, looking at the intricately painted details, as suddenly, Marie's smiling face peered from around the painting. She met the wonderous look in his eyes with sheer joy from her own.

Just as quickly, she was gone, soon to reappear at the front door.

Greeting her with a hug, he said, "Marie! That is incredible! How do you do that?"

"I imagine it's because I paint just like you write… with my eyes. I am blessed to have hands that follow their lead." Marie stepped away with faux indignance and said, "Speaking of writing, I'm wondering how long I'm going to have to wait until I get to read something you've written?"

Paul wasn't sure what to say. He had never shared his work with anyone but teachers.

After a moment, she said, "I get it, you're going to make me beg. Aren't you? Well okay…"

Marie dramatically fell to her knees in front of him with a sorrowful look on her face. She held her upraised hands together, prayerfully. Then, with her best English accent, she pleaded, "Please, sir? Might I have a look at your sonnet?"

Paul, embarrassed by her production, pulled her up to say, "Enough, already! I did write something last spring that I'm fond of, but you'd need to have been there to understand. You know, to hear it with *your* ears. I tried to write what I heard. It was *so* real, and although I tried to interpret it with words, it seemed impossible. But you're right, Marie. It is the job of the creator to portray a visual image, and that is possible with art or literature. I'd love to show my poem to you sometime, but maybe it would be best for you to hear it too."

"Can't wait!" she said.

They caught the next streetcar, and despite all the windows being open, the rain earlier in the day poured humidity over them and the entire city. As they traveled along, Marie fanned her face with her hands and commented, "I feel like we're riding through a greenhouse tonight!"

The ride to South Carrollton seemed unusually long. They timed their approach to Talulah's to be about the same time they had been there the last time. To their surprise, there was already a long line of people, and as they approached, they saw Talulah serving through the door.

"Looks like we're late this time," Marie said.

Paul looked at his watch, then back at her with a shrug of his shoulders. "We made it at the right time, maybe even a little earlier," he said.

Slowly, the line moved. Then, after they'd waited for a half-hour, the most terrible thing happened. The five people in front of them suddenly walked away without being served. As one of them passed them, Paul inquired, "Why are y'all leaving the line?"

A woman who looked like she was about to cry, stopped to say,

"Talulah sold her last pie, just as we got to the front. That's it for the night. No more till tomorrow." She shook her side to side with a downcast head as she walked away to catch her family.

Paul and Marie, unconvinced, hesitantly stepped up to the porch and approached the door. Just then, Talulah reappeared and began to close the upper half of the door.

"Excuse me," Marie said, "Miss Talulah, we were hoping to buy some of your delicious pies tonight?"

"Oh, honey, I'm so sorry for you. All my pie already been bought, but don't you worry, Talulah will have more tomorrow!" She smiled, then proceeded to close the door.

Marie impulsively reached out and pushed back against the door. This evoked a stern look from Talulah as she peered around the edge. With her hand still against the door, Marie frantically pleaded, "We were first in line the other day and even got here earlier tonight, but now you're sold out." Then she looked side to side before turning back to plead, "I don't see your hours posted anywhere. We tried to come at the right time, Miss Talulah. Could you *please* tell us what time you start selling your pies?"

"Missy, the onliest thing I can tell you is don't *never* grace you fingers on Talulah's door. You understood?"

Marie froze, her eyes wide with shock. The only thing moving in this standoff was her chin, which slowly nodded in agreement.

"But just so you know, my people's bones feel when the door gonna open, I spec cause 'o the smells! So, next time, lil lady, maybe you remember these words and can gets here on time for some pie. That'a ways you and Talulah will remain on terms!"

Talulah concluded with her broad smile just before the door shut solid. They heard the latch slide closed.

Pie-less, they stood there looking at each other.

Paul thought he, too, might cry.

Marie whimpered, "I don't think I've ever felt pain like this!"

"I feel it too," he said.

"What are we going to do? If we don't know what time the pies are coming out, how in the world will we ever get more? We have classes we have to attend, and we don't live next door! Is this how addiction feels?"

Not waiting for a response, Marie stepped off the porch and, predictably, kicked the gravel in the lot.

He could feel it too. It had only taken one dose of Talulah's pies to addict them both.

Paul remained on the porch, contemplating what to say next. Thinking hard, he said, "I have a plan. It may not be the best plan, but maybe tomorrow we'll get pie."

Marie spun to face him. Frustrated, she said, "I don't personally have enough money to go door-to-door paying people to stand in line for us if that's what you're thinking."

"No, Marie," stepping down to her, "both of us get out early on Wednesdays. We'll just have to count on getting pie one time a week."

Marie was incredulous. "One time a week?"

Paul had never imagined that pie of any sort could transform someone's personality so completely.

Standing in this lot longer would do no good tonight. As Paul walked away, he called over his shoulder, "I'll bet the Camellia Grill is open and still serving food... Oh, and I'm paying this time!"

Grabbing his hand from behind, she raced ahead, pulling him.

Never get in the way of a hungry woman, he thought.

9
GRADING DAY

At long last, Wednesday arrived. This day held not only anticipation but intimidation. Marie arrived in class before anyone else. This grade hung over her head like the sword of Damocles, but as she had told Paul on the way home last night, "No matter what marks Ms. O'Red-Ink places on my paper, it won't bother me much when I'm able to wrap my lips over more of Talulah's pie."

Paul, again impressed that Marie was seated when he arrived, wisely chose to walk directly to his seat this time. No need to risk provoking Ms. O. again.

"Good morning, Marie."

Marie impatiently blurted, "Did you go by my window on your way here?"

Paul knew it would drive her nuts, so he remained silent for a moment, pulling his things out of his backpack. Slowly, he responded with a simple, "Yes, ma'am."

"And?"

Looking admiringly at her, "You were busy again last night, it appears."

"Well, did you like it?"

"I loved it. You captured us on the blanket, studying under the live oak tree. How did you do that? You are amazing!"

Marie smiled at him. Then, just then, she caught a glimpse of the door next to the blackboard opening, and in stepped Ms. O.

Leaning over to Paul, she whispered, "Our teacher doesn't look happy today. I hope that's not a bad omen."

Other students walked in, and before long, it was time for class to begin. Ms. O. rapped her pen against the podium. When the class quieted, she spoke in a firm, measured tone, "Class, you need to know that I was disappointed in many of your assignments. Even though this is an introductory English literature class, I expect more from my students. I will pass your graded papers back to you before the bell at the end of class. If anyone takes issue with their grade, they should make a personal effort to meet with me."

Marie remained silent as she faced Paul to mouth the words, *"Oh shit."*

What followed was the longest hour of Marie's life. She heard nothing during the entire lecture. She'd instead dwelled on something she'd heard in the past; that some people, on the brink of death, can see their whole lives passing before them. Marie wasn't that lucky. She could only imagine herself drowning in a sea of red ink.

What would she tell her parents, she thought?

Marie didn't take her eyes off the professor for the entire class. Her mind, working not unlike a mental dousing rod, tried to divine what might appear on her paper. *Is there such a thing as an F-minus?* Finally, when the time came, she found it odd that Ms. O., the bane of her short college existence, approached her desk with a smile on her face. *How demonic,* she thought.

Wordlessly, Ms. O. placed the paper on the desk before her. Just like that, the teacher walked on, flying toward her next helpless victim like a vampire looking for another neck.

Marie was too nervous to look down at her paper. Instead, she looked at Paul's, which he had just picked up to read.

On his, she read: *A -. Again, great work.*

Oh no, she thought. *Even Paul came down a notch.*

Looking over, Paul asked, "How'd you do, Marie?"

The effort required for her to look at her paper was Herculean. Before her eyes could turn downward, she heard Paul say, "Great job! I knew you would get a better mark this time!"

On the page before her was: *B -. Nice improvement. You should keep this up. It might help to supplement your acting career.*

Marie lunged for his neck, a move he was learning to anticipate. She squealed with joy, causing Ms. O. in the next aisle to turn her way.

Marie waited until she looked away again to whisper, "This is *such* a wonderful day! First, *this* happened, and later we will hopefully be able to, *at last,* get some of Miss Talulah's pies! I can't remember such a nice day, like, *forever*!"

Paul nodded in agreement, whispering, "We should have a game plan. How 'bout I tap on your window around 3? Be ready to go. Bring an umbrella just in case it's hot or raining. I'll bring my backpack and a camping canteen with water. We'll pull a siege on Miss Talulah's shop!"

"I'll bring some aspirin too."

"Why would you need that? Are you feeling bad?"

"No, silly. Not for me! It appears that 'Mr. A +' dropped down a notch today and might be feeling the pain later!"

Later that day, he approached her dorm. In her window was another new painting. He had no idea where she found the time. On the canvas in vivid color was a beautiful mahogany sailboat, under full-sail. In the cockpit was him, sitting next to a smiling, jovial, Ernest Hemingway.

He stood there at the windowpane, looking in, paralyzed with amazement. Oh, what he would give to have been able to meet this man. The world around him grew silent and disappeared as the painting transported him.

Brought back by a tap on his shoulder, he turned to meet her gaze.

"That's incredible. Thank you!"

Smiling back at him, she held up a bottle.

"I've got that aspirin if you need it, but take it in a hurry because we need to get *your Lady* some pie!"

Laughing heartily, he loved the prankster in her. He also loved hearing her call herself *his* 'Lady.'

He grabbed her hand, and they began to walk, "I'm good for now," he said, "We should get moving!"

❧

As they rode along St. Charles Avenue, the traffic was light, and the operator was flying. The streetcar pitched wildly side to side on the aging tracks causing Marie to hold onto the brass handle on the seat in front of them.

"When's your birthday?" she asked.

"Every year." he replied flippantly.

"No, Mr. A -, *smart ass*, I mean, what is the date of your birthday?"

"June 18th. It's the same day of the year that Paul McCartney was born. My mom is a huge McCartney fan. She named me after him."

"I'd say she is! Maybe that's why I always want to 'Hold your hand!'" Marie giggled at her joke.

"So now it's your turn, when is yours?"

"Wait a minute, big fella, I'm not done with you yet!"

Paul reached up to pull the cord. As the streetcar came to a quick stop, they exited just as the operator started to ding his bell impatiently. A car had done the unthinkable, pulling in front of him, blocking *his* tracks.

As they crossed the street and proceeded toward River Road, Marie said, "What I wanted to say was that I'd make you a deal, Paul Morel."

"I'm getting the feeling that your deal has something to do with a lopsided share of pies coming your way."

"Wrong, oh, suspicious one. The deal is this. If you read something to me that you've written, I'll give you your pick of the window paintings, framed, for your birthday."

"Oh, dear Lady, you are making a huge assumption with your deal."

"What?"

"Well, who's to say that I'll even be dating you by June 18th of next year?"

Marie whacked him on the back of his head, hard. "And let that be a lesson to you, Mr. A -! I'll tell *you* how long we're going to date!"

He grabbed her hand, this time to be more assured he wouldn't get hit again, then, feeling safer, said, "Honestly, that is the sweetest deal, and I already know which one I want."

"Well? Tell me, please!"

Ignoring her, Paul snatched the blue umbrella from her hand and opened it over his head. "My, oh my! It sure is hot today. Thanks for bringing *my* umbrella!

They laughed their way along as they walked the few blocks to Talulah's, finding on arrival that there was no one else there. The top part of the Dutch door was closed, but smoke and a great smell billowed from the chimney.

"Looks like we're in luck, my lady!"

Marie smiled at his choice of words, and as she stepped up on the porch, she turned around in actress mode to declare poetically to the empty lot:

"Hear, Ye, Hear, Ye!
My man and I
Stand first in line,
And just about now,
It sure feels fine!"

Paul moved close to whisper in her ear, "Be careful what you say so close to the door, Marie! No telling what Miss Talulah can hear in there!"

The surprise by Ms. O. that one morning was still fresh in both of their minds.

Marie, sounding unfazed, asked him again, "So, which one of my paintings do you want?"

Paul challenged, "I can't consider any of your paintings mine until I fulfill my end of the deal."

Marie retorted, "Hell, the Café Du Monde will run out of beignets before that might happen. You say you are a writer, so where's the proof?"

"Well, Little Miss Artist-Poet, funny you should ask!"

Paul reached into his backpack, moved his hand around a bit, and looked up to catch Marie, who moved her head side-to-side, trying to see into the pack. The moment had arrived to tweak her again as he put his hand on the canteen, pulled it out, and with a surprised voice said, "Oh, look, I found it! Want a sip?"

Marie snatched the canteen from his hand and, with furiously squinted eyes, sneered, "You better hurry up and show me what else you got in there, or I'm going to use this canteen to put a big knot on your head!"

Smiling, he reached in again and pulled out a sheet of paper. Proudly, he stated, "This is the poem I mentioned to you. The genesis of it was something that happened one night at home this past spring. I was exhausted from working around my parents' house all day. It was hot outside, but our house was still comfortable because of the high ceilings. The window screen, open to the night, was all that stood between me and beautiful music shortly after dark. I collapsed on my bed, and what I heard inspired me to write this poem."

Marie, with childlike excitement, sat down, wiggling her butt into a comfortable, cross-legged position on the porch just in front of the door; her ulterior motive was to hold her place at the front of this line.

"Okay," she said, "I'm ready."

Behind her, they both heard the latch on Talulah's top door slide, causing them to look up, but the door didn't open.

Marie said, "I can hardly stand this excitement. First, you are going to read something you've written, and within moments, Miss. Talulah is going to spread all sorts of other joy! Oh, and don't worry Paul, I won't dare touch that door!"

Paul was also having trouble curtailing his excitement for the pies.

It wasn't easy to resist the urge to read quickly. He did his best to concentrate on the paper before him.

Standing with his back to the gravel lot, he didn't notice what Marie saw, as people began to come from nowhere, like locusts attracted to fresh wheat. They all smelled the same thing: Talulah's glorious pies.

Unaware of the people behind him, Paul raised his paper and closed his eyes. Reading from memory, he began:

"The Symphony
By Paul Morel
Spring 1978

It had been a long day,
And hard work calls for rest.
The sun worked hard too,
Slowly heading for its nest.

My pillow felt so cool,
On my face, freshly clean.
I could feel my body relax,
Even the muscles that felt mean.

Full darkness, oh so peaceful,
Forced my breathing to slow.
So quiet outside my window,
The dreams surely to flow.

The night traversed the portal,
Flowing in, from outside.
Filling every possible nook,
My ears, not to be denied.

Who could fall asleep,
During this beautiful melody?

As the clicks and the strumming,
Trumpeted familiarity?

Into my ears fell a sound so sweet,
None prettier had they met.
As the resonating voices sang,
Their infinite duet.

In time and as I listened,
The more relaxed I did become.
Then the symphony surrounded me,
Transforming us into one.

Open ears, eyes closed,
Feeling tired to the bone.
What joy would be sleep,
Within this harmonious tone.

Free was this concert,
For the world and for me…
Directed by a Conductor,
That no one could see.

So, I sat back and listened,
To this beautiful sound.
What a glorious production,
My window had found.

Cicadae and crickets,
Clicked and chirped,
Frogs croaked with passion,
Not to be usurped.

Their voices harmonized,
In and around my room.

No barrier could block,
Such a heavenly, pleasant tune.

Resigned was their voice,
To the night as they sang.
Day-dwellers, make way,
For my personal, symphonic gang.

Tired as I am,
To listen, oh, I must.
For someday, I may find,
My ears turned to dust.

But never will I forget,
This music sent just for me!
My ears, never the same,
Touched in the night, symphonically."

Not aware of the crowd behind him, Paul bowed to Marie, who had jumped from her spot to hug him. As she kissed him on the cheek, she whispered, "What a great poem. Thank you! Now, I think you need to turn around and acknowledge your audience."

As he slowly turned, the people in line began to applaud what they'd heard.

Then, the top door opened widely as Talulah beamed behind it. She said, "Mister, I can't say how many years Talulah been doing this, and never before, even when I weren't feeling right, did I not sing my open song. You see, it be planted inside 'a me. But this night, when I begins to open the door, I hear near 'bout the best poem I ever hear. So, sir, I thank you from the depths of my heart for your reading! Tonight, your words will do jus' fine!"

Again, the audience applauded.

Talulah looked out in the direction of the levee and clouds overhead as she bellowed, "NEXT!"

Marie jumped up to her coveted spot instantly, startling Talulah.

As she reeled backward slightly, Talulah sternly looked at Marie to affirm this familiar face, saying, "Honey, I know what you wants, a Chocolate for here and a chocolate for there."

Marie acknowledged by smiling and silently stepping aside, saying, "Talulah knows me!"

Under his breath, he replied, "She knows you, no doubt!"

Talulah was all business, and her look in Paul's direction let him know that any clout he had seconds ago had long-since expired, as she snipped, "You can't just stand in this spot. What you want, Mr. Peach Writer Man?"

From the back of the line rang out, "Talulah ain't got no peach, son, it ain't on the sign!"

Paul couldn't believe how sensitive some people's hearing was. Without risking further admonition, he said, "Strawberry and apple, ma'am. Oh, and I'm the one paying tonight."

Talulah turned away for only a few seconds, returned, and handed them separate bags. Looking at Paul, she held out her hand and said bluntly, "Five dollars."

Paul reached into his pocket while contemplating this mystery. He didn't understand why the price remained the same, despite getting one less pie tonight. He knew he couldn't leave without seeking clarification.

He handed Talulah the money before stating what to him was obvious and to Talulah was no less, "Miss Talulah, we only got four pies today, and for the same price the other evening, we got five. I don't understand, and I don't want to interrupt the line, but would you mind explaining your prices to me?"

From the back, a different voice yelled, "Son, you out your evah-lovin' mind? Don't nobody never question Miss Talulah 'bout money!"

Talulah hesitated at the counter before feeling compelled to respond to Paul. The crowd behind them, sensing imminent danger, grew deathly quiet.

"Mister, since you seem to be about as fresh here at Talulah's as a live crawdad thrown into boiling water, I'll explain this to you this time before those hungry customers behind you get riled up. You see, these peoples ain't going to wait much longer with all your questions."

From somewhere behind them, "Yeah, Mister, we being real nice, but we ain't gonna wait much longer."

As she looked out at the line, Talulah gave her other customers a stern look that demanded silence.

Paul's feet had retreated several steps already as he clutched his bag of pies.

Then she spoke. "Miss Talulah has the right to impose an advertisement fee on any customer. Now you best go ahead on while your pies be warm!"

From the back, "She has the rights!"

Paul and Marie thanked her *and* the hungry audience. Then they walked across the road and up to the top of the levee to eat their pies. The pies and the view of the river were out of this world.

Paul silently vowed to never again question the pricing of Talulah's pie. Each bite reminded him that they were priceless.

On the streetcar headed back to campus, Marie asked again, "So which of my paintings is the one you want?"

His response, "You never told me the date of your birthday."

Her response, "Every year, smart ass!"

Marie could tell by the look on his face that he was not going to give in unless she told him what he wanted.

"January first," she said.

"Thank you. Now I'll answer your question. The choice wasn't easy. All your paintings mean so much to me because almost all included you in them. But my favorite is that one of you and me, holding hands in front of Talulah's."

Marie nuzzled his ear as she whispered, "Really, Mr. Morel, I hope you know I've done them *all* for you. I was just wondering which one you wanted me to give you first."

It had been a fantastic night.

10

BEA

In the next few weeks, Marie came into her own in English Lit. It began the day she quit hating it, and from that day on, she set the trend in that class for better work and better grades. The couple, now inseparable, spent their free time exploring all areas of Audubon Park and local restaurants. No matter what direction they traveled off-campus, they reveled in the beauty of this city and its inhabitants.

One thing for sure, the only direction they went on Wednesday afternoons was toward Talulah's. Going early and waiting turned out to be the only reliable way they could arrive at the front of a long line in time to purchase pies. Some days were rainy, some days were scorching hot and unbearable, but those uncomfortable times were only a small price to pay for the incredible, mouth-watering taste that only Talulah could conjure.

On one Wednesday, there was an unusually talkative lady in line behind them. She informed them that "Although I be one of her best friends, she give me no special place in her line. When it come to her pie, all God's children be equal."

Everyone who wanted Talulah's pie had to wait in line.

Introducing herself, Beatrice continued talking through the next hour, almost non-stop. She did satisfy at least part of the curiosity about this jewel in the rough on River Road. When "Bea" stopped talking long enough to take a breath, Paul had a chance to sneak a question or two in about Talulah.

As they would learn, Talulah became a widow at a young age. She and her husband, Huey, both very much in love, opened this business together in 1966 when their daughter, Delilah, was four years old. It was Talulah's dream to have a bakery of her own. Her pastries would always quickly disappear during holiday meals with family, and they were the ones who encouraged her to spread her joy to others.

So, the couple eventually made plans to open this bakery shop. As Bea put it, "And the peoples loved it! But the poor lady couldn't bake fast enough to sell to all the peoples who wanted some." Bea nodded approvingly at her own words as she cast an occasional look to the door, watching to see it open.

Bea went on, telling them how Huey had gone door to door to sell his wife's fresh, warm pies, while Talulah stayed behind to bake. "Yep," she said, "The young'uns were makin' more money than they had *ever* knowed! But afta' while, not as many of Talulah's pies made it to them people's doors." Bea shook her head side-to-side to emphasize her disapproval.

"Where did they go?" Marie's wide eyes revealed genuine empathy regarding *any* consideration of lost pie.

"Well, Missy, it was her own man. He come a'dicted to her pies just like evahbody. Soon he be eatin' almost more than he sell and his sugar shore don't be happy, uh huh!"

"You mean Talulah?" Marie asked.

With a frustrated tone, "No, honey! He *had* the sugar! All his peoples had the sugar, and it caught him bad, eatin' all them pies!"

Paul leaned over and whispered in Marie's ear, "Diabetes."

"Oh, dear," Marie cried out as she placed her hand over her mouth in horror, "that's terrible! How did Talulah find out?"

"She knowed something not right cause the money weren't coming home like a'fore. But Talulah, she keep on working. Then she hear some of the peoples who be upset with no pie. They be axing her why Huey don't come round no more. And her man Huey, who be growing more wide than tall, could barely fit in his clothes, don't you know, and soon he gots so short of breaths that he couldn't even walk his route no more."

Bea shook her head again, looking at the gravel, then said, "It weren't no more than a week, and Huey be *dead!* They wonder what kill him! The docta' say maybe it his heart, a stroke from pressure, all I can say is I thinks it was his sugar! Either way, he was cold by the time they gots him to Charity Hospital."

Marie was speechless.

"Poor Talulah," Paul said. "What about their daughter, Bea? What happened to Delilah?"

Bea turned her head, looking off in the distance and didn't respond. Paul and Marie could feel another sad story coming their way.

Then, Bea began to speak firmly. "Talulah know what she hads to do after Huey went on to be with the Lawd. She began to do both the jobs herself *and* raise that child. The bakin', the deliverin', and she raise Delilah too! It weren't long before she couldn't do it all, and that be when this line out here began." Bea pointed up and back down the line with an arthritic finger.

They all turned to face the porch as they heard the top door open, then singing was heard from inside.

Marie, loud enough for Bea to hear, said, "We've never seen anyone else working with her. Surely her daughter is old enough to be of more help now?"

Just at that moment, Talulah appeared in the door to sing her song, and soon the line was moving.

Bea said, "It been real nice talking with y'all!" Looking directly at Paul, she added, "You certainly make one handsome couple *together*, and that be somthin' you best don't forget!"

"Nice to meet you too, Bea," Marie said as she nudged Paul forward. She added, "Maybe we'll see you in line again; we have lots more questions for later!"

This semester was flying by. Both families were looking forward to their "kids" coming home for Thanksgiving and Christmas. For now, the holidays had remained undiscussed between Marie and Paul. Both continued to ignore the reality of the pain they would feel when separated by more than a few hours.

After class on a Friday in October, the pair strolled through campus arm in arm. Marie, unable to hold back, said, "I'll be checking with my parents, but I don't think they'll have any issues with you coming to our house in Morgan City for Thanksgiving dinner!"

"Gee, Marie. That's nice, but Thanksgiving is a big deal at our home! It's the one meal every year that I never miss. My grandmother Morel cooks cornbread dressing just the way I like it, and it's the best food of the year. While I'm home, we wake up early and go deer hunting with my cousins and my dad. I really couldn't miss any of that!"

Paul didn't realize that he'd just shaken a giant hornet's nest. He believed that issue was done and continued to walk along, still holding her hand. Marie released his palm as she stopped in her tracks. Folding her arms, she turned around and, looking at her feet, began to cry. Still oblivious, Paul touched her shoulder to find out what was wrong.

Marie turned away and snapped, "Don't touch me, Paul Morel!"

"What just happened, Marie? You invited me to your parent's house, and I told you why I couldn't go. What gives? Why are you so upset?"

Marie started walking away from him.

Calling after her, "Wait a minute, can't we discuss this?"

Suddenly, she turned around. "I gave you an invitation to my home, and instead of accepting it, you would rather eat dressing, hunt, and be without me. Did I hear you correctly?"

Paul shrugged his shoulders as he sheepishly put his hands in his pockets. He'd been hit broadside and had the wind knocked out of his sails. Speaking slowly, he said, "I love being around you. You are the neatest person I've ever met. But this is family. It's not like we're married or something."

"Well, with that attitude, that's never going to happen! You'd do better to remember what Bea told you that day. We're a couple, Paul!" She turned away again and continued walking.

Marie heard her voice and couldn't believe the words that had just crossed her lips. *Who was this possessive person she'd become? Is this what relationships do to someone?*

"Marie!" he called after her. "Wait a minute, *please!"* Paul ran ahead of her, positioning himself directly in her path as she tried to walk around him.

He'd been holding something back, something he wanted to say but couldn't find the words. It wasn't until this happened that he genuinely understood Marie's feelings for him.

As she tried to dodge him by stepping off the path, he grabbed her shoulders and said, "I've avoided telling you something. I've never told any girl what I'm about to say."

For a moment, Marie thought she might faint. What she was about to hear was either going to be real good, or really bad. And the reality was, either way, she was unprepared mentally to listen to it. These were uncharted waters for her, and her mind had been taken over by emotion. Still, she said, "I'm listening."

"I'm in love with you, Marie."

She didn't move, but continued to look away from him as something inside her replied, "I'd love you more if you came to my house for Thanksgiving."

She had fired another volley, knocking him off balance again. He stepped back a little, looked away, then fired back, "Wait a minute. Did you say what I thought you just said?"

Marie turned toward him, placed one of her hands on her hip in a questioning pose to respond. "Do you think, Paul Morel, that I would stay up all night painting life-like pictures of us as a surprise for you, walk together holding hands with you every day, and dream about you every night *if I didn't love you? You need to get with the picture!" No,* she said to herself, *I didn't just say that!*

He was happier than he'd ever been, and this state she had catapulted him into prevented use of his mouth. Paul stood there, speechless.

She raised her arms to exclaim, "Well, don't you have anything else to say?"

Words formed on his lips none too soon, "What time is dinner served at your house on Thanksgiving Day?"

"Five o'clock in the evening. We pick at hors d'oeuvres and catch up with each other most of the day, then eat our meal late."

Paul grew quiet again. He looked aside, obviously thinking.

Marie appeared committed now. "So, what do you think, Paul? We are in a holiday crisis here, and where have you gone?"

"Uh, well, how about you come to New Roads on Wednesday, the day before Thanksgiving. You can spend the night with my family, have a meal with us at our normal time, at 11 am, and then we could be at your house in time for dinner! That way, we could meet each other's families."

Marie folded her arms again and said, "On one condition."

Sarcastically, "Just one? How'd I get off that easy?"

"You need to buy a bunch of Talulah's pies on Wednesday after you get out of your class so we can bring some to our families. I've been telling my parents all about them."

"Okay, that was easy."

As soon as those words catapulted across his lips, he knew that getting a bunch of Talulah's pies in one trip was going to be next to impossible. He needed a plan to pull that off. But for now, he chose not to show Marie any weakness.

"Oh no, wait just a minute there, Mr. Writer Man! There is something else included in my condition."

"Lord, what else could I possibly do or say?"

"This is easy. It's just something I want to know…"

Feeling defeat at hand, he said, "All my other answers have gone your way, I'm sure this one will too."

She was still battling her own emotions, trying to understand what was driving her toward him so intently. No question, he was handsome, smart, and a true gentleman. She'd just entered college with such high aspirations for a career. Several times already, she had questioned herself about her feelings for Paul. Was it her raging hormones that were manipulating her? One way or another, she needed to understand this strong pull for Paul.

Marie stepped up next to Paul, a position that he usually would embrace. The past few minutes, however, had been intimidating.

With her lips so close that they touched his as she spoke, she asked, "Do you think of me at night… you know, like the way I think about you?"

Paul thought he was dreaming. He'd never even remotely discussed feelings like this with a girl. Despite the intense warmth felt all over his body, with a straight face, he replied, "No, I don't."

He knew Marie and knew that she would not take that statement well. But he loved yanking her chain. Like a world-famous running back, he smiled and proceeded downfield quickly. He ran a short distance away so he would be a safe distance from any lightning-fast retaliations, and called back, "I think of you more… a lot more! See you tomorrow, Marie Elise Landry!"

And with that, he was gone. Marie found the nearest bench and sat down. Her legs became too shaky to trust. So much was just said, she needed a moment to catch her breath and digest it all. It was surreal. They had both, each in their way, just confessed love for each other. She had felt it for weeks, and knew he also had. She never felt this way, before Paul. It felt good to hear what he said. *Who wouldn't want to hear someone say those things?* Now, she didn't know what to do with it.

She had instigated this, and she had to decide what would become of it. One thing for sure, she was unsure where any of these words might lead. To stay in the moment, for now, felt so right.

The score was: Hormones – 1: Career – 0. Like many youthful as well as adult relationships, neither was privy to the other's complete thoughts.

11
PIE RUN

Not a moment had passed, since committing to Marie, that Paul didn't wonder how he would pull it off. Not the love part, but the pie part. Through trial and error, they had come up with a reliable system for acquiring only a small share of the Wednesday pie harvest. But to get enough of Talulah's pies to spread between two families for Thanksgiving dinner seemed next to impossible.

He couldn't bring himself to discuss his concerns with Marie. He had to figure out a way to pull it off because she was counting on him.

Marie understood the magnitude of this project. It was obvious. One morning, walking to class, Paul asked her if she had told her parents that they were bringing pies for dessert. Her response was, "I'm not saying a word to anyone until I see them with my own eyes!"

In the week before Thanksgiving, in desperation, Paul asked her if she was going to help him on Wednesday with his raid and siege of Talulah's.

"I'll be doing my nails Wednesday, they are looking pretty rough," she replied.

Sacrificial lamb, thy name is Paul, he thought.

By Wednesday, he awoke with a feeling of intense dread and trepidation. The reality of where this was going hit him squarely in the face when he made his usual stop at Marie's window. Weeks ago, she had started beating him to class, yet despite this, he still went the long way, taking him past her dorm. His effort was always rewarded. Each Wednesday, she continued to place a new painting in her window for him. He gladly continued to stop by to view her latest creation before meeting her in class.

Standing in the early morning light, he viewed a hopeful scene that he feared might be fictional by days end. Beautifully and realistically done, like all the rest, was a picture of him standing in front of Talulah's door, showing Talulah extending a huge platter filled with steaming pies to him. Talulah was pictured smiling broadly.

Despite the crisp air, as he gazed at this hopeful scene, Paul felt a bead of sweat form on his forehead as he felt a massive knot expanding in his stomach.

After a contemplative walk to class, he pushed open the door to see a smiling Marie, waiting for him.

She called out to him, "Did you go by my window?"

Just inside the door, "You did it again, didn't you? Your paintings are simply incredible. Good morning!"

He continued to his seat. Glancing along the way at the blackboard door to verify privacy, he arrived at his place and leaned over to greet her, planting a quick kiss squarely on her lips.

"What a nice holiday we have ahead of us!" Marie said. Then, she let loose, "When are you going to tell me your plan to get our pies? I can't wait to hear it! I'm not sure how I'll be able to hold myself back with all those pies in the car for the drive to New Roads, you may have to put them in the trunk of your Dad's car when he picks us up! You know, remove the temptation?"

The longer she rambled on, the more Paul liked it. Not knowing how to respond, he was in no way excited about this holiday yet. He couldn't be in holiday mode until the pies were in hand.

Aware that the subject needed to change, Paul asked, "Do you think Ms. O. will give us an assignment for the break?" Allowing no time for her to respond, he piled on a second deflection, "I hope not. We've been going so hard it would be nice to have a break, wouldn't it?"

"Paul Edward Morel, I don't appreciate you changing the subject away from our glorious pies." Louder now, she added with emphasis, "*I'm already on vacation!*"

"Good morning, Ms. Landry. Still acting, are we?"

Marie looked at Paul with eyes so full it was all he could do to keep from laughing. He had to look away and stared at his empty desk as though he was busy.

Marie was upset that she'd been "had" again. Things were going so well for her lately in Ms. O.'s class. As she slowly turned to face the voice, all she could envision was bringing her Dad's hammers and nails from home to seal this sneaky woman's private entrance.

Ms. O., acting a bit herself, met Marie's shock with an initial scowl, which quickly extended into a broad smile to say, "We're just going to be doing some reviewing today, so in a way, you're already on break. I hope you both have a wonderful Thanksgiving with your families! Oh, and I guess you can see there's a bit of an actress in me, too!"

After extending the same well-wishes to her, Marie turned back to Paul, who began to laugh as quietly as he could.

Marie gently slapped the back of his head as payback, and finally was able to giggle.

❧

Paul's next class on Wednesday began at 10:30, but he was doing well in History and planned to skip that class today. He had a friend from home in his class, and he could contact him to see if any new assignments appeared before the break. Today, he walked Marie in the direction of her next course, as he always did, but didn't mention that he was skipping his.

Just as he parted from Marie, she said, "I get the feeling you are keeping a secret from me. I've been asking about your plan for the pies, and you keep changing the subject."

He was worried enough without her asking and hoped she wouldn't keep pressing him, but he had to fess up. He replied, "The problem, you see, is that I have no plan. I don't know how I'm going to pull this off. I'm going to skip my last class and go now. Hopefully, I'll figure it out when I get there."

"I can miss my class; do you want me to come with you? And why are you going so early? You know that she only opens her door later in the day!"

Paul considered what she was saying and replied, "I have to go early to see what I can do, and it's probably best that I go alone. I'll call you later and let you know what happens." He started to turn away as he looked back to say, "Oh, and I'm really looking forward to sharing Thanksgiving with you!"

Reaching for his neck on her tiptoes, Marie latched her arms around him tight, kissed him, and reminded him that she loved him.

What was happening felt like a scene from a war movie. One where a young soldier leaving for battle has to say goodbye to his girl. Paul could only imagine his fate as he walked away alone. But he knew he'd made the right decision leaving her behind. If Marie were to come with him, odds were that they would both become a casualty by day's end. His mission today was to return the victor: with pie.

The streetcar ride down St. Charles Avenue was unusually rough today. The car seemed to sway side to side so hard that Paul hoped it didn't jump the tracks. Several times he thought the operator was going to jump out at blocked intersections and get into a physical altercation with people from the land of rubber-wheeled vehicles. He'd never heard as much clanging and banging on the bell from any operator before. None of this helped to calm his uneasy nerves.

There was another possibility concerning what was happening around him. Marie, who was never at a loss for mind-diverting words, wasn't with him. She could distract his mind in exciting ways, including from streetcars about to jump the rails.

He saw it ahead; his stop at South Carrollton. It was a sweltering hot day, and he didn't relish what was about to happen. He had his backpack with him, but it was half-filled with books. The realization hit him suddenly that he had no idea where to put these pies *if* he were able to get them.

❧

When he arrived at Talulah's, the lot was empty as expected, and the only positive sign was smoke billowing from the chimney. He approached the porch and held his ear to the closed Dutch door. After listening for a minute, he was disappointed that he couldn't hear singing.

It took a while longer to summon courage, and then he decided it was time for the frontal assault of this campaign to commence.

He knocked on the door twice, lightly.

Again, Paul listened across the door with his ear. No footsteps, no voice, no nothing. The next time, he knocked louder, but still no response. He stepped off the porch and looked around, wondering how he could find Talulah's real house to tell her of his predicament. *Surely, she didn't live here,* he considered.

Paul knew enough about New Orleans to understand that one doesn't go traipsing around the back of a stranger's house without an invitation. Only desperate people did such things. And that's why he knew it was his only option.

Talulah's bakery was in a typical shotgun style house. Classically narrow and long, the name came from the fact that if all the doors of the home were open, you could fire a gun through the front door, and the bullet could exit out the back door without hitting anything. Paul knew he would find a back door, and with a fire going in the fireplace, it was probably left open to a screen.

He was taking a considerable chance, possibly even a risk, but hoped he might find Talulah and plead his case. He began to walk around to the back of the house.

The windows on the side were all shut with curtains. As Paul arrived at the back corner, he peered past the corner to see a small backyard, filled more with dirt than grass. All it contained was a clothesline and what appeared to be a small tool shed.

Moving slowly, trying not to appear any more suspicious than he felt, Paul approached the three wooden steps at the backdoor. As he guessed, there was a screen door, and he could feel heat flowing out of it as he stood at the foot of the steps. Finding himself suddenly on the top step, he peered into the dark house and could faintly make out several tables with baking utensils and bowls. The heat from this kitchen was oppressive.

He called out, "Miss Talulah! Are you here?" Hearing nothing from within but the snap from a burning log, he paused.

Not yet defeated, he sat down on the step. *Surely,* he thought, *someone would be returning soon.*

Wondering what Marie was doing at this moment, he tried to ignore the heat, thinking about both of their families. He envisioned how they were each beginning the preparation of part of the meal for tomorrow. He looked forward to meeting Marie's parents and having her meet his family.

There are so many emotions and so much time invested in preparation for Thanksgiving. The day is part of the fabric of our American society; a day that family, love them, or not, gets together to share a meal.

Considering these things, it was still hard to ignore what Marie would think if he didn't return with pies today.

Reality bellowed from the other corner of the house as he heard, "Mr. Peach Writer Man, what you be doin', sittin' on Talulah's back step? You come here enough to knows that *if* Talulah had the peach, it'd only be served at her front door! Now, you be real smart to go back where you knowed you should be. Talulah, don't cater to no bidness through her screen door!"

Talulah was carrying a big box and appeared, for that reason alone, to be very impatient about entering her door. He was, at the very least, in her way. She didn't slow as she approached, and Paul was about to be run over.

Paul hadn't cried since he was a child. But he felt a good one coming on. Doing his best to hold it together, he promptly stood, preparing to jump from the step.

But he hesitated. Running and crying weren't options at this point. Standing his ground, he made a quick flanking maneuver. He reached out with an offer to help as he said, "Good morning, Miss Talulah… here, let me help you if you don't mind."

She ignored him.

Next, he said, "Here, let me open the door for you. That box looks pretty heavy!"

With sweat already on her brow from the exertion of carrying the box on such a hot day, Talulah's only expression was a faint nod, as Paul held his breath and opened her door.

Not used to help, Talulah said, "Thank you, sir, now best you go 'head on." She proceeded in, leaving Paul holding the door.

The first skirmish, having gone better than expected, encouraged Paul. He planned to wait her out quietly. This strong woman had one weakness: she needed help. He closed the screen and waited outside patiently.

The screen distorted his view as he watched Talulah table the box to extract the contents. From what he could tell, she was bringing more baking supplies for her cooking.

From this vantage, allowing him to see her fully, Talulah appeared larger than she did above the Dutch door. Much larger. Despite this, he watched in amazement as she delicately floated around her tables, seemingly unconcerned by his curious gaze.

He continued to wait and watch quietly. After fifteen minutes, he hadn't seen her look back at the door even once, yet suddenly she called out, "You still there, Mr. Peach Writer Man?"

"Yes," he called out, as though he was proud of his new name.

"Well, you must got something more to say, so why don't you come on in and get it out your system so Talulah can keep her mind on her cookin'!"

As Paul jumped to open the screen door, she added, "An don't you thinks that Talulah be letting anybody skip her line!"

His hopeful heart grew weary of leaping into his chest from his feet as Talulah sent it reeling back. As optimism sank again, he fearfully stepped into the inner sanctum of pie.

"Sit right over in my chair by the sink, and don't move less I tells you too." A faint smile appeared as she added, "I moves so fast sometimes, you needs to be careful. If you gets in Talulah's way, I be stirrin' you in the *fruit!*"

"Yes, ma'am," he said. He could tell she meant business.

Talulah was already mixing faster than he'd ever seen anyone before. His grandmother would be in awe. In separate, large cast-iron pots, she combined her fresh fruits and sugar and placed the pots on metal hooks close to her wood fire in the hearth. After a while, she looked over at Paul and said, "You sure be the quiet one, don't you mama teach you how to speak?"

"Yes, ma'am," he replied again.

"Then why you be holdin' back? Tell Talulah why you here so early and sneaking 'round her screen door?"

He cut to the chase. "Miss Talulah, I need some of your delicious pies."

"You think Talulah don't know that already? Son, I already done toll you, you be in the wrong place for that! You need to pick your hiney up off 'a Talulah's grand mama's chair and go park it in the fronts to get in line like all the other peoples!"

She continued to glare at him with her stern face and now sported an upraised, threatening spoon, adding with even more emphasis, "An Talulah don't want 'a hear no sass-mouthing!"

Things weren't looking good. Pulling all the stops, Paul tried one last flanking maneuver, "There was a nice lady that we met in line last Wednesday named Bea, and she said she was your good friend..."

"Well, you out you evah-lovin' mind if you be thinkin' that droppin' the name of Bea Carter, gonna get you somethin' special *through the screen door!"*

"No, Miss Talulah, that's not it at all! Miss Bea mentioned that you had a daughter, and said it was so sad that your husband Huey had passed away. I was wondering if I could swap with you?"

"Swap? With me? For what you say?" Talulah looked away from

him and continued her work. She began to mix a large bowl of unmeasured contents for her dough.

Paul waited, choosing his next words carefully.

Impatiently, Talulah said, "Well, Mr. Peach Writer Man? You best be talkin'! I knows you wants some pie; now what you got to swap with Talulah?"

"I go to college down the street, and I'm doing pretty well, so I have a lot of free time. I was hoping that I could help you somehow, in exchange for some of your delicious pies. I can't cook, but I can carry, lift, stir, and sell door to door!"

His words fell on silence from her.

He added, "Since you are so busy making ends meet, and your dear husband is no longer here, I thought maybe your daughter could use some help with homework and assignments if she's still in school. I could be a tutor! And maybe, at times like this, when I need more pies than normal, you could help me?"

Talulah stopped stirring and stared at him incredulously. She appeared dumbfounded. His pitiful plea was about to be crucified.

Pulling all the stops while continuing to pray nonstop, he added, "And the best part is, I will still pay you for the pies!"

She began stirring again, and her furrowed brow made it visible she was thinking either about helping him or whacking him with her spoon. Time would tell.

Suddenly, she looked at him and said, "You tryin' to tell me that you want extra pies, now and again, but you still willin' to pay, and you'll teach Delilah for free, and help me round here if I needs it?"

"Yes, Miss Talulah, that's what I'm saying.

"Did Bea tell you that Delilah just got out'a the juvenile jail a few weeks ago, for drugs, and finely 'greed to get her GED to keep out'a jail? Did you know she been kicked out the high school?"

"No, all she said was you had a daughter, and your husband passed away suddenly and way too young."

"Did she tell you 'bout the sugar?"

"Yes."

"Well, that says somethin' good 'bout'cha. Bea ain't got many friends, and it's cause she be tight-lipped. It appear she weren't tight-lipped with you."

"Bea is very nice, and she sure likes you, *and* your pies."

"Ain't you a flatterin' Peach Writer Man. You gots a name, son?"

"My name is Paul Morel."

"Well, Mr. Paul Peach Writer Man Morel, you gots yourself a deal. What kind'a pie you want, and how many?"

Paul stood, although still in disbelief of the outcome. He ventured, "An assortment of twenty, please?"

Talulah's furrowed brow and wide eyes couldn't adequately express her surprise with this request. "Twenty pies?" she asked, indignantly. "On the day before Thanksgiving? You sure gots you some highfalutin nerve!"

Talulah was stirring furiously, faster than any time while he'd been watching. With his eyes wide open, he waited patiently, thinking he should step back in case she started hurling things in his direction.

She finally responded, "When you gonna start the tutorin'? For twenty pies, it sure better be soon! I ain't never seen so many pies go out'a the screen door at one time, 'cept when Huey be alive."

Almost under his breath, Paul offered, "Would next week be okay, when we return from Thanksgiving break?"

She didn't respond right away as her stirring slowed. She placed the pot she was working on over the fire. Then, she looked at Paul and said, "Okay. You and Talulah gots a deal. Now sit yourself back down, take a load from your feets, and when the pies come out, you can go your way right after Talulah opens the top door in the front room. That's when the peoples eyes look nowhere else except at my door. It's the pies, don't you know? Them that's in line gonna be lookin' only at my door. You knows, distracted so you can sneak away with that big box full." Talulah raised her immense arm from the bowl to point the spoon at the large box she carried in earlier. She was allowing him to use it for his pies.

Paul sat down and remained quiet until the box brimmed with steaming pies. He couldn't believe his eyes. After she sprinkled them with powdered sugar, she motioned him over to the table, saying only, "Go 'head on now, I be seeing you on Monday."

"Talulah. It's been very nice getting to know you. I hope to get to know you better real soon. Tell Delilah that I'm looking forward to helping her, and we hope you both have a wonderful Thanksgiving."

Paul pulled his wallet out and began to open it to settle his bill.

Talulah placed her large hand over his and said, "I hopes you and your family have a blessed Thanksgiving, and I'm sorry I overcharged you the other day. It wasn't right, cause you poem was real good, and I been 'pologizin' to the Lawd ever since. This be my way telling you I really likes you poem, and you not too bad you selfs!"

Paul thanked her profusely and picked the box up to leave.

As he started to turn for the back door, Talulah said, "Oh, and Mr. Paul P. W. M. Morel, do you knowed what the name Delilah stand for?"

"No, Miss Talulah, I don't."

"It from the Lawd's bible. It mean 'Hope.'"

"It's a beautiful name. Thank you for that too, ma'am!"

With the large box in his arms, he waited for Talulah to move into the front room and open the Dutch door. As soon as he heard her begin to sing, he quietly walked out the rear and escaped toward the front. And like a leaf in a wind-storm, he drifted away.

Paul tapped on Marie's window, and she didn't appear. As he was about to rap again, she flew out the front door of her dorm and came running over.

Without a word, he proudly opened the box.

Marie stopped just inches from him and stared with disbelief at the bounty before her eyes. She looked up in amazement and asked, "How in the world did you do this, Paul Morel?"

He smiled and said, "Talulah likes me."

12

THANKSGIVING BREAK

Later that afternoon, Dr. and Mrs. Morel picked them up outside of Paul's dorm. His dad watched as his son carefully placed the box of pies in the trunk, stating, "You are handling that box so carefully, Paul, it must really have something special inside!"

"Very," Paul responded as he closed the lid and jumped in the car.

Marie found Dr. and Mrs. Morel, from the beginning, to be kind and gracious. Dr. Morel informed her, "Marie, Mrs. Morel, and I feel like we already know you. It's amazed us both that when Paul calls, we hear more about you than how he's doing in school."

As they exited the city, heading for Airline highway, Marie felt very comfortable with these people as she listened to Paul, bantering with his mother.

He said, "I didn't miss you a bit, Mom, or your cooking!" He winked at Marie as his mother playfully slapped his hand on her shoulder. Marie also felt that Paul had everything essential to him in this car, not to mention her and the pies.

Dr. Morel looked in the rearview mirror at Marie and asked, "Perhaps you know the answer to this question already, Marie, but I wonder if my son is still interested in Law School?"

Dr. Morel had caught her off-guard. She looked at Paul for a sign. It was the first she'd heard of this.

Paul smiled as she shot him a look, indicating she reserved the right to kill him later.

Then, from Marie, "I'm not sure, Dr. Morel. Your son plays his cards close to his chest! It sounds like you know more about that than I do about that subject."

Marie gave Paul another look that clearly spelled out, *English major my ass!* Her intelligence prevented her from sending up flares, just yet. She was aware that her share of pies was in jeopardy.

How dare him, she thought, *to withhold valuable information like that!*

Paul looked out the window, attempting to remain separate from all the commotion in the car. He understood there would be a price to pay for withholding such information. One he relished.

There is one thing familiar about a drive anywhere in south Louisiana: it is flat. But it is also a beautiful, fertile region, with people as lovely as the sugarcane is sweet. Only a couple of hours from New Orleans, New Roads, like many places in Louisiana, is historically French.

Dr. Morel, obviously very proud of his home, gave Marie a history lesson as they drove along False River. "The town hasn't always been called New Roads. The French founded a trading post here in the 1720s by the name of Le Poste de Pointe Coupée.

Marie chimed in, "Cut Point Post! I'm studying French as a minor, sir!"

"Correct you are! When Great Britain defeated France in the French and Indian War, France gave the region to Spain. That's when the Spanish built, as locals called it, a Chemin Neuf, or New Road, that connected the Mississippi River with False River. In 1803, the area became part of the United States again with the Louisiana Purchase. The name of our town bounced around many times, from St. Mary's to New Rhodes until the current spelling stuck."

Just as he finished his introduction, Dr. Morel turned down a stately driveway lined on each side by massive live oaks, covered in moss. At the entrance was a sign that said: Retraite de Pelican, or Pelican's Retreat. Marie could see a large, wooden home at the end of the long path. She turned toward Paul with eyes filled with anticipation as he smiled at her.

Paul said, "Welcome to our home! My great grandfather, a successful sugarcane farmer, built it. I love to come home."

"I can see why!" Marie said as they pulled up in the circular drive by the front entrance.

"Home again, home again, jiggidey-jog," Mrs. Morel sang.

"Mom, I never looked forward to hearing your little jingle more than today!"

His mom chirped, "Grab your things and let's go in. Your sister's been cooking since before we left. I'll bet it's starting to smell pretty good by now!"

The car came to a stop, and Paul almost ran to the trunk. He found Marie already there, about to grab the box.

"Back away from that box, Marie Landry!"

His father looked at him like he had a screw loose, and Marie's hurt look didn't help his cause.

Paul changed his tone, saying, "It's a heavy box, please let me help you with it."

Marie didn't want the varnish of her initial meeting with his parents to rub off too quickly, so she stepped away to make room for Paul, the pie guardian.

"Must be a precious cargo in that box," his mother said as she turned and walked into the front foyer, with Marie following closely on her heels.

Marie quickly forgot about pie as Paul's father took her by the arm and escorted her into the house. "My grandfather built this house around 1866, right after the Civil War. It took fifteen years to complete because the south was hurting badly." As they reached the grand staircase, he said, "Our room is upstairs, the kids and the guest rooms are in the back in a newer section added on after the turn of the century. I'll let my wife show you around upstairs later. Let's follow them back to the kitchen. I'd like to introduce you to Savannah, our daughter. She is an attorney in training at Tulane, but don't let her intimidate you; it's a holiday for her too!"

Walking down the hall, Marie said, "I know she's been busy. Our paths haven't crossed yet at school. Paul says she studies all the time!"

As they entered the kitchen, the other ladies were seen standing next to a counter as they worked. Dr. Morel introduced Marie to Savannah and her elegant grandmother, Memie. They were in the middle of making Memie's cornbread dressing.

Dr. Morel thought it was the right time to warn Marie, as he said, "Whatever you do, Marie, don't slow them down. It wouldn't be Thanksgiving around here without Memie's cornbread dressing!"

By the time Dr. Morel walked away, the ladies wasted no time approving Marie to help by fitting her with an apron. After that, they placed a beer in her left hand and a spoon for mixing in the other.

Marie found the warmth of Paul's family almost overwhelming. Within moments she felt at ease as their conversation took off where they had left it, while including her.

Savannah was a spunky lady and was even prettier than Paul had described. With long brown hair, pulled back in a ponytail, she was trim and athletic looking. Memie was more reserved, and her face shone with a perpetual and genuine smile. Her silver-white hair was accentuated by a gorgeous blue pants suit.

When Savannah noticed Marie intently looking at Memie, she said, "Marie, don't you just love Memie's silver rings?"

"Yes," Marie said, "but first I had to force my eyes away from her gorgeous necklace! I think that's the largest sapphire I've ever seen!"

"Keep your eyes on it!" Savannah said, "One year, it fell off into the dressing!"

Memie replied, "Yes, and that's the year it tasted better, wasn't it?"

They all laughed together.

Paul was already out in the sprawling family room adjacent to the kitchen, catching up with his grandfather, dad, and cousin, Gerard. All of them were planning on getting up before the chickens in the morning to go deer hunting.

It was a delightful evening and had been a long day for everyone. Shortly after dark, Paul's grandparents drove back to the smaller home they lived in now, one that was "much easier to maintain," his grandfather had said.

Savannah had studying to do, and the beer had lowered everyone's eyelids. The kids all shared a bathroom at their end of the house, and they gave Marie the right to use it first, "while it's clean".

After kissing Paul good night, she told him, "Your family is incredible, and your home is like a living museum!"

It had been a great day.

Marie felt at ease here, and the refreshing shower felt awesome after a hot day. She slipped on her nightclothes, only to find herself wide awake again.

His room wasn't far from hers, and she found herself innocently approaching his door. *Should she,* she wondered.

The next thing she knew, she found her hand gently rapping on the door. Then, from inside, she heard, "Come on in, Marie."

As she entered, the room was dark. When inside, she closed the door. Paul turned on a lamp by the side of his bed and surprised her by pulling the covers aside. He waved for her to join him.

Feeling like they were in a fishbowl with the light on, she quietly demanded that he turn it out, then she fumbled her way in his direction.

Except for grunts heard as Marie stubbed toes on objects in her path, she arrived between his bed and the window.

Then, like a child slipping under the covers to hide from the boogeyman, she slipped in as he wrapped the sheet over her. She kissed him, then immediately turned over and nestled her back against his chest as he wrapped his arm across her. His warmth made her heart glow like a piece of hot coal in a wind storm.

"I need to know something," she asked.

"Yes?"

"How did you know it was me at the door?"

"That was easy," he said. "My parents haven't come to my door after dark since I was nine years old! They live upstairs at the other end of the house, so unless there's a fire or something, they leave me alone at night. As for Savannah, her 'Palace' is down the hall. It would be beneath her to damage a fingernail or hurt her knuckles on *my* door! I knew it was you. You just couldn't stand it, could you?" He began to nibble on her neck.

"I hesitated to knock. I wasn't sure you would want me in your room *and especially* under your covers. You know, like this."

"Don't be silly, Marie, it's no different than that day in the park under the blanket, and yes, I was hoping you'd come."

"Great," Marie said, "I wanted to hear what you heard that night that caused you to write your poem."

"Then listen," he said.

With his home close to the river, there was never a lack of night-sounds, especially when temperatures were unseasonably warm. Tonight, they wouldn't be disappointed, as the symphony began.

Sounds filled the room. It was incredible, and Marie understood how difficult it might be to put words to what she heard.

Marie felt at home in his arms, easily allowing a strong feeling to overwhelm her. She had never made love before, and with her eyes closed, she attempted to sense every part of this body that so intimately touched hers. *Was this how it would happen? It felt so right...and with this intense desire, how could thoughts alone satisfy her?*

Tonight, she felt something very different than what they shared in the park. She was spooning with the man she loved, and this was possibly more temptation than either one of them could resist.

Her body had been ready for years, and its physical needs were not easy to deny. Before Paul, her ambitions for art, and grad school had been her only love. Now, a vicious competition took place in her mind. Tonight, her body's physical desire was winning. She found it strange how feelings this strong can so quickly dispel other hardwired goals for the future. She bit her lip as she listened to the beautiful sounds outside and imagined the glory of being with Paul: close enough that they could become one...

She knew all she had to do was roll over, and words would be unnecessary. As she tried to gain her courage, she noticed a new sound from behind her. It was Paul. He was breathing heavily. As she tried to listen over the increasing melody from outside his window, she soon knew that the sound from Paul was not from excitement. It was from exhaustion. He was asleep.

Instantly, relief washed over her. She listened for a while longer to the symphony and her beautiful man. It amazed her how at ease he was with her in his bed. She waited until he rolled over, then slipped out from under the covers as quietly as she could.

Opening the door slowly to the hall, she stepped out, only to meet Savannah exiting the bathroom, sporting a Cheshire grin on her face.

Seeing the guilty look on Marie's face, Savannah almost busted as she said, "Honey, no matter what happened in that room, I've got to give it to you! You've gotten much farther with him than any girl that I know!" Savannah was relishing this moment far more than Marie, as she added, "Girls and my brother have, till now, mixed about as well as a breakfast of French toast and Brussel sprouts!"

Embarrassed and blushing, Marie stuttered, "But... but... nothing..."

"It's okay, Marie! If it did or if it didn't, I'm happy for you both. I can see how happy you make my brother. That's good enough for me, and what I saw just now goes no further."

Marie still fumbled. "Savannah, it was crickets and frogs... they come through his window..."

"I've got to give my little brother credit. He's got one of the best lines I've ever heard! If you're through in there, why don't you come on back to my room for a while, I'd like to get to know you better myself! And by the way, we're all dying to know what's in that box y'all brought?"

Marie followed Savannah to her room. They played music, talked into the night, and left each other in the early morning as the best of friends.

13
THE FEAST

At 5 am, Marie's door opened to the sound of Paul. "Marie? Are you awake?"

She turned on her bedside lamp to see Paul standing in her room in full camo. He said, "I wanted to apologize for falling asleep so fast last night, but with all the excitement, beer, and fresh air, I fell hard into my pillow."

Marie sat up against the headboard, wiping the sleep from her eyes. Her hair was everywhere.

Looking at her, he said, "Your hair is incredible!"

"Excuse me?" she asked.

"Your hair, it's going in every direction imaginable. I love it!"

Still half-asleep, she said, "Must be the humidity or cricket chirps or something."

Paul laughed as he sat on the side of the bed and said, "I hope you were able to get some sleep last night, and I'm sorry to wake you so early, but I missed getting a kiss last night. You know, when I fell asleep?"

Marie brushed her hair away from her face, leaned over, and planted a sleepy kiss on his lips. She pulled away and said, "Part of me wanted to give you more than that last night. It's a good thing you went to sleep. I should thank you. With you being so tired, it gave me a chance to figure out that I wasn't ready for that anyway."

"Well, if you ever change your mind, I'll try to keep my eyes open! Thank you for the kiss, though. Your kisses alone are enough to keep me coming back, Marie Landry."

Paul stood to say, "We should be back by 10 am."

"Be careful and come back to me!" Marie rolled over and pulled the sheet over her as he walked to the door.

As Paul stepped into the hall, he saw his sister down the way, standing at the entrance to the bathroom, watching him as he shut the door to Marie's room.

Caught off-guard by her presence and her questioning smile, and not at all prepared to explain, Paul said nothing. As he turned to walk in the other direction, he heard a voice behind him ask, "Good hunting in the guest room, brother?"

The family wouldn't be hurting for venison for a while. Three shots made, and three bucks brought home to gut and clean, all before 9 am. This was a family of great hunters for generations.

Paul, dressed and ready for 11 am lunch, was as hungry as could be. The immediate family was there; parents and grandparents. After his father offered grace, no stomach went unfilled.

Midway through the meal, his grandfather inquired, "Y'all got anything worth eating for dessert this year? I've got a section of my stomach still vacant, and depending on what I hear, I'll either wait for something sweet or go back now for more turkey."

Looking around the table at the others, Paul said, "Okay, which one of y'all put him up to this?" Then, focusing on his grandfather, he added, "And Pappy, I've never heard you ask about dessert! You've always had room for it no matter how much you ate!"

Nobody commented as the rest of them continued to eat. None raised their eyes from their plate, but Paul noticed that several were doing everything they could not to laugh.

Paul's father hadn't opened the box his son brought, but his nose had gotten close enough to it to know something good was inside.

Paul was enjoying keeping this secret from them. He, too, returned to his plate and continued to eat.

Looking at his son, Dr. Morel said, "Paul, you should answer your grandfather."

Marie couldn't stand all this secrecy over dessert. She tapped on her crystal iced tea glass before announcing, "*We* brought y'all some of the *best* pies I've ever eaten, all the way from River Road in New Orleans!"

Mr. Morel said, "Well, with those words from my grandson's girl, I'm a believer! I can eat turkey later!"

With the dinner plates cleared, the girls served coffee to those that wanted it and removed the pies from a warming oven.

Dr. Morel took a bite, which brought a smile to his face. He asked, "Where in the world did these come from?"

Marie had to answer, "Your son had to sell his soul to get this many, sir. They come from a hole-in-the-wall bakery on River Road, close to school. It's named after the owner: Talulah's Pie.

Paul asked, "What flavor did you get, Dad?"

"Strawberry, and boy, it is good!"

"Wait till you try the apple!"

Marie inquired, "How do you know which filling is in which pie, Paul?"

"Miss Talulah has a code visible on the pies. If you look closely, you'll see a difference from how she applies her fork marks to the edges. Apple is straight and short, and the cherry is straight and long. Strawberry is angled and short, and raspberry is angled and long. Blackberry gets sealed by a knife mark parallel to the outer edge, and Blueberry gets a slight roll. Oh, and Marie's favorite is chocolate, and it has Talulah's pinky prints on it, sealing it tight. Now, if there are any other questions, you'll have to pay by giving your pie to me! I accept all edges!"

Marie pushed away from the table and walked around to whisper in

Paul's ear, "Paul, I'm worried there won't be any pies left for my family. Are there enough?"

He replied, "There are plenty. I took out only half of the pies to eat here. I hid the rest of them in my closet."

From the other side of the table, Savannah questioned what the couple was discussing, "Paul, are you and Marie talking about hunting?" She finished with a giggle that caught her mother's attention.

Savannah knew from Paul's silent stare that there would be no other questions like that at the dinner table.

❧

By 1 pm, it was time to go. Paul and Marie wondered how they could eat anything else later today. They said their goodbye's and left in his mother's Pontiac Bonneville. It was hard for them to go. The family waved until they were out of sight on the main road.

"Paul," Marie said, "your family is incredible. They are so gracious and welcoming."

"I am fortunate, Marie. And you seem to fit right in!"

"I feel that way too," she said. "Savannah and I are already the best of friends."

Paul thought for a minute, then replied, "She's a sweetie, but I've always found it's best to stay on her good side. She'll make a great attorney!"

His mother's car was almost new, a beautiful shade of dark blue, with lots of power. Paul loved driving this car. With minimal traffic, they would quickly arrive in Morgan City early, probably no later than 3:30. They'd have plenty of time to get to know each other over hors d'oeuvres before dinner at five.

As they drove along, Marie had time for a question. One that had been building inside her since the other day when Paul magically appeared with *twenty* of Talulah's precious pies.

She began, "Since I have you captive for a couple of hours, I think it's high time you told me how in the world you got Talulah to give you all these pies?"

"Well, funny, you should ask, Miss Landry! I'll have you know that our Miss Talulah is quite the businesswoman!"

"I know you had to pay, probably dearly. That doesn't surprise me, but how did you get so many pies, and so early in the day?"

"Getting my hands on so many pies that day was, as my high-school history teacher Brother Peter Barnes called, a 'sticky wicket'!"

Marie didn't have a clue what he was saying, and her silence and confused look allowed him space to continue.

"You see, my dear, as you said, I did have to pay for these extraordinary pies, but not with money."

"Well, Mr. Morel, you really have we wondering, what else did you use for payment if it wasn't money?"

Paul didn't answer. He was enjoying this and began to whistle.

Marie hadn't known Paul long enough to know what he might do in a desperate situation.

Driving through otherwise empty country roads on a holiday, Paul was able to steal a glance in her direction now and then. Marie had grown quiet with thought, and Paul was enjoying this.

She couldn't stand it anymore. "Paul Morel, when are you *finally* going to answer my question?"

"Just realize, I'm going to be very busy at Miss Talulah's when we get back to school. I'm not going to have much free time. You knew that her husband had passed away, didn't you?"

Fortunately, he didn't run off the road when she slapped him hard on the shoulder. It also didn't help that he laughed harder than he had in a long time.

Marie grew quiet again and faced her window away from him. Paul dug a deeper hole, as he asked, "I'm not believing this, Miss Landry! Were you jealous?"

She folded her arms tightly. It bothered her that he still hadn't offered an answer to her question. Nothing else had worked, so she decided to try the silent treatment. It was probably safer than hitting the driver anyway.

He let her stew for a while. Finally, when her silence continued, he told her all the details she'd requested. Marie was impressed with what he'd done. True, it would require a lot of time away from her, but she agreed it was a worthwhile thing for him to do.

As they drove along, Marie grew silently reflective about her family. She thought about her last conversation with her parents. Their only child had never been away for a holiday before, and Thanksgiving was very special to them. Her father was often hard-nosed and lately was very protective of his "little" girl. In his eyes, Marie could do no wrong; that is unless she defied *his* wishes. The night she called, he told her he was not happy with her going to spend the night with people they didn't know, especially the home of a new boyfriend. Her mother bravely came to her defense, saying from the other line, "Oh now, Lucien, go easy on our baby!"

She hated it when her mother called her their "baby".

Marie was a model student at her high school and graduated with honors. She only dated a few boys, and they were polite and kind, both to her and her parents. If they hadn't been, there was no way she would have agreed to go out on a date.

Typically, when they would arrive at their Acadian style home, her Daddy would be doing something close to the driveway involving power tools like his chain saw, or cleaning his gun. He was uniformly gruff with the young men. Her Daddy wasn't a small man, and she could only imagine how intimidated he was to those young men.

As they continued further south and closer to her home, the more intimidated she became concerning her relationship with Paul. She hadn't told Paul this part, but it was all she could do to gain reluctant permission from her parents to arrive so late, and she prayed that Paul's first meeting with them would go well. She feared the worst now.

As they passed up the turn that would have taken them over the Mississippi River to Baton Rouge, they continued a few more miles, almost to Addis, Louisiana. That's when things changed. Traffic came to a standstill. After sitting in one spot for a while, Paul considered turning the car off because the temperature gauge started to indicate the vehicle was overheating from using the air conditioner. Just about that time, traffic began to come from the other way, and soon they had arrived at the scene of a tanker truck rolled over that had spilled fuel all over the road. Luckily the driver was okay, but the State Police were turning everyone around.

The only way to get to Morgan City now was to take the interstate to Lafayette, then south, or go east across the river bridge to New Orleans, then south on Highway 90 to Morgan City. Either way was going to add several hours to this trip. There was no way around this: *they were going to be late.*

"Marie, it might be best to pull over soon and call your parents to let them know you are okay, but we're going to be late. I'm so sorry about this."

As they turned the car around, Marie placed her head into her hands and began to sob.

Pulling the car to a safe spot on the side of the road, he stopped and tried to console her, saying, "Surely your parents will understand? Let's stop when we see a payphone so you can call them."

In a few minutes, the crying ceased, and she said, "Paul, you need to know, my father is not the easiest man to get to know. He was upset that I wasn't coming home for the full day already and not at all happy that I spent the night at your parent's house. Arriving there late is not going to go well."

Always the optimist, he replied, "How bad could it be? Let's not make this worse by sitting here. I need your help to pick which way we go, and whichever way you pick, we're going to be late. It's okay; it wasn't our fault."

"That's great, but do I also get to pick which way you'll go when he sends you home immediately after we arrive?"

Paul ignored her negativity and asked, "So, is it left or right at the intersection?"

To his surprise, Marie opened her door and exited the car. She picked up a few blades of grass and threw them into the air. A slight breeze caused them to float over the hood of the vehicle. As she got back in, she said, "Turn left up here, at least we'll have the wind behind us till we get to Lafayette."

"Great minds think alike. We're off."

They arrived in Lafayette at 4:35 pm and found a payphone booth to place the call.

"Hello, Daddy?"

Paul watched her face as she spoke.

"Yes, we're okay, but there was a huge wreck just south of the intersection to Baton Rouge and Lafayette. We had to turn around and go one way or the other, and we chose Lafayette, thinking it would be…"

Paul watched as Marie held the phone away from her ear. Then, she started to cry.

"Daddy… now please don't…"

Now she was sobbing hysterically.

"I'm so sorry about Thanksgiving dinner, Daddy…"

It was all Paul could do not to yank the phone from Marie and give this man a piece of his mind. She may be his daughter, but she was now *his* girl.

Marie continued to hold the phone at a distance. For the longest time, she said nothing. At one point, Paul could hear her father yelling.

Paul approached Marie suddenly, with the intent to intercede, and Marie stepped farther away from him, holding her hand out to halt his approach. Paul was more than ready to give this man a piece of his mind. The crying was mostly over, and for the next few minutes, Paul heard nothing more from Marie other than the words, "Yes, Daddy," repeated over and over.

Paul went back to the car and waited for her to return. When she did, she slid in next to him and held him as though she would never let go.

In New Roads, they had all been on such a high. It amazed Paul how things could change so quickly on such a special day.

After they sat together for a few minutes, she said, "I'm sorry to tell you this, but Daddy says I need to come home, and you will need to return to New Roads right after you drop me off." Tears returned as she sobbed into his shoulder. "I'm so sorry," she said.

Paul knew that there was nothing that he or Marie had done wrong, but it was not yet his place to argue with her father's wishes. He placed a call to his family, then joined her in the car for the painful finale of this trip to Morgan City.

Arriving after dark to her driveway, her mother came out to greet them as her father stood in the open front doorway with his arms folded. Marie wasted no time exiting the car. At her request, Paul remained behind the wheel as Mrs. Landry followed her daughter to his side of the vehicle. Her mother apologized to Paul, and after shaking his hand, told him she hoped he could come again soon under different circumstances.

Paul had trouble imagining that day. He reached out through the open window and touched Marie's hand. Her fear forced her eyes to the front porch. Unable to speak, she again began to cry. Paul backed out into the street and drove away.

Emotionally, it was a long trip home. Heading up Highway 70, he hoped to find no delay. Continuing down the road, he realized that the rest of the pies traveled with him. *Fitting,* he thought.

14
THANKSGIVING'S REMORSE

Savannah felt so sorry for her brother that she allowed him to drive her car back early to New Orleans. Her parents would follow with her the next day.

Paul was on edge, and everyone understood why. Ready to be by himself back at school, he returned before Marie. His parents and family were concerned about what the young couple had been through, and before leaving home early Sunday morning, his father took him aside and gave him some advice. He said, "Remember, son, to always be the bigger person. It's the best way to navigate through life's storms."

Driving the familiar route to New Orleans, he thought a lot about his family. He'd found himself disagreeing with his parents less as he aged; because he *always* found their counsel to be right. As he reached the intersection of indecision that he and Marie faced together on Thanksgiving Day, his choice this day was clear. He turned in the direction of the bridge headed for Baton Rouge. He'd seen enough of Lafayette and Morgan City for a while.

He'd not spoken with Marie since he backed from her driveway in Morgan City on Thursday evening. She hadn't called, and neither had he. Who in their right mind would want to upset her angry father even more? Because of expense, long-distance calls were frowned upon by many families, and he imagined that angry fathers set that bar even higher.

As he drove down Airline Highway to New Orleans, he said a prayer of thanks for a family that was universally kind to everyone. He'd been raised in a bubble and hadn't realized the full extent of sheltering that occurred growing up in a rural town. He'd experienced differences a few times when he and his parents visited Savannah in the big city of New Orleans. Most people didn't share the blessing he took for granted. Not everyone came from a kind family and a comfortable home. He'd grown up in an idealistic, protected way compared to many who survived day by day in an oppressive atmosphere.

It suddenly hit home to him, the price he paid for the pies from Talulah. An amount that would require him to enter a new world, one possibly filled with pain and even anger. His mother told him in the past, "Plans and choices that you make for yourself, son, may not coincide with those made by others around you. Everyone travels their own path in life." Again, wise words that traversed generations.

When he arrived at school in August, a feeling of loneliness crept over him after his family left. It remained with him until he met Marie. She quickly became that person that so many people are still searching for, the one that you think of when you first wake and hold in your dreams when you sleep.

A rift had occurred in this relationship, caused by something outside their control. What Paul didn't know was whether this obstacle might prove to be a major one for both him and Marie. Uniting as a couple in the face of these latest events seemed daunting.

Paul parked Savannah's car outside her apartment and took the streetcar back to school. He lugged his duffel up the stairs, hoping that Nathanial wouldn't return until late tonight. He sat down at his desk and wrote Marie a letter:

My Marie,
You soften my days and light up my nights. I hear you talking to me when you are not there. I see you everywhere, my eyes settle, and you make me smile in ways that only God could have imagined. I miss you so.

Love,
Your Paul

When he finished the letter, he grabbed his backpack and left for Marie's dorm. Arriving there while the afternoon was young, he taped the message to her window with the words facing her room.

After delivering the letter, he wasn't ready to return to his room. Soon, he found himself waiting at a stop on St. Charles Avenue. As he stepped onto the broad step leading up into the streetcar, his ears heard content, playful voices from a young family, possibly headed back home from a Sunday in the Quarter. They looked terrific in their Sunday clothes. Two young daughters with long, braided hair and dresses with ribbons and bows. Their clothing revealed bright colors of yellow and light blue. He imagined that they might have attended Mass at St. Louis Cathedral, perhaps afterward having lunch at any one of several places that served world-class food. They might have finished their excursion with beignets at Café du Monde.

Wherever they had been or were going now, they appeared to be a happy family. A family like his, brimming with mutual respect and kindness flowing like a creek that never ran dry.

He didn't know Marie's family but hoped that what he witnessed the other day was just a fluke, an anomaly. He wished only happiness for Marie.

He watched the family with joy as they bantered and interacted with each other. Suddenly he found himself stepping off the streetcar at his normal exit. Within minutes, he was standing in the lot, staring at Talulah's bakery. He wasn't sure why he was there, but something about this place had become part of him. His previously sheltered life was no more. A chance meeting with Talulah had somehow changed him, providing the focus for his path forward. He knew Talulah didn't want him to feel sorry for her; she was a fiercely proud woman. He could tell that from the first encounter. But she was as kind as she was determined, and her life, in some ways, was no different than his. They each had decided at some point to live life one day at a time.

He stood in the middle of her gravel lot, looking at the levee on the other side of the road. From down the street, he heard, "Hey there, Mr. Peach Writer Man, what you be doing on Talulah's property on the Lawd's day? Ain't you got no religion?"

Paul turned toward the voice and saw Talulah walking down River Road, carrying a sack slung over her shoulder, and headed to her shop. Whatever she was holding looked heavy.

He ran to help her, which made her stop and even back up a step or two. As Paul came to a stop in front of her, he said, "Please let me help you, Miss Talulah, that looks heavy.

"I do this every day, son! Talulah ain't no wilting daisy. You just go 'head on now. I got me some works to do. Ain't no fresh pies for you to barter today."

"Well, Miss Talulah, I've been thinking about our deal…"

"Oh, you wait just a minute, Mr. Peach Writer Man! When Talulah make a deal, it be so done that there ain't no going back. Even Moses be havin' second thoughts 'bout partin' the water before he even think 'bout undoin' a deal with Talulah!"

As Talulah walked on, Paul jumped in front of her again, bringing a furrow to her brow, and said, "Oh no, Miss Talulah, I'm not trying to break our deal; in fact, just the opposite. I'm here to tell you that I'm ready to get started! Will Delilah be ready to start tomorrow afternoon?"

Talulah had never met such a strange man. In her world, she was used to men trying to get out of deals they'd made rather than showing enthusiasm toward settling them.

Even in the short time since Wednesday, distrust bred from a distance had grown in her bosom. Her instinct, born from experience with men, was displaced by a renewed comfort as she thought, *why would he come here if he didn't mean what he say? I ain't got no pies tonight, and he knowed that.*

Against her better judgment, she said, "I'm just gonna drop these things in the shop, and go back home. This sack here, it be heavier than Talulah think. I don't want 'a turn up dead like Huey. You can carry it for me if you likes."

Paul swung the sack over his shoulder; it must have weighed more than fifty pounds. Respectfully and quietly, he followed her to the rear door of her shop.

She fumbled with the keys from the pocket of her skirt, finding the one to unlock her inner door.

Stepping into her shop in the faint light, she said, "Jus' put the sack on my table. Talulah thanks you for you help, Mr. Peach Writer Man."

Paul couldn't believe how cool the shop was without the fireplace blazing. He did as she requested, then turned to her and said, "Miss Talulah, I really am fond of that special name you gave me, and I'll always remember it, but if you don't mind, especially in front of your daughter, I believe I'll get more respect from her if you call me by my real name, Paul."

"I understand, Mr. Paul. Yes, I do."

"No, Miss Talulah, you don't have to call me Mr. Paul, just Paul."

"Oh, Mr. Paul, you needs to understands, you be fightin' a whole lot'a years 'o tradition 'round here to have me *or* Delilah talks at you that way."

"Well, Miss Talulah, I want you to know I don't expect it. My family calls me Paul, my teachers call me Paul, and that's who I want to be to you and Delilah."

"So, Mr. Paul, why don't you plan be 'round here along 'bout 3 pm tomorrow. I do my best 'ta have Delilah here, but she be difficult for me without a man round to help."

"I'll be here tomorrow, Talulah, and whatever happens, happens."

Paul walked past Marie's dorm, viewing the letter as he passed, still taped to her window. *She must not be back yet,* he thought.

Proceeding to his room, he walked in and switched on the light. Grumbling from under his covers was Nathaniel.

"Hey man, shut the light off, I'm trying to get some sleep here."

"I'm so sorry to disturb you, and I hope you and your wonderful family had a great Thanksgiving!" Paul shut the door as quietly as he could as he entered.

From under his covers, "Oh, and a girl called again and again for the past couple of hours. She sounds like she's gonna be pissed if you don't call her right away, man. But hey man, use the party line down the hall, I had a rough last couple-a-days."

"I'll bet you did! So sorry to disturb you in your room. Sleep well!"

Paul exited the room; the heavy wooden door seemed to slam itself. From within, he heard his roommate yelling, "Are you deaf, man? I told you I was sleeping!"

Ignoring him, Paul walked down the stairs and proceeded out the exit on the first floor. He was going to tap on someone's window.

He only took a few minutes to arrive, and he didn't understand why his letter was still there, taped in the place where he'd left it. If Marie had returned, why wouldn't she have come out and removed it herself? It was apparent she was there; the lights were on in her room. As he approached the window to tap, her smiling face appeared suddenly from inside.

Marie held up one finger to him as she mouthed the word, *Wait,* then again disappeared. Paul approached the entrance door, expecting her any second.

Soon, she was there, standing before him. The first words from her mouth were two familiar ones.

"Paul Morel," she said, "If you love me like you say you do, then I want you to romantically hand me that beautiful letter you left so I can read it."

"Wait a minute. You say my letter is beautiful, and how would you know that if you hadn't read it already? Oh, and you, Marie, are not the only judge of romantic."

Despite his protest, he walked over to her window and reached up to peel the tape off, being careful not to rip the sheet of paper. Carrying it like parchment for the Queen, he carefully turned and attempted to hand it to her.

She didn't try to take it from him. Standing there with a smile and folded arms, she said, "No, I want you to read it to me… please."

"Jeez, if I'd have known about all of this, my paper would still be in my notepad without ink on it!"

Insistently, she added, "You heard me, I said, *read it to me*."

This whole situation seemed odd to him. He was the one that returned home with his tail between his legs after what her father had done. But here she stood, being demanding, and certainly not eating any crow. *At least she seems happy to see me, that's a consolation.*

He looked at the paper in the faint illumination provided from an overhead light close-by, and began to read, "My Marie…"

Marie swooned, "I love that part, it's so very romantic. Did you mean for it to be so romantic?"

"Yes, I know, but I thought you wanted me to read my letter to you, and again, you implied that you'd never read it."

"Go on, please."

"My Marie…"

"You read that part already, *please* keep going!"

"Do you want me to read my letter or not?"

She didn't respond and looked at him with wide impatient eyes.

"You soften my days, and light up my nights…"

"Do I? Do I really? That is just so wonderful for you to say! Thank you so much. I can't thank you enough; you'll never know how much this meant to me: seeing your letter when I returned to my dark room tonight."

Despite her stated joy, Marie proceeded to sit on the grass outside her window and sob.

Paul sat next to her and finally realized what only fortunate men ever learn; knowledge passed to them, *not* one male to another but absorbed and recognized by mere chance and observation. Marie was trying to tell him something without telling him.

Compelled to speak, he asked, "How are you doing?"

She remained silent for a moment, then asked him if they could walk for a while.

Paul stood and extended a hand to pull her up. They walked together for the next few hours, up and down quiet streets adjoining the university.

Before returning her to her dorm, Paul learned that Marie's father had always been emotionally abusive but never physically. Her words comforted his concerns that she and her mother might be in danger from her father's eruptions. It became evident that her father was an intense man whose long-held family shrimping business had fallen victim to competition from corporate fleets. Marie said that he had become progressively more irritated and possessive of his family as business pressures escalated.

She asked him, "What did your family say when you returned home that night? Were they upset with me?"

Paul turned to her and held her shoulders, looking her in the eyes as he replied, "They know you. They would never judge you based on something your father did."

"Do you think we will ever have such a magical time at your parent's home again?"

"Soon, yes, I hope so."

"Do you still love me, Paul?"

Paul responded with what he considered a given, "Does Talulah make delicious pies, Marie Landry?"

15

TUTORING DELILAH

Promptly at 3 pm the next day, Paul approached Talulah's screen door at the rear of her shop. The heat from her fireplace poured through the screen like a river from a collapsed dam.

He hesitated outside the door, contemplating what would come of this session. *Would Delilah be receptive or resistant?* He'd never know until he entered. He grabbed the metal door handle, which was as hot as the air tumbling out the screen, and pulled the door open as the springs barked with protest.

Inside, Talulah was hard at work, several dozen pies already perched on the warming racks. She must have started early today, and was probably close to opening her top door for business. Without looking up, Talulah said, "Hello, Mr. Paul."

"Good afternoon, Miss Talulah." He was so happy to have moved beyond his other name. Paul looked around and saw no one else present.

"Give me a spell so's I can stir in my fruits, and then I introduce you to my daughter." Paul took another look around, wondering if he had overlooked someone.

"Less I accidental-like slap you upside the head with Talulah's spoon, why don't you sits outside on the step and wait where you'll be out'a Talulah's way. It's cooler out there, too. When I finish my stirrin', I'll gets you student." Pointing her spoon at the far corner of the room, she added, "Someone be catchin' up on sleeps under my table, and she ain't real nice when she first wakes up!"

Paul nodded receipt of that valuable information and walked out the door.

He was too restless to sit and instead slowly walked around the backyard. From every direction, he saw run-down houses and buildings. The poverty all around Talulah's shop was just blocks away from some of the most expensive real estate in New Orleans. Again, he gave thanks for how he'd been blessed and sheltered growing up. A father who was a professional, a stay-at-home mother who was always there, extended family close-by, all helped to shape him into who he was today.

He realized that was precisely why he was here today, to try to pass some of his good fortunes to someone else. Talulah's daughter happened to be just one of the innocent victims of inner-city poverty. As for so many others, she had no father. In her case, it wasn't because of a "hit and run" ne'er-do-well or person unwilling to step up to his responsibilities. Her father had been there for her and her mother until his premature death. Talulah was a hard-working mother who did her best to make ends meet, sometimes probably at the expense of time away from Delilah. Raised within a society that chewed young people up only to spit them back out, he hoped he could offer her some glimmer of hope that even her name hadn't provided.

Suddenly, the springs on the back door squealed to announce movement. Out walked Talulah. As she stepped down to the yard, the springs slammed the door closed again. With a surprised and impatient look, Talulah quickly turned and said, "Girl, you best be walkin' out that noisy door real soon!"

The door opened again, and a skinny young girl squinted as she hesitantly walked out into the sundrenched yard.

"Mr. Paul Morel, let me introduce to you my girl, Delilah."

Paul stepped up to her with his hand extended. Ignoring him,

Delilah looked only at her mother, blurting, "Mama, this man be white! You knows rite now this ain't gonna work!"

After saying this, Delilah spun around and started back to the door.

In a flash, Talulah grabbed her arm, turned her back around, and pulled her up close to her face to say, "Mr. Morel be a real nice man. When I looks at him, you mama don't see no color. I just see nice. He don't have 'ta be here, and certainly, he don't have 'ta help any ungrateful peoples, so I suggest you tries be a bit more polite to this man who be ma friend."

Talulah had a way about her. It was Talulah's way or the highway.

Delilah stood, still facing away from Paul, with her arms folded and her face looking at her feet. Talulah's hand had not abandoned her arm.

Talulah was growing impatient. She didn't have time for insubordination. "Nah, girl, I thinks you needs to off'a ma good friend, Mr. Morel, apologies."

Delilah pulled her arm away from her mother's bear-sized hand. Begrudgingly, with her eyes focusing on the ground in front of her, she said, "I'm sorry, Mr. Morel. Thank you for comin' to help me."

"That be more like it," Talulah said, as she quickly turned toward the door. "I gots to get back to my bakin'."

After the springs grew quiet again, Paul and Delilah stood in their places for a few long moments. Paul knew he needed to take charge of what would happen next. "Delilah," he said, "I'm not here to judge you, just to help. Today, we're not going to do any school work. I'd like to get to know you better first. Would you take a walk with me? We could walk along St. Charles Avenue for a little while."

Delilah nodded, and Paul began to walk in the direction of the street. After a few steps, he looked back and saw that she was following at a distance. Delilah was sixteen years old, and at an extremely fragile stage in her life.

Paul didn't say anything to her for the first few blocks as she walked several steps behind him. As they arrived at St. Charles Avenue, he turned to face her and said, "In my school Delilah, I can't pass unless I do the work. If I'm going to be your teacher, you should know that unless you do the work, I can't tell your mama that you passed." He had her attention.

They waited for the light to turn so they could walk across the intersection, and he added, "So my only assignment for you today is that you talk to me so I can better understand how I can help you. Starting today, it is pass-fail, and you can't pass unless you talk, and I can't hear what you say unless you walk next to me. Okay?"

Delilah nodded.

"Excuse me?" Paul said.

"Yes, sir. I hear what you say."

Paul continued, "Gentlemen walk next to the road when they are walking with a lady. They do it out of respect to help keep the lady safe. So, please walk on my right side. And another thing, Delilah, I'm only two years older than you, so I'm not a 'sir,' I am Paul. Okay?"

"Okay, sir… I mean, Paul."

And so, the class began. As they walked for the next hour, Paul could see signs of a beautiful flower trying to grow from the hardened stump of a child. He heard that she had always dreamed of being in a business like her mother, and hoped that she might own a beauty parlor someday. He learned about her struggles with math, reading, and writing, and she sounded very disappointed about being expelled from school. She did say that being away from some of the students at school was a good thing. As she became more open, he heard that lately, the bad influencers were seeking her out again. They needed her to sell their drugs.

Paul had to ask, "Do you have a drug problem, Delilah?"

"Aw, no, sir, Mr. Paul." Catching herself, she smiled and said, "I mean, Paul."

"That's better," he said.

This was the first time he had seen her smile. With the hour about to end, they walked back to her mother's shop and stood outside the screen door. Paul asked, "Which subject would you like to work on first when I return on Wednesday?"

"How 'bout English?" she said.

"Sounds perfect. I'll bring a book for us to read." Paul looked at

Delilah intently, adding, "I just have one request from you, between now and Wednesday."

"What's that, Paul?"

He looked her in the eyes and said, "Please be safe between now and then."

He held out his hand, and this time she grabbed it. Delilah shook it vigorously then bounded up to her mother's back steps. "Opening the door, she turned back to say, "Thank you, Paul!" then she disappeared inside.

This day had gone much better than anyone expected. Like a moon landing, it had been one small step for a man, and one huge leap for Delilah. He stood there, relishing the moment. Just then, Talulah appeared from inside the screen with a surprised, almost shocked look on her face. Paul smiled widely and extended her a thumbs up before walking away.

Paul barely tapped on Marie's window, which brought her flying out the door before he could blink.

"Tell me all about Delilah, Paul!" she demanded.

"Can I tell you first how much I like your latest painting?" Paul asked.

"If you must," she said, trying to act indifferent.

Paul knew better.

Her painting deserved praise. What greeted him today was Marie's depiction of Talulah's shop. It was different, much more whimsical than her usual style. In the painting, Marie had transformed the dull, unpainted exterior of Talulah's to be a new gorgeous shade of yellow. There were flowers and trees, and he could visualize the top door about to open.

"Your painting is fabulous, as usual, but not very accurate."

"What? Oh, you mean the style, well I'm trying something new!"

"No. That's not it. You should know already that there's not a drop of paint on that entire shop!"

"Artists have 'Artistic License', my dear. And we can imagine unforeseen potential, too!"

"Well, it's beautiful, but that license of yours seems to be a little premature and over-extended. I'm not sure Talulah needs your help."

"I beg your pardon, Mr. Morel?"

"If you would have painted what Delilah looked like today, you could have spared some yellow paint." Paul puffed his chest like a proud peacock.

"But it's the bright yellow paint that made her shop look happy!"

Paul grabbed her hand and began to walk away, pulling her, as he crowed, "At the end of the hour, when Delilah was going back into her mother's shop, she was smiling big enough to brighten her mother's shop without paint!"

Marie couldn't pass up this opportunity. Stepping up next to him, she quietly stated, "Oh, I get it. She was truly that happy to get away from you, wasn't she?"

Marie was not only smart but agile as she darted away from him, giggling as she went.

❧

As they walked together through the campus, Paul told her details about his first session with Delilah.

"She is as skinny as Talulah is large, but underneath her tough exterior, she's sweet mush just like her mother."

"When are you going to go back?"

"I'm going to try to go three times a week unless it starts to affect my grades, so my next visit will be Wednesday afternoon."

Marie hesitated, then thinking out loud, said, "If you're going to go early, maybe I could take the streetcar down to meet you after my last class, and we could catch dinner at the Camellia? My treat?"

Paul turned away from her abruptly and started to walk in the direction of his dorm. Calling over his shoulder, he yelled, "Okay, sounds great. See you Wednesday!"

Marie placed her fists on her hips and called back, "You just turn that cute butt of yours back around right now, Paul Morel! I'm already jealous of your time away, and if you keep walking that way, I'll be the one putting a black mourning drape up over my window permanently!"

Running back to her, he raised his hands prayerfully, as he sarcastically pleaded, "No, dear Marie, anything but the black mourning drape over the window, treatment!"

This guy was too much. Marie couldn't help but kiss him.

Then she said, "I'm so happy you had a great visit with Delilah!"

16
CHRISTMAS APART

On Wednesday, by the time Marie arrived at 3:45, Talulah's top door was shut, and there was no one in line. She was sad because she skipped lunch today and was really looking forward to some tasty pie.

Marie had made plans to meet Paul here and wondered if he was around back. From the front porch, she looked around the side and thought she heard someone at the rear. As she walked around the corner, she found herself at the back part of the shop. Arriving there, she peeked around the corner and saw Paul sitting next to a pretty, young girl on the bottom step. They were reading a book together. They were both so mesmerized in what they were doing that she was able to move closer, and soon stood directly in front of them just as they looked up.

Paul gave her a surprised smile, and Delilah appeared disappointed that Marie had interrupted something she was enjoying so much.

Marie looked at the book and said, "I always loved reading *Where the Red Fern Grows*!"

"One of the classics, isn't it, Marie." Paul looked over at Delilah and said, "Delilah, I'd like to introduce you to my girlfriend, Marie Landry."

Delilah politely stood to shake her hand, then said, "Very nice to meet you, Miss Landry, and I don't means no rudeness, but can you waits over there till we finish this chapter?" Delilah pointed at the broken-down fence at the back of the yard.

Paul smiled as Marie said, "Why yes, that's not a problem at all, and please forgive me for interrupting. What a wonderful book to read on a beautiful afternoon. Please enjoy it!"

Marie smiled at Paul, then walked out into the yard and found a place to sit, leaning against the shed by the back fence. Over the next fifteen minutes, she overheard Delilah, struggling to read the book to Paul.

At 4 pm, Talulah cracked the screen open a little, causing Delilah and Paul to stand. "You axed me, let you knows when it be 4, so here I is!"

Looking out into the yard, she added, "An look like we gots another pie monster out there. Y'all blink a time or two, and Talulah be back with pie for you boths."

Soon, she appeared with a bag and handed it to Marie with a smile. Paul pulled out his wallet, and again Talulah placed her hand on his, shaking her head. "Just so happen, Talulah had one cherry and one chocolate left, and y'all know how she hate when they go to waste!"

After saying their goodbye's, the pair took their bag and waited briefly for a table at the Camellia Grill. They'd not seen Clarence since the very first visit, and he immediately asked them about the contents of their bag. "Is that one of Aunt Talulah's bags?"

"Yes, Clarence. Your advice has proven to be life-changing!" Paul looked at Marie and asked her if she was ready to order.

"Catfish please!" she said.

Clarence looked at Paul and said, "I'm so sorry, sir. We just ran out of red beans and rice with andouille sausage."

The smiling waiter waited only a moment for the hook of his joke to sink in. And it did. Paul stared at him in disbelief.

With a live one on the line, Clarence added, "Got c'ha, sir!"

Paul thumped his hand loudly against his chest next to his heart and said, "Oh Lord, you scared me there! That was a good one!"

"So, Aunt Talulah is taking good care of y'all?"

"Yes, she is."

"The way Aunt T. described the new tutor for Delilah, I'd say you fit the picture pretty close. So, are you the fella named Paul she told me 'bout?"

"The same! I've enjoyed getting to know Delilah."

"She's had a tough road, my cousin. She started hanging out with a bad bunch, and I hope she don't go back near them. Thanks for what you're doing. Y'all's food'll be right up!"

❧

When they finished their meal, they ordered Café au Lait and pulled out Talulah's pies. Marie checked for the one with a fingerprint border as they enjoyed dessert.

Marie hadn't had a chance since Thanksgiving to discuss something with Paul. "So, tell me, Mr. Tutor Morel, from what I remember when we first met, you were an English major."

"Yes, that's right." He took another bite of cherry pie that sent filling streaming over his fingers.

"Well, why did your father say you were going into Law?"

"Oh," he said, "*now* I remember the surprised look on your face that day. We never did get a chance to discuss that again." Paul took another bite of pie.

"So, is it English, or is it Pre-Law?" Marie got the distinct impression she was being played with again.

"I guess I need to make up my mind, but really, there's no hurry. Part of me was following the path of my sister, you know? But part of me is enjoying being a teacher."

"Couldn't you be both?"

He replied, "Like many things in life, there's no real rush now, is there?"

There was a certain ambivalence Marie perceived from Paul concerning some things in his life; he held much close to his chest. The time it hit home was when they were in his bed together that night in New Roads, and he fell asleep just as *she* began to feel primal stirrings. Now, he spoke in vague ways about decisions involving the rest of his life, *with no mention or inclusion of her.*

Interestingly, she knew that her future was just as uncertain, but the difference between them was that if he had asked her, she would have told him that. She was asking for details, and he refused to give her a straight answer. She'd had just about enough of that for tonight. The door was calling her name.

As she stood, she said, "No, Paul, certainly no rush. Ready to go? I'm getting tired."

Before Paul could cram the rest of his pie in his mouth, Marie was out the door. He caught up to her just before the streetcar pulled up.

"Marie, is it something I said?"

"Actually, no." Marie stepped up into the car as the door opened. What Paul didn't know was that it was something he *hadn't* said.

The ride back to campus was quiet between them. Marie wasn't sure what had bothered her so much at dinner. *How could Paul help her with if she didn't know herself?* They quietly walked back to her dorm, and he thanked her for coming to meet him, kissing her goodnight before she walked in.

For Paul, there was so much going on right now. He knew that something frustrated Marie at dinner, and although he'd played dumb, he had a pretty good idea what it was. His thoughts indeed were betwixt and between concerning his major, but this was a decision he would have to make on his own. He hadn't come up with a polite way of telling her that yet. He'd also never had a steady girl, and sharing his life in this way at the tender age of eighteen was not easy. He honestly didn't know about tomorrow, concerning *anything*, and the last thing he wanted to feel was: rushed.

Marie's father was a huge red flag for him regarding a future with her. *How could he tell her that?* He couldn't. But did he love her? *Yes!* She was so different than any girl he'd ever met. She was gorgeous, but gorgeous by itself was nothing to him. The most important thing for Paul was, *did he like her?* He did: tremendously. Was she funny? Yes. Did she make him smile and laugh? Constantly. Was she honest? Yes. Did the dimple under her left cheek appear when her eyes twinkled? Yes.

Marie was his cat's meow, the other pea in his pod, the frick for his frack, the Minnie for him, the Mickey. She was one of a kind, and he was so blessed, and he knew it.

It was just that he was in no rush to move on with his life too quickly, and yet the thought of losing her scared the bejeebies out of him.

Hopefully, Nathaniel would be "out" when he arrived at his room, and he could call her. He needed to speak to her again before he would be able to go to sleep.

❧

Soon, in his room alone, he called her. "Hello, Marie?"

Gruffly, "Who is this? Is this just another prank call?"

He laughed awkwardly, "You know who this is. I wanted to hear your voice again before bed."

"Thanks for calling, I needed you too…"

"Listen, Marie. I have an idea. We are going to be away from each other for close to a month during Christmas break.

"I know. I'm already having trouble with that."

"Well, I'm going to miss you tremendously."

"Me too, Paul."

"So, I have an idea. All our classes finish on Thursday, and most other kids are leaving that afternoon to go home for Christmas. Why don't we spend the day together on Friday the 22nd, and go out on a dinner date that night? We can ask our parents to pick us up sometime on Saturday, and that will give us an extra day together."

Marie skirted her concerns about her father as she replied, "I think that sounds do-able. My parents *usually* just ask what day to come, not when school is over."

Paul was unsure if he would be able to see Marie during the holiday, especially considering what happened during Thanksgiving. He wanted to get her a present but didn't want her to feel obligated. He said, "Please understand that I'm not saying you must get me a present, Marie, but if you do, we could exchange gifts that night? Just in case, you know. What do you think?

"That sounds wonderful. So, from what I'm hearing, it sounds like you're going to get me a present?"

"You'll have to wait and see."

"Will you, at least, tell me where you are taking me for dinner?"

"Out to eat. That's as far as this plan has gotten."

Marie giggled. "Well, that sounds delicious. It sounds like a great date night to me! I hope you sleep tight!"

"I'll sleep better now, that's for sure." He waited a moment to garner courage, then summoning his best attempt at a deep, sensual voice, added, "Good night, Miss Tight-Butt."

"Paul, you better watch yourself, you've never discussed any part of my anatomy before. I'd almost thought you hadn't noticed. And right before bed? You bad boy!"

"Sorry, Marie. It wasn't your anatomy, I meant. That's the name Talulah gave you. She told me that calling you 'Miss Tight-Ass' wouldn't sound polite, so that's why she gave you the name, 'Tight-Butt.'"

After a few moments of silence, Paul said, "Marie… Marie? Are you still there?"

Through the receiver, he heard the essence of frustration as she huffed, "Men!" just before the line went dead.

Paul smiled; his mission accomplished. They had a date.

17

END OF THE SEMESTER

The last few weeks of school were a blur for them both with the growing lists of projects, papers, and final exams. They suddenly found themselves approaching the final week of the semester. As had become his routine, on Wednesday morning, Paul made his round-about trek past Marie's window on his way to meet her in class. He never knew what treasure he would find waiting for him.

Marie was an incredible artist. She amazed him with the speed and the clarity that she could capture moments in time or snapshots of her imagination, making them come to life inside her window pane. Even better, she did them all for him. How incredibly special.

He could barely believe his eyes as her offering this morning came into full view. It was a hopeful rendering of him, Marie, and Talulah sitting in the front row of an auditorium, clapping for a proud Delilah standing on the stage before them, receiving her diploma.

If only… he thought.

As he hurried toward class, he recalled the last few weeks with Delilah. She was trying hard. Paul knew that for her to advance, she needed to learn to write and speak using proper English. It was like trying to teach someone a new language. These efforts hadn't come without resistance, not from Delilah, but her friends.

One day recently, he found her sulking on the step outside the screen door. What she eventually shared with him was that some of her friends were mocking her for the new way she was speaking with them. They were not happy with the changes they heard and began referring to her in derogatory ways, telling her she was a traitor to her race.

All he could tell her was, "I never told you this would be easy, Delilah. You've got to want it enough for yourself to make it *your* future. Their choices don't have to be yours."

He'd not told Marie about these recent concerns for Delilah, and how it weighed heavily on him.

As he pushed open the door to English Lit class this morning, he found Marie, sitting in her usual seat, but she was not alone. Standing in front of her was Ms. O., and they appeared to be having an engaging conversation.

As he approached them, he told them both good morning. Trying not to interrupt, he sat down.

"Oh, Paul!" Marie exclaimed, "I've got some great news this morning!" She looked at her teacher as she continued, "Ms. Oglethorpe has commissioned e to do a painting for her!"

"That's great! I'm sure she won't be disappointed!"

Ms. O. wished them a personal, "Merry Christmas" and proceeded back to her podium to get ready for today's class.

Marie, still excited, asked Paul, "Did you see it?"

"Yes. It was another incredible painting. Thank you so much!"

"I had so much fun painting this one. You and Delilah have been working so hard! I can just see that day, and it will all be because of you!" He didn't respond and opened his notebook to prepare for the last class.

Paul was acting strange, and it didn't go unnoticed by Marie. She said, "Everything okay?" He continued to look at his notebook.

She persisted, "It's been a while since you've said much about your sessions with Delilah, is everything going well?"

He couldn't hold this back anymore. Paul turned to her to say, "I hope so. It hasn't been easy for her; she's being picked on by some friends." He took a deep breath and sighed, "I loved your picture, but graduation day for Delilah is nowhere near in sight right now. Unfortunately, I am concerned that the odds are stacked against her."

"I'm sorry."

Intentionally changing the subject, Paul asked, "How did Ms. O. find out you were an artist? I don't remember that ever coming up between the two of you."

"It was from our last assignment. Remember? When Ms. O. asked us to write our final paper using only the topic of 'surprise encounters,' I wrote about the night of our first date but confined my paper to the discovery of Talulah's bakery. I included a small 8 x 11 sketch of her shop at the end of my writing."

"That's amazing. I have no doubt your final grade will be a good one!"

Ms. O. tapped her pen against the podium and began. "I want to start by telling you all, being your teacher, this semester has been a joy for me. From where some of you started," she looked over at Marie as she hesitated, "there has been gratifying improvement noted, which I believe you will see reflected in your final grades. I will pass your papers back to you at the end of our class today, and the slip of paper included with it will have your final grade for this class."

Today's session ended with much anticipation as Ms. O. moved quickly up and down the rows. As she returned Marie's papers, Paul was more interested in her grade than his own.

"Let me see it," he pleaded. A smile extended across Marie's face as she handed Paul her assignment.

"You got an A + on your paper Marie and an overall grade of A -. That is incredible!

Paul looked at the last page, where he found a smaller version of the "artistic license" Talulah's. It looked just like it had appeared in her window. "Wait a minute Marie," Paul looked at her with a questioning face. She knew what was coming. "This is your painting of Talulah's painted in vivid colors; yellow, with beautiful plants in front… it's an awesome painting, but it's not the Talulah's we saw on our first date."

Marie smiled and reached out for his hand as she said, "It is

Talulah's. It is how I see it in my eyes, someday, for Delilah and her mom. It's what Talulah's *can be!* For me, it's also symbolic of our surprise encounter in this class. Who would have thought we would be where we are together, or that I'd even like English Lit? If *we* can 'blossom', who says Talulah's can't?"

"And what a wonderful day that will be, Miss Landry!"

"So, dear sir, what, pray-tell, might your grade be?"

"Oh, I was so excited about yours, I hadn't looked." Paul turned his paper over, and on it was an attached slip indicating an A +, which also was his final grade.

"Why am I not surprised, Mr. Writer Man!" Marie was genuinely happy for him.

"You never told me the topic of your paper. Let me see..." Marie grabbed the page out of his hands and began to read."

He watched her face as her eyes widened and a blush washed over her. She looked up as she read the title of his paper out loud, "My Marie."

Incredulously, she asked, "Paul, was I the subject of your paper?"

"Yes. You are everything to me, including a surprise!"

Marie sat motionless as she read the entire paper. When she finished, she looked up with tears of joy in her eyes. She reached for his neck and held him tight.

Almost everyone had left, and Paul said, "Come on, Marie, our teacher is waiting to tell us goodbye!"

As they walked to the back of the room, Ms. O. was standing at the exit door, shaking everyone's hand. She had proven herself to be a gracious lady and an excellent teacher. After extending well-wishes to each other, she handed Marie another slip of paper.

As they proceeded out of class, Paul asked, "What was on that slip of paper?"

"It's the address of the Oglethorpe's home. She and her professor husband live close by, and I'm going to walk by later so I can make a quick sketch of the front of her home. She needs the painting done pronto as a Christmas gift for her husband. It wasn't until yesterday when she was grading the papers that she saw mine and knew what to get him. She wanted it to be something special. So, before you came in this morning, she asked if I could do a painting on short notice, and I said, 'Yes.'"

"That's great, Marie, but when are you going to have time?"

"I'm going to get started later tonight after my initial sketch this afternoon. I'll have to use acrylic paint so it will dry fast enough for Ms. O. to get it framed on Saturday. She has a friend at a frame shop that owes her a favor, and although it's cutting a fine line, I think we can pull it off!"

They stepped outside into an unseasonably warm and sunny day, soon to part ways. Each had a busy day ahead.

Paul arrived by 3 pm at Talulah's and sat down on the wooden step outside the screen. In short order, he heard Talulah calling through the door, saying, "Afternoon, Paul, you gots one more session with Delilah, then y'all gone be off for what you say? A month?"

"Yes, Miss Talulah. We're going to miss seeing y'all, and I hope Delilah keeps up with her reading while I'm away. I'll try to reinforce that with her today."

"An' I'll do my best to keep her gone in the right direction till you return!"

"I'm sure you will, ma'am."

"Don't you gets out'a here this evening without this bag I'll have by the back door when you through, you hear?"

"Yes ma'am, Miss Talulah, and thank you!"

What remained unspoken was that neither one of them knew where Delilah was.

It was hot, and the heat pouring out of the screen didn't help. When Paul looked at his watch, it read 3:35 pm. Delilah was very late, and as each minute passed, his fears for her grew.

Talulah peeked out the screen at 3:50 pm, to check on progress. There had been none.

Paul stood as he heard her sigh, then said, "She's not here yet, and I'll need to be going soon."

"I'm so sorry we be wastin' you time, Paul. Something mus' be wrong, and it won't be the first time. I fear she be hangin' 'round them boys again."

"Is there anything I can do to help you, Miss Talulah?"

"The onliest thing is to jus' pray. She old enough now, and that's all we can do." Talulah opened the screen partially and passed a brown paper bag out to Paul, smiling as she said, "Merry Christmas to you and Lil Miss Tight-Butt."

Despite all her misery, she was still trying her best to put a smile on Paul's face, and it worked.

"She's fond of your name for her," he said.

"I'll bet she be!" Talulah laughed as she added, "Bless you and yours, Mr. Paul!" Then she disappeared into the heat. As he passed around the front lot, he heard her singing to a long line.

Life continued for Talulah: no matter what. Despite witnessing her faith, he was truly worried for her daughter.

Paul knew Marie was busy and would call him when she was free. He was so disappointed about Delilah and thankful for the time alone. Thankfully, his dorm room was unoccupied since Nathaniel had already left for home. There were a few things he'd left behind, nothing immune from pitching if he flunked out.

He took off his shoes and stretched out on his bed to think about his day. He hadn't been sleeping well for the past week, and with the window open, it wasn't long before his lids grew heavy and he fell asleep.

His room was dark when his phone rang, and he had no idea what time it was. Nearly stumbling in his half-sleep state, he reached the obnoxious device, picked it up and held it to his ear.

"Paul, is that you? I've been worried to death, are you okay?"

"Yes, I'm fine. What time is it?"

"It's after 10 pm! What's going on?"

"I figured you were busy and would eventually call. I'm glad you did. I must have fallen asleep. I've been anxious for Delilah. She didn't show today."

"I'm so sorry! I hope she's all right! Did you learn anything from Miss Talulah about what's going on?"

"Not yet, except she's hanging out with some creeps lately. So how is your project going? Did you find their house?"

"Sure did, it wasn't hard. I finished my preliminary sketch in about 30 minutes, then I came back to my room and have been busy ever since. This painting is a tough project because of the timeframe. It's going to be tight for me to finish this and get it to Ms. O. by Saturday morning. And we both have classes tomorrow!"

"Will you still have time for our date on Friday, Marie?"

"*Is the sky blue?* Wild horses couldn't keep me from going to dinner with you! How could I miss such a special date! You know, with Airforce One picking us up, to have dinner at the White House? Who in their right mind would miss that?"

Paul was fully awake now. "Hallucinating again, are we? I believe that our dinner will be somewhat shy of a State Dinner."

Marie giggled and replied, "Then maybe I *should* reconsider. I have standards, you know."

"Well, will your 'standards' understand if I don't have a present for you? I'm going to be so busy tomorrow. I need to go back over to Talulah's after class to see if Delilah is okay."

"You are my gift, Paul. And you are a gift to Delilah. If you keep kissing me and me alone, I'm fine till Friday!"

Paul was ready to play now, too. "I am your gift… For true? Would you like your gift to come over, like right now? All I need to do is brush my teeth, put on some fresh clothes, and sprint over there. Would 30 seconds from now be too late for your gift to arrive?"

"Silly man. I love you so. Keep me posted on our plans and pick me up Friday evening."

Before hanging up, he said, "I love you too, *Tight-Butt*. Talulah *and* I are very fond of your new name! Good night!"

On Thursday afternoon, Paul planned to pay Delilah an unexpected visit. It wasn't his typical day for tutoring, but out of concern, he took the streetcar down to South Carrollton and exited at the Camellia, as usual. After the short walk, Paul arrived around 3:15 to the house. He heard a commotion even before he rounded the back corner. Talulah was fussing loudly at some young boys and girls that were hanging around, just outside her screened door.

Paul heard Talulah yelling, "Y'all get on out'a here *now!* Ain't gonna be no loitering or selling none 'o that devil potion back here at Talulah's!"

He saw Delilah standing with the other young people on rounding the corner. They all grew quiet as he stopped in his tracks to assess the situation. There, he saw three young men and two young girls in a group, which included Delilah.

Delilah, looking embarrassed, called out to him, "Mr. Paul, we's not havin' no class today."

The tallest of the young men looked directly at Paul as he spoke harshly, "Delilah, why you be callin' this man, 'Mister'? He ain't nothin' to you!"

Out of the corner of Paul's eye, he saw the screen door slowly begin to open. Paul saw Talulah, and she had a dough roller held high in her right hand. He was confident that she knew how to use it.

The tall guy wisely backed up as Paul held up his hand, motioning for Talulah to wait. Looking at Delilah, Paul said, "I know today is not our day Delilah, but you weren't here yesterday, and I just wanted to come by to tell you Merry Christmas, and that I look forward to working with you more."

Delilah looked down. She didn't respond and looked scared.

The next tallest one chimed in, "You best go 'head on back to you university. If Delilah need help, she gets it from her own."

Talulah had reached her limit. She was out the door faster than dough could hit a cast-iron skillet. Down the steps, she went, with her rolling pin held high as the other kids scattered and ran.

She grabbed Delilah's arm, and said, "Nah, you gonna 'pologize to this nice man who worried for you, or this dough roller gonna knock some sense in'ta you noggin, you hear what you mama say *Lil Miss drop-out?"*

Part of Delilah looked relieved, and part didn't.

The repentant side focused on him and said, "I'm sorry, Mr. Paul. Thank you for worryin' for me, and I hope you has a real nice Christmas."

It was apparent she was trying. Her mother's hand released her arm, and Delilah, without further prompts, went into the shop.

Talulah, embarrassed, thanked him as only Talulah could, with a generous bear hug. Then, she wished him a "Merry Christmas" and disappeared into the heat.

❧

Thursday evening, his phone rang. "Paul, are you okay? Are we still going to spend the day together tomorrow and go to dinner? How did it go today, was Delilah there?"

"Who is this?" Paul asked, knowing the answer but still half asleep. "What time is it?"

"Past time for you to call me, I'd say!"

"Sorry, Marie. I'm okay, Delilah is kind of okay, and I think Talulah has been better."

"Did you get to talk with Delilah?"

"Not much. I had to have my words interpreted by her punk entourage. She's hanging around with some real losers."

Paul went on to tell her the whole story. Marie was impressed with Talulah and her use of the rolling pin.

"I'm sorry." Marie said, "For everyone's sake, I hope that all changes soon."

"Yep, me too. So why do you keep calling and waking me up? I'm detecting a trend here that is disturbing!"

"Well, Mr. Writer Man, I could quit calling if you prefer."

"Jeez. Decisions, decisions. Let me sleep on it!"

They both laughed. Then, Marie said, "You should know, I'm way behind on this painting. I want it to be perfect, and it's not nearly there yet. I'm sorry even to ask this, but can we make an earlier dinner, maybe around 4 pm tomorrow? I'll need to work the entire day even to come close to finishing, and if you could get me back home early, I'll have more time if I need it. Will that work?"

Paul felt let down. Their entire day together was just turned upside down. But understanding what her art meant to her, he said, "Sure, Marie."

She worried about him even before requesting this of him tonight. It didn't make her feel any better that he sounded so distant.

Marie still didn't know where they were going for dinner or how she should dress. She asked, "So, where are you taking me for dinner tomorrow?"

Paul suddenly realized that time had gotten away from him. Trying not to sound panicked, he said, "I'll let you know in a little while. I'm going to have to see if four works for our reservation. I'll call you back."

Without waiting on her response, Paul hung up the phone and started a frantic search for a phone book. They didn't have a reservation anywhere at any time, yet. This wasn't like him at all. Preoccupation with Delilah had caused time to get away from him. He needed to get busy and make some calls.

After an hour of calling, he found no restaurants in his price range that had an opening for Friday evening. None. Paul was frantic. *How in the world would he explain this to Marie?*

Pulling all the stops, he started dialing the expensive places. He had a savings bond he could cash from his grandparents. He phoned Commander's Palace: their response, "No." Arnaud's? The same. There were no reservations available despite the early hour he requested.

Paul was almost ready to admit defeat. He had always heard great things about Broussard's in the French Quarter. They were one of the six oldest restaurants in New Orleans. As luck would have it, they had just received a cancellation. He wouldn't have a penny left to his name after the meal, but this was a special dinner, and money didn't matter.

He called Marie and told her about the excellent shrimp served at Broussard's, and how gracious they were to accommodate an earlier time.

"That's wonderful, but where've you been? What took you so long to call back? I thought maybe you'd fallen asleep again. It's been over an hour since we spoke!"

He said, "I'm a busy man, Marie. You should feel fortunate to get a phone call from me no matter when it comes."

Firing back, she said, "I wonder if Talulah will let me borrow one of her rolling pins? I'm feeling the urge to change someone's attitude!"

It was unimportant for Marie to know the rest of this story. All that mattered to him was that she was happy and that they had a reservation. She didn't have to know the other details.

Marie added her opinion about his choice of restaurants, boasting, "I reserve the right to judge the shrimp myself. I know good shrimp, Paul."

Paul knew he was lucky to find a great restaurant at the last minute. He told Marie he would meet her outside her dorm the next day at 2:30 pm. That would allow them time to take the streetcar to Canal Street, and it would be a short three block walk down Bourbon Street to the restaurant on Conti.

"Good night, Marie. Try not to stay up too late. I can't wait to see you tomorrow!" He hung up the phone and went back to bed. It would be another long night for him.

18

THE LAST SUPPER

Paul woke early and took his savings bond to the bank. He said a silent prayer for his Morel Grandparents and would thank them again for their generosity when he arrived home.

Early in the afternoon, Marie called him while he was getting ready for dinner. She sounded unusually excited but lacked details to confirm. He was trying to get prepared, and for some reason, Marie seemed to be interested in talking about mundane topics utterly unrelated to their date.

This perplexed him. For someone as pressed for time as Marie sounded last night, she sure seemed to have an abundance of time now. He continued to comb his hair with the phone pressed to his ear, as he realized she had been talking non-stop for at least the past five minutes. He wondered, *Why, on earth, is she telling me all this stuff now? I'm going to see her in less than an hour!*

Soon, he couldn't hold his tongue any longer. As she took a deep breath, he broke into her one-sided discussion of "what causes tickles in the back of your throat at inopportune moments," to ask, "Marie, you know we're going to see each other in just a little while. Wouldn't it be easier to discuss these pressing topics in person? You know, over dinner." There was no response.

"Marie, are you still there? I didn't mean to offend you…"

A muted voice returned as she finally said what she'd been trying to build up the courage to say, "When you arrive to pick me up, I want you to climb through the window into my room before dinner. I want you to see my painting. It's still wet, and I'm afraid to move it."

Paul didn't know what to say. Soon, he heard her take a deep breath before she added, "I don't think anyone is around to see you climbing in. I don't think you'll get in trouble, just come in, please. I'll leave the window unlocked."

Before he could respond, she hung up. That was good because he still didn't know how to react, or even what he would do when he arrived at her window.

His face froze in the mirror, and he didn't recognize the person that looked back. He had never parted his hair on the left side and wasn't sure how or when he'd done it. *Marie,* he thought.

As he recombed his hair, he wondered, *what is happening?* He wasn't sure the risk for them both was worth it, just to see her painting. If found in her room, they could both face expulsion from school. Then again, the odds were in his favor that his entrance would go unnoticed since most people had already left the campus for break. But the Campus Police weren't going anywhere, and they kept a closer eye on the girl's dorms. He didn't know what he would do.

His gait felt odd as he hurried along. Several times he looked down to confirm that his shoes were on the right foot. At the appointed time, Paul arrived at her window. Today, no painting waited to greet him, just a piece of cardboard blocking any view.

The last thing he wanted for this special event was to disappoint Marie. He was going to go in. He glanced in all directions, and on verifying that the coast was clear, he tapped a few times to warn her, and immediately raised the pane. He had to jump up a little. Then as he swung his leg over the threshold, his foot felt a hand grab it unexpectedly, guiding it down to a chair, positioned just inside.

"Quick, she said, we need to shut the window right away!"

Her implied haste caused Paul's inexperience with breaking and entering to manifest itself as he clumsily lost his balance, falling in a heap on the floor.

Marie covered her mouth to stifle her laugh as she reached up and slid the window back down. Sitting on the floor next to him, she congratulated him with, "We did it!"

"Don't be so sure," he said, "I'm still waiting for a knock on your door."

Paul couldn't believe what he'd just done. Eagle Scout, member of his church's youth league, honor student... was temporary insanity or just stupidity that hurdled him through her window? Looking at her, he believed there had been another incentive: the intoxication of Marie.

He stood abruptly and could feel sweat beading on his forehead. Suddenly the impact hit; that of being in a girl's dormitory room alone... with a girl... his girl. Reality knocked him in the face like a welter-weight pinned against the ropes.

"Paul, are you okay? Did you hit your head on something when you fell?"

This room smelled different. It smelled great, like a girl, not like dirty socks and musty unwashed towels. Everything about this room seemed foreign; the color of the paint, the size of the room, and a distinctively pleasant odor. He couldn't get over how great this room smelled. It smelled like, Marie.

"Paul!"

"Hi, Marie... your room is very nice."

In a take-charge mode, she said, "We need to keep moving if we're going to get to Broussard's in time for dinner! Just do what I say, okay?"

"Yes, ma'am."

"Go over there and sit on my bed. I've hidden the painting in the bathroom on my easel, so just sit down, and I'll do the unveiling!" Marie disappeared into the bathroom.

Odd, how quickly things can trigger thoughts from the past. That same old feeling began to creep over him. As he sat down, he recalled the days back home, when as a much younger, "Guinea pig, Paul", his older sister took advantage of him. She made him sit in her room, on her bed, as she paraded all her dressed and undressed baby dolls out in front of him. All he had wanted to do was go outside with his friends and play G. I. Joe. But Savannah was older and big enough to thump him if he didn't do as she demanded.

He hoped this would end soon. Being in this sacred place was becoming more uncomfortable by the second, and he could have done without the Savannah flashback.

He heard Marie before he saw her, "Here I come, Paul!" She backed out of the bathroom door, then carefully moved the easel and art into view.

Instantly, his fear disappeared as he gazed upon a magnificently done painting, that if sold in an antique shop on Royal Street, might bring thousands of dollars. It was so real; he felt he could step right through the front door.

"Wow! I can't believe you did that!"

Paul was the first person to see the result of her hard work. She beamed with pride.

Moving off the bed for a closer look, Paul reached out with his finger to point at one of her details.

"Don't touch it! It's still wet!" she yelled.

Paul took a few steps back. "Sorry, Marie, I wasn't going to touch it, I just had a question."

"I better get my purse, we need to go. So, you like it?"

"I love it, how in the world did you make it look so real?"

"When I paint, I'm in that spot where I'm not happy until everything in front of me is crystal clear."

"Funny. That's how I try to write."

Marie went to her door and placed her ear against it. Hearing no one in the hall, she said, "Here's how this is going to work. You stand here with the door cracked after I walk out. I'll signal you from down at the exit if we are clear. Got it?"

"I don't want to go to jail, Marie."

She leaned in, kissed him, then opened the door, and walked into the hall. Paul's stomach was doing cartwheels.

"Pssssst!" came the signal from down the hall. He jumped out, slammed her door to make sure it closed, and started to run."

"Shhhhh!" he heard next.

As he rounded the turn at the exit, he nearly knocked Marie over as he bounded out the door. As she watched in amazement, he didn't stop. When she blinked her eyes, he was out of sight down the sidewalk.

Paul didn't slow down until he arrived at the streetcar stop.

Marie eventually caught up to him, laughing hysterically.

"Why are you laughing at me?"

"You crack me up, Paul Morel!"

"What? Why do you say that?"

"Because I was just imagining inviting you back over when we return from dinner. You know, just to watch me put the finishing touches on my painting. But after witnessing you run out as you did, I'm not sure you could survive another visit!"

❧

In less than an hour, the door of Broussard's was opened for them as the maître d' met and ushered them to their table.

Never one to miss an opportunity, Marie looked at the menu quickly and said, "I'm not sure how you're going to like this restaurant."

Without lifting his head from his menu, he replied, "Why do you say that?"

"Because they have every Cajun food here *except...*"

"I've already noticed. Except for red beans and rice with andouille sausage."

Trying her best impression of Scarlett from *Gone with the Wind*, Marie fanned her face with her napkin as she asked with an exaggerated drawl, "Oh Paul, how on earth will you survive?"

Not missing a beat, "Don't worry, Scarlett. I'll survive just fine with the southern fried chicken and waffles. And you, Scarlett? Are you going to eat tonight, or just sit there and pine away over that ne'er-do-well, Rhett?"

Fanning her napkin faster this time, "Oh, dear Suh, you are far, far more handsome than that scoundrel, Rhett." Marie giggled. Remaining in character, she added, "Just for you, I'll be stepping down a bit from my normal fare, to admit that the Barbequed Gulf Shrimp and Grits look acceptable."

They were having a blast together. The laughs and great meal removed the tension they both felt from just a short time before. They both needed this care-free time together. Dinner was fabulous, and Marie was duly impressed. With the drinking age being eighteen, they had wine with dinner. Relaxed and satisfied, they too-soon found themselves on the streetcar returning to campus. Paul's pockets were much lighter, but it had been well worth every penny.

They were both unusually quiet on the way back. Both knew the time was approaching when they would be apart for weeks. They stepped from the streetcar together and began a challenging walk back to her dorm. They held each other's hand tightly.

Marie wanted to invite Paul to Morgan City again but didn't want to risk extending another invitation without permission from her father. She feared that one more lousy visit for Paul might make him run away and never return.

As if trying to prevent her from arriving, Paul stepped in front and caressed her face with his hands. He looked into her eyes, to say. "I'm going to miss you, Tight-Butt." He leaned over and kissed her in a way that she had never felt before. His lips against hers spoke without words.

She placed her hands around his waist, holding on as she leaned away to say, "You've never touched my butt, Paul Morel. How would you know whether it's tight or not?"

She saw a gleam in his eyes as she felt his hands slowly slide down her back, coming to an intentional rest on her cheeks. Then, without hesitation, he pulled her into him firmly and whispered, "I've admired your butt before, and have now confirmed by touching," Paul nibbled on her neck, causing Marie to giggle, as he added, "that you, Marie, deserve that nickname!"

Marie felt something else pressing between them. She kissed him passionately.

"Marie?"

Between kisses, "Yes?"

"Earlier, when you were kidding me about going back to your room... you know... to do a little more work... well, were you just playing, or were you serious?"

Marie was surprised by his sudden courage. *Possibly the wine,* she thought. Suddenly feeling out of breath, she pushed away from him to say, "I *was* teasing you then, *but not now*. See if you can keep up!"

Marie grabbed his hand and moved at a slow run along the sidewalk leading him to the dorm entrance. As they approached, both looked side to side as she said, "Let me go in and see if it's safe. Don't you go *anywhere!"*

Within seconds, they closed the door behind them in her room as Marie pinned her man against the door with her body.

In an instant, they became the only two people in the world. Two hearts, consuming each other to form one. Hands touching and feeling, senses on full alert, this night without end came alive.

Only after the fact, could they realize how this moment caught part of them both unaware. Each wanted the other, no doubt, and each held the key to unlock the other's soul. But, typical of young love, neither was at all prepared for tomorrow. How could they be? Their minds had not yet caught up to their bodies. To physically bond to another person is the glue that unites humanity. No small responsibility there. But with such desire, who might consider that the bliss and personal connection formed by the physical act of love carries no more guarantee than each heart *might* offer?

It is incredible, all the moments two separate lives experience, only to arrive at a place in time together, like Marie and Paul did this night.

Just one small glitch in the past could have prevented them from being in this place behind her door, alone, together.

Words exchanged between these two young people over the past few days, spoken with no more intent than to test the waters of young love, were the kindling to ignite this blaze of passion.

Many things quickly passed through both of their minds after the door to her room shut. *The only thing not filtered out was desire.*

Marie drew away to catch her breath. In the darkness of her room, she spoke directly to his lips while holding his face. She whispered, "I didn't know while we were out tonight that our dinner would be my last supper."

He had to ask, "Why would you say that? We can go there again sometime, that is… until I run out of savings bonds."

She playfully pushed him away. "I need to use the restroom, but first, I'll move the painting in there, so we don't knock it over in the dark." There was just enough light from the streetlight outside, shining through the transom for Marie to carefully move her work.

"Sit on the bed and wait for me, I won't be long," she said.

Her silhouette moved away, and he heard her ask, "Is this what you wanted, Paul Morel?"

Without hesitation, he answered, "More than anything."

He did as she requested, and sat on her neatly made bed, to wait for her. A few minutes passed, allowing the reality of this night to sink in for Paul. He had imagined this with her. He had dreamed repeatedly of Marie. Now that the moment arrived, it still felt like he might awaken at any moment from a fantasy. But touching her was real, and he knew that there was no place on earth he would rather be tonight than in her arms. Like her, he could not see past tonight.

Then he heard something that he hadn't heard since their second class together: that time she became upset about the homework assignment on the blackboard. Inside the bathroom, Marie started to cough loudly and sneeze. It continued non-stop for at least five minutes. He hoped she didn't consider intimate time with him to be comparable to an intimidating English assignment. It had to be her nerves.

It seemed like forever until the coughing stopped, then the bathroom door opened. The transom's light cast the form of a beautiful woman against his pupils. She was in her nightgown, and this was happening.

Marie walked over in her bare feet and kneeled next to him. She reached down and unlaced his shoes, removing them, then his socks. She stood and leaned him back in the bed as he made room for her to lay down next to him.

Her silk nightgown hid nothing underneath from his touch, and her skin responded to his touch, urging him to explore. As her beauty unfolded, all hesitancy for either to resist evaporated.

Marie felt warmth and firmness pressing against her leg, which begged her for comment. "Mr. Morel, I'm getting the impression you are happy to be here."

"Marie, sometimes you talk too much. Please don't break my concentration; I can tell there are parts of you that need my urgent attention."

She smothered him with her mouth as she rolled over on top of him.

Paul felt like he could explode. He'd never felt like this before. Whispering in her ear, he asked, "Marie, why did you call dinner tonight your 'last supper'?"

"I thought you said I talk too much!"

Paul rolled her back over and said, "You need to finish at least that sentence, please."

"Silly man," she said as she ventured her hand under his shirt, "before dinner, I was a virgin, the next time I sit down to eat, I won't be."

Marie was happy to learn that she was not the only virgin in the room. Tonight, they explored each other in kind, delicate, patient ways. Inexperience can be both awkward and meaningful. As his touch caressed every inch of her body, the passion ignited consumed them both with complete satisfaction.

❧

Paul stole out the door in the middle of the night. As he passed her window, he tapped briefly, then moved on. Marie lay back in her bed, so tired, yet so not ready to submit the rest of this night to slumber.

With her arms crossed behind her head, she thought about every second that had transpired tonight. Every word, every sensation from this evening replayed behind her closed eyes.

Unlike other girls she'd heard before, she hadn't been disappointed with her "first time". She had never forgotten what one girl said in high school, "I blinked my eyes, and it was over. No thunder, no fireworks, just over."

Marie smiled with the thought that she had shared a completely different experience with Paul. Something she would forever keep to herself. No, tonight had been better than she imagined.

Paul had loved her entirely, filling her heart to the point that it still wanted to jump from her chest.

Unable to sleep, Marie pulled her easel from the restroom, turned on the light, and went to work. She would apply the love she felt to her brush and finish the painting she needed to deliver in the morning. She turned up the heat in her room to help dry it quickly as she applied the finishing touches.

Paul turned the key to open his room. His space was lacking before, but now, it was empty. It contained no Marie.

Gold and rare stones are precious but can be easily lost. True love lasts. It fills your heart, makes your soul sing, and washes your entire existence in warmth. There is nothing else you can take with you when the day comes to leave this world, and not to have experienced it was unthinkable.

Paul had no expectations that this would happen tonight. Life's experiences can vary infinitely, and things that occur spontaneously have the potential to cause either incredible joy or pain. Something as simple as a kind word, a smile, or the gift of time can change a person's life.

Even more powerful, the human expression of love through physical intimacy is a rare and beautiful thing. Paul reveled in great joy tonight. Marie offered her complete heart to him tonight. She let him know that she wanted to be as close to him as is physically possible. There is nothing more special than that.

He lay down on his bed, still smelling her perfume. Paul didn't want to go home tomorrow. The future for him would be nothing, without his Marie.

19
CAJUN SANTA

It was like he had just closed his eyes, and the phone was ringing. The clock said, 9:03 am.

"Hello?"

"Paul, she loved it!

Still half asleep, he replied, "I'm glad you loved it, I did too! It must be a coincidence because I was just thinking…"

Exasperated, "*NO,* silly! Of course, I loved… *that!* But I was referring to Ms. O. and the painting!"

"Oh, that," he said. "That's great, sweetie!" Paul was awake now and happy to hear her voice, "But did you get the money? And could I have a loan?"

"She was so impressed with it that she gave me *extra* money!" Playfully, she said, "I'm rich now! Maybe next time you cash in a savings bond for Broussard's, I can spring for a cab!"

"That's great! I knew she would love it!" Looking at the clock again brought a feeling of panic. He said, "I just realized what time it is, my Dad is going to pick me up at 10 am, I've got to get moving, Tight-Butt!"

"Oh, that's a shame, I was just going to ask if you were interested in a little more of… *that?"*

"Very unfair, Marie. Not only did you wake me up, but you had to torture me also?"

Her laughter in his ear forced him to hold the phone away.

She grew quiet, waiting on him as he confessed, "I'm going to miss you, Marie. I can't believe we have to be apart for a month."

"I'll call you if I can. It won't be as often as I'd like, but I don't want Daddy to go ballistic about his expensive phone bill. The best time for you to call me would be during the day while he's at work."

"Okay. I'm happy for your painting and that it pleased Ms. O. I also want you to know I couldn't stop thinking about you last night. Thank you, Marie,"

"I hope I talk to you soon! I'm glad you can't stop thinking about me, and I'd love to at least talk more about *that*."

It was hard for both to end this call. It heralded the beginning of a long separation.

As the line went silent, his smile remained as he recalled their magical night together.

❧

He could hardly concentrate on anything but her. After finishing last-minute packing and showering, Paul was waiting at the curb with his loaded duffel when his Dad arrived.

"Goodness gracious son, you're normally a pretty happy fellow, but I've never seen you smile like that before! Are you showing me how it looks from the top of the world?"

If his father only knew, he thought. Perhaps he already did. He had been a young man at one point.

"Things have been great here, Dad. It's been an interesting semester, and I can't wait to get started again after Christmas."

"Your mom and I had no doubt you would do well here. We're both proud of you, son."

As they turned onto Airline Highway, his Dad asked, "How is Marie? Do you think you'll get to see her over the break?"

"Glad you asked, I was wondering if I could borrow one of your cars Christmas evening?"

"Destination, Morgan City?"

"Yes, sir."

"You have my vote, and I'm sure your mother won't be hard to convince."

They rode along in silence for a minute before his father felt compelled to ask, "Are you sure her father is on board with this?"

"I'm not sure, but there is only one way to find out."

Driving along, Paul told his father the latest regarding his tutoring with Delilah and his concerns for her. His father listened carefully to what he said and waited until he finished before he spoke.

"I admire you for what you are doing. Not many people would go the distance for Delilah as you have. She's had a tough life, losing her father at a young age and growing up in the inner city. She has a lot going against her. You know you need to be careful, though. It is a fine line to juggle to keep their problems from becoming your own. Your priority should always remain with your education. Speaking of that, have you made any decisions about Law School?"

"I'm still leaning that way, but I love the teaching part. I helped Marie at the beginning of our English class, and all she needed was a spark. Then she took off on her own. Delilah is more of a challenge. She's gotten so far behind on the fundamentals. But it's thrilling to see her improve. She has a real desire, and helping her gives me such great satisfaction."

"She's lucky to have your attention, son. You, too, are lucky in so many ways. Few people discover their passion for a career at such a young age, and some never find it. One avenue to consider is that lawyers need teachers too." His father looked at him earnestly, and added, "That's how the lawyers get educated. A passionate teacher would be a real asset to any Law School."

Paul smiled at his father, then looked out the windshield at the path ahead. He said a silent prayer of thanks for parents and extended family who had shaped him through love and kindness, a blessing that not all young people share. Now, more than ever, he felt a deeper appreciation for his family.

He looked back at his father and said, "I should have a firmer answer for y'all soon, Dad. Thanks to you and mom for making this opportunity possible for me. Delilah never had this chance."

"We love you, son."

"Thanks, Dad. I love y'all too."

Christmas Day arrived, and for the fifth time, Marie's mother called to her as she sat in the den, looking out the window. "Honey, you look like you're in a trance! Are you okay?"

"I'm doing great, Mom. It's just that I really miss Paul. We've spent so much time together. Being here without him, I feel like a part of me is missing."

"Marie Elise Landry, it sounds to me like you are in love with him!"

Marie answered, "I am. But I'm afraid to call him because Daddy will be upset. It's frustrating because I don't know what to do now. It's Christmas Day, and all I want is to hear his voice."

Her mother sat beside her and said, "Your Daddy is like a little puppy. His bark is far worse than his bite. He tells me all the time that he can't believe how old you've gotten. And it's not just him. Others, including me, have said the same thing: you were a child not too long ago, and now you've become a beautiful young woman. In your *father's* mind, you will always be his little girl. I've tried my best to talk to him, but he won't listen to me. You need to delicately remind your father *yourself* that you're a grown woman who is capable of making her own decisions."

Marie couldn't hold her tongue, and she felt compelled to say something she knew she would regret, "You want me to speak to him in a way that you can't even bring yourself to do, momma. I've wished for years that you would find the strength to stand up to him! For both of us!" She had never spoken to her mother this way, but her frustration had moved past resentment.

From the living room, they heard her father yell, "Who is this person coming down our driveway on Christmas Day? *Marie! Did you invite that young man here today?*"

❧

Paul had enjoyed a wonderful Christmas with his family. At the Morel home, Christmas tradition began on Christmas Eve. Even after their kids became adults, their mother continued to remind her children of the true meaning of Christmas. The "Preparation of Santa's Gifts", as his mom, Ella, called it, could not begin until her "children" were in bed. Their children knew from a young age that Santa would not arrive until the sheet was up, and the sheet wouldn't go up until they were in their beds. His mother, despite her children being adults, steadfastly demanded this tradition.

Where the large bedsheet had come from in the middle of the night, remained unspoken. The kids knew their parents had erected it, but never saw them do it. From the kid's standpoint, it just appeared the next morning. What the children saw when they arrived in the den on Christmas morning, was this large sheet, preventing any view of the Christmas tree or what Santa had brought.

Paul could still hear his mother's defense argument. Her solid reasoning never changed or wavered. "Christmas is not about the gifts under the tree from Santa. It is about the birth of our Lord, Jesus Christ. We will give proper thanks and praise for the birth of our Savior before the sheet will come down."

So, every year since he could remember, their Christmas morning began at the dining room table, saying a blessing of thanks to God for the birth of his Son, sent to take away the sins of the world. She even had a birthday cake with a candle.

Only after giving thanks during breakfast would their parents allow the sheet to come down, to reveal the gifts.

It wasn't as if he and Savannah hadn't protested, citing that the sheet was just for children. Their mother held firm. She wanted to emphasize that Santa wasn't the real reason for the day, no matter their ages, a point that made far more sense to him now than when he was very young.

There were no gleaming new bicycles behind the sheet this year, just smaller gifts, including shared love and reflection. His grandparents arrived just after breakfast, in time to witness the sheet coming down. They would never admit the genesis of this unusual tradition. Savannah irreverently called it, "The Jesus Sheet".

Later, after lunch, Dr. Morel knew that his son had a long trip ahead of him and asked him what time Marie expected him. He had told them that he was going there that afternoon, but had left out the part that it was a surprise visit.

"Soon, Dad," was his reply. And within the hour, he was driving toward Morgan City. Traffic, as expected, was light. He didn't know what awaited him on this next trip to her home, but he knew he yearned for her family to know how he felt about Marie.

❧

Now, sitting in Marie's driveway with the engine turned off, he sat for a moment to muster the necessary courage. He didn't know what he would say and hoped the right words would form on his lips.

Without recalling his steps, he found himself at the front door. It opened without a knock. It was Mr. Landry, and he didn't look happy.

The best defense is a good offense; he again recalled his father's words. Paul summoned a smile and kept his chin up as her father stood, big as a mountain, blocking the path through his door.

Paul said, "Merry Christmas, Mr. Landry! I'm Paul Morel, one of Marie's classmates. I hope I'm not intruding, and I won't stay but a minute!"

Mr. Landry stood there, silently.

Things could be worse, Paul thought, *at least he hasn't pulled a gun, yet.*

"Sir, I just wanted to surprise Marie today. She didn't know I was coming, so I guess you didn't either!"

Her father wasn't laughing, much less smiling.

Marie and her mother had moved quickly into the living room to see who had arrived. Looking out the window, Marie gasped and turned back to her mother. "It's Paul," she said frantically. She parted the drapes to look, adding, "I hope Daddy doesn't kill him!"

"Oh honey, let's not talk worst-case scenarios! Your father can be nice too! Give him a chance; it's Christmas!"

Marie held her breath as she continued to look out the window.

Mr. Landry continued to stand motionless, with his arms folded. From Paul's perspective, it wasn't going well. Mr. Landry was as big as a grizzly bear, and Paul had always heard that you should never run from a bear.

Within arm's reach, Paul held out his hand and repeated his greeting, "Merry Christmas, sir!"

The silence seemed to last forever, as Paul's hand remained empty.

Then, at last, her father uttered, "That's a pretty far drive for just a quick hello."

Mr. Landry unfolded his arms and extended his hand. The frown on his face remained unchanged.

The bear-sized paw that grasped his hand felt powerful enough to crush it. The handshake offered was manly but polite, and Paul was relieved.

"Lucien Landry is my name. You can call me, *Mr.* Landry." Without taking his eyes off Paul, he yelled, "*Marie! That boy is back!*"

Marie appeared behind him, sporting a sheepish grin as she held her Daddy's shoulders from behind and peered from around his torso. The man was so large he blocked almost the entire portal.

"Hi, Paul! Merry Christmas! I see you've met my Dad."

"Yes, we've, uh, met. Merry Christmas, Marie!"

Mr. Landry huffed, "Okay, you've said your 'hellos', now you'd best be getting back down the road, Mr. Morel. It's going to be dark soon."

"Daddy, please. He's come a long way, can't he stay for a few more minutes?"

Mr. Landry shook his head but stepped aside as Marie grabbed Paul's hand and led him into the house.

"Here's my mom," Marie yanked Paul into the living room, "remember my mamma? Y'all met Thanksgiving Day in the driveway."

Paul quickly grasped Mrs. Landry's extended hand as she said, "Welcome back, Paul! My husband and I…" Mrs. Landry gave her husband, who continued to lurk nearby, a cold stare, "we'll be out in the kitchen if you need anything."

Looking at Marie, her mother said, "Why don't you go get Paul a glass of that wonderful sweet tea you made earlier?"

"Yes, ma'am."

As her parents exited, Mr. Landry said, "Better take this opportunity to have a seat and take a load off, son," then he smiled as he said, "you'll be leaving soon."

Mrs. Landry slapped her husband's arm playfully as she shooed him from the room.

Paul sat on the sofa just as Marie returned with his glass of tea.

"You should be proud of yourself!" she said, "The last boy that made a surprise visit here on a holiday, he mounted on the wall in the family room!"

"I believe it!" Paul took a long sip of the tea, which wet his nervously dry mouth. Looking first at the door, he surprised Marie as he leaned over and kissed her.

She smiled shyly, then quietly cautioned him, "Better be careful, love. Daddy's got eyes and ears that a mountain lion would be envious of!"

Throwing caution to the wind, he leaned over and whispered, "I can't stop thinking about you, and us… I love you, Marie!"

Circling her arms around him, she said, "I love you too. And I can tell that Daddy likes you because you've been here for more than two minutes. That's a record!"

"And my head's not on the wall yet!"

"It'd be best not to get cocky," Marie giggled.

They spoke for a while longer before Paul asked, "Would it be okay if I walked back and told your parents goodbye?"

"I can tell you that my mom would love it, and Daddy is… let's just say that with him, you'd be pushing your luck!"

Before he left, he handed Marie a folded piece of paper, stating, "It's your present. Sorry, it's not much."

Marie unfolded it. It was the poem he had written and read to her before, The Symphony.

"Thank you from the bottom of my heart for that and coming to see me today. You are a brave man, Paul Morel."

Paul drove back to New Roads relishing the thought that he'd gotten his foot in the door. After what happened on Thanksgiving, the only direction he could go was up, and Christmas turned out better than he expected.

During the next few weeks, he visited Morgan City one more time. He asked Mr. Landry if they could go to the dock with him to see his shrimping business and boats. With Marie in tow, the 3 of them had an unusually pleasant visit as Mr. Landry gladly showed off his passion. He was a hard-working man who was highly respected by his crew and his competition. The shrimping business had been as good to him as he was to it.

Paul arrived at school a week early. He remained worried for Delilah through the break and was anxious to check on her. Arriving at Talulah's rear door at 3 pm on Monday, it was damp and cold outside; the warm air flowing through her screen felt good for a change.

From inside, he heard, "Is that you, Mr. Paul Morel?" Talulah floated over to the door, "Come on in here and gets out'a the cold air!"

She had already opened the screen, and he gladly walked in.

Talulah immediately continued with what she was doing: baking. It was her true passion. She repeated the same process six days a week, but each time she exuded excitement as though it was her first.

"Sits yourself down over there," Talulah rarely pointed without using her spoon, "outs the way, and tells me all 'bout you family Christmas!"

They had come such a long way together. This generous woman was genuinely interested in his happiness and his family.

Paul looked under the table for Delilah, then craned his neck to see if she were sleeping anywhere else.

Talulah was anything but unobservant. "She ain't here. You and me'll talk 'bout her after while. Now tell Talulah 'bout Christmas at your home!"

They talked for a short while, while Talulah worked her magic. Like a highly trained surgeon, each move she made was so precise that any wasted effort or steps to complete her task left years ago.

After Paul told her about his holiday and Marie, she said, "Sounds me like you and Lil Miss Tight-Butt be getting real tight, *together!* And don't you worries about her Daddy. You's a good man yourself, and he gonna come 'round."

"Please tell me about Delilah ma'am. I hope you and she had a good Christmas together."

She grew silent as she leaned over under the hearth to stir all the cast iron pots of fruit fillings cooking over the fire.

Stated without emotion, as if only a matter-of-fact, "Delilah ain't been 'round much since you left, Paul."

This statement by Talulah was Paul's worst nightmare.

"Sure, she comes home late to sleep and even come here now and again to sleep under my table in the back, but she don't say where she go, or who she be with. But I think we both knows, don't we?"

The words his father told him recently, "remain at a distance so that their problems don't become your own," kept echoing through his mind.

"Things was different when I was growin' up. I had a momma and daddy that never been to school. They made sure I was in school every day. But still, I had to quit after the sixth grade. Mamma died from sugar; and daddy was kilt in'a accident on the river. I hads to work. I still be workin' for me and Delilah. I worry 'bout her every day. There be so many bad peoples 'round her. Boys that never had chances cause 'a no father at home. What's goin' wrong with this world, Mr. Paul? The last few times I sees her, she so tired she can't stand, and she sleeps for a long time. I looks at her arms while she be sleeping, they be skinny as bone, like the rest o'her, and she gots red marks everywhere."

This wasn't good. It concerned Paul that Delilah could be doing dangerous drugs. With marks on her arms, it sounded like she could be using heroin.

"I sure appreciates what you have tried to do to help her, Paul. But until she gets herselfs squared away with me and the Lawd, I think you just wasting your own valuable time coming round trying to help. I's afraid too, for you. You can't get you own education if one o'dem boys knocks you upside 'o the head! You gots to think 'bout youself!"

Paul left Talulah reluctantly that afternoon but placed his dorm room phone number on the table on a piece of paper that said: call me if I can help you. She hugged him like a mother before he walked out the door, and he saw a tear in her eyes as he turned back to wave.

20

NOTHING REMAINS THE SAME

Paul had never felt so depressed. He walked back to the university the long way; down River Road and from there, through Audubon Park, then back to his dorm. He felt so helpless; he could only imagine how Talulah felt. Delilah was the product of love between her and her husband, Huey, and with his premature passing, she was Talulah's only living reminder of that union.

He recalled his father urging him not to become involved personally. Prudent advice for a father to give a son. *But is it possible for a person to purge something this significant from their mind,* he wondered? *Is it possible to not care, or try to forget like it never happened?*

He was convinced that there were some things you could never forget: for him, it was childhood experiences. He knew that no matter how old he grew, he would always remember his childhood during Christmas. He and his sister knew, starting at a young age, that Santa couldn't arrive until the sheet appeared to hide the Christmas tree from view, and the sheet never appeared before Christmas morning. His mother, steadfastly upheld this tradition. *Is it possible to just forget something so central to your life?* His concern for the daughter of his friend was no different. They had both become part of his life.

Paul reasoned that forgetting and ignoring were two sides of the same coin.

He knew that Delilah's problems left a massive void in Talulah's soul. It was hard for him to imagine how any person, especially a mother, could come to grips with the inability to help their child. It was a natural urge, desire, and need that began even before the child was born. Certainly, Talulah could never forget the innocence and potential that her little girl was born with, nor her own desire to be there for her.

For the next few days, Paul walked in every possible direction, getting to know the entire area around Tulane University. The wealth nearby, and the magnificent homes it bought, amazed him. Street after street, he walked, seeing signs of affluence, bounded by sections of stark poverty.

During the day, he felt relatively safe. But he knew that there were many areas he wouldn't have walked through after dark. His travels were a constant reminder of the world trying to consume, Delilah.

Marie returned the same day as the other students. It was the Sunday morning before classes began for the spring semester. When she called to tell him she was back, she could tell right away from the tone of his voice that something wasn't right. Her concern began before she returned when he seemed short with her and distant during his calls to her house after Christmas.

Trying to sound upbeat, she said, "Meet me outside my door in 30 minutes. I know it's cold, but it's sunny. Let's go for a walk!"

His kiss this morning lacked the enthusiasm she expected from being apart for so long. Paul wasn't acting right, he was distant, and Marie wondered if he was getting ready to break up with her.

They walked together to a coffee shop nearby that he'd found during one of his recent walks. Paul remained very quiet, and his hand felt limp to hers.

Inside, over steaming coffee, he loosened up and broke from his shell, confessing his concerns for Delilah.

The news distressed Marie, but she was relieved that his funk was not about her or her father. She commented, "The price you paid for those Thanksgiving pies was very high, Paul."

"I know," he said, "but it was my choice. No one twisted my arm, and I'd do the same thing all over again if I had the chance. Delilah didn't have the same opportunities you and I had, Marie."

Paul said something else to her this morning that made her think. He said, "I believe that Talulah overpaid me for what I did. Not only did we receive all those delicious pies, but along with it came another gift… something priceless. I learned how lucky I am to have a loving family. When I was growing up, I thought that everyone had the same thing, the same blessings, and support that I had at home, but they don't. There is a world living close to us where life is a constant struggle and threat. We are so blessed."

Relieved to have unloaded his burden, he and Marie spoke together about other things.

Marie was excited that her curriculum had more than basic core classes. She would be attending her first college-level art class that would involve many mediums; paint, as well as stone, wood, and glass. She was beyond excited.

During the second cup of coffee, Marie asked Paul a very pointed question. She'd held back, asking until she couldn't wait any longer. "So, tell me, Mr. Morel, are you going to be an English major or pre-Law this semester?"

"That decision, Miss Landry, was also a beneficiary of my deal for Thanksgiving's pies."

Marie could never anticipate what Paul might say next. She looked at him and said, "I believe you are the most interesting man I've ever met. That statement begs for an explanation!"

"Well, I love to write, and I love to teach. I discovered that fact not just with you but also with Delilah. In my mind, that has narrowed my choice down to something that involves teaching. In regards to writing, although it's a passion for me, not everyone can be Ernest Hemingway. Just look where that success got him? He committed suicide, probably right before his liver gave out from all the alcohol!"

"Okay! So, you're going to be a teacher, and you love to write, but you don't see that as a profession by itself. Will you be an English teacher? What, pray-tell will you teach, Professor?"

"You mean, after Law School?"

"Wait just a cotton-picking minute! So, it's Law School again? I'm confused."

"Well, a light bulb went off after speaking with my dad. He reminded me that law students need teachers too. Also, a university has many privileges and grants leeway to Professors to pursue their passions. I've chosen my path to become a Professor of Civil Rights Law."

Marie sat back in her chair with an astounded look on her face. "Just like that? Not only do you know you want to be a lawyer, but you've refined your search to Civil Rights? Amazing. You are so focused! I'm impressed! I understand teaching, and I understand Law, but why did you choose Civil Rights?"

He passionately explained his reasoning to her. "It circles back to the pies and Talulah. I want to help break down the barriers that still exist between rich and poor, mainly related to their opportunities for education. I'd like to help to throw a legal wrench in the spoke of poverty, a vicious wheel that just keeps turning. That circle is the one still trying to consume Delilah."

Paul took a deep breath and continued, "My passions have come in a big circle, Marie. It was an English class in high school where the teacher gave the class an assignment to read a book called, *Black Like Me*, by author John Howard Griffin. It changed the way I looked at the issue of civil rights. The author was a white man who used various means to disguise himself as a black man in the deep south. He performed his own social experiment, then wrote about it. Mr. Griffin knew that only one thing had changed about him: his skin and hair color. He was the same person underneath, but that one difference: the way he looked, caused horrendous treatment by some whites."

"That's terrible! Perhaps everyone should read that book."

"Yes, they should. Ever since I read it, I've made even more of an effort to judge a person, not by what my eyes see, but from what my ears hear, and my heart feels. It doesn't matter what color a person's skin is, some are good, and some are bad, but everyone should start with a chance, shouldn't they? I've been treated poorly by some whites *and* blacks in my own life. I believe that there is such a thing as reverse racism."

"What do you mean?"

Paul said, "Listen to Muhammad Ali's famous quote, *'Hating people because of their color is wrong. And it doesn't matter which color does the hating. It's just plain wrong.'* You see, Marie, racism knows no skin color. No race alone owns it. Who knows where it all started, but I refuse to spread it any farther by the way I live my life. I can't change the actions of other people as much as I can change my own. So that's why I've chosen Civil Rights Law. We were all endowed by our Creator with 'certain unalienable rights', so I'd like to help level that playing field. We are not born with hatred; we learn it. Bias or hate based on skin color or any other physical difference should be shunned from our society, by law if necessary."

Marie was impressed. "What a wonderful goal. I am so proud of you and your passion."

They spoke for a while longer about their upcoming semester before leaving. As they walked back to school, Marie nervously asked, "How do you see *my* place in *your* life?"

"Everywhere," he responded. "There is no place without you. I'm sorry I've been so preoccupied. The old Paul is still here; just thrown for a loop, that's all."

Her heart soared. "I've been worried, with the time away from each other… you know… right after we made love. I wasn't sure. You know how doubts can creep in. We couldn't see each other for so long, and the way my Dad acted…"

"Your dad is great. I'm still working on him, but I'm trying to take it slowly! I think we're growing on each other!"

Marie suddenly became serious and turned to face him with a frown as she said, "I wouldn't be so sure. There is a new mounting plate that recently appeared on the den wall, and it has your name on it." She started to giggle.

"Yeah, right." Playing along, he felt his head with his hands, then said, "From what I can tell, I don't think he's mounted me on it *yet!"*

Marie was still concerned about Paul. With a more serious look, she said, "That night before we left for Christmas, I hope you didn't think I was too forward? You know, with me asking you back to my room? I guess it's obvious to you now that I'd also been thinking about *that*. Everything was happening so fast, the end of the semester, us leaving the next day, my feelings of how much I wanted you…"

"Don't beat my lady up! I hoped you would invite me back. If I'd had the nerve, we never would have made dinner! And that probably would have been safer than sneaking in the second time! Oh, and I would have invited you to my room long before that, but I was worried that once you saw it, you'd dump me!"

"As if!" They walked a little farther, and she stopped again. She had another pressing question, "I need to know something. I didn't disappoint you… I didn't… did I?"

"It's not possible for heaven to be a disappointment. Come to think of it; we need to visit that beautiful place again soon!

Marie needed this reassurance from him this morning: at least. Content, for now, she cast her eyes at the pavement as they continued.

21
A MOTHER'S FEAR

It was the last full week in January when they found the time to venture to Talulah's on a Wednesday afternoon. Both found themselves very busy with their new schedules, and it was rare that Marie didn't work late in the Art lab. Her projects were very satisfying to her, but also quite time-consuming.

Rarely did Paul speak about Delilah: he couldn't. Marie knew what Paul was doing. Intense study became his deflection: an emotional band-aid too small to cover his unhealed sore. They both knew that distracting his mind from Delilah didn't relieve his concern.

Plans this afternoon were Marie's idea. She knew that if she mentioned pie, Paul would want to go. The timing was just right. She had just turned in a significant project, and Paul had phoned her earlier, hoping to take a break for a while. After thinking about what she'd like to do, she called him back, and soon, they were off to Talulah's.

It had been a few weeks since Paul learned that Delilah was not doing well. As they rode the familiar path down St. Charles Avenue, he mentioned to her that he was surprised that Talulah hadn't phoned him since the last time he'd seen her.

"Maybe that's good news. Perhaps she's doing better?" he thought out loud.

"I hope so too," she said.

Arriving in the front lot, they hoped there would be pies left to purchase. A hopeful sign was the sight of several people standing in line already, and smoke coming out of the chimney. Things were looking promising.

They stood quietly in line for a couple of minutes before anyone else arrived. When Marie turned around, she exclaimed, "Miss Bea! So nice to see you!"

Paul turned to see the beaming face of Beatrice, Talulah's friend, they'd met in line before.

"I be wondering where y'all at! I ain't seen y'all in the longest!"

Paul said, "We've been busy, Miss Bea. We'd be here every day if we could, and if that were the case, I'd be as wide as that levee over there!"

Marie knew that Paul wasn't telling Bea the whole truth. Coming here each day would only worry him more.

Beatrice laughed, her white denture teeth gleaming. "Well, I shore did miss seeing y'all, but nobody 'round here gonna complain 'bout havin' more pie for them selfs!"

"Miss Bea, how is Delilah doing?" Paul asked. "Is she okay?"

"To tells you the truth, Mr. Paul; I is surprised to see the smoke coming out'a Talulah's chimney today. Delilah, she got 'rested last week by the police for drugs. Not long after they takes her to the jail, they takes her straight to the Charity Hospital for rehab. The last I hear, she might still could die!"

It was worse than Paul imagined. He was speechless and could only look at Marie.

Suddenly, the top door opened. They were both anxious to see Talulah's face and hear her voice. But there would be no song tonight from Talulah. Clarence appeared in the door. He announced that he only had a limited number of pies to sell tonight because Talulah had to leave early to see Delilah.

Marie held her hand over her mouth as she looked up at Paul. She could see tears in his eyes.

"God has a plan, Marie," was all he could say, "and we have to trust His plan."

Although the line wasn't very long in front of them, it took a while to reach the front because everyone had questions for Clarence.

They were next in line on the porch, and they both turned around to tell Beatrice that it had been nice seeing her. But Beatrice was gone, possibly to Charity Hospital to be with her friend.

When they turned back, Clarence was waiting for their order. Paul handed him twenty dollars and said, "I'm sure Talulah could use a little extra cash right now. Sell our pies to the next person, Clarence."

"That's real nice of y'all. I look forward to seeing you both at the Camellia soon!"

❧

The next Saturday, February delivered almost spring-like temperatures. Marie called him before 9 am, risking the verbal wrath of his roommate for, as he would typically say, "crashing my best sleeping time".

Nathaniel hadn't returned last night until 2 am, so he showed no sign of life when the phone rang. Paul had tried to get to know him months ago, but Nathaniel was on a path chosen for himself. In a way, it was almost like having a room to himself; they had so little interaction together. His roommate didn't schedule any classes before 1 pm. By contrast, Paul loved his early classes, and only rarely on the weekends would he sleep past 8 am.

Paul, already awake and lounging in his bed for the past hour, was unable to sleep with the bright morning sun filling the room around him. He jumped from bed to silence the ringing phone. "Hello?" he spoke quietly into the receiver.

Marie told him she'd been up since midnight tossing and turning, and had been ready to start this day hours ago. She'd waited "as long as she could" before calling.

Paul wasn't surprised by her inability to sleep. He'd figured out early in their relationship that she lacked the "coma gene". That being his description of the genetic blessing he possessed: to be able to pass completely out when his head hit the pillow, and not wake until the alarm went off. It had been quite a while since the last time he gloated to her about his superior ability, and this beautiful morning was not the time to bring it up again.

She called to invite him to the park with her for the day. Although he had some work he needed to do, it would be much more enjoyable doing it on a blanket in the park with Marie. Despite the crisp feel to the air, the sun was out in full force. He anticipated a beautiful day with his girl.

Marie was again uninterested in breakfast, so, Paul loaded his backpack with his books and traversed to the cafeteria before picking her up at her dorm.

On arrival at her window, to his delight, he found a new painting. It was a very detailed view of the large, low-lying branches of two separate live oak trees. They'd grown so close together that they almost touched. There were two squirrels, one on the end of each branch, shown with their delicate paws reaching out toward each other. One squirrel was passing an acorn to the other. It was beautiful. No wonder she wanted to go to the park today.

He tapped on the pane, and soon they walked together to the park entrance.

Paul said, "That was a beautiful painting on your window this morning!"

"Thanks. I couldn't sleep, so I painted something special for you to see."

"It was *incredibly* special, thanks so much! I'm sorry you couldn't sleep last night. Are you feeling okay?"

"Mostly," she replied.

Paul didn't press, knowing that Marie was usually an open book, and whatever it was that was bothering her would surface soon.

For a change, it was Paul who today jabbered on about this and that. He could tell that Marie was tired. It would be great if she might be able to catch up on lost sleep while he worked. They were both drawn to the same live oak from their first visit. It was somewhat off the beaten path, and no one ever passed them here.

After Paul spread the blanket for them, Marie was the first to stretch out, resting on her back with her eyes closed to the warming sun. He heard her say, "I love this spot, Paul. I'm glad we came here today."

Paul, still standing, took his backpack off and kneeled to rifle through it, looking for something inside. Proudly, he pulled out the delicacy he had carefully packed from the cafeteria and opened the napkin for display.

"Look what I brought you, Marie!"

Marie turned her head sideways, squinting in his direction, to see a smiling Paul holding a banana nut muffin toward her with his outstretched hand, one of her favorites.

Without warning, Marie turned away suddenly and began to retch.

Paul, shocked by her response, retracted his hand. He returned the muffin to his backpack, and seconds later kneeled at her side. Gently, he pulled against her shoulder, turning her to him. She was crying.

He thought about her statement earlier concerning her sleepless night. Then, he offered her one of her favorite breakfast foods, at it made her nauseous. *The painting: it was symbolic,* he thought. *She had been trying to tell him what was happening, through her art.*

A shiver shot through him, almost taking his breath away, as the words tumbled out, "I didn't realize at first what your painting meant, Marie. Is it true?"

Marie, still unable to answer, continued to weep.

Paul stroked her back, and she responded by rolling over face down. She was exhausted. He continued to rub her back gently, and soon she relaxed beneath his fingertips and fell asleep.

All thoughts of his assignments vanished. As this delicate, distraught, worn-out woman that he loved was comforted by his simple touch, his mind raced.

The rough outline of the life that he'd awakened to this morning, one that he had spent eighteen years developing, had suddenly turned very complex. The aftermath of their passionate sharing of souls had not granted them any semblance of carefree, added time.

He knew that the choice they made was made freely by both that night. He'd heard of this happening to others, usually kids in high school. But the two of them? They should have known better. Again, he reminded himself that God has a plan.

Comforted that she was asleep, Paul rolled away. He needed to think. In the past, he'd taken pride in being a good problem solver. And this was most definitely a problem for them both. Their families would be disappointed. No question. He knew his family would be there for them. Just how much, he wasn't sure, but his family would never abandon him.

After a few minutes, a hand rested on his shoulder. From behind, he heard, "Hold me, please."

Rolling over to her, he smothered her in his arms. She wailed next to his ear, and her tears ran onto his shoulder.

He asked her, "Are you sure?"

"Yes," she replied.

After a few minutes, her breathing slowed as she tried to calm herself. Her voice broke as she whimpered, "I'm so sorry."

"Oh, no, you don't!" Paul backed away enough to look her in the eyes. He waited until she opened them to look at him.

"*This happened to us both*, and we will get through this the same way!"

The floodgates opened.

When she could speak, Marie said, "But your dreams of becoming a lawyer, my dreams of being a successful artist… you know my daddy will shoot you, don't you? How could this happen? It was the first time for us both! Now, our families are going to *freak out,* and our futures are down the drain."

Paul stood and said firmly, "Stand up, please."

The comforting man who had just held her had suddenly sounded cold and demanding. He must want to leave; this place, and her, she thought.

She stood slowly, wondering who this man had suddenly become, feeling even more alone and helpless.

As she stood, Paul went down on one knee. Her eyes widened.

With tears in his eyes, he held her hand and said, "In my wildest imagination, I never envisioned this: not in this way and certainly not this soon. But I did envision it happening *someday* with *you. Someday* has come early for us. Will you marry me?"

Without hesitation, she replied, "Absolutely."

22

FAITH

One thing was clear. Both Marie and Paul believed that all life was precious, even an unplanned one. There could be no priority in their lives to take the place of this child, no matter what the other consequences were.

Amazingly, this decision was far more comfortable for them to make than the more pressing one: how to present it to their parents. They knew this conversation needed to be in person.

They took a few days to discuss their options, then decided to invite both sets of parents to New Orleans for dinner. Valentine's Day was this coming Wednesday, so they used it as an excuse for their request and picked the evening of Saturday the 17th to make it convenient for their working fathers.

Paul phoned his parents first. His father would jump at any excuse to come to the French Quarter for a great meal. Dr. Morel loved The Court of Two Sisters restaurant on Royal Street and said he would be delighted to make reservations there for both families. Paul asked his father to stop by the university and pick them up on the way.

Marie's parents had more questions, which, when not answered adequately, caused hesitation, mostly from her father. He didn't understand the need for this sudden and extravagant trip to the big city, just for dinner. They refused to commit until she told them that she and Paul had a surprise for them that they would only say in person. Despite her father getting firm with her on the phone, she refused to divulge any details.

After hanging up, Marie turned to Paul and said, "My Dad sounds very upset with us already. He was angry. Probably because I wouldn't tell him why it was so urgent that they have dinner with your parents. He said, 'You're not getting serious already with that boy you just met, are you?'"

Paul was silent. This confession wasn't going to be easy and had virtually no chance of going well.

He turned to Marie as they sat like statues on the bench outside her dorm. Neither of them had slept much since their visit to the park on Saturday.

Marie said, "I'm going to go back to my room and see if I can close my eyes for a little while. Otherwise, the mother of your child is going to turn into a zombie right here on this bench!"

"Just a minute, I want to ask you something." Paul put his arm around her and said, "I'm just guessing, but I don't believe that dinner Saturday will be a very memorable first Valentine's Day for us, so would you come to dinner with just me tomorrow evening, on the real Valentine's Day?"

"Well, of course I will." Marie was pale and looked like she might fall asleep at any moment.

"Okay, it's a date. I'll pick you up at your dorm at 3 pm."

"Three? That early? I'll have to skip my last class!"

"Won't you, Marie, please?"

She couldn't argue, she was so tired. With her eyes half-closed, she said, "Yes, okay. But only because it's you. And it would be nice to make our first Valentine's together, memorable!"

Marie was unsteady on her feet as she stood. After a moment, she was better, and Paul walked her to her door.

She turned toward him to say, "I'm not sure I'll be able to hold anything down tomorrow, so don't pick an expensive restaurant." She turned, still thinking, then looked back at him to say, "It must be the pregnancy, but I've had a real craving recently for a Lucky Dog."

Paul was perplexed. Lucky Dogs were an inexpensive gastric staple in New Orleans. Sold from mobile carts that could be found all over the French Quarter, there was nothing special about their recipe. But there was something stellar about their reputation in New Orleans. They were the official Hot Dog of the city.

"It's your pick, Marie. That will certainly be an easy reservation to make. We just have to find out which street corner they're serving from!"

As she turned to walk through the door, he called, "Come to your window to let me know you made it to your room, please."

"I will if I'm still awake!"

Moments later, she smiled through the pane and blew him a kiss.

Paul went directly to his room, then made a trip to the bank. It was his last savings bond from the Morel grandparents. He would need the cash soon.

The next day, Paul arrived at her window to find that Marie had been productive. There was a new painting—an optimistic interpretation of them sitting at dinner with their parents. Everyone had smiles, and they were making a toast.

Paul tapped at her window, and she appeared, the corners of her mouth more upturned than down.

Outside, she appeared less pale and reported that she'd gotten some sleep, which felt, "Heavenly." She said that having a plan to move forward with their families helped to ease her mind.

They boarded the next streetcar that was heading downtown. It was a gorgeous day.

"Where are you taking me to dinner, Paul? I'm finally getting my appetite back!"

"Lucky Dogs you requested, and Lucky Dogs you shall receive! From my last recollection, even if we close our eyes while we walk, we'll run into one of their stands in less than five minutes! We're almost there."

As they exited the car on Canal Street, Marie grabbed his hand and said, "So let's go, I'm hungry."

"Hold on there, Miss Landry! First, you will pick out your Valentine's present."

"Oh! That sounds like fun! Can I shop anywhere I want?"

"Yes, after I choose the shop and the display case."

"What?"

"Come on, Marie! Let's get going; these shops don't stay open all night!"

As they walked down Royal Street, Paul stopped suddenly in front of Royal Antiques.

"Here it is! Valentine's Central!"

Marie was incredulous. She stopped walking and placed her fists on her hips to say, "Wait just a minute, Mr. Morel. An antique store? Aw, come on, that's cheesy." Pointing down the street, she said, "Let's go down to one of the art shops so we can see if you really love me."

As if he hadn't heard a word, he pulled her inside. At the cashier's station, there were glass cases with beautiful rings inside.

"Let's look here for a Valentine's present for each other." Paul dropped down on one knee, adding, "Something that looks like a ring… a wedding ring."

Paul smiled at her as tears appeared again. "Oh, and we should hurry. The magistrate down the street closes at 5 pm."

"This is truly happening, isn't it? Do you mean it, Paul? We are really getting married today?"

Word spread through the store like a benevolent virus as clerks gathered to witness this special event.

"Yes, Marie. I love you with all my heart! Now let's get busy. They told me when I called that if we don't find something we like in the display case, the owner will open the vault and help us personally."

It didn't take long. Marie chose a simple gold band with a small stone.

The person behind the counter commended her choice, "That stone is an amethyst, how appropriate! It is the birthstone of February and Valentine's Day!"

Paul chose a simple gold band that looked like it was made to accompany her ring. Her ring fit perfectly, his took a few bangs with a rubber mallet on the sizing post, and they walked out with both rings, polished like new in a small velvet bag.

And, so it was. At 4:48 pm on Wednesday, February 14th, 1979, Marie became Mrs. Marie Landry. For now, retaining her family name seemed like a good idea to them both. Her father would have enough trouble with all the other changes, and Paul, comfortable in his heart they were together forever, readily accepted this.

Lucky Dogs was found just down the street, and none too soon for the famished bride; Marie wanted hers with mustard and sauerkraut. Paul had mustard, ketchup, and onions. The simplicity of this moment was in keeping with their shared happiness on this day.

Nothing and everything had changed. No one on the streetcar had any idea about the significant event that occurred tonight for these two young people. It seemed a shame that no one besides themselves had a clue. Arriving at her dorm a little while after sunset, they sat outside on the bench, laughing as they reminisced Marie's initial reaction to the antique store.

It wasn't long before Marie yawned, and Paul asked if he could walk her to her door.

Marie would have none of that. "Paul Morel, this is our wedding night, and you are not going anywhere except with me. That is unless you would prefer to spend your wedding night with Nathaniel!"

She grabbed his hand as she stood, and they both looked in all directions reflexively before they dashed for the door. Trying to focus on today only, they made tender love for the second time, now as a legally married husband and wife.

Paul and Marie stood at the curb, anxiously waiting as his parents arrived on Saturday afternoon. Paul wore his Sunday suit, and Marie a beautiful pink dress.

"Wish me luck," Paul said to Marie.

They grasped each other's hands tightly.

As Dr. and Mrs. Morel slowed, approaching the curb, Mrs. Morel said to her husband, "I'm afraid you were right, Winston. I can already see a ring on Marie's finger. She's such a beautiful young lady!"

"Reminds me of someone else at that age," Dr. Morel smiled at his wife as they pulled to a stop by the curb.

His parents both got out to greet the couple, but Marie's feet felt frozen to the pavement.

Paul hugged his mother and shook his father's hand.

His mother said, "You look beautiful, Marie, and it's so nice to see you again! Isn't she beautiful, Winston?"

Her husband nodded approvingly.

After hugging them both, Marie replied, "It's great to see you both. Thank you for coming so far for dinner and picking us up."

Dr. Morel noticed a gold band on Paul's ring finger but chose not to say anything yet. He said, "Well, let's go; we can get caught up on the way."

Paul opened Marie's door, then when she was seated, closed it, and walked around to his father's side of the car.

His father said, "It's good to see you, son."

"Thank you for coming to pick us up, Dad."

"I've been hungry ever since you called, Paul. It's been too long since I've eaten at my favorite restaurant. Hop in and let's go, we don't want to be late."

His mother and Marie were already talking as Paul entered the back seat. He placed his right hand over Marie's after she rested hers on his thigh. He listened to them cordially conversing as he felt the amethyst from her ring against his palm. This spot, where his parents picked them up this afternoon, was the same spot they dropped him off just a few short months ago. They delivered him to this university so he could build a future for himself, and had wished him well.

Sure enough, he thought. He had built a future; not the one any of them had imagined, but a future for sure.

The minutes seemed like years since just the other day when they had invited their parents to dinner. Now the anticipation, the dread, the fear of a few simple yet incredibly impactful words, would soon pass. The time had arrived for an admission that he had failed. Failed his parents and hers, and upended the hopes of many. He had never felt disappointment from his parents, and couldn't imagine how tonight would end without it being the first time.

The car moved away from the curb.

Dr. Morel glanced at his watch and said, "We're a little ahead of schedule, I'm going to meander our way to the restaurant. Some of these side streets are beautiful. I'm not sure I ever showed you the house your mother and I lived in while we were in school."

Paul had never heard anything before about his parents living together while in school. As they drove, the streets and the outside of the homes looked familiar in passing, each one guarding many generations of personal history. Motoring through a maze of quiet humanity and progressively smaller homes, they arrived in front of a one-story house a block off South Carrollton. It had a "For Rent" sign in front of it.

His father came to a stop in front of the home and turned off the car.

"This is where your mother and I lived for two years while I finished college. This house has seen a lot. It's where we brought your sister after your mom delivered at Touro Infirmary."

"What are you saying, Dad? I didn't realize you and Mom were married in college."

"It wasn't planned, son. Sometimes things happen. And when they do, that's when a family steps up for one of their own. Have you and Marie got something you want to tell us?"

"Yes, Dad… and Mom… but it appears it's not something you don't already know."

Mrs. Morel looked back at Marie and asked, "When are you due, Dear?"

"September, ma'am."

"Well, you and I will need to go shopping soon for some new clothes for you!"

Dr. Morel asked Paul, "Do Mr. and Mrs. Landry know?"

"Not yet, sir. And I hope they take this news half as well as you and Mom did." Paul reached forward and threw his arms around his father from the back seat. "Thank you, Dad."

Dr. Morel turned the key and said, "Let's go; I'm starving."

As they pulled up to the restaurant on Royal Street, they were promptly greeted and ushered into the restaurant. The Maître D' said, "Hello, and welcome back, Dr. Morel. Your other party is seated at your table, and have been made comfortable with a round of drinks."

Mrs. Morel led the way. Dr. Morel reached for his son's arm and whispered, "There's no easy way to tell the Mr. and Mrs. Landry this news, so my advice is you just do it and get it done."

With the confidence of a man who couldn't swim, about to escape a sinking ship with no life jacket, Paul jumped.

The Terrace Room, just off the Courtyard, was a room filled with light. As they walked past smiling couples and happy people, Paul's eyes followed Marie to a larger, circular table in the corner of the room. Dead ahead, sat a stone-faced Mr. Landry, who remained seated as they approached.

Paul felt the first wave crash over his head as he reflexively held his breath.

His father, who noticed that his son had slowed, passed him and followed the ladies to the table, saying, "Hello, Mr. and Mrs. Landry. I'm Winston Morel." Placing his hand on her shoulder, he proudly added, "And this is my wife, Ella."

Slowly, Mr. Landry rose, still no smile, and said, "Hello, Mr. Morel…"

Mrs. Landry, sounding very embarrassed, interrupted her husband to say, "It's *Doctor* Morel, Lucien!"

Accompanying his sudden turn toward her, she recognized an all-too-familiar glare, with the obvious intent, to again, seal her lips.

Paul's nightmare began as his visual and auditory senses locked onto Marie's father.

With no change in his demeanor, Mr. Landry turned back to say, "*Doctor* Morel, I'm Lucien Landry, and my socially correct wife is Rebecca."

"Y'all can call me Becky," Mrs. Landry said warmly. She shot her husband a look comparable to his own.

Before Dr. Morel could respond, Mr. Landry sat down and raised his tumbler to his frown for another sip. It was apparent that Mrs. Landry was horrified.

Dr. Morel, typically an optimistic man, instantly realized that dinner in his favorite restaurant tonight would be no less than awkward.

Mr. Landry looked around Dr. Morel, searching for Paul. As their eyes locked together, Paul could almost feel his hulk of a hand pushing his head further under the surface as he gasped for air.

Marie, hiding her ring from easy view, hugged her parents, then sat next to her father.

The Morel men sat next to each other, as Paul's legs shook under the table.

Deflecting as best he could, Dr. Morel inquired, "Mr. Landry, what are you drinking today?"

"Vodka tonic," came the somber reply.

To the waiter standing by patiently, Dr. Morel said, "Sounds good to me, I'll take the same, and I'm sure the ladies are thirsty!"

As requested, the waiter returned with a bottle of red wine for the ladies and vodka for the doctor.

Their table remained very quiet, a stark contrast to a virtual sea of gaiety from tables in every direction around them.

Mr. Landry's drink expired with his next gulp as he searched the room impatiently for their waiter. Paul, not yet willing to make eye contact, did steal a glimpse of a man with the appearance and demeanor of a racing stallion. One that had been prodded by force into a starting gate. His father-in-law was being held tentatively by invisible and inadequate restraints and was ready to lunge at the first opportunity.

Suddenly, a glass fell from a table close by, shattering against the floor. All the tables became quiet, reflexively scanning for the culprit.

It was then, as the chatter from the other patrons began to return, that Mr. Landry declared his real impatience by saying, "Marie, you said you had something to tell us, and now would be the time for you to do that."

Marie's wide eyes filled her face as she turned to meet her father's voice, ready to confess.

Before she could respond, Paul began to rise from his chair, a move his father quickly halted with a firm hand on his son's thigh. Paul remained seated, yet resigned as he extended his left hand across the table toward Mr. Landry, showing him the wedding band as he said, "Love brought Marie and I together, and our marriage will sustain the child we created. Your daughter and I, Mr. Landry, eloped on Wednesday and are now husband and wife."

Mrs. Landry reached out and grabbed her husband's forearm, not to console, but as her attempt to restrain.

As Paul's words sank in, everyone at the table awaited a response from Marie's possessive father. He was dangling over the edge of his tenuous hold on composure.

Lucien Landry rose from his chair, placed his napkin on the table in front of him, and without taking his eyes from Paul, said, "Rebecca, we have a long drive to get home. We've heard all we need to hear, and it's time for us to go."

Mrs. Landry looked at Marie, already sobbing into her napkin, then looked back at her husband, who had already pushed his chair back under the table and extended his hand to her.

"Please, Lucien, can't you sit for a little while longer? This is a time to talk, not walk away."

"Talk, you say? Well, yes, I have something to say." He turned to face his daughter, "Marie Landry, I have worked hard to provide a college education for you at a costly school. Your mother and I didn't have that luxury. And tonight, you come here to tell us at this expensive restaurant that you've thrown all of that away. Your family's wishes, your education, your future, and for what? An impulsive fling with a boy you just met? Well, I, for one, didn't work this hard to sit by and watch this happen to *my* daughter. But then again, you're not acting like my daughter, and haven't since you left for this school. Your father will never be a doctor, and I break my back every day for my family. Your mother and I chose to help support you at this expensive university, but only if you did your part. Now that you defy our wishes, all you will have is your scholarship money, but that alone doesn't cover all the bills. Either way, you've made your choice and are on your own. Becky, I told you we are going home."

Mrs. Landry couldn't move.

Everyone remained quiet, focused on Mr. Landry.

Mr. Landry's face was red. His anger was directed at his wife now, "I'm warning you, if you don't come now, you will need to find another way to Morgan City."

Mrs. Landry was unsteady as she rose slowly from her chair. Her husband was already on his way around the table.

As he intentionally brushed Paul as he passed, Dr. Morel turned to say, "Mr. Landry, please don't leave like this, these two young people need our help."

Mr. Landry continued toward the exit without response.

Mrs. Landry said, "Please forgive our reaction to your news." As she walked past Marie, she leaned down to hug and kiss her daughter, saying, "No matter what was said tonight, we'll all get through this."

As she walked past Paul, she placed her hand on his shoulder. And just like that, her kind touch, and the Landry's, were gone.

Paul and Mrs. Morel moved closer to Marie to console her. She was already head down and crying into her folded arms against the table. She had never been hurt so badly by someone she loved.

Dr. Morel raised his glass to the nearby waiter, shook it, then made a sweeping gesture with his other hand toward all the others at the table; his move quickly interpreted as the universal sign for another round.

❧

Dinner after the Landry's left was quiet at their table. Dr. Morel devoured his entrée as Ella and Paul picked on a shared appetizer. Marie couldn't eat. On the ride back to the dorm, Dr. Landry said, "That house we drove by earlier is for rent. I'm going to pass by there so we can get the phone number. Paul, you can call the owner and investigate renting it for you, Marie and the baby."

"Thanks, Dad. I'll call them tomorrow."

Paul looked over at Marie. It was the first time in weeks that her tears fell from joy.

Doubts arose as Paul stated, "But, it doesn't sound like Marie's father will be supporting her with tuition anymore."

"It's okay, son. Your grandparents supported your mother and me when Savannah surprised us, so what goes around, comes around!" Smiling as he looked back at Paul, "And since it doesn't look like you're going into medicine, I'll just have to hope for this grandchild!"

Marie said, "Dr. and Mrs. Morel, I can't begin to thank you."

His reply, "Welcome to the family, sweetie. It would be wonderful if you could get to New Roads soon. I'm sure Father Muldowney would expedite the blessing of your marriage in the Church."

Paul said, "Spring break starts in a few days, we'll see if we can make that happen."

23
CHANGE

Together, they watched his parents drive away. Paul held Marie in one hand, and the phone number for the rental in the other.

He'd never questioned his parent's love for him and never would. When times get tough, you should at least be able to count on family, and his family had not let him down.

His heart ached for Marie as he planted a kiss on her head. She was his wife, and they were a family now. Through his actions as well, he would show that he was there for her.

She looked up at him to say, "You are so fortunate to have a family like that."

He knew he was fortunate, and as his wife, she was the beneficiary of that. "They are your family now, too. Let's get you back to your room. You must be exhausted. I'll sleep in my room tonight. I'm also going to call the owner to ask about renting that house. It's not too far from campus, so would that be okay with you?"

"Yes, that would be perfect. I'll go to the Administration Office tomorrow. They'll need to see our wedding certificate so we can get permission to move off-campus."

Arriving at her dorm, Paul held Marie for the longest time, then kissed her good night, saying, "We knew what we had done wouldn't be received well, and now we have at least that behind us. It wasn't easy for either one of us to do, was it?"

Marie couldn't speak. She shook her head side to side.

"It won't be possible to anticipate everything that will happen now, but I want you to know that I love you with all my heart. I will always be there as your husband *and* the father of our child."

Marie hadn't had a chance to react to the ball of fire that the catapult of life had just launched over her wall. It was coming at her faster than her eyes could track. She admired Paul's optimism and his attempt to comfort her with words. But as she gazed into the eyes of her eighteen-year-old husband, she could only see a reflection of herself, the scared girl who felt alone, connected to a body that was already changing. What had happened had modified her life and career suddenly, bringing everything dear to her to a screeching halt. This new soul inside her had taken over the vessel of her youth. It commandeered every molecule and every moment, demanding of her to not only survive but thrive. *She wasn't ready for this,* and as much as she wanted to scream at this fireball hurtling over her fortress wall, her mouth was paralyzed. Even worse, she had no idea how she could ever confess this to Paul. She hated how she felt, but couldn't help that either. *All she felt was resentment.*

She kissed her protective knight, then closed the door, sealing herself off again. A world she couldn't imagine was storming her walls, and she hoped that from within, she might find the strength she needed to survive.

❧

It was only 7 pm, so Paul placed the call. After a few rings, an automated voice picked up, requesting that a message be left. That done, he stretched out on his bed, hoping that Nathaniel wouldn't be back to the room until late, as usual. He needed time to think.

Paul laid on his bed to wait for a possible returned call. Wide awake, he considered all that had happened during the past few days. There was no question that the kind, loving acceptance from his family helped to ease his mind significantly. As fulltime students, he could only imagine what he and Marie would face in the coming weeks, and now this painful, yet crucial, first step of informing the families was done.

He already had less time for the things he wanted to do. Spending time with Marie, trips to Talulah's… *where would they find the added hours needed for this transition?* Moving from the dorms would only be the beginning. They'd have to set up a house, fix meals, and schedule doctor visits, all while juggling their school load. It seemed impossible.

Back home, he knew a young couple that became parents of a child with significant health issues. From birth, they remained on call 24 hours a day for their son born with cerebral palsy. Often, he had wondered how parents and families of children with such problems seem to muster to the task. He'd heard stories like this before where the parents selflessly do what their child needs. *Did God pick just the right parents for this child, or were they average parents who stepped up to the need?* Perhaps a little of both.

With new concerns and obligations surfacing daily, he hoped he and Marie would find a way to be like those other parents, ready to care for their child, no matter what.

He'd not slept well in days. As his tense body relaxed, the offensive light from the sidewalk lamp, casting a haze through the transom, disappeared with his falling lids.

The phone rang.

"Hello?"

"I'm dog tired, but I can't sleep. I need to know something, and then maybe I can get some rest."

"Anything," he responded, "you can ask me anything."

"Okay." The line went silent, almost making him think they were disconnected, then she spoke rapidly, "Have you ever looked at me and wondered why my nose is crooked?"

Now Paul was quiet for a moment. He had no idea where this was going.

"Well… no, I haven't noticed that."

"Well, we haven't known each other very long, that's all. So, how could you know that I broke my nose when I was eleven years old? It happened when I fell against the kitchen counter after slipping on an ice cube."

"Is that so?"

"Yes, and have you noticed that one of my eyes doesn't blink as fast as the other?"

"Why no, did that happen during your fall in the kitchen too?"

Impatiently, "*No!* I was born with that. The doctor said that one of my nerves was stretched and injured during my mother's difficult delivery. She *almost* died giving birth to me! But how could you have known that."

"I'm sorry it bothers you. But you failed to consider something."

"What?"

"The possibility that it makes your face even prettier! You see, I have absolutely *no* problems looking at you!"

Suddenly, he could hear sobbing on the other end. He gave her a moment, allowing himself one too. Nothing he'd said so far seemed to help. He hoped for words from her that might provide clarity to his confusion.

Then, she blurted, "You just don't understand, damn it! Oh... *how could you?* We just met, for God's sake! You couldn't possibly know that I have ingrown toenails... or that my Aunt Seda had bunions. And have you heard me snore yet? My family says I snore like a grizzly bear!"

Paul hadn't seen this coming. A tenuous silence caught him further by surprise as he listened to her rapid breathing. Just then, he discovered that she'd held back the real reason for her call until the end: the crowning blow.

"What about the plans I had for my career in art? *You should know, that meant more to me than almost anything!"*

Paul was afraid to open his mouth. His words, up till now, seemed ineffective to comfort her as she waited for his response. "I wasn't aware of any of the things you said first," he said, "but was very aware of your passion for art."

"Well, how then? How can you say you love me when you don't even know me?"

"Here's how. My grandmother and my mother influenced me as they showed me who they were: intelligent, strong, kind, and beautiful women, just like *you*. As a child, the important women in my life provided a template for the caliber of a woman I would want to spend the rest of my life. I've known *you* all my life. It was you, all along. You dazzle me with your talents, and never is there a dull moment. You keep me on my toes… and you make me smile constantly. So, no, I can't see the things you're talking about today because that's not who you are. I love *you,* Marie. I love *all* of you."

Still sniffling, "The nose?" she asked.

"Especially the nose."

"I think it's the nose that makes me snore…"

He heard a yawn on the other end of the line. "Say good night, Marie."

"Good night, Paul. Thank you for loving me. I love you too."

After hanging up the phone, Paul jumped back in bed. As soon as he did, the phone rang again.

Picking it up, he said, "Marie? You've got to get some rest!"

The voice said, "Hello, is this Mr. Paul Morel?"

"Yes, sir. This is Paul."

"I'm sorry I missed your call; my wife and I were out at dinner, and we just got home. I understand that you are interested in renting our little house?"

After a pleasant conversation with Mr. Guidry, Paul had an appointment to view the house the next day at 6 pm. He would tell Marie about it tomorrow, and hopefully, she could come along.

He called home to speak to his parents. They already knew the house and encouraged him to make his best deal.

❧

Marie was like a new woman the next day. "I was worried about you last night," he said as they walked toward the streetcar stop.

"I was worried about me too! I was so tired I couldn't see straight! Luckily, I wasn't a sobbing mess when my mom called me this morning. Thank you for listening to me last night. I'm sure that wasn't easy. I was in a bad place."

"I could tell. I'm happy your mom called. How did that go?"

"Okay, I guess. Mom waited until my father left for work, and went to a nearby phone booth to call me using cash. That way, Dad wouldn't learn from the phone bill that she called. We had a good talk."

A streetcar pulled up, and they jumped on. When seated, Paul asked, "What did your mother say?"

"Mom paid a high price to try to make me feel better this morning. My father must never find out what was said, but she told me that when they were in high school, they had been going together for half a year, and there was a time that she thought she was pregnant."

"Wow, Marie. How did that make you feel?"

"I instantly worried about her feelings and the fear she had all those years ago. I could relate to what she went through. She didn't have to tell me what she did. She recognized how I feel now, and called me to tell me that she understood how these things happen and that she will always love me."

"Did she say how your dad is doing?"

"Yes. Not well, unfortunately. My father is a caveman."

"Excuse me? What do you mean?"

"When he gets upset, he goes into his cave, and it can take him a long time to come back out. Mom says he still refuses to discuss anything with her."

They sat together as the streetcar jostled them side to side. After rounding the turn onto South Carrollton, it was about another ten minutes to their stop. The rental house would only be a block away.

After they got off, Paul asked, "When your father comes back out of this cave, do you see him changing his ways… with you?"

Almost instantly, Marie looked at him and said, "If you knew my dad, you'd know that Mr. Lucien Landry's pride is far more important than anything else to him. So, no, it's highly unlikely."

Paul felt terrible for Marie.

Mr. and Mrs. Guidry were both delightful. The previous renters moved out a few months prior, and the owners had just finished repainting and replacing the old appliances. When Paul told the story about his parents renting the house, Mr. Guidry admitted that his last name did sound familiar. The prospect of the next generation of the Morel family living in his rental appealed to him so much that he even reduced the monthly rent by a hundred dollars.

Not only did the Guidry's give them a ride back to school, but they also left them with a set of keys. They could move in any time they wanted.

Walking back to her dorm, she said, "Oh, I've got some more good news I forgot to mention. I went by the Admin building this morning, and all I had to do was show them our marriage license, and not only can we move out right away, but our parents will get half a semester refund on the dorms."

"That's great, thank you for looking into that! I don't think it will take more than a few streetcar rides to haul our stuff over there. If you feel up to it, let's move in this weekend. I miss sleeping with my wife!"

24
PLUM STREET

Paul didn't have to ask for help. When his family inquired and found out the date of the move, they were there to help. Dr. and Mrs. Morel picked up Savannah at her apartment and were waiting outside Paul's dorm Saturday morning before 8 am. Marie was there too. Dr. Morel used any excuse he could find to get behind the wheel of his extended cab pick-up truck.

Savannah ran to greet them as the newlyweds walked over. She wrapped her arms around Marie and said, "Welcome to the family, Sis! I've liked you since the first time we met, and I've always wanted a sister!"

Paul couldn't resist, "Watch out, honey, the next thing you know, she'll have you quarantined in her bedroom, watching a parade of barbie dolls… for hours!"

They laughed together as they walked to the truck to greet their parents.

With the truck, it only took one load to transfer their belongings to their new residence on Plum Street. The biggest problem was listening to the grumbling from Paul's roommate, who never rose before 2 pm on the weekends. Paul wouldn't miss Nathaniel, and never truly understood why he was in school except to delay his entrance into the real world.

As he and his father looked around his dorm room one last time preparing to leave for good, Paul walked over to Nathaniel's bed and whispered, "Sorry if we disturbed you, but we're leaving now. I wish you well, Nathaniel."

From under the covers came a muffled, "Yeah, man, later."

Paul turned away, feeling sorry for him. Not once had family come to visit, and the phone never rang for Nathaniel. His only "friends" displayed their names on lighted signs outside of bars within walking distance of the campus. Nathaniel was a victim of a different type of poverty: an absence of love. Paul walked out of the room, shutting the door quietly to a part of his life he was happy to leave.

The house was immaculately clean. That didn't keep Mrs. Morel from scrubbing the kitchen anyway, "You can't be too careful with a baby coming!"

It was one thing to move a few things in from their small dorm rooms, but something entirely different to make this tiny house into a home. It had a small front and back yard, two bedrooms, one bath, and a small living room. A cozy kitchen with windows led to the backyard.

Savannah, at large and in charge, surveyed the property. Like the director of a Broadway play, she marched around the house from one end to the other, her family as her entourage, while making suggestions combined with waving arm gestures.

"Oh Marie, I can just see it! A small table right here!"

She jumped into a spot right in front of the kitchen window then turned back to the others to proclaim, "It would be the perfect place for a table! A chair on either side. I can just see y'all sitting here with your highchair pulled up between you. It's just *perfect!*"

Mrs. Morel glanced at her husband, knowing what would be said next.

Looking at Savannah, Dr. Morel said, "Your mother and I sat you in a highchair in that same way, years ago. I think that's a perfect idea."

Paul couldn't resist. "Savannah, our new house is not a naked Barbie Doll for you to dress!"

Savannah countered by directing her response to Marie, "Sis, you got your work cut out with this man! He needs to get with the picture; a woman is living here now!"

They all laughed.

"Your sister is right, Paul," his mother said.

Dr. Morel met his son's eyes with a look that implied; *you'd be smart to listen to your mother!*

Mrs. Morel continued, "Now that your things are in, we need to find y'all at least a bed and a table. No mother of my grandchild is going to sleep on the floor! I'm not sure you noticed that box we brought from home, but there are enough linens in there to get you started. We've got our work cut out for us still." She looked at her husband to add, "If your daddy lets me drive his precious truck, we girls can go on a mission to see if the thrift stores I remember from before are still in business."

And so, it began. The next flock of Morels occupied a familiar nest. Wishing the girls good hunting, father and son went on a walk together around the new neighborhood.

Little had changed for Dr. Morel. The area in all directions looked very much the same to him as they walked block by block. They walked around Carrollton Cemetery and stopped to read the plaque at the entrance.

After reading the plaque, Paul said, "I didn't realize this part of New Orleans had so many German immigrants."

"Yes, it did. They fled civil war in Germany at first, then more came after our Civil War, providing workers during the industrial revolution. Many went west from here, but many stayed."

As they walked further, Dr. Morel felt compelled to talk with Paul about the future. "Son, I know you have a lot on your mind right now, but you need a plan. Since your mother and I will be helping you financially, it's something that we should discuss."

They walked for another hour before returning home, discussing the priority of his education continuing, and the need for one of them to stay with the child as well. It was evident to Paul that Marie's education was also a priority to his father, but the template that his father laid out involved Marie finishing the semester they were in, but not registering for the fall semester when the baby was due.

It was what needed to happen, Paul knew, but with everything going on, he told his father that he and Marie hadn't had the time to discuss it.

Dr. Morel wasn't surprised. He made it clear that he was only suggesting to Paul what he and his mother had done. For them, this plan had worked well. "Your mom," he said, "was able to return to school that next spring. I'll be the first to admit, for you and Marie to do this, it won't be easy. It surely wasn't for your mom and me. There will be times that you'll wonder how you and Marie will keep going, but you will."

As they continued to walk along, the vision of the Titanic came into Paul's mind. The people on board that night were on top of the world. After all, they were in an "indestructible" ship, filled with privileged people, on their way to New York with chandeliers and champagne. The imagery reminded him of his less gilded but austere path a mere month ago. Just like what happened to those on the Titanic, something unexpected had also happened to him. The part of that story that would continue to haunt him was that when the world changed so dramatically for those people, some survived the night, but many didn't. His father's story was his alone. For Paul's to turn out well, he needed to avoid any new icebergs.

When they arrived home, the truck was on the street out front, filled almost to the brim with furniture. As father and son walked inside, they followed the sound of happiness to the kitchen. There the three sat with a spread of Chinese food on a quaint table in front of them. Spooning some Lo Mein from her container, Savannah said,

"Your chairs, gentlemen, are outside on the truck. Y'all would be wise to get them before all this great food disappears!"

Mrs. Morel chimed in, "And as soon as y'all get it unloaded, there's another load waiting for us to pick up before 5 pm! Oh, and the living room sofa will be delivered next week."

Dr. Morel looked at Paul. Turning toward the front door, he said, "Come on, Paul. We best get busy. I don't see much food left, and they are still eating!"

This late afternoon meal was what they all needed. After that, it didn't take long for them to put together the queen-sized bed in the larger bedroom. Before his family left, the basics of utensils, thrift store plates, silverware, and essential furniture were in place. They discussed plans to pick the newlyweds up next Friday evening, so they would be in New Roads early Saturday morning for Father Muldowney to bless their marriage.

Savannah was going home with her parents for the rest of the weekend, and shortly after sunset, their family left them on the porch with full hearts. It had been a glorious day.

They were exhausted. Paul showered and brushed his teeth and was in bed before Marie could blink. When she walked by the door, he was already snoring. In no hurry now, Marie spent a few more minutes walking around their new home, not yet willing to release the day's excitement that had temporarily taken her over. Yes, she had thought earlier in the day about how nice it would have been to have *her* mom here to help. But she wouldn't allow that disappointment to displace her smile tonight.

She turned the light on in the empty nursery, then closed her eyes to imagine how it would soon look.

She entered the bedroom with her husband fast asleep. Marie approached the dresser and opened a drawer where she'd hidden something that Savannah helped her pick out this afternoon. It was the only purchase made from a unique store.

After changing, Marie exited the bathroom but left the light on with the door partially cracked. She slowly moved to what was now Paul's side of the bed, leaned over, and kissed him. He felt so warm to her; it sent a shiver down her spine.

"Hi, sweetie," he said, still mostly asleep, "you coming to bed now?"

She kissed him again. "You should open your eyes, Mr. Morel."

Paul squinted into the light as he cast his eyes on his beautiful wife. She was wearing a revealing, gorgeous red negligée.

Savannah hadn't allowed Marie to choose the conservative one she had picked up first at the store. Thankfully, her new mother-in-law had politely waited in the truck while the two shopped in the exotic shop.

She blushed when she put it on in the bathroom, it was, to say the least, revealing.

"Yep, that's the one, Marie," Savannah had said.

The amount of material used bore no resemblance to the cost. Savannah was so excited to help, and she didn't hesitate to pay.

Now, in the dim light, Marie stood before her husband, who grew more alert by the second.

She backed up enough for him to see her fully.

As he pulled the covers aside and moved over, she said, "You know Paul, we've never really had a honeymoon… but if you're too sleepy…"

He was *fully* awake.

Marie slipped the silk straps off each shoulder in the dim light, allowing the sheer gown to fall to the floor. Paul knew she was beautiful but never had been witness to such a magnificent silhouette. His eyes feasted upon her as his wife glided across the floor in slow motion. Holding the covers up for her, she eased in, as he swallowed her in his arms.

Paul woke to the sun streaming through the window. He reached out, but she was not there. Rising to a new day, he sleep-walked through the bedroom door leading to the living room. There in the morning light, was Marie, sitting on the floor cross-legged.

Hearing the door open, Marie turned around with a smile. As he looked around, it was obvious what she'd been doing. Using thumbtacks, she had transformed the walls of the living room into a gallery of her paintings: the one's from her dorm window. But there was one he hadn't seen before, hung closest to the front door. It was a painting of her family home in Morgan City.

"Good morning, husband! Come sit with me in our living room."

As he sat next to her, he nibbled on her neck, saying, "Do you have any idea how hungry I am?"

Marie giggled as she tried to get away, "All we have for breakfast, is Chinese leftovers in the fridge unless you were interested in something healthier…"

Paul came after her, leaning in, pushing her back against the hardwood floor. As he pursued the same vulnerable spot on her neck, this time, he whispered, "This long nightgown you have on this morning doesn't look as edible as the one last night… maybe I'll just have to go get that food in the fridge…"

Marie rolled him back over, pushing him away as she said, "Suit yourself." She gazed with delight at the apparent contradiction noted in his boxers. Pointing with her finger, she said, "I don't think the fridge will satisfy *'that'*, Mr. Morel."

"Well, don't blame him. He's hungry too."

"Very, it appears."

An hour later, he woke again; this time, she was still there with her head resting against his chest. His back was stiff from falling asleep on the floor after their early-morning lovemaking. As he stretched and yawned, she woke.

Rolling away, she pulled her nightgown, their only cover, with her as she said, "Good morning again, husband!"

"It is a great morning! And now I'm really starving!"

"Why am I not surprised?" Marie smiled coyly at him as she began to reapply her nightgown.

Paul leaned over with his head propped up against his hand. "No, little lady, I need other nourishment before you can count on *that* again. Our main goal today is to go grocery shopping." He pondered his own words for a moment, then said, "I guess it's about time we discussed meals. You do know how to cook, don't you?" Paul covered his face with his hand, expecting that she might find something to throw at him.

Rising off the floor suddenly and wrapping her gown around her like a Roman Emperor, she replied, "How dare you question a real Cajun woman if she knows how to cook? This begs further inquiry, Sir Jester, do *you* know how to cook? I do believe you will have to start fending for yourself if you keep questioning my abilities this way!"

"I can poach a mean egg, and pour the best bowl of cereal you've ever had! So yes, ma'am!"

Smiling coyly at him, she turned in the direction of the kitchen. As she walked away, she said, "Then, it sounds like you, *Sir Jester,* will go hungry. I'm going to eat leftover Chinese!"

25

MOVING ON

By later in the day, the pantry and refrigerator were filled. Savannah called to let them know she would return soon with her sewing machine. Together, she and Marie planned to make curtains.

The next days passed quickly. With good weather, they walked to school together in the mornings. Paul imagined this was the same path his parents took when they were in school. The ride on the streetcar was longer and more circuitous, and they met at the end of their day for a leisurely ride home together.

Spring break would begin Friday afternoon for them and include Mardi Gras. As Wednesday arrived, they both realized that their recent concerns had distanced them from another: Delilah. As they walked to school that morning, they discussed meeting later for a streetcar ride and a planned exit for Talulah's.

From a block away, they saw no smoke exiting Talulah's chimney. The shop where she sold her baked goods had always looked run-down, but today appeared even more so. As they drew closer, there was no line, and the Dutch door remained shut.

They walked around back, hoping to find Talulah inside, but the inside door was closed inside the screen.

Paul knocked, and with no response, he tried again.

"I don't like this one bit. Come on, let's walk to the Camellia and see if Clarence is working today. Maybe he can fill us in. It's dinner time anyway, and I'd love to get some beans and rice…"

"With andouille sausage…" Marie added with a smile.

❧

The Camellia Grill, typically busy this time of day, overflowed with customers this evening, less than a week from Mardi Gras. They waited patiently for their table, noting that Clarence was working this evening. After a while, he saw them and nodded in their direction, that being his indication that he'd make sure they'd be seated in his section.

When seated, he came over with his usual smile and two glasses of ice water. "Happy Mardi Gras! Long time no see!" he said. "I hope you folks have been well!"

As Paul took the glass of water extended to him with his left hand, Clarence looked in amazement, then looked at Marie's hand resting on the table. "Looks like there have been some changes since you were here last!"

"Yes, sir," Paul proclaimed proudly, "we're married!"

"Well, ain't that special! I can't think of two other people I know that deserved each other more than y'all! I'm very happy for you both! Dessert is on me tonight!"

Marie said, "That's very nice, Clarence. Thank you so much. We wanted to take some of Talulah's pies home tonight also, but she was closed. Is she okay?"

"She's okay as she can be, but Delilah ain't. She's going through the withdrawal something fierce. And on top of that, those boys she was sellin' drugs for, they been talking on the street 'bout hurting her if she tells the police 'bout 'em. Talulah's bakery been shut down for days cause she been sittin' by Delilah's bedside at Charity Hospital."

"Oh no, is there anything we can do to help?" Marie asked.

"Just pray, that's all. Pray hard. I'll be back in a minute to take your order."

As good as dinner always was at the Camellia, it just wasn't the same tonight in several ways. They were both in a funk about Delilah and Talulah.

Marie ordered a salad and only ate half. Her queasy stomach was still hit or miss, and even the thought of fried catfish tonight gave her a rumble. Sadly, she could barely tolerate the smells of this delicacy from surrounding tables.

Paul had a slice of the best coconut cream pie he'd ever had, but Marie gave Clarence the excuse that she'd had a big lunch at school and asked for a "rain check". They thanked him and bid good night to Clarence, then somberly boarded the next car to Plum Street.

Marie looked at her quiet husband and asked, "Do you miss the carefree days that you had just a few weeks ago? It seems like all our days go by so quickly now. You know, like suddenly there's not enough time in the day to get everything done."

"It's only going to get a lot busier when our baby arrives, Marie."

Paul hadn't found the courage to broach the topic of Marie skipping the fall semester. He hoped she would gain that knowledge on her own, and he hoped it would be soon.

"Well," she said, "I'm starting to wonder how I'm going to waddle into class next semester. And then, when the baby arrives, how I'm going to take care of it *and* go to class!"

Paul pulled the overhead cable but remained silent, allowing her own words to sink in as the streetcar jostled to their stop.

"Let's go, 'Mrs. Red Lace!'" Standing, Paul bowed and held out his hand to her as he whispered, "Daddy needs attention."

Laughing together, they stepped onto the pavement as she commented, "Better hold on there, big fella, Mom needs a break tonight! I'm sorry, but I'm *exhausted!* I need to get some rest. I'm afraid I'm going to have to put that negligee under lock and key for at least a day! And don't forget, tomorrow your sister is coming, and I want to be bright-eyed and bushy-tailed for our curtain extravaganza!"

"That's okay; I think I'm going to need to skip school tomorrow and make a visit to Charity Hospital. I need to see how Talulah and Delilah are doing."

❧

Thursday was overcast with rain showers. Paul quickly finished his breakfast cereal. Marie, still not hungry, asked for his help to move the kitchen table out into the larger living room to give her and Savannah more space to work. Kissing her goodbye, he told her he hoped to be home by noon. Donning his raincoat, he ventured out to the streetcar line. He could have gone the other way, but it would have required bus transfers. Instead, he got on the car headed toward school that would eventually go further into town, through Lee Circle, then on to Canal Street. In less than an hour, he pulled the cord to exit on South Villere Street, and it was just a few blocks walking distance to the entrance of Charity Hospital.

Nicknamed "The Big Free" because all treated there received care at no charge, Charity's roots went back to 1736, funded from a grant included in the will and last testament of a French shipbuilder, Jean Louis. This massive, gray, "H" shaped building was an imposing place on the outside, and within, it symbolized a refuge against human suffering. At Charity Hospital, L.S.U. Medical students and residents competed for responsibility to treat deadly diseases with student equivalents from Tulane medical school.

Paul walked through the main entrance and into another world. Overhead were the words, *Where the Unusual Occurs & Miracles Happen*. As he looked around, there was no reception desk for patient information. His bewildered appearance didn't slow a continuous stream of people flowing through from every direction. Almost dizzy, he stepped out of the way, to lean against a nearby wall, as he tried to make eye contact with someone.

Having no luck, he stepped in front of a tall person wearing green scrubs and a white jacket highlighted with red lettering that said, "General Surgery".

"Excuse me, please," Paul said.

The man stopped reluctantly, appearing to have no time for interruptions.

"Could you help me find someone here?"

"Which department are they in?" he inquired as he looked at his watch impatiently.

"I'm not sure. My friend is here because of a drug overdose. Her name is Delilah."

"Last name?"

"I don't know."

"Then I don't know, either. You can check up on the third floor. The overdose patients usually get locked up for a while in the Psych Ward."

"Okay, thank you."

"Oh," the man said as Paul started for the elevators, "Watch what you say up there, or they won't let you out of there!" He smiled and went on his way.

Other than the one reluctant angel, there appeared to be nothing inside these walls, but chaos. Little did he know that he hadn't seen anything yet. The elevator filled quickly with twenty stories worth of people going up, shoving Paul into the back corner. Exiting the elevator on the third floor was almost impossible; he barely made it to the door in time.

A nursing station situated just outside two large locked doors brought him to a mandatory halt.

The nurse behind the desk was on the phone, so he waited. Her conversation was impossible to ignore. She blurted, "*Are you crazy?* What do you mean, trying to tell me Thorazine is back-ordered? If you don't find me some right away, I'm going to haul your raggedy-ass up here to hold some of these people down yourself!" She slammed the phone into its cradle.

Turning her head up to the fresh meat standing in front of her, she yelled, "*What can I help you with?*"

He was frozen, but managed, "Uh, ma'am…"

"Come on now, Mister, speak up! I haven't got all day!" She turned away to hand some papers to another nurse passing by.

Looking back at the irritation before her, "Well?"

"I'm looking for a girl named Delilah, and her mother Talulah is probably here with her."

"Last name?"

"I don't know. All I know is that my friend had a drug overdose."

"Do you really think I have time for this?" As the nurse buzzed the door, she said, "You got ten seconds to go through that door; then it's gonna' lock again. You get one try. When you get inside, feel free to look around. There are at least one hundred and twenty people in this ward, and probably none of them know their first name, much less their last! Good luck."

She hit a button under her desk, and a loud buzzing noise sounded.

Paul stood there trying to process what was happening as he heard, "Mister, I told you: you only had ten seconds, and that was four seconds ago!"

Paul stepped through the door into a world of chaos as he heard it lock behind him. The loud sounds all around him stopped momentarily as eyes from every direction focused only on him. People wandered around aimlessly and without apparent purpose, displaying bizarre states of mental distress, some dragging bed sheets. One pair in the middle common area were slinging food at each other gleefully like children. No one seemed to find this odd. From another direction, he heard yelling and screaming, an apparent fight about to break out between two patients arguing about which ice cream flavor tastes better.

As he questioned his sanity for electively walking into this place, he frantically searched for the two familiar faces that drew him here. Peering around a barrier slowly, he was met instead by a wild-eyed inmate staring back at him. Caught off guard, Paul slowly reversed his path just as the man's face followed him, saying, "Hey man, look here." With wild eyes, he pointed at his nose with his head cocked-up, then with a hushed tone, almost as if in confidence, said, "I got a fly up my nose!"

Paul assumed that the man wanted him to comment. But no one had ever said such a thing to him before. As the man continued to look at him, seemingly waiting for a response, the last thing he wanted to do was disagree with or provoke the man. As calmly as he could, he smiled and said, "I see!"

Wishfully hoping that was it, he continued to slowly back away. The man, again pointing at his nose, screamed this time, "HEY!"

When Paul said, "Yes?" the man repeated what he said before, this time yelling, *"I GOT A FLY UP MY NOSE!"*

Realizing that this patient couldn't possibly be seeking a rational response, Paul continued to back away, while hearing him repeat his statement over and over, in various intensities, as he regressed into his spot to wait for the next passer-by.

Paul walked up and back down aisles in the next section of the ward, and just before giving up, spotted her. Seated at the entrance to Delilah's small space was Talulah. Despite the chaos around her, she appeared to be asleep. The poor woman was probably keeping a vigil day and night.

As he approached, both mother and daughter were asleep. Paul worried about causing even the slightest provocation, as he gently touched Talulah on the shoulder.

Without moving her head, one of her eyes opened to appraise the threat before her.

Then, looking up, Talulah realized who was standing next to her. It was a friend, not a foe that she saw as she reached up to cast her arms around Paul for a hug.

It was intimidating when Paul leaned over. Not because of Talulah, but because his focus would be distracted from the other patients temporarily. He'd come so far now, the last thing he wanted was another sneak attack.

Talulah could feel his hesitation as she proclaimed, "These people in here are harmless. Ain't nobody gonna bother you."

Talulah thanked Paul for coming to visit them as she reached over and tried unsuccessfully to wake her daughter.

This frustrated Talulah, causing her to proclaim, "They got her drugged with other drugs to help her get through the drugs that brought her in here. Now she can't stay awake. But they say she's gettin' better, and I thank the Lawd she ain't screamin' and tryin' to pull out her hair no more. A few days ago, they say she might could die, but she still here with us. Praise the Lawd!"

Paul sat, leaning against the partition that separated Delilah from the next patient.

Talulah focused on Paul as she asked, "Where's Lil Miss Tight-Butt?" No sooner were those words out of her mouth; she focused on his hand resting on his knee, and his wedding band.

Excitedly, she said, "*Boy, lemme see that hand 'o yours! Is that a new ring on your finger? Your wedding finger?"*

"Yes, ma'am." Paul, seemingly embarrassed, looked down at the floor as he said, "Tight-Butt… I mean, Marie and I married just a few days ago."

Talulah looked at Paul, whose eyes still avoided hers. Slowly, she sought clarification, "I gots the feelin' that this happen all a sudden… for a reason?"

He looked up to say, "Yes, ma'am."

"So, tell Talulah, when you be 'spectin'?"

"September."

"I sees," she said. "You loves her, right?"

"Yes, ma'am, very much."

"That's all that matter. All the rest'll work itself out."

"I hope so. Right now, her father is so mad that he wants nothing to do with either of us. He's even stopped sending her money for school."

Talulah took a moment, thinking as she looked out around the ward. Then she refocused on Paul. Calmly she said, "Everything we do in this world make a ripple. There be good ripples and bad ones too. We all make'em every day. That ripple Marie's daddy sent away ain't with him no more, and it will go on and do whatever it want to do. It ain't in your power to stop the ripples other peoples make. But for them hurtful ripples, you just got'a keep you chin up, and you head high."

Paul looked at this wonderful friend as he considered what he'd just heard. This kind woman had an intuition about things that had a way of putting everything in perspective.

Rather than suffering or feeling oppressed by hardships, Talulah turned life's vinegar into wine.

Talulah said, "Now, you listen to me, son."

She had his attention.

Talulah leaned forward and placed her ample hand under his chin, lifting it. As she looked intently into his eyes, she said, "That father of your wife, only he can turn what's his ripple into something good. The only thing you can do is pray and give it up to the *Lawd*."

During the next hour, he listened to Talulah describe how she and Delilah felt trapped between fear for their lives from the boys and fear of incarceration for Delilah for selling drugs. He heard the details of how Delilah had almost died going through the delirium tremens, or DTs, and how Talulah had nothing but praise for the nurses and doctors at Charity Hospital.

Paul also knew that this mother, who fiercely loved Delilah, was also the reason she was still alive.

Within the next few days, Delilah was discharged to the juvenile detention jail to await trial. Her mother hoped she would be safe there from the punks, and planned to return to her bakery.

Paul promised to find her again as soon as he could. His visit today meant the world to Talulah. He had no way of knowing that a new ripple began that night. It was from Talulah. It was a good ripple — one of constant prayers for him and his entire family.

❧

Arriving home later than expected, Paul immediately noticed that the front windows had new coverings. *Good riddance to the fishbowl,* he thought. Walking in, Savannah and Marie were finished and found sitting at the kitchen table, which they had moved back in place. It was apparent from the laughing and carrying on that they were having the best of times.

As he entered the kitchen, Marie said, "Hi Hun! It's a good thing you got home to defend yourself! I've heard so many stories about you from Savannah. You're lucky I didn't hear them before our first date!"

"Gee, thanks, Sis, I knew I could count on you! And by the way, y'all did a great job with the new curtains. You did it so quickly. I'm glad I was out of the house! You must have been sewing so fast that if I was here, I'm afraid I'd be hanging in the living room!"

The girls chuckled at that thought.

Savannah said, "Best for you to remember that, brother! Never forget the power that the women in your life have over you!"

Paul, feeling outnumbered, called back as he walked away, "I'm going to take a shower. What's for dinner tonight?"

"Egg sandwiches with lettuce, tomato, and mayonnaise," Marie called to him. "And hey, how's Delilah?"

"Thankfully better. Much better!"

"What wonderful news! I'm so happy you went to see her today."

Poking his head back in the door, Paul smiled and said, "Oh honey, by the way, Talulah said to tell 'Tight-Butt' hello, and congratulations!"

Marie rolled her eyes as he quickly disappeared.

26

SPRING BREAK

Marie had to wake Paul when she came to bed. She couldn't wait until morning to tell him about the new plans.

"Tomorrow, when we finish turning in our work, Savannah is going to drive us to New Roads! I can't wait to get away!"

The excitement he heard in her voice was the happiest she'd sounded in weeks. Between the curtains and the new plans, this had been an excellent day for Marie. He was pleased for her. But he was concerned she was running on spent fuel. He'd noticed over the past few days that her energy level had begun to fade. She had been going to bed earlier and was the last to get up in the morning. She had several major projects due recently, and because of that, she'd been arriving home later. After eating, she would usually jump right into bed. He wondered if she was just tired or if something else was going on. Maybe tomorrow they would finally have a chance to talk.

After brushing her teeth, she came to bed. Paul, physically spent, kissed her goodnight and rolled over.

Marie rolled over with him, and from behind his head, confessed, "This is taking more out of me than I expected."

He rolled back and wrapped his arm over her shoulder just as she burst into tears.

"I knew this wasn't going to be easy," she sobbed.

Suddenly, she jumped from the bed and began to walk to the bathroom. Her demeanor changed just as quickly as she said sarcastically, "I'm sure this is quite a surprise for you, seeing your wife melting down again."

"Under the circumstances, I believe my wife is holding up admirably."

Marie grabbed a hand towel and blew her nose loudly into it. She returned to the side of the bed and spoke through the darkness between them, "Savannah and I had fun looking out the kitchen window today. The sun came out in the late afternoon, and it was beautiful in the backyard. With only a few days to go before March, the most beautiful time of the year in Louisiana has arrived."

Continuing to stand next to the bed, she spoke with a serious tone, "It won't be long until we have a little one playing in the yard outside that window. Are you ready for that, Paul?"

"Yes, I'll be ready. But is that what you really want to know? Aren't you asking if I would have purposely chosen this time in my life to be married or have a child? No, I wouldn't. But listen, Marie, I can't imagine anyone else in the world I'd rather be married to, or have a child with, than *you*."

"Well," she said, "I've asked myself that same question time and time again. I have this new life growing inside of me, getting larger each day, and the mother inside of me demands that I love it. But there is a selfish, angry part of me that wasn't ready, a side that resents what I have to do."

The tears flowed again, in earnest. Sobbing into her towel, Marie said, "I just wasn't ready, Paul."

Paul stood, went around the bed, and gently coaxed her back under the covers. He said, "You need some rest, dear lady. Tomorrow will be a better day. We'll take the streetcar to school, complete our assignments, and be ready for spring break to begin tomorrow evening. You and Savannah have come up with a wonderful plan. I'm always ready to spend a few days in the country."

Marie didn't respond and settled under her covers. Soon, he heard her breathing heavily. She was asleep.

Despite how tired he'd been, what she had said kept him awake most of the night.

❧

As they rode to school in the morning, things mentioned last night were left alone. At least one of them had rested well, and Marie was in a much better mood. She was happy about seeing Savannah later, as well as the trip away from New Orleans.

Paul mentioned that he was curious to know if Talulah was able to reopen her shop. "Would you mind if I stop off on the way back home this evening? You can continue home in case Savannah arrives before I get back. I'll try to get some pies for the trip to New Roads."

"That would be wonderful," she replied. "If you like, why don't you ask Talulah if she'd like to come to our house for dinner sometime soon? We'll probably be home by Saturday, a week. Tell her, 'Tight-Butt' is fixing roasted chicken! I can't tell you how many times my mom made that dish while I was growing up, and I can't wait to make it for us!"

The Garden District of New Orleans was about to explode with color. March was only days away.

❧

By 4 pm, Paul was standing outside the Art Lab as Marie exited. Although she looked tired, she appeared content with her project completed.

Before long, he kissed her goodbye as the streetcar dropped him in front of the Camellia Grill, and Marie continued home as planned.

Paul walked onto Talulah's lot later than expected. Because of that, he wasn't sure he would be able to get pie but still hoped to say hello to Talulah. Smoke poured from her chimney, but the lot was empty, and the door remained closed.

As he walked around the back corner, the familiar feel of heat billowing out the screen door gave him hope she was there.

He knocked on the screen door.

"Hello? Miss Talulah?"

She was moving slower than usual, but still extended a smile as she opened the screen door to invite him in.

"Gets yourself in here, Mr. Paul, and take a load off them feet!"

She walked back to the large sink where she was washing her pots as Paul sat at her mixing table.

"How is Delilah?" he asked.

"She fine. She be just fine now. Just the other day, they move her to the Juvenile Detention jail. She gone be there for a while, yes she will."

Paul asked, "What about those boys? Have they been causing you any trouble?"

"Those boys, they ain't nothin'. They come 'round the other day sayin' this and sayin' that… but I pulled out my trusty guardian, I did!"

"Guardian? Do you mean a gun, Miss Talulah?"

"Better 'n' that," she said. She reached down into her soap suds and pulled out a large rolling pin and started to wave it around. Soap-suds went everywhere.

"Yep, my Guardian cause all them boys to roll rite on out'a here!" Boisterous laughter roared from her prideful chest.

"Sounds like those boys are smarter than I gave them credit for!"

"Yes, sir!" she said, "Talulah ain't no pushover for punks!"

"Agreed!"

They spoke for a while longer, and when Talulah finished washing, she said, "It be time for me to get on home, Mr. Paul. I gots to do this again tomorrow."

"Before you go, Miss Talulah, Marie and I would like to invite you to dinner Saturday a week. She wanted me to tell you she is fixing her mother's roasted chicken. Will you come?"

"I shorely will, and that was mighty nice of the boths o'you!"

As Paul leaned over to write down the address and phone number, he asked, "Six o'clock be okay?"

When he looked up, Talulah was standing in front of him, with a bag held close against her bosom.

Holding it out to him, she said, "Six o'clock be perfect for dinner. I hoped you'd be stopping by soon, so I been keepin' a bag of fresh pies ready just in case. Delilah and I means to tell you again what it means to us that you comes to see us at the Charity."

He took the bag and wrapped his arms around her, "You take care of yourself, Miss Talulah. We'll see you in a little more than a week. We're going to get out of this town for Mardi Gras."

As soon as he hopped on the streetcar, he opened the bag. There were probably a half dozen pies, but the one on top was apple. It didn't survive the trip home, and was beyond delicious, as expected.

Paul's mother and father loved the way Marie and Savannah bonded. They behaved like sisters that were best friends. Mrs. Morel knew that Savannah's feelings for Marie were real. She fiercely loved her brother, and they all cherished the newfound happiness seen in Paul's eyes.

Mrs. Morel, based on her own life's experiences, still couldn't help but worry for this young couple. She was confident her son would muster to any need that arose; it was who he was. He'd been easy to raise, rarely straying out of line. She could only remember one time he *almost* got in trouble, and even that, to this day, made her chuckle.

As she sat at the table sipping coffee, she reminisced as father and son watched television in the den. She recalled one night when Paul was in high school that he took his daddy's tractor into the cane field late one weekend night and used it to cut a pattern of circles. The next day he showed his cousin Jeremy the "alien crop circles" that had mysteriously appeared. Only when Jeremy wanted to tell the Sheriff did Paul confess it was just a joke. The funniest part was hearing Winston and his father laughing about it later that night, lamenting that they could have sold tickets if Paul had allowed it to hit the newspaper.

Concerning Marie, she wasn't quite as sure. Only time would tell how her daughter-in-law would manage her new truth. It was impossible to know; she'd only known her for such a short time. The surprise of an unexpected child was a shock that she, too, was all too familiar. She didn't know what she would have done if it hadn't been for her husband's family. Like Marie's, hers hadn't taken it well. Those days were, thankfully, long gone, and something that to this day remained so hurtful that she refused to talk about it.

After a long, but good day, Paul and Marie said their goodnight's to family, leaving them still discussing school with Savannah in the family room. Savannah was mixing another round of Moscow Mules, which would surely make any school-related issues sound better.

Paul and Marie returned to a room that, until only recently, belonged to a single man. On his first night back home as a married man, he and his bride closed themselves behind the door to his childhood room. Marie circled her arms around his neck, pulled him to her, and asked, "So, Mr. Morel… how does this feel?"

Marie was the only girl his age, besides his sister, to ever step foot in this room. To him, closing the door with her inside was an incredible new privilege. In the light provided only by the moon shining through his window, he coyly replied to the beautiful woman in his arms, "What do you mean, Tight-Butt?" Paul squeezed her butt-cheeks hard with his hands.

She cooed to his touch, then whispered, "Well, you grew up in this room as a child, so now, how does it feel to have a sexy woman alone with you here? One who not only wants you but *really* needs you tonight?"

Paul was ready to play, but not exactly the way his wife might have wanted. "Well," he said, "if you're not too tired, we have some other options! We could go back to the family room. There is a good show on T.V. My dad said he would be up for a while watching it. I guess we could…"

Marie shoved him aside playfully. She walked over to his bed and turned to face him. Then, she looked at him seductively and began to unbutton her blouse, saying, "I wondered if instead, you might consider staying here with me so we could finish what we started the last time we were in this bed together?"

The practical joker in him had her just where he wanted her, "Let me see," he said, "I do remember that I finished doing something last time. Let me think… Oh, yes, *sleeping!* That was it! I had a full night's sleep after you left me, so what is there to finish this time?

"These!" she said. Marie threw her blouse to the floor and reached behind her back to release her bra. Paul remained speechless as she unfurled her breasts; her lovely curves all silhouetted in the moonlight. Then, she gracefully removed her pants and laid on the bed, facing him.

This night was young. Unwilling to give up an opportunity to play with his best friend, he slowly removed his wallet and keys from his pocket, placing them on the credenza, "It's obvious to me, Marie, that you're not at all interested in watching television. You must be tired, so sure, we could get some sleep. But remember, if I fall asleep first, and you're having trouble getting to sleep, you could still follow tradition and go off to talk with my sister!"

"Hurry up, shut up, and get in this bed," she demanded. "I've got a few spots that need attention."

He'd long-since squeezed the last drop of lemon from this joke. As he undressed, he responded, "Yes, ma'am, we aim to please here in the fair town of New Roads."

By the next day, Paul felt that the decision to come home during the break was a great one. Each day they were here, Marie appeared more relaxed. His parent's initial impression of her proved accurate. She was a welcome addition to the Morel clan.

Father Muldowney blessed their marriage in the Church after mass early Sunday morning. It was a simple but meaningful service, and in the eyes of the Church, their marriage was not official until this service was complete. Paul's family, including his grandparents, were present. Marie silently lamented the absence of her own family.

At dinner that evening, Paul informed his family about Talulah's problems with Delilah. They all felt his pain for his new friends as he expressed his frustration and concern for their well-being.

Paul knew that some things have no solution in plain sight, but having a family, to at least listen, is a good start. Savannah's grace over their meal included a prayer for the mother and daughter she hadn't met.

While they shared a great meal of his mother's famous meatloaf and mashed potatoes, Marie heard many stories about her new husband. She had no idea what a prankster he had been his entire life.

Savannah told Marie about the time three girlfriends came over for a slumber party. "My friends and I were thirteen, and he was only nine. We stayed up most of the night, talking and laughing in my room, and we didn't realize Paul had been waiting up until he knew we were all asleep."

"It served you right!" Paul said. "Y'all were making so much racket that the walls were shaking in my room!"

Marie gave her husband a suspicious look, then scooted her chair further away from him and closer to the safety of Mrs. Morel. "What did he do?" she asked Savannah.

"Well, after what he did, none of those girls ever came back for a sleepover, I can tell you that!" Savannah picked off a piece of her dinner roll and threw it at Paul.

Paul must have been pelted like this by his sister before. He was ready. His chin dropped suddenly, and his mouth opened in a flash to catch the piece of bread. Smiling, he said, "A little more butter next time Sis, please?"

Savannah looked at Marie while pointing directly at her brother in an accusing way to say, "That little bread gobbler came in while we were all passed out and put toothpaste all over our faces. When my friends woke up, they were all furious at me! It was humiliating!"

"You've got to be kidding me!" Marie said, "Paul seems so straight-laced and proper!"

"She has no fingerprints to confirm this hogwash!" Paul testified in his defense.

All but Savannah laughed, as she kicked her brother under the table.

"Owe, that hurt, Sis! Dad, make her quit!"

Dr. Morel looked at his wife and shook his head. "Some things never change, do they, hon?" Now, all laughed.

Paul encouraged Marie to tell them of her plans to fix roasted chicken for Talulah.

"That's a wonderful idea," Mrs. Morel said, "I'd be happy to help you with planning if you like?"

"No, ma'am, but thank you! It's a special recipe that I've learned from my mother. Even if, *God forbid*, I was laying in the hospital in a coma, I could whip this dish up, serve it, and have the dirty dishes cleared before the doctor came back!"

Both Paul and Marie enjoyed the visit to New Roads tremendously. The trip home had been a relaxing time that they both needed. Time there, passed like a blink. Soon, Savannah would drive them back to New Orleans. They had no way of knowing that this trip had merely been the calm before the storm.

27

ROASTED CHICKEN

Friday morning, they loaded up Savannah's car with clean clothes and leftover food in a cooler to return to New Orleans. They both stood in their doorway on Plum Street and waved as Savannah drove away. Paul loved walking into his living room. Today was no different. He would always stop there, no matter how much of a rush he might be in, to view Marie's paintings. They displayed the amazing chronology of their relationship. Each time he entered their home, in full view, he saw their short but meaningful courtship.

Part of him missed passing by her dorm window. His living room allowed him to recall his feeling of anticipation of what might appear next. From the beginning, her brush on the canvas said more than words could; reflecting her feelings for him and what they shared.

No doubt, this home of theirs heralded a new phase of their lives together. Paul lingered in the living room as Marie took her travel bag to the bedroom. The only thing he didn't like about this rental house was that there was no more space for new paintings on their walls.

As he turned to follow Marie, his eyes fell on the door to the other bedroom. Soon, furniture would transform that space into a nursery. He took a deep breath and followed her with the other bags. A baby was on the way, and he hoped they'd be ready.

Marie had been unusually quiet during the ride back. He worried there was a part of her that didn't want to return. It wouldn't be long before their brief, carefree honeymoon of time spent with each other was replaced by a lifetime of obligation as parents.

They returned a day early so they would have time to shop for groceries. Tomorrow evening was the planned dinner for Talulah. He hoped Marie would be ready to go before long, so they could get the shopping done early. When he walked into the bedroom, the curtains were closed, and Marie was in bed.

"Marie, are you okay?"

She was lying on the bed, facing away from him, toward the window. Without turning, she said, "Yes, I'm just tired. I'm going to sleep for a while."

Paul quietly placed the bags inside the door and went to her side of the bed. Leaning over, he kissed her forehead. She didn't respond.

"I'll shut the door," he said, "just sing out if you need anything."

Paul closed the door quietly as he left and went out to the kitchen table to read.

Marie stayed in the room past lunchtime. It was approaching 2 pm. Paul had fixed himself a peanut butter and jelly sandwich earlier. Every few minutes, he would look up from his book to glance at the bedroom door. He wondered, *surely, she must be getting hungry by now?*

By mid-afternoon, the door opened, and she shuffled into the kitchen with shoes in her hand. "I'm starving, Paul. Have you had lunch yet?"

"Yes, about two hours ago. Did you get caught up on your sleep?"

She nodded as she sat to put her shoes on.

"How about I fix you a sandwich?" Paul asked.

"I've got an urge for some Kipper Snacks; didn't we get some of those the last time we went to the store?"

Paul didn't know how she could stand canned herring. *Possibly a pregnancy thing?*

"Let me look." He knew they were still there, but part of him hoped the cans had magically disappeared.

He walked to the cabinet, knowing that he would have to leave the room while she ate. "Yep, there's a couple left. Why don't you finish them up?" He grabbed both tins and placed them in front of her.

Marie opened one as he opened the drawer to get her a fork.

Paul felt the urge to exit the kitchen, and said, "I'm gonna check out the backyard while you eat, and maybe you'll be ready to go grocery shopping when you finish those things?"

Marie stabbed her fork into the tin and pulled out a chunk, only to wave it at Paul menacingly as she giggled.

He jumped back, trying to avoid the smell as she circled her fork into her mouth, releasing an exaggerated, "Mmmm! Don't you want some?"

"Thank you for asking, but I'd rather eat a dead mouse!" Paul was happy that his wife had returned. She was awake, finally, and playful again. Now he hoped the "snacks" would disappear soon.

He gave her a wide berth on his way out the kitchen door to the yard. She called to him, "These are so good, it won't take me long! Promise me you'll come right back and give me a big kiss for dessert!"

Paul rolled his eyes.

Marie added, "Only after a good kiss will I be ready to go shopping! And please don't let me forget to get some more Kipper Snacks while we're out!"

Paul grabbed his book and retreated to the backyard, his refuge, taking note of the need for chairs and a small table someday.

Better late than never, they made it to the grocery store before they closed. Paul pushed the cart as Marie searched for the ingredients for her roasted chicken recipe. Marie's creative instincts awakened with this dinner project for Talulah. The planned roasted chicken was a favorite dish of her family, and because the recipe called for a whole chicken, there would be leftovers for days after. Although Paul was fond of peanut butter sandwiches, lately, he'd had his fill.

Marie found a chicken that was unusually large, and even better, *it was on sale!* She hadn't remembered her mother's chickens being this big; it was as big as a small turkey. She reveled in her good fortune. Lettuce and tomatoes for a salad, green beans, potatoes to mash, and vanilla ice cream with strawberries rounded out the menu.

With dismay, Paul heard her squeal with joy when she found the aisle where her prized canned delicacy resided. As she placed an excessive number of tins in the cart, he confessed, "Sweetie! I'm getting worried."

As if she hadn't heard him, she continued to grab more tins. By the time she stopped, there were more in their cart than remained on the shelf. When she straightened up, she looked directly at her husband and asked, "About?"

"I looked around, Marie, really I did. But I couldn't find that sign that you must have seen, the one that said, 'Herring in a can – get it fast, before we run out!' I'm concerned that I'm going to have a nightmare of our child being born with fish eyes and gills!"

For some reason, his fear didn't deserve any comment from her other than, "I think we have everything we need, let's check out! We need to get home so we can start cleaning the house."

"Oh, great. Why didn't I think of that?"

At 4 pm the next day, Marie had everything almost ready. She planned to put the chicken in her oven promptly at five.

A flood of emotion tried to overwhelm her. Marie longed for the lost connection with her own family. The roasted chicken dish was one her mother had taken such great joy in preparing since before Marie could remember. As a little girl, she stood on a stool to be able to see over the top of the kitchen counter as her mother worked. Wide-eyed, she would watch her prepare this dish for her and their family. These thoughts, from not long ago, threatened to send her running from this kitchen in tears. It seemed unfathomable that she lived in a house that her mother might never see. *How was this possible? To be in a kitchen where your mother couldn't visit or share in the joy of her daughter preparing a special family dish for the first time? How could she find comfort, knowing her mother could never taste it?*

Several times already, this dinner had almost been too much for her to bear. She knew how much this meant to Paul, and the last thing she wanted to do was upset or disappoint him or Talulah. As she reached her hand into the cold carcass of her chicken, searching for the plastic packet of giblets and neck as her mother had taught her, Marie resolved herself to positive thoughts only. That was the only way she would get through this evening.

Paul tried to stay out of her way by studying in the living room. Marie did her best to remain focused. Setting the oven to 325 degrees, she transferred the chicken to her only cooking pan, which was barely big enough. She spread salt, pepper, minced garlic, and butter inside and out, then, just like her mother, added large pieces of celery and onion into the cavity, too. Her mother would be so proud. She had followed the recipe by heart.

As her mind began to work against her, she jolted back to the present, hearing a voice from the living room, "Honey? How's it going in there?"

Needing no added pressure, Marie called back, "You just mind your own business out there. It's only 4:45 pm. If I need your help, I'll send up a flare!"

Paul didn't like being in "Chicken Quarantine" and silently vowed to be much more involved next time. He did want Marie to feel accomplished by preparing this meal by herself, but he also loved to cook, something that they had not been together long enough for her to know.

Promptly at 5 pm, Marie loaded the pan into the oven and shut the door. Almost able to taste the delicious meat that would fall off the bone, all she had to do now was wait.

Marie busied herself peeling the potatoes while imagining the satisfied look on Paul and Talulah's faces. They would all soon dig into the feast she was preparing.

Potatoes peeled and soaking in the water soon to be heated, Marie looked at the clock on the oven door. It said 5:23 pm, and the chicken appeared no different than when she had put it in. She recalled being a child, using a stool to peer into the oven at home, and her mother saying, "Marie, you can't cook that chicken with your eyes! Be patient and leave it be!"

She turned off the oven light and tried to wait patiently. She had the salads ready and covered in the fridge, and wouldn't start the potatoes until 5:45. She took off her apron and went into the living room to sit for a few minutes.

"Hi baby," Marie surprised Paul as she sat down on the sofa next to him. He closed the book he was reading.

"Well, the chef emerges!" Paul kissed his wife. "I can't wait till the aroma reaches out here, then I'll know we're getting close! Talulah will be here in twenty minutes or so. Do you need my help with anything?"

Marie, distracted, was surprised that after almost an hour, there was no aroma. It was time to take another peek.

"I'll check back with you in a few minutes. Just go back to your book, sweetie." Marie returned to the kitchen.

It was time to start the potatoes, and looking at the chicken through the oven window didn't help at all. The chicken didn't appear any more cooked than when Marie first put it in the oven. Concerned that the appliance wasn't working correctly, Marie opened the door briefly to check, and feeling a gush of heat escape, she quickly closed the door. *Well, that seems okay,* she thought.

Concerned with how long it was taking to cook, she increased the temperature to 375 degrees, believing the thermometer on the oven was not working correctly.

She started heating the water for the potatoes at the appointed time, and in a heartbeat, the doorbell rang. It was 6 pm on the nose, and she heard Paul greet Talulah at the front door.

Marie, leaving her apron on, went to greet their guest in the living room.

Talulah wore a flowing, colorful dress, and had brought them fresh eggs from her laying hens.

Graciously taking the eggs, Marie said, “Thank you so much, Miss Talulah! We are so happy you could be with us this evening for dinner!”

“Thank y’all for the invite! I’m smellin’ somethin’ good comin’ from your kitchen, Marie!”

Marie thought, *Finally, it does smell good!*

“Can I helps you with anything?” Talulah asked.

“We’re having my family’s roasted chicken and mashed potatoes, ma’am. And tonight, is *your* night, so sit back on the sofa and talk to my good husband. I’ll let y’all know when its supper time, it shouldn’t be too long now! Oh, and would you like a glass of water, tea, or soda?”

Smiling politely, Talulah said, “Thank you kindly, Marie, I’ll just have some water with my dinner.”

Marie retreated to the kitchen.

By 6:15 pm, the smell of cooking chicken was not nearly as profound as Marie recalled from her mother’s kitchen. She hesitantly turned on the oven light and viewed a chicken that still looked very much like it had when it entered the oven. *This is so odd,* she thought.

She was still staring into the oven at 6:23 pm when Paul called from the living room, “Sweetie? How’s it coming? Are we almost ready?”

Marie went to the entrance of the living room, disguising her concern with a smile, and said, “Honey, could you come here for just a minute?”

Paul excused himself and waltzed into the kitchen where Marie stood close to the back door, waiting with folded arms and a scowl.

Whispering through pursed lips, she demanded, “Come over here right now, I have something to say to you.”

Paul, taken aback, slowly approached her. He knew now that he’d hit at least one of her nerves without trying.

“Mr. Morel, you need to go back out, entertain our guest, and quit rushing me. I've never used this oven, and I think there is something wrong with it. I'm doing my best here."

Marie was acting like she was in a pressure cooker herself. Paul nodded and left right away. Marie returned to the oven and the chicken that looked no more cooked than it had earlier. It needed to be brown, and it had been cooking for almost an hour and a half. She turned the temperature up to 425 degrees, and in a few minutes, it finally looked like it was beginning to brown.

The potatoes were ready to mash, so she busied herself with that and started to heat the green beans.

Marie went to the door with a mustered smile and said, "Dinner should be ready in just a few minutes!"

Paul said, "Marie if you've got a few minutes, why don't you come out, Talulah has been waiting to tell us about Delilah."

The chicken appeared to be cooking so slowly in this oven; Marie felt comfortable sitting with them for a minute or so. She was relieved that it was finally starting to brown but didn't understand why it didn't smell as good as her mother's.

Talulah barely began to share the news about her daughter when she noticed a smell that didn't seem right. Something was burning. Calmly she said, "Marie, how 'bout you and me go to the kitchen and check on that chicken? We can talk more 'bout, Delilah, later."

At that moment, Marie smelled the same thing. She bolted from her chair.

With Paul close behind, they rounded into the kitchen, to see smoke billowing from the oven.

Marie slung the oven door open as Talulah stood by, and Paul, speechless, watched as the kitchen filled with smoke.

Grabbing her potholders, she pulled the smoldering carcass from the oven, releasing it with a loud crash on the range top.

Paul had never seen his young wife with such a horrified look on her face.

Marie backed away from the sizzling black mass. Holding her hand over her mouth in disgust, she mumbled, "I prepared it and cooked it just like my mother did. There must be something wrong with the thermostat on this oven. It just wasn't cooking right from the beginning!"

Talulah, as always, tried to see the good that could still come from this dinner. She was surprised by the size of this chicken. She moved closer and placed her hand on Marie's shoulder, saying, "Aw, honey, don't you worry your pretty little face over this bird. Where I come from, we just cut the burn skin off, and the meats underneath still be real tasty! Let Talulah show you."

Talulah grabbed the knife and fork nearby and started to remove the black skin, casting it quickly into the garbage pail that Paul readily held for her.

"Oh, no, honey, lookey here, this ain't right," Talulah said with surprise, "the meat underneaths, it still be pink!"

As Talulah cut into the meat, it bled pink. The big bird was raw inside.

"Miss Marie, what did the wrapper on your bird say when you bring it home?"

"Chicken," Marie said.

"But is that all it say?"

"The wrapper is still in the trash. Let me get it," Paul said. He searched briefly and pulled out the plastic bag. "It says, 'Chicken, whole – Hen.'"

They both looked at Talulah, who had the makings of a smile on her face that she was trying to hold back.

"You see, Missy, a hen, she be a tough old big bird that takes forever to cook and never will tastes right. Lots of peoples who cook a chicken like this don't realize what they gots and turns up the heat too much just like you did. You ain't the only one! You did it cause it don't look to be cookin'! Then, they comes out just like this."

With a smile, Talulah added, "Y'all like egg sandwiches?"

Responding much too quickly, Paul replied, "I do!"

Marie, feeling hurt and at least a little betrayed by her husband, said, "You'd better go to the corner store and get some bread if you want a sandwich, and put this chicken in the garbage outside on your way."

28
THE SOFA

As their dinner walked out the door with Paul, Marie couldn't move from the chair at the kitchen table. Along with a beautiful tablecloth, the three place-settings continued to wait patiently, like palace guards for their princess.

There was smoke everywhere. Even with the back door open and all the fans spinning, a haze of burnt chicken still tainted the air.

Hurt and embarrassed, Marie felt like a punching bag that had taken one too many hits, forcing the seams of her life to separate. What lay beneath her surface was never meant to be exposed. It was the hen that had cemented Marie's reality that she was unprepared for everything that was happening in her life. At the age of eighteen, she was pregnant, married, and overwhelmed.

Marie's eyes released a flood of tears proportional to the shrieking wails that she could no longer contain.

Talulah sensed that the chicken dinner was only part of this emotional hurricane. She walked behind Marie and rested her hand on her shoulder.

"Child, I hope you knows that Talulah ain't upset 'bout dinner."

Marie continued to wail as Talulah massaged her back and neck with both hands.

Slowly, Marie's crying calmed. Talulah took advantage to step over and retrieve a hand towel from the refrigerator door and placed it in front of Marie's face on the table. She resumed rubbing Marie's neck.

In a little while, Marie raised her head and wiped her face.

Talulah moved to sit across from her. She spoke slowly and softly, "You knows, child, you and Mister Paul gots more okra in front of you than your pot can handle right now. But you don't want that okra to goes to waste! You gots to cook a little at a time to make a big meal that everyone can enjoy. There ain't nothin' worth doin', goin' be easy.

"Paul probably doesn't even like okra, Talulah, and right now, he probably doesn't like me either."

"Child, I hope you knows that this be 'bout more than okra, it certainly ain't 'bout him not likin you! Why don't you tell Talulah what be on your heart? Don't do no good holdin' it in, it just get all balled up like a spool been threaded wrong."

"I don't think I am ready for this… being a wife, a mother… it all happened too soon, and I have to force myself to be happy now. I know I've upset Paul."

"Has you let him know? You know… 'bout how you feels?"

"No, Miss Talulah, I'm too ashamed. I've become angry, not only at myself but at Paul."

"You knows that Mister Paul be a good man, Marie. It hard on him too, you gots to know that."

"But he's not the one whose body is changing. He's not the one that will have to suffer through labor and delivery. He's not the one who can calm a crying baby in the middle of the night, or leave its side for months. *He's not the one who can't move on with school, his dreams, or his future because of this.*" Marie placed her hands on her belly and looked at Talulah as tears began to flow again.

Talulah remained silent, allowing Marie time to calm. She stood to move her chair across the table so she could sit closer. She reached for Marie's hand, wrapped it in hers, and pulled it against her belly. Then, she said, "Miss Marie, I've liked you…" she hesitated because she had to speak honestly, "*almost* since the moment we met, so Talulah's goin' share something with you, and I think *you* should think hard and long 'bout these words."

Marie wiped her eyes with her free hand and focused on her other hand, resting against Talulah.

"We all makes a choice when the Lawd grants us the blessing of opening our eyes to a new day. We can choose to look for the good in what he puts before us or dwells on the bad. I choose that they ain't nothin' but good that the Lawd has me see. Everything has itself a silver coatin' if only you looks for it. The Lawd give you Mister Paul, and now you be blessed with his child too. All I sees in front'a you is silver coatin's, honey. But you gots to start bein' able to see them for youself. Even this supper, it ain't nothin' bad! This supper started cause o'you boths lovin' me enough to invite me to share a meal with you. It ain't the food; it be the *love* that's important. It be a long time since Talulah been invited to a meal with such love. That child, growin' inside you, gots two good parents, and that child be blessed with that. I wants to thank you for goin' to all this effort for Talulah tonight."

They both turned in the direction of the living room as they heard the front door open. Paul called, "I've got the bread. How are you ladies doing?"

When Paul entered the kitchen, Marie had moved to the refrigerator and was guarding her eyes.

Talulah said, "Marie is goin' use the lettuce and 'mata from her salad, and you just need to tell Talulah if you want mayo on your sandwich. We's half a shake from bein' ready to eat. Best, you wait in the other room, so my fast-movin' skillet avoid collidin' with your head!" Talulah smiled broadly at Paul as he began to realize the delicacy of this moment.

Marie's face remained hidden in the fridge, as Paul looked back at Talulah who silently raised a finger to shoo him back in the direction he'd come. Paul handed her the loaf and wisely retreated.

With Paul gone, Marie turned around to Talulah, walked over, and placed her arms around her neck. "Thank you, Talulah. I miss my mom and my family so much. I can't tell you how much your words helped me tonight. I'm going to try harder."

"Sure, honey, I knows you will. Now you sits down over there and gets out'a Talulah's way too. My skillet don't discriminate when it start movin'!"

It wasn't long until Paul returned to the table. The egg sandwiches were delicious, as was the dessert of strawberries and ice cream.

Not long after dinner, they said their good-byes, and Paul walked their friend back to the streetcar stop.

He hugged Talulah, and as Paul withdrew, she grabbed his arm to hold him close for her parting words. "That wife o'yours be goin' through a lot right now, Mister Paul. I hopes you knows that."

Paul nodded and looked down the tracks; the lights of the approaching streetcar were a block away. Talulah continued to hold his forearm tightly as he said, "That was an expensive meal we had to throw away today. It was embarrassing that it was your first-time having dinner with us, and you had to be the one to cook our meal."

"Now you listen to Talulah, son. That beautiful child be your wife, and I don't want hear no more disrespect like that, you hear me?"

"I'm trying, Miss Talulah, but I've got feelings too."

The streetcar pulled up and opened the door. Talulah ignored it. Holding Paul's arm so tight he flinched, she said, "What y'all gots now ain't 'bout your feelin's, yours or hers, it be 'bout that new life you made. You gots to be a team, and your wife be at home, alone, thinkin' she be in this game by herself. Just like you, she be upset, but for a different reason. You can't know her reason, less you speaks to her. She can't know yours, less she does the same. But one thing you should never forget. Never goes to sleep with anger between you."

The operator dinged his bell, and Talulah stepped up into the car. Before the door could shut, she said, "Thank you for the invite to supper, and to your beautiful home."

And with that, the doors slid closed.

It wasn't long until Paul opened the front door at home. He had paid loose attention to what Talulah had said as his thoughts churned. On edge with a night that had gone so poorly, he hoped to contain himself as he walked through the front door. His thoughts continued to dance around Marie on pins and needles, ever since they returned from New Roads, and that had grown exhausting. Marie was finishing up in the kitchen as he sat at the cleared kitchen table. Neither one had any idea what the other was thinking.

As he walked in, he found Marie sitting at the kitchen table. He asked, "Is there anything I can help you with?"

Silence remained between them.

"Marie, did you hear me? I'd like to know if you need my help?

"I've heard you all evening. It's clear what you were *really* saying. You were making a statement. You said, 'Marie, how in the world did you mess up a chicken dinner? A dinner that you watched your mother cook countless times? How could you offend our friend, Talulah? Aren't you embarrassed?' That's what you said. I heard it loud and clear. Don't you think you've helped me enough? You're not the one that must carry this child as your body distorts. You're not the one who will have to stay out of school for at least the next semester to care for it. You just sit back and yell from the other room, 'Is my supper ready yet?' How inconvenienced *you* are! I heard what you said."

Paul, wisely, didn't allow his thoughts to turn into words. Instead, he violated the last piece of advice that Talulah had given him as he walked away, turned the living room light out, and laid down for the night on the sofa.

Marie closed herself into their bedroom and cried herself to sleep.

29
EATING CROW

Paul woke around 6 am. Before he opened his eyes, he was impressed by how the smell of burnt chicken lingered. The reality and guilt of a night spent without Marie assaulted him when he opened his eyes, revealing the view of her paintings all around him in the dim light.

He had heard, but not listened to Talulah last evening, by going directly home and violating the last bit of gold she gave him before parting. She had said, "Never go to sleep with anger between you."

It was early, and even before the argument last night, Marie had been sleeping later. Paul went to the kitchen to make coffee.

As the percolator worked its magic, Paul sat at the kitchen table and admired how the morning sun sent sabers of light through the mist rising from the grass. Birds flitted past the window, thriving in this beautiful space. He could see why his parents loved this place. It was in this home, during equally trying times, that they had thrived and grown more in love with each other. He prayed it would be the same for Marie and him.

Marie liked her coffee to taste more like cream than roasted chicory beans. Sugar for her was a necessity. With a cup made, he turned the knob on the bedroom door and entered. The room was still dark, but as his eyes adjusted, he could see that she was lying on her side of the bed, facing away from him. He walked over slowly, trying not to spill her full cup.

Reaching for her, he felt her leg under the cover and touched the back of her calf softly. "Marie, baby, I've made some coffee if you'd like some?"

She rolled toward him, stuffing the pillow behind her back as she said, "I missed you last night." Reaching for the cup, she thanked him.

"I missed you too, and I'm so sorry for what happened," he said.

Marie smiled before taking a sip, then replied, "Thanks, Paul. You fixed it just right… *just the essence* of caffeine!"

"I'm going to fix mine, and I'll be right back."

Propped against the headboard, they talked for over an hour. Marie could finally laugh about her roasted chicken and what she wouldn't do "next time," and each in their way sincerely apologized for what happened between them last night.

Marie admitted that it hadn't been easy for her to accept that after this semester, she would have to remain at home until they could come up with a new plan for her to return to school. Paul, at the same time, promised that he would do everything in his power to make that happen. Together, they planned to focus on getting the nursery ready for their child.

"I think you should call your mom tomorrow while your dad is at work, and tell her about your chicken. Surely that story will remind her how much you miss her! It would help you both."

"It's been a while since we spoke, so yes, I'll consider that. My mom doesn't even know the address where we live, so I'd like to give her that and our phone number."

Paul leaned over and kissed her. Then, he whispered, "Plan to be seated in the kitchen in ten minutes. I'm going back out to fix you some of my famous scrambled eggs, 'à le Paul' and French toast. We both need to wash the taste of crow out of our mouths!"

As he flew from the room, Marie called out, "This crow-eating pregnant woman better find enough coffee left in that pot for my second cup!"

Breakfast settled well with Marie, and after they both finished their school work, they planned to revisit the thrift stores, this time to look for a crib.

❧

March in south Louisiana is the prettiest time of year. Azaleas were Marie's favorite, and soon she planted several in their backyard. *With them*, she thought, *their love for each other would bloom again.*

The next few months brought the end of the semester, along with a hot, humid summer. Despite the high ceilings in their home with fans in each room, the heat made sleep at night difficult until Paul installed a small window air conditioning unit for them.

By June, Marie was at the end of her second trimester and was becoming much less comfortable in any position. She had never experienced migraines before, but now had days that she would have to spend in the bedroom with the lights off and a cold towel on her forehead. Paul helped her when he was there but had elected to take courses in the summer to speed up his future graduation. Marie was often at home alone.

Marie's ankles disappeared with swelling. She wasn't sure how her belly could stretch any tighter with three months to go. Often at night, insomnia would force her from the bed, and she would spend time in the nursery, checking and organizing the necessities they had slowly collected in a small chest of drawers.

Since the night of the chicken dinner, Marie remained unable to discuss her jealousy issues with Paul. It all centered on his ability to move on with *his* life and *his* dreams, while she couldn't. Sure, she wanted to have children someday, but this pregnancy made her wonder if *her* life's roller coaster would ever have the momentum needed to coast over the high peak ahead. The summit of her ambitions appeared to grow higher, and more out of reach, each day. The words needed to tell this man that she loved how much she also resented him, eluded her. The fact that he could soundly sleep when she couldn't sleep at all didn't help.

As she sat in the antique rocker by the side of the crib, Marie reread the letters she recently received from her mother. They had spoken several times after Marie called her to share the address. When they spoke, Marie always asked about her dad, and if his thoughts had softened for her. Her mother made light of that as if the months of separation would end at any moment. "Your daddy loves children," she would say, adding, "He's said before, he can't wait to be a grandfather!" Her letters always expressed how much she loved her and how much she looked forward to seeing the nursery.

The latest letter had been weeks ago, and there had been no visit. Marie knew her mother was skirting a fine line.

Baby Morel was kicking harder and more frequently inside its confined space, reminding her that uninterrupted sleep was gone, indefinitely. Marie knew her mother had good intentions about visiting, but now held little hope that she would arrive before the baby.

They had seen Talulah several times over the past weeks, but not nearly as often as they tried. Sometimes it would be Clarence, poking his head from the top door, sometimes, Bea. They heard that Talulah was doing as well as could be expected, and her absences were to be there for Delilah in Juvenile detention as often as she could. The word was that it wouldn't be long until Delilah was released.

When, by chance, they did see Talulah, she delighted in seeing how Marie was "showing" and always had something positive to say about it. Talulah had a way of remaining upbeat, despite the hardships swirling around her. Marie wasn't sure how she did it. Marie chuckled to herself at the thought of the last brief sermon dispensed. The latest Talulah-ism she'd heard was, "Always let that ray of sunshine in your belly shine out your face! Don't never keep that joy from spreadin'!"

She knew then that Talulah was right, of course. But the teachings of even the best professor can be hard for some students to emulate. Talulah's age, mixed with wisdom, had allowed her to master what she preached. *But how?* Marie wondered as she tried to focus on that kind of optimism through her latest migraine headache pain. Somehow, she knew that finding joy in her predicament wouldn't be possible until she was able to release her resentment. The letters from her mother were a reminder that her mother wasn't coming in person, and only magnified her negative thoughts. Words, written by her mother's hand, bore no semblance to what Marie heard from them. Her mind forced her to read between the lines. There, all she saw was the loss of her family, her freedoms, and the delay of her education. Marie couldn't move past how this child had alienated her from *her* life. She knew that her selfishness was what prevented her from feeling joy, and it would not allow her to be happy. Her head felt like it might split at any moment.

There was another way of thinking that occasionally tried to surface. She knew things could have been worse. Paul's family had stepped up financially for them. That was a huge blessing, one that not all young couples shared. The doctor visits were paid promptly by his parents. With any hint of something needed for Marie or the baby, Mrs. Morel and Savannah made sure it arrived in a few days either in person or through the mail.

Others around her were excited and joyful for Baby Morel, *so why couldn't she feel the same?* Marie feared that she internalized her unspoken feelings to the point that only she and the baby could hear them. Her selfishness, almost overwhelming, forced her to view the baby as separate.

She thought, *Poor child, it's alone also.*

30
BABY MOREL

Marie's due date was Saturday, September 22nd, and she was very ready long before then. His parents had driven two cars down, leaving one for them to use in case they needed to get to the hospital quickly. The Louisiana heat in August remains unrelenting, and rest for Marie still came only minutes at a time. The headaches were also constant. Kicks from the baby were much less frequent, but when she called the doctor about that, the nurses didn't seem concerned. She thought maybe her belly was so tight the baby didn't have room to kick much anymore. But the way it felt when it did, she half-way expected to see a foot appear through her skin.

Dinner was ready when Paul arrived home. That was Marie's main challenge for the day, and after they finished eating, she would need to lie down.

As Paul served his plate of meatloaf and mashed potatoes, he brought up something that had been overlooked for too long, "Honey, I believe it's time to begin the discussion of names for our child."

Paul tried to discuss this with her several times before, each time retreating when she seemed impatient or upset with his timing. Marie knew why she was resistant but had never mentioned it to him: it was her denial about what was happening to her that prevented that discussion. Now, approaching the end of her last trimester, she had changed her tune, stating, "I've been thinking of some already, so tell me first, what you've come up with."

"Well, if it's a girl, I'm very fond of Camille."

"Do you mean like the hurricane in 1969? That thing was ferocious! With all the kicking I felt a couple of months ago, that name would seem fitting."

"No, Marie. You've got to give me more credit than that! The name 'Camille' means '*Perfect!*'"

Impatient to be done with this, Marie said, "Okay, well, go on. Don't you have a few more choices?"

"None that I'm fond of except, Little Marie!"

"Very funny. Well, girl names aren't going to be useful here."

"Why not? How can you be sure?"

Marie folded her arms over her protruding belly and said, "I just know. Call it a mother's intuition."

"Then tell me! What name would you give our son? Larry? Gary? Bill? Les? What about Bruce?"

"You are so far off base! Our son can only be named Ernest. As in Hemingway. But we'll call him Ernie."

"I'm on board with that," Paul said.

"Okay, fair enough, but what if it *is* a girl? I'm not sure I'm okay with people wondering why we named our daughter after one of the worst storms Louisiana has seen in decades! Do you have any other choices than Camille for a girl? I mean other than Little Marie?"

"No."

Marie caved. She was ready for bed. As she stood, she said, "Then Camille, it will be, unless Ernie writes himself a birth certificate first!"

Two nights later, Marie's headache suddenly became severe. It woke her from an unusually sound sleep, to find their bed soaked between her legs.

"Paul… turn on the light, something's wrong."

He flew from the bed, and Marie was already standing with the covers pulled away as the light came on. They both noticed a large volume of clear fluid mixed with flecks of blood.

Her eyes met his as she said, "It's time. We've got to go *now*."

With a horrified look on his face, Paul said, "But it's over a month early!"

"Tell *that* to your son!"

He was stunned. It was at that moment that Paul became convinced that she knew the gender of their child.

It was Sunday, August 12th, 1979.

"Please help me to the car, we've got to get to Touro right away, I'm scared."

At 3:18 am, traffic was almost non-existent, and Paul sped the few miles to Touro Infirmary Hospital. He arrived it the drive-up emergency entrance and ran inside for help. In short order, Marie was in a private examination room. Her OB, Dr. Robichaux, had been paged and would arrive shortly.

Paul, looking pale himself, was escorted to the waiting room as the attending ER doctor examined Marie.

It only took a minute for the doctor to remove her gloves and squeeze Marie's hand as she said, "It looks like you are going to be a mother this morning!"

"Oh no, doctor, it's too early!"

"Just relax, Marie. Dr. Robichaux is only minutes away, and everything will be just fine."

"Would you ask the nurse to bring my husband back?"

"Surely. I'm Dr. Elizabeth Nelson, and I won't leave you until Dr. Robichaux arrives."

"Thank you, Doctor."

Paul returned in short order. Marie asked him to contact their families as soon as possible. In a few minutes, Dr. Robichaux entered the suite. Paul and Marie liked this man the first time they'd met. He exuded cool. With a huge smile and a warm reassuring "hello" for the young couple, he leaned over and said, "Everything is going to be just fine, Marie. Your baby decided to come early, but we're ready!"

Dr. Robichaux thanked Dr. Nelson for her help as she left the room. Paul excused himself this time to make the calls.

Within a minute of his arrival, Dr. Robichaux had greeted them, examined Marie, and spoken to the staff standing by, saying, "Mrs. Landry is at eight centimeters. Let's get this room ready for a delivery."

There was a payphone in the lobby. Paul pulled the slip from his wallet and made his hardest call first: to the Landry's.

After accepting the collect call, Mrs. Landry, with concern in her voice, asked, "Paul, is everything okay?"

"We think so, but they are saying that the baby is going to be born tonight even though it's a month early."

"We're leaving in just a few minutes," she said, "It'll take us a while to get there. Which hospital?"

"Touro," he said.

"That is a wonderful hospital. Please give Marie our love, and we'll see you soon."

Before making any other calls, Paul wanted Marie to know her parents were on their way. He knew how much it would mean to her. When he arrived outside her room, a nurse was coming out as he tried to go in. She held up her hands to stop him and said, "Wait a minute, Dad, that's it for you until after the baby is born.

"But, I need to give my wife a message!"

"Better tell me, and I'll go right back to let her know."

"Tell her that her parents send their love, and they are on their way. Oh, and so do I!"

"Consider it done, now you go back out to the waiting room and let us do our jobs! We'll take great care of your wife!"

Paul's next call was to his parents. His father sounded concerned about the premature delivery, and they both would be coming as soon as possible.

Marie's exam room quickly transformed into a mini-operating room. People were hustling around, preparing for the delivery as the nurse gave her the message from Paul, one which brought tears of joy to her eyes.

After the call home, Paul sat in the nearly empty waiting room. Every minute turned into a week as the reality of these moments began to take hold.

Just then, an older nurse approached him from the station nearby, checking to see how he was doing. She asked, "Is there anything you need, Mr. Morel?"

"Just two things," he replied, unable to take his eyes off the door to Marie's room. "A healthy baby and my wife… that's all."

He heard her words, and they sounded nice, but Paul had a clear view of the door to Marie's room. It wasn't long before the traffic stopped going in and out. Tension gripped his spine, and he wondered if he would collapse if he tried to stand.

At 4:03 am, the doors burst open from the inside, and a bassinet surrounded by six people hustled his baby down the hall.

The older nurse appeared again with a huge smile. "I am pleased to inform you, Mr. Morel, that you are the father of a beautiful baby boy!"

Almost stupefied, Paul said, "Ernest."

"Yes, sir!" The nurse replied, "There is nothing about your son we would ever joke about! He is doing very well and your wife too!"

Paul stood there, almost unable to respond. He thought he and Marie had given their child an easy name. *You just never know,* he thought.

He looked at the nurse and tried again. "Ernest," he said. "We are *naming* him Ernest, like the author Ernest Hemingway."

"Oh, well… you don't say! What a 'novel' name!" The nurse giggled at her pun, then added, "Congratulations, Mr. Morel," as she spun in her spot and started to walk away.

Paul called after her, "When can I see them?"

"Just wait right here, another nurse will come to get you soon!"

Paul's mouth was dry as a bone. He walked over to a water fountain close by and took a few sips.

A moment later, he heard, "Paul Morel? Mr. Paul Morel?"

He raised his head from the fountain to see a nurse standing outside the entrance to Marie's room. Seeing him, she waved him over. "Your wife is ready to see you, Mr. Morel. Dr. Robichaux said you could come in for only a minute; then, we need to get her up to her room."

Nodding agreement to her as she opened the door, Paul entered to find Marie was in the same spot he'd left her. He couldn't help but think, *so much had happened in that spot in such a short time.*

Walking up to his wife, she appeared pale and sleepy.

The nurse said, "After she delivered, the doctor gave her a mild sedative."

"Sweetie, are you doing all right? I hear we have a son!"

"Ernest, yes," Marie slurred, eyes half-open. "Where is he?"

The nurse said, "Your pediatrician, Dr. Cummings, took him to the neonatal intensive care unit because he is a preemie, Mrs. Landry. He's in great hands there!"

The nurse asked, "Does he have a middle name?"

At that moment, it hit Paul that they'd never gotten that far in discussing names.

Before Paul could utter a reply, Marie said, "Winston. Ernest Winston Morel." It was Paul's father's name.

She looked back to see Paul's smile of approval just as her eyes glazed over, and she became unresponsive.

Paul yelled, "MARIE!" The other nurses came running over. The Head Nurse took one look at Marie and called out, "Get Dr. Robichaux back here, ASAP!" She reached up and opened the I.V. fully for added fluid. As they looked down at the sheet, in horror, they observed a dark red, rapidly expanding circle of blood in the area between Marie's legs.

Again, the nurse yelled, "Call the O.R., we have an acute post-partum bleed, we need O negative blood, NOW!"

Paul loudly said, "Would somebody please tell me what's going on?"

The Head Nurse turned to Paul and said, "Please, sir, it's not the time for questions that I can't answer. Please go directly back out to the waiting room so we can care for your wife."

Paul was frozen in a tunnel and could only look at Marie, whose life was draining out, literally before his eyes.

"SIR!"

Another nurse grabbed his arm and led him out the door to a waiting room that had begun to fill with people complaining of chronic aches and pains. Paul stood, mouth agape, as his wife's lifeless body hurtled through the double doors on a gurney headed for the operating room.

31
NO MORE

His parents arrived first, followed quickly by Mrs. and Mr. Landry. The distraught parents and Paul quietly waited for news. The O.R. soon phoned and called him over to the nursing station. Paul listened intently to the nurse as she quickly appraised him of Marie's status.

Paul returned to his anxious parents; his face was no less grim as he considered what to say. *How do you inform parents and in-laws that you have just witnessed a scene that has shaken you to your core, and you have no idea what will happen next?* The nurse had informed him that they had stabilized Marie. That felt like more than a white lie to Paul. He had seen the blood.

As optimistically as he could, he told the parents what the nurse told him. "The nurse told me she is still asleep in the operating room, and the doctor will speak to us as soon as he can safely leave her side. He wants us to move upstairs to the surgical waiting room."

Soon after they arrived upstairs, a nurse from the neonatal intensive care unit, or NICU, found them and delivered the first positive news they'd heard in the past hour. Ernest was doing well. She alerted them that he still had a breathing tube in place, "As a precaution only, and just until his lungs develop more."

After the nurse left, Dr. Morel tried to comfort his son by saying, "It's just routine, Paul. They'll remove the tube as soon as he's able to breathe on his own."

Minutes turned into hours. Paul's parents and Mrs. Landry had spoken freely with him and each other, but Mr. Landry remained quiet. When her father first appeared in the Emergency Department waiting room, it had sparked hope that harsh words from the past might stay there. Paul couldn't imagine a father turning his back on his daughter as Mr. Landry had, but, as his father had said, "Not everyone thinks the same way about family the way we do, son." Still, Paul knew how much it would mean to Marie when she learned that her father came this morning to be here for her. *But it would be so much better if he would speak.*

Just then, Dr. Robichaux barreled through the double doors from the O.R., pulling his mask down as he approached.

They all stood to greet him.

Walking directly up to Paul, the doctor said, "I'm going to give it to you straight, Mr. Morel. Your wife is lucky to be alive. We had to resuscitate her on the table. I wasn't sure I would be able to stop the bleeding.

Mrs. Landry began to cry hysterically as her husband, and Mrs. Morel did their best to comfort her.

The doctor continued, "Marie has a rare congenital malformation called a unicornuate uterus. I'd have to say that her first miracle was getting pregnant so quickly. Many women with the same issue can't ever have children. Luckily, Ernest was able to hold on until near term, and that was the next miracle. It must be a fitting name for him. I understand that Ernest means '*determined*'.

"After I delivered him, everything seemed pretty routine at that point. Because of his premature birth, he would just need a little help for his immature lungs for a few days, and I was already in the next room, dictating my note. For Marie, the real problem began *after* delivery. Her postpartum bleeding came from another rare problem, called placenta increta. Her placenta was attached deeply to her uterine muscle and was just going to keep bleeding until it was all removed. But then, the uterine tissue had an arterial bleeder that was almost impossible to see and stop. We were running in donor blood as fast as we could. Just as I was about to remove her uterus as an emergency hysterectomy, the third miracle happened: the bleeding stopped."

Mrs. Landry stepped toward him and declared, "*I did this to her.* It was because of me that we almost lost Marie when she was born. I had the same problem with her, and I never warned her about it." Mrs. Landry looked at the others individually, adding, "You know, I thought I had years to build up the nerve to tell her about this. Then, once she was pregnant, I didn't want to scare her and chose to pray for her instead." She turned to look at her husband, who hung his head and stared at his feet.

"Lucien wanted a son, and because of the bleeding I experienced when Marie was born, the doctor had to do a hysterectomy to save my life. There would be *no more* children for us."

Dr. Robichaux removed his surgical cap and used it to wipe the sweat from his brow. As he gathered his thoughts. For now, he didn't have time to pursue Mrs. Landry's grief, as he continued, "I'm still not sure why Marie's bleeding stopped. But with her being so young, I'm glad we didn't have to do the hysterectomy. She'll have fewer hormonal issues." The doctor placed his hand on Paul's shoulder as he said, "You should know, Paul, that because of the trauma and damage from today, even though her uterus is still there, it is highly unlikely Marie can ever have another child. There is a high probability that she will have *no more children.*"

Paul said, "Thank you for helping us, Dr. Robichaux. We don't know what we would have done without you today."

The doctor nodded and stepped back to say, "Although she won't be out of the woods for a few days, hopefully, the worst is over. But don't stop your prayers just yet."

As he walked away, the family all breathed a sigh of relief. Dr. Morel asked Mr. Landry if he would accompany him to the cafeteria to bring back coffee and snacks. They left together, leaving Mrs. Landry, Paul, and his mom to wait on other news.

Paul sat, holding his head in his hands. He'd not had the chance to take a deep breath after the birth of their son.

Mrs. Landry sat next to him and placed her arm over his shoulder. "Thank you for loving our Marie," she said.

"She is my heart and my soul," he replied. Paul rubbed his eyes and sat up.

"I like our grandson's name. Who picked it?"

"Marie did. She picked it because I'm an English major, and I like to read Hemingway's works."

His mother-in-law thought for a minute before she said, "Isn't he the author who killed himself?"

The events of today fueled courage in Paul's words. He didn't hesitate and looked directly into her eyes before replying, "Yes, but even a name deserves a second chance. And speaking of second chances, Mrs. Landry, do you think Mr. Landry is ready to give Marie one?"

Mrs. Landry folded her hands in her lap and looked at them. Hesitantly, she said, "All I know is that he is here today, and I'm surprised about that. On this day of blessings, I count that as one. He knows he was wrong; he's just too hard-headed and embarrassed to say anything yet."

Paul had much more he wanted to say but made a silent vow that he would not escalate any issues with his volatile father-in-law today. Looking over at his mother, she winked at him, approvingly.

Later that evening, relatives were allowed in one at a time to the surgical ward. Paul went in first and alerted Marie that her father was still there if she wanted to see him. She was happy he had come and was anxious for him to visit with her. Paul would let her father know. He cautioned her that the doctors didn't want her upset by anything that might cause the bleeding to return.

Paul smiled as he informed Marie that they had all visited the window outside the NICU, and Ernest was sleeping comfortably. Dr.

Cummings told the nurses that the breathing tube would probably come out within the next 24 hours.

Paul sat for a moment on the side of the bed, then said, "You scared me today, Marie."

"I did? I didn't mean to."

"Well, you did! It's because I can't imagine life without you."

Marie smiled. Today had been a blur, and she couldn't imagine tomorrow. She was still exhausted, but thankfully, the headaches were gone. Paul kissed her and told her he would give others a chance to come in and would return as soon as he could.

Marie's mother entered next, having already decided to delay her confession until much later.

Mr. Landry had tears in his eyes when he left Marie's room. Paul was happy that he had come for his daughter but found it odd that he had never said one word to him. He hoped beyond hope that he had at least been able to speak to Marie. She deserved that moment of peace.

By 8 pm, after Dr. Robichaux made his final rounds for the evening, the Morels returned home. Mr. Landry, also on his way home, dropped Mrs. Landry off on Plum Street, where she would get some sleep and be ready to give Paul a break in the morning.

If everything continued to go well, Marie would be discharged before their son. The nurse said she would have to follow the orders for strict bed rest for the first week. They both looked forward to their son, given the nickname of "Ernie", coming home soon.

Early the next morning, Paul returned home for a well-deserved nap, then he and Mrs. Landry drove back to the hospital together. By the afternoon, the baby's breathing tube was removed, and he quickly became the star of the NICU. Ernie had already mastered different coos and facial expressions that delighted the nurses. Paul was allowed into the NICU to see his son after donning a gown, mask, and headcover. He was ecstatic. The bottle he held of Marie's expressed breast milk brought mother and son closer together.

Marie was anxious to hear of Paul's visit with their son. Vicariously, she listened as her excited husband used words to paint that scene for her. It was driving her crazy that she hadn't yet held her son. Her questions about him came faster than Paul could answer. "Does he look like you or me? Are his toes and fingers cute like mine? Does everyone like his name? What color is his hair? Do you think he'll want to go to Tulane someday?"

❧

The evening before her discharge was the first time Marie was allowed out of her room. The color was returning to her face. Paul escorted her in her wheelchair to the nursery, and there, she saw Ernie and held him for the first time.

Marie was in awe. She remained speechless until the nurses placed him in her arms, then she said, "Hello, Ernest Winston Morel, I'm your mama!" She looked at Paul, in amazement, and said, "Look at him, he's so little!"

Paul silently acknowledged how he would never understand even a fraction of God's mysterious ways, as he watched the interaction between mother and child. There was no question that his son knew that Marie was his mom. It was instant. He'd been fussy in his crib when they entered, then one second after being placed in her arms, he went to sleep. In a short while, Marie cried when they were told that it was time to leave.

Later, after returning to Marie's room, the Morel's arrived to surprise them just before discharge. Dr. Morel handed Paul a folder and said, "This is our baby gift to your new family.

Paul sat on the edge of the bed close to his wife and opened the envelope. He pulled out the papers, and they read the cover sheet together.

"Mom, Dad, this is incredible. Thank you so much!" It was the deed to their house. His parents had bought it for them.

His father said, "I've always wanted someone in our family to own that house!"

Hugs filled the room before the Morel's left again for home. Marie demanded one more visit to hold Ernie before leaving, then, with hesitation in their hearts, the nurse wheeled Marie to their car for the trip to Plum Street. Paul knew he would return soon; he would be the courier for Marie's milk. Mrs. Landry waited at home with dinner prepared. Later, she would hear Marie's infamous roasted chicken story, and much laughter was heard in their kitchen tonight.

It hadn't been easy for them to go home without Ernie, and they couldn't wait to bring him back home where he belonged.

32
REALITY

Paul readily relinquished their bed to Marie for the short term. It was hard for her to find a comfortable position to sleep, and the living room, split in two by bedsheets hung from the ceiling, wasn't far if she needed help during the night. Mrs. Landry slept on the sofa, and Paul had a pallet on the floor.

The fall semester had begun for him, and he'd made a trip into school to speak with the administration to explain his absence. After that, he had a lot of catching up to do, and now had less time to get it done. He stopped by and spoke to several professors that he could reach on short notice, then returned home with an update on the work he needed to complete as soon as possible.

Shortly after returning home, he learned that his workload had only increased.

Marie's mother had only been with them for a few days when Mr. Landry demanded that she return home. She was upset as well as compliant and promised to return home as soon as she could.

Mr. Landry didn't enter the house when he arrived to retrieve his wife.

Marie's emotional wound reopened to the closing of the door when her mother left. Again, she cried.

A week after discharge, Marie and Paul visited Dr. Robichaux's office and received his blessings to end the regimen of strict bed rest. Marie was free to move around, but with lifting restrictions.

Paul learned later that evening when he dropped off more milk to the NICU, that Dr. Cummings would release Ernie for home in the morning. It would be such a blessing that both be present for this momentous event.

❧

The next day, it was an emotional release for the NICU nurses and Dr. Cummings, but a good one to see another set of miracles on their way home together. Paul and Marie thanked them profusely. While there, Marie and the lactation nurse went to a private room but didn't stay long. As they came back out, Paul overheard the nurse tell her, "Don't worry. He's probably not that hungry yet. He'll catch on soon!"

Paul saw the worry in his wife's face.

After the ride home, Paul opened the front door for mother and son, and they introduced Ernie to his new home. Marie spoke softly to him as she cradled the precious, small package on his first tour around the house. She spent the longest time at the kitchen window with its view to the yard. Paul overheard her explain to Ernie that it would be his yard soon, and that she was sure he would find many buried treasures there.

The last stop on tour was his room. Paul had picked up a variety of colored poster board sheets from which he had cut letters spelling "Ernie". Paul taped the rainbow forming his name to the outside of his door. Paul stood in the doorway as Marie welcomed their son to his room, rocking him gently in her arms until he fell asleep. She placed him on his side, covered him, and quietly left the room, leaving the door open. They both moved to the living room sofa, knowing it wouldn't be long until it was time for another feeding. Marie hoped that breastfeeding would work better this time.

As they sat together on the sofa, the new normal of constant exhaustion began as both fell asleep. Mother and father awoke too soon to the rising crescendo of an upset child.

The lactation nurse was right. Ernie caught on to breastfeeding.

So, the cycle began. Rest was suddenly a thing of the past. Ernie always came first.

❧

Marie's mother soon returned to help. Paul replaced the partition in the living room, separating it in half.

One evening the phone rang. Paul answered it quickly, trying to prevent waking Marie and the baby. "Hello," he whispered.

The voice on the other end said, "I ain't seen you in so long, did y'all have that child already?"

"Talulah? Is that you?"

"You did, didn't you? Ain't that something! But why you didn't let Talulah know!"

Paul replied, "I'm very sorry, Talulah, but we've just been so…"

"I don't want hear no excuses, Mr. Paul Morel! That mule done left the cart!"

"Ernie came home with us a little over a week ago. He was born on August 12th. We are thrilled and can't wait for you to meet him!"

"How 'bout I come over for just a few minutes tomorrow evening? I gots something I want to show y'all too."

"That'd be perfect, Talulah. We want you to meet Marie's mom too!"

"All right then. I'll see y'all round 6 pm. Bye now!"

❧

Mrs. Landry and Marie together made roasted chicken for dinner. It was fantastic, and the banter about Marie's misadventure with the hen kept them all laughing. As they cleaned up the kitchen, they put several containers in the fridge for leftovers, and one was to give to Talulah tomorrow. Marie especially wanted her to try the dish as it was meant to taste.

The next day, Paul disassembled the partition and brought the kitchen chairs into the living room.

Promptly at 6 pm, Marie answered the door. To her surprise, Talulah wasn't alone. There, with her, stood a smiling Delilah.

Introductions flowed with the sound of Ernie wailing in his room, as they moved into the living room.

"Sound like somebody be upset!" Talulah said as she reached into the basket, she was carrying and pulled out a plate of her fresh pies, holding them out to Paul.

"Lookey what I broughts y'all!"

"You're the best, Talulah," Paul said.

"Now they ain't all for you, Mr. Paul! And before you leave for the kitchen with them, there's something else in Talulah's basket."

She had everyone's attention as she held the basket in front of Delilah, so she could reach in.

Carefully, she pulled out a handmade baby quilt and held it out for Marie. "My mama and me made this for your child. It's the first one I ever made, and we want Ernie to have it."

Both Marie and her mom had tears in their eyes. Reaching beyond the quilt, Marie grabbed Delilah, hugging her tight.

Marie and Delilah spread the quilt open. The hand-stitched needle-point appeared expertly done and depicted an intricate scene of Marie sitting in the grass, watching as Ernie chased his father.

Marie said, "Wow, ladies, I thought I was an artist… this is incredible! Thank y'all so much!"

Talulah and Delilah beamed with delight.

Talulah looked intently at Paul and said, "Cause nobody calls me to lets me know, we had'ta stitch Ernie on last! Could a'been a girl, for all we knowed!"

A hush came over them as Mrs. Landry appeared from the nursery with their inconsolable baby. Ernie hadn't stopped crying all day.

As they sat together in the living room, Talulah said, "That child gots him some lungs!" She looked at Delilah, chuckling, "Let's sign him up for the Church choir!" More serious now, "Miss Marie, he so small, has he been eatin' good?"

"He came a month early, Miss Talulah, and he wasn't a good eater at first, but I think he's getting better!" Marie sounded like she was trying to convince herself.

"Well, he gots time. He be a cute lil thing, ain't he Delilah?"

Delilah agreed as she reached over to stroke his cheek with her finger.

Trying to be discreet around Mrs. Landry, Talulah said, "Since Delilah return from camp, she been helping her mama in the shop. It been real nice havin' her back! She been listenin' and learnin', and I ain't even had to threaten her with my rollin' pin once in the past few weeks!"

They all laughed, barely louder than Ernie's cry.

Marie scooped Ernie into her arms from her mother, saying, "The doctor says Ernie has colic, and he'll grow out of it."

"How he be sleepin'?" Talulah asked.

"An hour here, an hour there," Marie replied.

Talulah said, "You poor, poor honey-child! But don't you worry 'bout it. Delilah was a cranky child, and look at her now…"

Delilah smiled on que.

"Well," Talulah and Delilah stood, "we best be goin'. We wants you to know we very happy for y'all. We hopes to see you soon!"

Paul went to the kitchen for the roasted chicken. Returning, he said, "Something for your basket, Miss Talulah."

Marie added, "It's what roasted chicken is supposed to taste like!"

After Talulah and Delilah left, Mrs. Landry made a bee-line for the kitchen. Marie had told her mother about Talulah's pies, and that she and Paul had brought them for Thanksgiving, but they had never made it out of his car.

Paul spread the pies on a plate, then interpreted the crust markings to tell Mrs. Landry what her options were. Handing her a raspberry,

Mrs. Landry ate until she finished it. Wiping her face of powdered sugar with her napkin couldn't remove her smile as she commented, "That was incredible. I wonder if she would hire me to help?"

Marie was in Ernie's room feeding him again, then she put him in the crib and tried placing him on his belly after burping him. She wondered if he might sleep better in that position. She spread the new quilt over him and quietly stepped away with renewed hope for a little rest tonight.

The three chatted in the living room for a few minutes, then Paul held his fingers to his lips and said, "Shhh! Listen!"

Marie and her mother looked around for a moment, then Marie asked, "Listen to what?"

"It's quiet, finally. What did you do to calm Ernie down?"

"I placed him on his belly. Maybe that's the ticket?"

"Fingers crossed for you all," Mrs. Landry said.

33
THE FIRST COLD

A few more weeks passed. Marie greatly appreciated the help and rekindled relationship with her mother. Her father did finally come inside to see his grandson when he picked her mom up, but only briefly. Marie believed that her father timed his visit to miss Paul, who was at school.

Mrs. Morel arrived early the next day, bearing thoughtful baby gifts, stuffed animals, a cushion for the rocking chair to ease Marie's back, and a cooler full of pre-cooked food from home. Marie shared her husband's joy in her arrival, as she stepped right in to help with her knowledge and care.

Paul's class obligations, which became progressively harder to juggle, didn't end when he walked through the front door. His mother worried for him, noting the pale light from his lamp shining through the partition at all hours of the night. She knew he had been running very low on sleep.

It was on a Thursday that he came home from school early, and without a word, shut the curtains facing the street on his side of the partition.

Concerned, she peeked around the sheet, separating them, and found him already sound asleep on his pallet.

By 6 pm, Marie kneeled next to him and rubbed his shoulder to ask, "Paul, aren't you getting hungry? I'm sorry to wake you, but your mom fixed some great spaghetti, and it needs to go in the fridge soon. Won't you come and eat some?"

With a scratchy, deep voice, Paul responded, "Thanks, baby, but I just need some sleep. I'm not feeling the best."

Marie rubbed his back as he rolled over, and soon he was asleep again, snoring loudly.

Back in the kitchen, Marie told Mrs. Morel that Paul was coming down with something, and offered to sleep on the sofa so her mother-in-law might sleep better in her bed.

"No, honey, but thank you. When either Savannah, Paul or myself get a cold, the other ones have it in a heartbeat. I'm probably close to sniffling already just being in the same house with him, so I'll just sleep in my usual spot."

And so, by morning, not only did Mrs. Morel have the congestion from a cold, but so did baby Ernie.

Paul felt so poorly; he made the wise decision not to go to school the next day. He spent the day blowing his nose so much that it remained red. Marie had to work overtime to cook for them all because Mrs. Morel was in no better shape than her son.

Ernie was miserable and cried almost non-stop. He was exhausted, irritable, and hungry. His tiny clogged nose prevented him from being able to breathe while he was sucking. The poor child was unable to feed more than a few sips before his tiny hands pushed to unlatch his red face, allowing him a breath. Ernie shrieked at the top of his lungs as the milk he was unable to swallow, ran down Marie's chest.

Mrs. Morel helped when she could, as did Paul, but after the first day, this, unfortunately, proved to be more than a 24-hour bug.

Marie was luckily not susceptible to this virus, but with her added responsibilities because the others were sick, there was no time for sleep. After the second day, her eyes could barely stay open while rocking Ernie in the nursery. She grew fearful of dropping him from her lap if she relaxed too much or fell asleep. Tomorrow, she promised herself that she would call the pediatrician's office for advice.

Marie forced herself to stay awake by singing any nursery rhymes she could recall until inevitably, her exhaustion won. There was no way she could continue to care for her child if she didn't get some sleep. Ernie cried whether he was in her arms or the crib. She decided to put him down for the night.

With love, Marie lowered him into his crib, placing him on his belly, the position he seemed to sleep best. Ernie wailed louder, as her tears flowed. It was all she could do. Marie covered him with his new quilt and left the room for some much-needed sleep. She knew that without rest, she couldn't help Ernie or anyone.

❧

Somewhere in the middle of the night, a blood-curdling scream filled the air, followed by the words, *"NO, GOD NO!"*

Paul and Marie jumped through Ernie's door almost simultaneously, finding Mrs. Morel standing in the dim light next to Ernie's crib, holding him in her arms. She was sobbing hysterically.

Paul went to her side, as Marie, frozen with fear, stopped at the doorway.

As her raw emotions caused her to shake uncontrollably, Mrs. Morel's crying barely allowed her to say, "I woke… it was so quiet… I was just coming in to check on him, and hoped he was finally getting some rest…"

Paul refused to believe what he thought she was trying to say. Abruptly, he reached for Ernie, quickly taking him from his mother's trembling arms. Mrs. Morel collapsed on the floor and began to pound it with her fists.

He now knew what his mother did. His precious child was cold and unmoving. Paul looked over at Marie as he broke down into tears, saying, *"NO, MARIE,* this can't be happening, please come over; we need to wake Ernie up...

Marie looked at the shocked, unblinking eyes of her husband as he extended the product of their love out, begging for her help. His voice dropped into a deep tunnel and faded away.

Paul's anguish didn't allow him to see the blood drain from Marie's face as her pupils dilated, and she collapsed to the floor.

❧

The emergency doctor at Touro couldn't revive Ernie, who, on arrival, presented cold with no heartbeat. He pronounced the child "deceased", noting the time for the death certificate: Sunday, October 7th, 1979, 3:53 am. The cause of death the doctor listed as "SIDS" or Sudden Infant Death Syndrome.

"It was classic." Paul overheard the physician telling the nurse, "A history of premature delivery, two months of age, an upper respiratory infection; very sad."

The only one that received medical treatment was Marie: an intramuscular injection of sedative for the trip home.

It wasn't until much later in the morning that Paul summoned the strength to make phone calls that no father should ever have to make. His first call was to his father, who, through cracking and distraught words, promised to come right away. The next call was answered by Marie's mother, who dropped the phone as she fainted with this news. Paul remained on the line as Mr. Landry revived her, only to hear his wife cry out to God for their grandchild. Soon, all knew that the unthinkable had happened.

Marie had spoken to no one since the doctor pronounced Ernie's death. More than Ernie died that day.

34
THANKFUL

The spotless white hearse pulled into the circular drive in front of the steps to the church in New Roads. The end of one nightmare and the beginning of another was upon them, and Marie could barely breathe. She had not fully recovered from Ernie's birth, and the physical pain she felt was a constant reminder of his recent birth. Motionless now, and inside the hard casket, her mind's eye could see her infant son, still and cold, wrapped in his beautiful new quilt. The priest, family, and close friends lined the path as Paul, Dr. Morel, Mr. Landry, and Paul's grandfather Morel became the pallbearers for the small white casket.

After entering the church, within a few minutes, the pews filled behind them as most of the town of New Roads came to pay their respects. What they all felt that day was similar, that the funeral of an adult was difficult enough, but of a child was immeasurably sad.

Father Muldowney, a priest that knew this family well, officiated the Requiem Mass. He never had the chance to meet Ernest Winston Morel. During the Homily, Father Muldowney made special efforts to ease the minds of those present, especially Paul and Marie. Concerning the loss of their not yet baptized son, Father began by saying, "The Bible reminds us, God only wants what is good for all His children.

God knows each of us by name before our birth." He continued, stating emphatically, "I believe that each human soul receives an opportunity to either accept or reject God, especially a child lost before the opportunity of Holy Baptism. As proof, I challenge you to question how a loving God could condemn an innocent baby who himself had committed no actual sin? The Lord baptized Ernest Winston Morel. The Lord granted him a Baptism of desire. In our frail and limited human thoughts, this child we knew for such a short time may have seemed ill-equipped to make an eternal decision. But in meeting his Maker, who could say that at the hour of his death, our loving God wouldn't give Ernie the maturity to choose whether to accept Him and come home or not?

"We are not joyous in our loss of such a young person, yet we rejoice his new life with our Lord and that someday we will all meet him again. We should be *thankful* for even a short glimpse of any of God's creations. Praise and glory, Ernest Winston Morel has risen with our Lord."

Father used the aspergillum to sprinkle Holy Water on the coffin before the pallbearers escorted Ernie to the waiting hearse for his last earthly ride.

Later, Talulah and Delilah stood directly behind Paul and Marie at the family gravesite that was nestled under the live oaks on the family property. After prayers, the priest extended his sincere condolences to Paul, Marie, and the family. People were invited by Dr. Morel back to their home for a lunch prepared by family members and dear friends.

Paul and Marie lingered at the gravesite. Savannah and his parents asked if Paul wanted them to stay with them, but he asked them to go back with the others to the house. They watched in silence as the funeral director and workers opened the above-ground family tomb. The young couple both broke into tears as their son disappeared behind the cold marble.

Neither Marie nor Paul wanted to leave after they were all gone.

Paul said, "I don't know how we can leave Ernie here like this, Marie. It's like we need to try to do something to help him. It's just not fair."

At that moment, a dragonfly magically appeared, and it hovered at the closed door to the tomb. They both watched as it landed on the marble base at the entrance.

Paul felt a warm hand grab him from behind. Turning, he saw Talulah and Delilah.

Talulah said, "Mr. Paul, Miss Marie, your precious son, he ain't in that box, and he ain't in that cold tomb. He be sittin' next to Jesus, and now, he be worried for you. You gots to take care 'o your own self. The Lawd, he giveth, and he taketh away. It ain't for us to know why except that He knows best."

Talulah drew Paul into her bosom and hugged him so hard he wondered if he could catch his breath. When she released Paul, she wanted to hug Marie, but she had turned away.

Before he or Marie could say anything, Talulah intervened again, saying, "Now, Mr. Paul, you all needs to show us round that beautiful home you family been blessed with, and it should be soon." Talulah turned to her daughter and said, "Just you looks at Delilah! If we don't feeds her soon, she gone blow away! She be starvin'!"

The four of them walked together through the back door, and it didn't take long for Talulah's presence to mysteriously chase the sadness away. She and Delilah began an impromptu, a cappella of gospel songs that soon had everyone singing along. No different than the upbeat music played *after* the burial at a New Orleans Jazz funeral, Talulah and her daughter serenaded and praised the beautiful new world into which Ernie had arrived.

35

SIXTEEN PERCENT

Although invited, the grieving young parents never planned to stay overnight in New Roads. Savannah was doing very well in school and had arranged to take the next few days off. She planned to return to New Orleans with Paul and Marie today. Long before the other guests left, they were escorted quietly to the front door by Paul's parents. Savannah invited Marie to ride with her to New Orleans, followed by Paul, Talulah, and Delilah in his mother's borrowed car.

The late afternoon drive proved too short for Marie to express her vast array of pent up emotions. Barely out of her parent's driveway, Savannah mostly listened as Marie poured out her anguish and guilt; beginning as a trickle, and transforming quickly, to a torrent of emotional pain.

"I can't believe Ernie is gone," Marie said. "Savannah, he was just born! How can Paul and I deal with this pain? Sure, we were too young, and it wasn't the right time, but we both loved him the moment he arrived." Placing her head into her hands, she added, "I just don't know what we will do. How can we just go back to school when our infant son lies in a cold grave?"

At times, it was hard for Savannah to concentrate on driving. The emotions were simultaneously heart wrenching and distracting. At one point, she missed the turn to Baton Rouge, having to slow and turn around. Paul knew she would realize her mistake and pulled over to wait on her.

Marie's emotional outpouring never slowed.

Savannah patiently listened to Marie's description of falling in love with her brother. Like many young people, they had wanted to share the closeness and joy of real love. Soon, this love story began to sound different. In it, it was hard for Savannah to recognize the brother she knew. Marie's story of being "smitten" with Paul became disturbing to Savannah as she detected vague but definite hints of him having cast some spell over her. Marie was casting blame with statements like, "I just couldn't help it that night. I was powerless."

Marie was all over the map. One second, she claimed to be helpless, and the next, her words described their "mutual feelings". Savannah was taken aback at how quickly the "mutual" part of her story took a back seat to Marie's other self-centered feelings. As Savannah continued to listen, it became apparent when Marie's resentment sprang to life: it was the afternoon she took the pregnancy test.

Several times during the trip to Plum Street, Savannah found herself caught up in the intensity of Marie's confession. Suddenly, she'd find her foot pressing harder against the accelerator as they flew past other cars. She knew that Paul had to be wondering about her erratic driving today.

One thing was sure, Marie felt resentment for how their love had placed her in a position of "alone" on the night Ernie died. Savannah continued to listen as her own anger grew for how this was being turned around on her brother.

It had never been Marie's plan to have children until much later in life. She spoke of her own goals and ambition to become a commercial artist. Compounding her frustration was her supposed knowledge that several of her girlfriends in high school had experienced unprotected sex on multiple occasions, and none had to deal with such life-changing decisions.

Mile after mile of hurt and anger followed until they were on the outskirts of the city. It was then, just when Savannah thought she had heard it all, that Marie said what she really wanted to say. Savannah was thankful they were close to Plum Street. She was ready for Marie to be out of her car. When Marie let loose on her brother, it was almost too hard to hold her tongue.

Marie said, "I'm still angry that Paul was able to go on with his life, and I wasn't. He got to continue his dreams of becoming a lawyer, while my plans, my hopes, and my future were put on hold."

Then, anger and guilt morphed into betrayal when Marie said, "Even though I wasn't sick the night Ernie died, I was exhausted to the core. Paul had slept most of the day already. If I'd had more help… if Paul could have woken up and checked on him, maybe Ernie would still be alive."

Savannah smiled at her politely and sped up intentionally this time. Her first thoughts of strangling Marie while trying to drive, wouldn't help anything and would probably kill them both. Tapping into her kinder, gentler side, she knew that there was nothing she could say right now that could help this poor, distraught woman. She also knew that her brother and his wife would need counseling. She would make sure to talk with him soon about that. The rest was for her ears only until Marie could find a way to broach these issues with her husband. Savannah could only hope that with time, Marie would realize that none of what had happened was anyone's fault.

They pulled to a stop in front of the house, arriving before Paul, and only Savannah exited. Marie handed the keys for the house to her out her window but made no effort to open her door. She said, "Please go on in. It will take me a while to summon the strength to follow you."

❧

Talulah and Delilah sang most of the way back, which helped to take Paul's mind off the next stage ahead. It was a blessing that his sister was returning with them. He and Savannah had been close since he could remember, and now he was confident she was there for Marie.

He felt that he had little time to grieve with all the course work that awaited him, but he also chose to see a positive side in that.

Paul continued straight on South Carrollton when the girls turned onto Plum. It wasn't far now to get Talulah back, and she requested that he drop her off where he'd picked her up: at her shop. He'd never seen her home but heard that she lived nearby.

He pulled the car into the small lot in front of the shop, got out, and opened Talulah's door.

She said, "Mrs. Morel taught you how to treats a lady, I notice. We wants to thank you for the ride today. You were kind to allow us to pay our respects like God asks, with humility and joy!"

Paul replied, "I'm not sure how we all would have gotten through this without the two of you. Thank you for being there with us today."

Paul hugged them both and turned back to his car. Then he heard…

"You just waits one more minute there, Mr. Morel! Talulah gots another piece of humble pie for you to swallow."

Turning back, he said, "Yes, ma'am?"

"That wife o'yours in a heap o'hurt. We so happy that you beautiful sister come home with y'all. But you gots to know that even with her there, Marie gonna need lots 'o help. You gots to be easy with her, specially rite now. You hear what Talulah be sayin', son?"

"Yes, ma'am. Loud and clear." Paul stepped into the car and watched as mother and daughter disappeared around the back corner. He pulled out of the lot, hoping that the worst was over for today. Barely over his cold, this long day had been exhausting, physically, and mentally.

This last leg of the trip was the hardest. Returning home was far more complicated than he imagined. When he arrived, the lights from his car illuminated Marie, still sitting in the passenger seat of Savannah's car. Glancing at the porch, he saw his sister sitting in a chair by herself. No words of explanation were needed.

Paul parked, walked over to the other car, slowly approached

Marie's open window, and said, "Baby, I feel the same way you do, but we need to go on in. We all need some rest."

Marie sat quietly without moving.

"This is not easy for me, either. Come on now; we'll walk in together." He waited for her response, which came quickly. Marie rolled her window up.

Paul attempted to open the door, but Marie held it from the inside. The last thing he wanted to do was hurt her more, so he let go of the handle. He raised his voice enough for her to hear him easily, and said, "I love you, Marie. We all do." He walked up to the porch and thanked Savannah for her help. Asking her to come in the house with him, he said, "Marie will be fine out here, and I'll keep an eye on her through the window."

After entering the house and turning on lights, Paul made sure the door to Ernie's room was closed. He removed the colored poster board letters that spelled out Ernie's name, then he and Savannah sat on the sofa together.

Savannah knew she would have to handle her next words carefully. She was distraught with what Marie had told her and needed to warn him somehow. "Paul," she said, "I researched some books in the school library before I left. I found a psychology book that had valuable information about couples concerning the sudden loss of a child. It's information you should be aware of."

Paul looked at his sister. He knew she meant well, but this day from Hell didn't seem to be cutting him any slack. Mustering a kind response considering how he truly felt right now, he replied, "Go on."

"Studies have found that as many as sixteen percent of marriages won't survive the sudden loss of an infant, for any reason. Even in cases like yours where it's not due to anyone's fault or neglect."

"Sis, where are you going with this? Marie and I are very much in love. We aren't blaming each other for what happened; it just happened. Our marriage will be fine!"

"Yes, brother, I'm sure it will." Savannah hesitated again before saying, "But would you do me a favor? It's something that would at least ease my mind…"

"Okay, Savannah," he said, "you've always been my favorite sister." Paul just wanted to be done with this.

Savannah knew she was getting under her brother's skin. Trying to add some levity, she slapped his arm and said, "We both know I'm your only sister!" A small smile crossed his lips as they heard the car door outside open.

"I want this to remain just between us, okay?" Without waiting, she added, "I want you to consider seeking grief counseling for you and Marie."

He had no time to respond before the door opened, and Marie walked in. Immediately she looked at Ernie's door and appeared relieved that it was vacant of letters. She looked at them and said, "I have a splitting headache. I'm going to bed. Thank you, Savannah, for coming back with us."

Paul stood and said, "I'll get you an aspirin, Sweetie. Is it okay if I sleep with you tonight?"

"Yes, okay, we'll see how that goes... it's still hard for me to find a comfortable position."

Paul found a sheet and pillow for Savannah, kissed and thanked her, then closed himself into the bedroom with Marie.

36

STEPS

The better part of the next week remained awkward. Paul stayed home for the first couple of days, then returned to school. Despite encouraging her to talk to him, she continued to only vent to Savannah. During rare moments alone with his sister, she continued to urge Paul to push Marie to consider counseling.

Soon, Savannah decided it was time for her to return to school. Her suitcase waited by the front door, and when Paul arrived home from school, he walked her to the car. His sister carefully reminded him of what was at stake if Marie remained in a state of depression.

Savannah was dismayed to find that Paul's attitude had hardened. He had grown angry with how Marie was treating him. As Savannah had feared, Marie's anger passed to Paul in hurtful, non-verbal ways. She was closing a wall around herself.

Paul was trying. "I've tried to speak with her," he told Savannah, "truly, I have. I've begged her to see a counselor with me, but she has refused. Marie thinks she's the only one who lost a son. And the worst part? She acts as though what happened was all my fault."

"You know I love you both, brother. But if your marriage is going to survive this, you need to start loving each other again. You should take steps that will bring you closer together, not further apart."

Paul hugged his sister hard. As Savannah drove away, she left an expanding emotional void behind.

Paul moved back to the sofa after she left, by his own choice. Marie never commented about that.

Marie's mother called each day, always offering to come to visit. This day, when her mother called, Marie had a different idea. She wanted to go home for a while.

Mrs. Landry inquired, "What does Paul think about that?"

"He'll have to be fine with it," Marie replied.

❧

On Friday morning, Paul had gotten a better night's sleep, and with a more optimistic mood left a poem for Marie on the kitchen table before leaving for school:

"The Spark

The lost Woodsman had
Just one match left.
One to start a fire
That might save his flesh.

Soon the wind
Did howl and moan.
His rain-soaked skin
Chilled to the bone.

When to strike the match?
His mind raced to know.
"Certainly not now,"
Said the wind that didn't slow.

But if he delayed too long,
And he froze to death in wait…

He'd chosen the wrong choice,
One to seal his fate.

The wind slowed a bit
As he struck the match and prayed.
Then his arm done froze,
And this is what he said:

I knew how cold it was
When I lit out here to hunt.
Now my only match is gone…
When I thaw, they'll find a skunk.

I love you with all my heart, Marie. We need to talk this out.
I'm tired of smelling like a skunk.
Can't wait to see you this evening,
All my love, Paul."

Marie's alarm clock woke her at 8 am. She slowly moved her sore legs off the side of the bed, and on opening the door to the living room, was relieved to find Paul gone. She went into the kitchen for a glass of water and saw the sheet of paper he'd left on the table.

She sat, leaning over to read it, and the symbolism in his words summoned tears that fell on the page. She quickly stood and grabbed a hand towel, dabbing it and unintentionally spreading the ink into a blur wherever a drop had landed.

She understood the meaning before her. Like the Woodsman, Paul felt damned if he did and damned if he didn't. She was sorry for what he was going through, but she, like his powerless match, was incapable of resisting the winds which were pushing her away.

The tears this morning were for more than his words. Marie had never deceived Paul in any way, but today she was about to. She was going home with her mother and didn't know when or if she would return. Marie and Paul hadn't discussed anything since returning from the funeral, including her leaving today. She couldn't. Right now, Marie could only do what she needed, and what she needed most was space from this house and all memories of what happened, including her husband.

Her mother arrived close to 10 am and found her waiting on the porch. As she exited her car, Marie met her there, where they exchanged a quiet hug. They placed her suitcase in the trunk along with one other thing; a protective cardboard tube used to carry a rolled-up painting.

Mrs. Landry looked at her daughter as she closed the lid and asked, "Which painting is that?"

"My favorite," Marie replied.

Two hours later, they were in Morgan City.

Paul was slowly getting caught up with his course work, and that was a good feeling. It hadn't been easy, considering the state of his emotions. The past weeks had been a blur. There wasn't anything either of them could have done to prepare for what they experienced. But today was a new day, and for him, it had been better.

As he rode home on the streetcar, none of the windows were open because the autumn air was steadily growing cooler. The days were growing shorter as the late afternoon sun began to retire early from the sky. He would have the upcoming Thanksgiving break to catch up completely… possibly even get ahead. He dearly hoped that Marie had a better day too.

With the cool evening air, the homes he walked past on Plum Street were vacant of the porch sitters that warmer temperatures invite so readily. Just another sign of fall, he thought. Toward the end of her pregnancy, he would routinely find Marie sitting on their front porch waiting for him to return home. He loved it when she did that.

He wasn't surprised that she wasn't outside, but as dusk settled outside their home, the house was unlit inside, a sure sign of her continued depression. The optimism of his day raised his foot to the porch. As he pulled the screen door open, his key turned, and the door parted. Silence greeted him—no smell of an early dinner, no radio, no Marie.

He called her name, softly at first. With no reply, fear chased optimism away as he loudly yelled, "MARIE!"

Still, no reply.

The bedroom door was open and dark inside. As he passed, he saw that the bed made and empty.

He flipped on the kitchen light to find his poem moved to a different spot on the table from where he had left it. The paper was distorted, crinkled from watermarks and smudges. There was no question who had read it; she signed it with her tears. Only his stained, heartfelt plea remained.

Her suitcase was missing from the closet, along with her clothes from the dresser. He scanned the living room, and his eyes gravitated to the blank space where a painting was missing. This absence would prove to be a bellwether. Marie would not return soon.

When they first moved in and displayed her paintings, she placed them in chronological order. Her choice today had not been random. This painting signified the birth of a beautiful relationship. It captured the beginning of their love, an evening with such great potential that chose, in time, to transform into something else, like a butterfly in reverse. He and their life together were no longer beautiful to her. The painting that was no longer there was the second one Marie had done for him, but the first one painted that showed them. It was the two of them on their first date, standing together on Talulah's porch. She took the one she knew was his favorite.

Paul steadied himself on the arm of the sofa as his body forced him to sit. There was no place left to look because it wasn't there. Marie left no note, no explanation for him to read. No response to his outpouring of love.

She didn't even say where she'd gone. But he knew.

❧

Mr. Landry didn't know that his daughter waited at home, anticipating his arrival from work and his response to her presence. His day had been a long one, due to two of his largest boats sent to dry dock for repairs. This meant that the largest half of his fleet was out of commission.

Stepping up to the porch well after 8 pm, Lucien Landry was tired and hungry. All he needed on his plate, was food. He heard his wife talking to someone in the kitchen as he walked in, but then there was silence as he rounded the kitchen doorway. There sat Marie.

She wanted to rush to the man who had been like a mountain to her as a little girl. But she waited, not knowing what he would say as he stopped just inside the kitchen door.

His face remained expressionless. He looked first at Marie sitting at the table and then glanced at his wife sitting with her. As he looked at Mrs. Landry, his eyes hardened. He walked over to his chair and sat. Her father was like a dormant volcano; there was always the potential for an eruption at any moment.

Marie felt her legs tremble.

He looked at Marie as if she was a dirty picture window, obscuring his vision. Then, without taking his eyes from her, he blurted, "Becky, I hope you have a plate warm for me."

Mrs. Landry's wordless response was to sheepishly rise from her seat and open the oven door. As quietly as she could, she transferred his dinner to a plate and placed it in his spot at the kitchen table as her husband cast a resentful gaze at their only child.

"Why are you here?" he asked as he sat down opposite her.

Risking further wrath on herself, her mother said, "Lucien, our daughter was in a bad place, and needed to come home. She asked if she could, and I said, yes."

Mrs. Landry placed his hot plate in front of him and returned to her chair next to him. He picked up his fork to approach his meal, then set it back on the table.

He crossed his arms and sat back in his chair. He only spoke to his wife, saying, "It's late, and I don't want you on the road tonight, but unless we come to terms before I finish my dinner, you can take your daughter back to her home in the morning."

Always the appeaser, Mrs. Landry tried to lighten his mood by saying, "Now Lucien, you know Marie is welcome here for as long as she wants to stay! She's been through a lot, and she needs us both right now."

Mr. Landry silently began his dinner of sliced ham and green beans.

Marie and Mrs. Landry knew one thing about her father. If he said something, he meant it. Now the clock was ticking.

Her mother asked, "Just what kind of agreement do you mean, honey?"

As he continued to eat without responding, she tried to deflect, "You're home late, did everything go okay at the yard?"

Lucien Landry was consuming the large plate in front of him at an alarming rate. Already half done, he stopped momentarily to say, "Marie Morel, you are no longer a Landry. You left this home and this family the day you ignored my wishes. Now, you return with your tail between your legs, looking for a place to hide. Well, you can't stay here unless you commit to the rules you were raised by, and as I said, if you don't agree right now, you can leave in the morning."

Marie's thoughts turned to this morning when she intentionally left Paul without any notice. Deep down, in the tiniest portion of her heart left without cracks, she knew she was blaming him unfairly for everything that had happened. But she couldn't change that now for one reason: she wanted her future back. The only path she could see that would lead her back to that future was going back to school.

"Okay, Daddy, I'm hoping you'll accept me back as a Landry. Remember, my name was not legally changed. I hope there's a way I can make up for the embarrassment I've caused you."

Mrs. Landry started to whimper between them softly. Mr. Landry thought it was because she was happy that their daughter had come to her senses. But he was wrong.

Becky Landry stood and said, "Goodnight" to them, went to her bedroom and shut the door. For so many years, she had played the part of a dutiful wife to this oppressive man. Now her daughter had fallen victim. *Poor thing,* she thought, *Marie had almost broken free.*

In the kitchen, Mr. Landry had been contemplating how to respond to Marie. He speared the last piece of ham with his fork and chewed it slowly. He shoved the plate aside and said, "Here's what you have to do. You, Marie Landry, need to go back to school, not to that Ivy League place that cost your parents a fortune, but to a great state school. You need to sign up for the spring semester at L.S.U. in Baton Rouge. In the meantime, you got plenty of mourning to get out of your system. It should give you time to get your head on straight for what will be your last chance for me to help you financially with college."

It was what Marie had hoped. She could now return to school with her father's help. She had strongly considered changing her major to Design. Then, she could use her artistic talents and possibly make a living too.

"I'll do what you ask, Daddy."

And with that, the deal was done. Both had gotten what they wanted. After speaking with her father for a while longer, she went back to her room to plan out her way forward.

It was the first glimmer of hope she had felt in months. She thought about calling Paul just to let him know where she was, and that she was safe, but didn't want to anger her father with the expense of a long-distance call. She could always call tomorrow.

Earlier that evening, Paul had spoken to his neighbors, finding one who had seen Marie leaving earlier that morning with her mother and her suitcase. He also considered calling her but thought it best to wait until he wasn't upset. He called Savannah, who bit her tongue while she listened.

37

HOLLOW

H*ow easy it is for battered emotions to allow days and weeks to pass; time spent intentionally ignoring the impenetrable fortress built around our hearts. The invisible walls rise quickly, with or without our consent, and soon surround us.* Paul wrote these words in a notebook as he watched the sunrise from the kitchen table. The world outside and Marie were unaware of the pain he felt.

The anniversary of when they had first met had already slipped past them both. Lost in the blur surrounding Ernie was September 8th.

He looked out the window in early November. It was becoming harder for Paul to remember the good times that followed their awkward introduction in Ms. O's class.

Try as he might, each day that passed with no contact from his wife extracted another scoop of life from deep within. He feared that soon, only a hollow shell would remain.

Sitting there that morning, all he could do was guess what she might be thinking. He was unaware that Marie had nightmares every time she closed her eyes.

For her, it was always the same. In her restless state, she was outside her body, watching… seeing herself, as if in slow motion, unable to move as she was awakened from a sound sleep by a blood-curdling scream. What she saw was always the same. Her legs wouldn't move, and no one came to help. Time and time again, Ernie died. Each time it happened, she would wake drenched in sweat. What had been real returned to her as if in vengeance, every night.

She made excuses to her parents for staying up late. Sitting in their living room, she kept an open book from their bookshelf next to her, pretending to read. Her mother knew what was happening and didn't comment when she noticed that Marie's latest choice was *Carpentry Made Simple*. Her parents went to bed hours before Marie could summon the courage to move to her bedroom and close her eyes. More than once, Marie's parents heard her scream early in the morning. One time, her mother distinctly heard her call out for Paul.

Neither Paul nor Marie understood why the other didn't call. Anger, fueled by blame, coupled with time and distance, breeds apathy. Both knew the longer this continued, the easier it was to perpetuate. Paul struggled with being abandoned by his wife, and Marie's thoughts only allowed her to feel responsible for killing a child she didn't want.

One day, Marie and her mother sat at the breakfast table together. Her mother's guilt for not speaking with Marie sooner came to a head. Mrs. Landry wanted to make sure that Marie knew what Dr. Robichaux had told them about Marie's reproductive future. "Honey," she asked, "did Paul have the chance to tell you what the doctor told us after he stopped your bleeding? Did Paul tell you about my history… or why you are an only child?"

"No," she replied flatly. Marie continued to eat as though this topic held no concern for her.

"Well, I first need to apologize to you for not telling you before now, especially after I learned you were pregnant. Everything was happening so fast. I had just hoped… truly prayed, that you wouldn't have the same curse that I'd had."

Marie continued to eat without comment or expression.

Her mother realized she had verbally cracked open a rotten egg between them and began to try to clean up her mess.

"Marie, we were both born with a misshaped uterus. You got it from me. It was almost a miracle that either of us could get pregnant. Also, after delivery, our placenta attaches in a way that puts us at risk of bleeding to death. In my case, they had to remove my uterus to keep me from dying after you were born, and because of that, I could never have another child. In your case, they were able to stop the bleeding without removing your uterus, but the doctor believes that the trauma and scarring will prevent you from ever being able to have another child. I'm so sorry to tell you this."

"It's okay, Mom, I don't ever want another child anyway."

Her mother couldn't imagine the pain her daughter still felt. She wished that the gentle soul, now hidden deep inside her daughter, would eventually return. Only then would she be able to discuss her feelings openly.

She didn't just feel sorry for Marie. She hoped her daughter, with time, could remember that there were others involved in this pain.

Mrs. Landry chose her words carefully, then said, "I just want to tell you again how sorry I am for you, Paul, and Ernie. What I told you today is something that I should have discussed before you ever left home for school."

"Don't beat yourself up, Mom." Marie stood, grabbing her plate and cup, and placed them in the dishwasher. She turned and said, "I love you for being such a great mother to me, but I'm not sure I ever had it in me to offer the same to my child. I don't think it was ever meant to be."

The phone rang. They both looked over at the intrusion to their quiet breakfast together. Mrs. Landry winced with pain as she rose to answer the call. Walking had become progressively more painful for her, but despite Marie's encouragement, she stubbornly refused to see a doctor.

"Mom, I wish you'd see someone for that knee of yours!"

Her pat response, "I don't have time to be laid up from surgery."

Reaching the phone, she added, "It's probably your father calling. He calls me when he needs something."

Picking up the phone, she said, "Hello?"

Greeted only by silence, she repeated, "Hello?"

"Hello, Mrs. Landry, this is Paul. Is Marie there? I need to speak to her… please."

Marie turned around after drying her hands and saw her mother, holding the phone to her chest, quietly mouthing, "It's Paul."

Marie felt the room closing in around her as it squeezed words from her lips, "Tell him I'm not ready."

Her mother looked at her with sympathetic, hopeful eyes as she said, "Marie, it's time. He did say, 'please'."

Marie slowly walked over and, with a trembling hand, took the phone from her mother. Holding it to her ear, she could hear him breathing, almost assuredly from inside the house on Plum Street.

That, to her, seemed ironic. She left because she could no longer breathe there.

She said, "Hello?"

A torrent was released. "Marie, thank you for coming to the phone, it's so good to hear your voice. I've missed you so very much and worried about you every day. It's been so hard not to call, I've tried to leave you alone and give you the space you needed, but I had to call today. I just had to. How are you doing?"

Distantly, Marie replied, "Hi Paul. Thank you for calling. I hope you're well. Everything is fine here."

He quickly realized from her tone that he was trying to swim upstream in a raging river.

Trying to remain upbeat, he said, "I'm glad you're well. I know you won't have an answer for me right now, but I was hoping I could stop by for a little while on Thanksgiving Day? I'd like to see you."

"I'm not sure," she said, "I'll have to check with my parents. Call back in a few days, okay?"

It was not the answer he'd hoped. He responded, "Sure. I'll call in two days. Thank you… Oh, and Marie?"

"Yes," she said.

"I'm upset too, but I've never stopped loving you. I wanted you to know that. I'll call back on Wednesday."

"Goodbye, Paul."

She hung the phone on the cradle against the wall.

Returning to the table where her mother sat, Marie said, "I don't think Paul understands yet."

All her mother could think was, *he's not the only one!*

❧

During breakfast the next day, Marie reminded her mother that Paul would call again tomorrow. She knew he deserved closure too, and despite her pain, she was starting to see beyond her darkness enough to recognize Paul's need.

Her mother said, "I'm not sure what your Daddy will say, Marie. I'm leaving this completely up to you. Tonight, at dinner, you need to ask him yourself. I can tell you, as well as I know your father, I have no idea how he'll respond to this. Let's hope he has a good day in the yard."

At dinner, Mr. Landry seemed in good spirits. Marie matter-of-factly informed him that Paul had called and would call again in the morning. "He just wants to know if he can stop by for a short visit next week for Thanksgiving," she said.

Mr. Landry looked up from his dinner at his wife, who could only offer a sympathetic stare. As he turned to his daughter, he placed his fork on his plate and asked, "Is this what you want, Marie?"

She looked at him blankly and said, "I think, considering everything, that it would be good for Paul."

"And you, Marie? Is this going to help you, or make things harder?"

"I owe him this, Daddy. Paul is hurting too. I think he should be allowed to come."

Mr. Landry thought for a long minute before he picked up his fork to scoop another bite of potatoes. He looked back at Marie and said, "One hour. He can come for an hour early in the day, so it doesn't interrupt *our* Thanksgiving."

That ended the discussion. Her father went back to eating, as did the others.

38
THE TWILIGHT ZONE

Each time Paul saw his parents, he offered to give them back their car. Before long, he found out from Savannah that their mother had gotten a new car, so the Bonneville was his to keep and use as he needed.

Paul visited his family and informed them of his plans, which would delay his return home until the afternoon of Thanksgiving Day. They reassured him that they would hold dinner until he arrived. Despite their optimism and cordial words about Marie, he learned from Savannah that even his parents had mixed feelings about her. To Paul's face, they seemed genuinely happy he would finally be allowed to see his wife.

This trip home was his third since the funeral, but the first time he could bring himself to visit Ernie's tomb. While there, he silently prayed for God to watch over his son and thanked the Lord for what Talulah had said to comfort him. He truly believed his son lived on in light, not darkness.

"Everything happens for a reason," Memie reminded him before he left, "Ernie came into your life as part of God's plan. No father can forget the pain of such a loss, but it's also not possible for your life to ever be the same. I hope that things will change, bringing you nothing but good. God works in mysterious ways; my grandson!"

Savannah's words also rang in his ears as he slowly drove back to Plum Street. She was livid with what was happening to her brother. "One hour? That's the best Marie and her family can manage? For her husband? What planet are they from, Paul?"

Paul never doubted for which team his sister played. He didn't understand why he and Marie suddenly wore different uniforms. *Didn't they grieve for the same loss?*

The next 50 miles passed unseen. Soon, he sat on his sofa in New Orleans as this day passed, and the next. He managed to turn in his assignments before Thanksgiving break, knowing that what he presented to his instructors was adequate, at best. For now, he was just trying to maintain; and that by itself seemed superhuman amid the tribulations of real life.

The day before Thanksgiving, he stood in line early Wednesday afternoon, waiting to purchase some of Talulah's pies. He thought he was early enough to be first in line, but nine people were already waiting. The line quickly grew behind him. When he glanced over his shoulder one time, Bea was behind them, waving at him with a smile.

There was a reason why Paul hadn't told Talulah about Marie leaving. It simply boiled down to his belief that she would return soon. Now that belief was unfounded, and he knew Talulah would ask about her.

Soon, the upper door opened. It wasn't only Talulah. Delilah stood with her. Paul knew her song by heart now, as he, Delilah, and the rest in line sang along.

A short while later, he stood second in line just before Talulah yelled, "NEXT!"

Then, a volley of questions flew his way, "Boy, where you been?" Talulah said as she opened another bag ready for his order.

Delilah added, "How is Marie, Paul? Why ain't she here with you?"

Paul couldn't lie. "Marie moved home with her parents for a while, and I'm taking her family some pie for Thanksgiving tomorrow."

Talulah blurted, "How long she been gone?"

"A few weeks," said Paul.

"A FEW WEEKS?" Talulah and Delilah blurted simultaneously.

Talulah added, "Well, I hope you gonna shake some sense back into her head cause that ain't right, Mr. Paul! Now you listen up here, and you listen fast. I expect you to visit Talulah when you return, you hear? You be like a son to me, and a son don't stay 'way from their mama for weeks neither! Now, son, we be ready for your order."

Paul said, "I'll take the usual, please. All of them are going to be for the Landry's Thanksgiving dinner. I'll get to see Marie for a little while before they eat."

Talulah stopped what she was doing and leaned over the lower door, close to Paul. She spoke in a much lower tone of voice, asking, "You means tell Talulah that you ain't gonna share they Thanksgivin' meal with them?"

Sheepishly, "No, ma'am. I can only stay for an hour. That's all her daddy will allow."

Talulah stepped back and looked at Delilah as she shook her head and said, "Them people of Marie's be crazy." Then she looked back at Paul to add, "An if you putting up with that, you be crazy too, son!"

She grabbed his pies, quickly placed them in the bag, and handed it to Paul as she said, "That be five dollars. And if you come back here next time with crazy news like this, the price gonna double. Happy Thanksgiving, Mr. Paul Morel."

Talulah yelled, "NEXT!"

His allotted time to visit his wife was to begin and end between the hours of 10 and 11 am in Morgan City. Arriving late was not an option, so he left New Orleans at 7 am, which hopefully would allow room for holiday traffic or road incidents.

As much as he looked forward to seeing Marie, another thought kept entering his mind: Savannah's last words to him on the phone last night. "Paul, it's like you will be driving into a scene on the set of *The Twilight Zone*! The problem is, they aren't acting!"

He recalled how much the two of them looked forward to another episode of the hour-long weekly show. Rod Serling created a masterpiece of altered reality, revealing that the world reserves the right to shock us when we least expect it. The clarity of her analogy amazed him.

The closer he got to Morgan City, the more his resolve began to crack. *He couldn't turn around,* he thought, *there may never be another chance.*

Paul arrived early to town, but rather than upsetting her father by arriving before the appointed time, so he drove around the outskirts of town past the docks and yard that proudly bore the sign "Landry's Fleet". Paul knew that this outspoken man was highly respected, but he also was so protective of his only child that it was unclear if Paul would carry any weight as her husband; today or ever.

He stalked his watch as he sat in his car a block away, and promptly at 10 am, he pulled into the drive. Marie sat on the porch, like a mannequin posed in a store window. As he walked up the path to greet her, she remained seated and quiet.

He continued along the front walk, smiled when close, and said, "Hello, Marie. Happy Thanksgiving."

As he stepped up to the porch, his concern for this visit ramped up. She hadn't replied or even looked at him. He stopped in front of her chair, feeling the need to break whatever spell held control of her. His attempt to touch her arm on the armrest only caused it's retreat to her lap. Marie seemed almost frantic as she glanced at the front door, expecting her father to burst forth at any second.

She spoke, finally, "Please just sit, Paul. It would be best."

He obliged, then placed the bag of pies on the small table between them as he said, "Talulah, Delilah, and I wish you and your family a Happy Thanksgiving."

Marie's eyes gave her away. "Thank you," she said, as she smiled and began to reach for the bag. Suddenly, she stopped herself.

Her shallow offering of kind words was sweeter to his ears than a drop of water to a man dying of thirst.

But he could feel the truth. She had just given him the distinct impression that she missed the pies much more than him.

The humid cold of the morning did nothing but remind him that everything about this meeting was out of place. The separation of their chairs sent a message to Paul, accentuating the apparent strain imposed by distance.

"Do you know I've missed you?" he asked.

"Yes," came the monotone reply.

"Do you know I love you?"

She stared at the pavement beneath her for a moment, hesitating before again saying, "Yes."

"Do you know I'd love for you to come back home soon, today, for instance?"

Marie didn't respond.

"Marie, I know that everything happened too fast for us both. I'm so sorry about it all, first with Ernie, then with us. But I believe our relationship is strong enough to move through this. You know, though, that it will take two people to make that happen."

Marie just looked the other way, with a blank demeanor that would make a mask envious.

"Honey, do you understand what I'm saying? Aren't you willing to admit how special we are together? I just want to know how to bring our love back… Marie, please…"

Marie finally turned to face him and began to speak. "I've had time to think Paul. I'm not sure I can return as if nothing happened, *and I'm not sure I can ever be your wife again*. What brought us together came at the wrong time in my life, and my pregnancy with Ernie felt wrong from the beginning. I was sick, angry, and moving in a direction that I wasn't ready to go. Returning to you now is more than I can imagine."

Paul was stunned and speechless.

"There is something you need to know," she said. "My father has agreed to pay for my education if I transfer to L.S.U. next semester.

I've decided to change my major to design and continue my education. It's what I must do. I'm sorry it didn't work out for us, Paul."

She stood and said, "It's much colder out here than I thought, but it'd be best if you didn't come inside. I hope you have a safe trip home. Thank you for the pies, we hadn't figured out what dessert would be today till you arrived."

He'd been there less than ten minutes as he watched her pick up the bag and walk inside. The door closed, then he heard it lock.

Paul sat on the porch alone until 10:59 am. Then he stood, walked to his car, and drove away.

Marie soon noticed what Paul didn't even know. After she arrived inside, she showed her mother and father the bag of pies he'd brought, saying, "Now we have dessert!"

"Wasn't that sweet," her Mom said.

As her father walked away unimpressed, Marie pulled the six pies from the bag, placing them one at a time on a platter. Her taste buds watered as she searched for Talulah's pinky print on the edge of at least one, but that tell-tale sign was not present anywhere. All six pies displayed the short, straight edge markings of Paul's favorite: apple. Talulah had sent her a message. None were chocolate.

39
L.S.U.

Paul called his family from a payphone in Morgan City to let them know he was on his way back to New Roads. Savannah answered the phone, and he poured out his battered heart to his sister. Two hours later, he found her waiting for him in the front foyer, barely able to control her rage. Savannah was livid. "You've got to be kidding me, Paul! What do you mean they didn't invite you inside? And the measly hour they offered suddenly turned into just ten minutes after you drove all that way? I think we should sue!"

"I've had enough drama today, Sis. Come on, we should join the others in the kitchen. I could really use a beer. Let's try to salvage the rest of this day, and we'll talk more later. I don't want to put any more of a damper on everyone's Thanksgiving."

They walked together into the kitchen. There, Paul was circled and greeted by his devoted family. He didn't say much to his parents, but they knew he was upset by his appearance. They surrounded him like a cocoon as a reminder of how love feels. Soon they enjoyed the excellent food prepared.

Late that evening, he and Savannah continued their talk in her room. He did more listening than speaking, but when he retired to his room, he knew one thing for sure. Today proved that he needed to worry less about Marie and more about *his* future. If his grades suffered any more, his shot at Law School would be history. On Sunday, he would return to New Orleans and try to knock the rest of this semester out of the park.

❧

During the next month, Paul accomplished his goal and better. He finished his semester with excellent grades and accolades from his professors, who were aware of the loss of his son. None were privy that he'd lost his wife too.

In his spare time, he painted Ernie's room, gave the crib and furniture to Goodwill, and made plans with Delilah to begin tutoring after Christmas. Gaining Talulah's permission, Ernie's room became transformed into a quiet place for Delilah to use, a comfortable and safe place for her to study. With wisdom born from experience, she was ready to learn and anxious to obtain her GED.

Paul spent a well-deserved Christmas break with his family in New Roads. While there, he had many conversations with them individually and collectively. Their main concern was him. Savannah was a warrior in defense of her brother and encouraged Paul to consider a divorce from Marie. "She left you months ago," she said, "and shows no sign that she wants to be married anymore. You need to move on with your life, Paul. You don't deserve treatment like this!"

His parents and grandparents took a similar tack, focused on their faith. Their opinion was that their religion would be open to an annulment of the marriage. Because neither Marie nor her family was open to dialogue, an annulment was an option.

Paul, in his way, let all know how much he appreciated their concerns for him. He told them that he just wanted to enjoy the rest of his break so he could mentally prepare for his next semester. They all respected his wish but planted a necessary seed for him to consider.

On Christmas Day, he tried to call Marie, only to have an answering machine pick up with her father's voice requesting that a message be left. He hesitated as the device waited for him to speak, saying only, "This is Paul. I just wanted to wish Marie and you all a Merry Christmas." Then, he added his parent's phone number and said he hoped he'd hear from Marie.

There would be no return call from his wife, and he had no way of knowing whether she had even received the message. Although he'd considered it, there would be no unannounced trip to Morgan City today. He just couldn't put himself through treatment like that again.

❧

Marie heard his message as she stood by the phone in the kitchen. Her parents did also. She was finally in a better place now and felt sorrier for what Paul was going through by the day. Her father's presence at the kitchen table nearby, caused any sympathy for Paul to be quickly displaced. Things were going well with her dad, and she didn't want to risk his wrath on Christmas Day. She walked away from the phone as Paul left his message.

Her mother tried to divert by stating, "Just a few weeks until you go off to Baton Rouge for school, honey!"

"Yes," Marie said, mustering a smile, "I can't wait!"

Marie was anxious for school, yes, but she was also ready to leave the oppressive atmosphere of walking on eggshells always in this home. Her father had become more possessive by the day. The answering machine was his doing, all because he feared that Paul would try to "worm his way" back into her life.

She spent most of her time in her room over the next few weeks and had packed well ahead of her move. This time, she took only the essentials, a change that surprised and perplexed her father when they loaded the car. She suddenly found joy in simplifying her life.

They arrived on the first day of check-in. Marie would have a private room again in the dorm. They ate a free lunch at a restaurant that was a regular buyer of shrimp from her dad, then her parents dropped her off, said their goodbye's, and left for home.

Alone in her room, Marie laid in her bed only to find the walls closing in around her. She had gotten her wish: a second chance. *But at what price?* The emptiness in her heart made her lightheaded.

❧

In March, Marie was sound asleep in the middle of the night when her phone rang. When she picked it up, she only heard wailing. It was her mother.

"Mama? What's going on? Why are you crying?"

As her mother gasped for air between sobs, she said, "It's your father, honey… he's had a massive stroke." A silence fell over the line. Then, "The doctors say he won't live through the night." Her mother muffled the phone against her chest as she sobbed hysterically.

Marie began to cry also, "Oh Mama, no! Please tell me this isn't happening.

There was silence from the other end for the longest time. Marie kept trying, "Mama? Mama, are you there? What's happening?" Then, Marie heard someone, possibly a nurse, speaking to her mother, but she couldn't understand what was said.

She heard a rustling noise as her mother moved the phone back to her lips, "He's gone, Marie. Your daddy is dead."

40

SWEET SORROW

Paul and Marie hadn't spoken since that day on her parent's front porch in 1979. It was now the middle of October 1981. The second anniversary of Ernie's death had recently passed, and although he'd been better at distancing his thoughts from her, Marie was, again, front and center in his mind.

His family was pressing him harder for disposition on his marital status, and he continued to brush that aside with his broader concerns over the entrance to law school.

Unbeknownst to his parents, things had been looking up for him. He hadn't told anyone yet, but he'd received a favorable nod concerning his application to Tulane Law School. That was not the only place he had applied. Any confirmation could still be months away, but this news certainly eased his concerns about the future.

On Friday evening, he celebrated a great week with a couple of beers and homemade tacos. Finishing his meal, he took the last sip of his beer and stared at the phone on the kitchen wall. The next thing he knew, he was dialing her parent's number.

"Hello?" It was her mother.

Paul thought, *at least they got rid of that silly answering machine!* "Hello, Mrs. Landry," he replied. "This is Paul… I was wondering…"

"Oh, Paul! It's so nice to hear your voice! I hope you're doing well! Marie isn't here; she is at L.S.U. Would you like her number?"

Mrs. Landry's cordial nature took him by surprise. This conversation was going much too smoothly. "Uh, yes, ma'am. I would. I hope you and Mr. Landry are well?"

"I guess you couldn't have known, Paul. My husband passed away over a year ago, shortly after Marie went off to L.S.U."

"No, Mrs. Landry, I hadn't heard this. I'm so sorry for you and Marie."

"Thank you. I know you might not miss him as much as us, but he was a good man. He just wanted to protect his little girl, you know."

"I don't blame him for that. I do wish we could have gotten to know each other better. I'll let my family know, and we're very sorry."

"If you've got a pen, I'll give you her number. Marie is doing very well in the Design School. She is much happier now, and I'm sure she'll be happy to hear from you." Mrs. Landry gave him the number, then said, "You take care!"

With her number in his hand, he placed the phone back in its cradle. He briefly considered walking to the store for another beer for more courage. Then, he visualized his hesitation to pick up the phone to be comparable to entering a pool of freezing water. There was no easy way to get in; *he just needed to jump.*

The phone barely had a chance to ring on her end when she picked up. When he heard her say, "Hello," Paul realized how much he missed her voice.

His words poured out, "I miss you," he said.

"Paul, is that you?"

"Yes."

Intentionally ignoring his opening remark, "Hello, it's great to hear from you. I think of you often and wonder how things are, you know, with getting into law school and everything?"

"Things are going pretty well. And you? How is school?"

"I'm having a blast, and I'm so happy to have changed my major to Design! I can use my artistic abilities in every aspect of what I'm doing."

"That's wonderful news, especially after what your Mom told me when I called. Your Dad, you know. I was unaware of what happened. I called to get your number, and she told me about him." There was an awkward silence before he added, "That's rough, Marie."

"Yep. It was a shock. God knows we've all had enough of those! Mom has been struggling, but she was able to sell the business and will get royalties for years to come, from letting the new owner use Dad's name on the sign."

"She sounded good," he said.

"My mom seems different now, in a good way. Without my father's thumb constantly pushing her down. She is finally able to do things *she* enjoys instead of just waiting on him hand and foot."

"And you, Marie?"

"Me what?"

"You sound better to me, almost like that spunky girl I met in Ms. O.'s class."

"Yes, Paul. I'm much better. I'm finally getting to do what I want, and that does feel good."

"So, what would you think about me coming up to see you this weekend? I can drive up on Saturday the 24th and get a motel room close to campus. We could meet for dinner?"

She hesitated longer than Paul liked, then said, "I would be interested in a platonic dinner visit, yes."

On hearing these words, Paul lowered the phone for a moment, wondering why he was putting himself through this again. Then he heard her voice faintly, "Paul, are you still there?"

Raising the phone, he said, "Uh, yes! That sounds great. Everybody could use a friend for dinner, and it will be nice to see you. I'll call your number Friday afternoon. I can either pick you up or meet you at the restaurant of your choice. Your call."

"Perfect. Talk to you later, thanks for the call."

"Oh, and Marie?"

"Yes?"

"Again, I'm really sorry about your father."

"Thank you," she said. Then, she hung up.

❧

Paul didn't tell anyone of his plans, especially Savannah.

Friday afternoon, he checked into the motel about a mile from the L.S.U. Campus, and called her room. He didn't have any expectations other than trying to spend a little time with his wife. He'd done his best to damper all expectations about this evening, but did wonder if the Marie he'd first met might return. *A long shot,* he thought, *but still his hope*.

He arranged to pick Marie up outside the student union for the short drive to a seafood restaurant and bar not too far from campus.

When he arrived, he came to a stop close to where she stood. Excitedly, he jumped out of the car to go around and open her door. She didn't wait for him.

As he rounded the front of the car, he heard, "I got it," as she seated herself and shut her door.

Paul circled back to the driver's seat, and as he entered, he said, "It's nice to see you, Marie."

Ignoring what he'd said, she commented, "I remember these wheels."

As the interesting evening began, Paul was still trying to wrap his head around a platonic visit with his wife.

He had never removed his wedding band, but stealing a glance while he drove, he saw no ring on her finger.

It was surreal. She was spunky again, acting just like the Marie he had fallen in love with several years before. Or, she was putting on a great show. *Would the real Marie please stand up!* This one took the term "platonic" to a new level.

It was odd that she requested that they split a pitcher of draft beer together over dinner. He'd never seen her drink.

"Everyone does it here," she informed him as she poured another glass for herself.

He had to admit; the draft beer did taste good. As she drank, the platonic part of Marie crumbled. Somewhere during the second pitcher, she poured out her guilt for being such a "bitch" to him. She tearfully admitted that unless she acted the way she did, she would never have been allowed by her father to return to school.

By the time the beer was gone, Marie was wobbly, and Paul was uncomfortable with the thought of driving. His motel was much closer than the campus and her dorm. He told Marie that he would sleep on the sofa, but that they could spend the night "platonically" in his motel room. She was in no place to argue.

Soon, Paul placed the key into the door of room 109. He sat her on the bed, removed her shoes, then eased her under the covers, and took his place on the sofa.

From the bed, he heard, "Thank you, Paul… for taking care of me. I never deserved such a great guy."

"You're welcome," he said. He heard her breathing heavily long before he fell asleep.

In the middle of the night, a hand touched his shoulder. He rolled over to see Marie standing next to him.

"Are you okay," he asked?

"Yes, I had to use the restroom, and wanted to ask something."

"Okay. Shoot."

"I noticed the wedding band on your finger earlier. Are we still legally married?"

His head, still spinning from the beer, said, "Yes."

Marie grabbed his hand, pulled him up before he could imagine what was going on, and led him back to her bed. "I have needed a Paul hug for the longest time… that is, if you're okay with it."

He was unsure what the definition of a "Paul hug" was but held more than a passive interest in finding out. Before he knew it, they were under the covers and entwined in a way that he hoped one of them wouldn't regret.

"How I've missed you, Paul," she said.

As he entered her, she gasped. Paul froze, wondering if he had hurt her. She whispered, "I'm okay, please don't stop."

❧

Morning light poured through the curtains. Paul had been awake for the past hour, listening to Marie sleeping next to him. He was on top of the world.

Noise from the parking lot pounded in Marie's head, as she woke and saw Paul lying next to her. The reality of being in the same bed with him, naked, infuriated her.

Marie was out of the bed in a flash, picking up her clothes as she almost ran for the bathroom.

"Marie? Are you okay? Is there something wrong?"

There was no reply as the bathroom door slammed shut.

Paul rose and gathered his clothes, putting them on as quickly as he could. He had the worst headache. He sat on the sofa just as the bathroom door reopened.

Barely into the room, she said, "I'd like you to take me back to my dorm *right now, please.*"

Stunned, he responded, "Yes, but could we talk for a moment first?"

Marie was avoiding eye contact. She paced around as she said, "I need to get back; there's a lot I have to get done today."

"Okay. Do you want to walk to the car with me?"

"Your car isn't here? Where is it?"

"We both had so much to drink last night that we walked here from the restaurant. It seemed like the safest thing to do."

Marie was angry. She said, "Well, I guess you're happy about that! It feels to me like you got what you wanted. What happened to our agreement to keep this platonic?" Marie winced from the pain of her headache and grabbed her head with both hands.

Now Paul was pissed. He stood and walked to the door. With his hand on the knob and his back to Marie, he spoke firmly, "This time, like always, it was me that upheld the deal. I was very platonic until you woke me on the sofa last night and pulled me to your bed. So, you can just sit down for ten minutes and wait until I return with the car, and then I'll be more than happy to bring you to your dorm."

With that, he slammed the door and left.

In fifteen minutes, he had returned, picked her up, and shortly after they arrived back at the student union.

As Marie grabbed the door latch to exit the car, Paul grabbed her wrist and said, "Before we made love last night, you told me you missed me. Now you act as if you hate me. Which one is it?"

She pulled her wrist away from him and said, "I never told you I missed you last night; you're making that up."

"I've never lied to you, Marie, and I never will."

"Well," she said, "there's something you seem to have never figured out, so let me spell it out for you as clearly as I can. At first, I didn't return to you because of what happened to Ernie. It freaked me out. Then, it became easy to allow my dad to take control of me; that way, I got what I wanted. All I had to do was play his game. It wasn't long before the freedom I found here to pursue my dreams allowed me only to look forward."

Paul was stunned. As he sat, frozen in his seat, he looked at Marie as she opened the door, thinking, *who is this person?*

As she exited the car, she turned back to say, "What we had was a mistake. We were too young to know better, that's all." She shut the door and turned to walk away.

Through the open window, Paul called out, "One of us was too young, that's for sure! Oh, and one of us still is! I hope you find what you're looking for, but it probably won't be until you stomp on a few more hearts. It shouldn't be a surprise to you that you've completely shattered mine. Thank you for walking away, now keep going and don't ever turn around. There will never again be a part of me that would care."

Paul drove away, vowing two things to himself. He would never return to this campus again and never say anything to his family about this visit.

He drove backroads all the way home, in no hurry to return to New Orleans. The one thing he couldn't reconcile about the new Marie was that she bore no resemblance to the old one; that is until she let her guard down with the alcohol. New Marie acted hurt, angry, scared, selfish, and mean. It wasn't the real Marie, but Paul didn't know if she would ever be able to act like her true self with him again. She reminded him of the kind old hound he had while growing up. That dog loved him with all its heart, but one day, it viciously snapped at him when he didn't realize the area he was petting was swollen and infected.

Marie had a deep sore that still festered, and having sex with Paul last night, no matter how it happened, was regrettable. At least she was comfortable with the knowledge that pregnancy couldn't happen.

Paul drove away, quickly regretting the words he'd said. Despite that, he wasn't sure that regret would keep him from doing what his family wanted him to do: divorce Marie.

41
PERSNICKETY

It didn't take Paul long to make himself busy. For at least a year, Delilah had been ready for the GED exam, but remained hesitant. Paul knew she was ready, but Delilah had to believe that, too. With new determination, he reviewed with her again one evening and finally convinced her to schedule the exam. Within days of taking it, she received the news that she was a high school graduate.

On a Sunday evening, when the bakery was closed, Paul and his wonderful new friends laughed together over a celebration dinner at the Camellia Grill. After the meal, Delilah, proud as a peacock, felt compelled to ask her mother a question that she'd been too shy to ask before. "Mama, why didn't you ever get your high school diploma?"

Paul remained quiet, just smiling at Talulah as he awaited her answer. He knew… but then again, he didn't know.

After the words slipped from Delilah's mouth, the silence that descended over the table began to feel very uncomfortable. Filling the void, Delilah added, "I hope I didn't offend you with my question, Mama."

"No, child," Talulah said, "I was just thinkin' what to say."

Talulah cleared her throat, then took a sip of water before responding, "Not getting educated always be a stain on my soul.

Before now, I didn't think I'd ever have a chance for more educatin'. But because I be the beneficiary o' such a smart girl for a daughter, I thought I might could go back to school in the evenin' whilst you finish up in the shop? If you could help me, maybe we boths could get smart! Maybe I can get Mr. Peach Writer Man to help me too?"

"Yes, Ma'am, it would be my honor," Paul said.

Delilah chimed in, "I'd do anything for you, Mama!"

Paul knew that there was more to this story about lack of education for Talulah. Growing up in the inner city, surrounded by poverty and parents with little education, Delilah's mother faced a steep hurdle at a young age. Families needed help to make ends meet, and children were called away from school to help.

Although Marie never left his mind, Paul was bestowed with some great distractions. For the first time in a while, he went home with a full heart.

Marie threw herself back into schoolwork. Soon, the evening with Paul played second fiddle to her studies. One of her design labs was in conjunction with the Department of Architecture. During the semester, different teaching interns rotated through her lab course. In mid-November, there was a new teaching assistant assigned to that class, and in short order, he stirred up quite a buzz. He was handsome and flirtatious. Soon, she discovered that all the other ladies in her lab were smitten with him.

Yes, he was good looking, and he knew it. Still, he was not someone who would interest Marie. She would seriously consider placing her tongue in scalding water before beginning a new relationship, good looks or not. Her plans didn't include a man anywhere in the foreseeable future.

The other ladies presented no challenge for the new assistant named Billy. They were like dead mice to a well-fed cat. Billy seemed interested in the "mouse" that tried to run away. Aloof Marie was much more of a challenge to him, like forbidden fruit.

His interest in her didn't go unnoticed by the other women. If she were on fire, none of them would have lifted a finger to throw water on her.

Marie didn't understand. She was doing anything but flirting with this guy. Yes, she knew *she* was pretty, but so were the other girls that Billy walked right past to check on her.

He made a point of placing his face very close to hers on the rare occasion she asked for help. Several times he told her how good she smelled, and she'd purposely not used perfume.

This class was tough, but all Marie needed was enough time to finish her work. She went to the lab in the evening on occasion and often worked there on the weekends. It was only a matter of time before Billy found her there alone.

She didn't realize he was there as he approached from behind. "Hello, Marie, working again, are we?"

Startled, but appearing unfazed, Marie said, "Oh, hello, Billy. What brings you in on the weekend?"

"I'd tell you it was you, but I could get in trouble for that," Billy displayed his famous smile filled with white teeth.

"Well, even if you don't get in trouble, you'd be wasting your time," she said.

Billy stepped in front of her table. With a smirk on his face, he asked, "Why so persnickety?"

Taken aback, "Persnickety?" This snarky comment was the last strike for this guy. He had already struck out in a game she wasn't even playing. He was using words that she didn't understand, which reminded her of Paul. "What do you mean, why don't you speak real English?"

"I'm just trying to be nice and helpful, and you act like a snob. Why can't you lighten up a bit?"

Marie stood, wishing that someone else would arrive soon. "Listen, Mr. … what is your last name?"

"Trieger."

Marie nodded her understanding, "Mr. Trieger, I would like to keep any relationship with my teachers completely professional. Now, if you don't mind, I have a lot of work to do."

Marie, obviously done with this conversation, looked only at the project in front of her.

"I understand, Marie. I'm sorry if I offended you, and I just want you to know I'm here to help if you need it."

Marie sat at her table, and Billy went to the teacher's spot at the front of the room and opened a book to read. He remained seated when she left, waving goodbye to her from his desk.

She stopped by the student union on her way home. She rarely checked her mail, but it was a beautiful evening, and the walk to the union was pleasurable. As she entered the mail area, her eyes squinted to read the small numbers on the boxes. She found hers, #682. It was crammed full with a large manila envelope. On the return address, she read "Plum Street".

42

THE BEGINNING AND THE END

Marie wasn't surprised when she opened the packet from Paul. Opening it, she found a folded, empty, postage-paid return envelope addressed to him. Awaiting her signature, were two documents. The first was a petition for divorce under the laws of the State of Louisiana, generated from Paul's New Orleans attorney, Mr. Charles Beckworth. The second document was from the Archdiocese of New Orleans, requesting her permission to proceed with an Annulment of their marriage in the Catholic Church.

It was odd that Paul had not included any other message in the packet. Marie believed that meant he was completely through with her.

She didn't understand why, but she began to cry as she signed the papers. *I guess these tears are for Ernie,* she thought… *or maybe the failure of everything? Either way, it's time.* As hollow as moving on felt, she placed the signed documents in the envelope but needed to return to her dorm. There was one more thing she wanted to add. By the next day, she sealed the envelope and pushed it through the slot for outgoing mail.

A few days later, the envelope arrived at Plum Street. Paul noticed it protruding from the mailbox as he approached the house. Ignoring it, he entered. He'd had his share of stress for today. Finals were close at hand.

Over the next few days, the mailman continued to place mail in and around the envelope that remained otherwise untouched. With no room for new mail, Paul approached the box and removed the contents. He opened the other letters, but couldn't bring himself to open the return envelope from Marie.

Despite the clear message she had sent him, he was having significant problems with accepting the finality that the envelope demanded.

The pressure from Savannah to move on with his life had been constant. Her last words to him still echoed, "Do you think any new girl would be interested in a guy your age that is still married? Come on, brother, you need to get with the picture!"

Like I have an interest in someone new... he thought.

His parents were less pushy. The primary concern for them and his grandparents was his soul. Memie said, "An annulment of your marriage would be best in the eyes of the Church, you know?" His mother kept reminding him, "It's not your fault, son, you tried your best, but it takes two people, not just one."

He could open the envelope any time he wanted but now was not that time. He placed it in the top of his closet, just wanting it to be out of his sight for now. As he found, the longer he ignored it, the less interested he was in opening it.

❧

One week before Christmas, Marie packed her clothes. Her mother was coming to pick her up from school. Her professors allowed her to turn in the end of semester assignments early, allowing Marie to assist her mother with elective knee replacement surgery. Mrs. Landry had put it off for so long; she was barely able to walk. It was scheduled two days before Christmas.

Marie hadn't been taking very good care of herself, recently eating more fast food than she usually did. As she dressed for her mother's arrival, it felt that her blue jeans were unusually tight this morning. But, shopping wasn't on her priority list right now.

Her mom arrived right on time. Marie threw her bag in the back, and her mom, needing to stretch her leg, was willing to allow Marie to drive. They were on their way to Morgan City, and it was a beautiful day.

Mother and daughter spoke freely with each other like the friends that they were. Marie informed her about school and the projects she'd recently finished. Her mother loved to hear the excitement in her daughter's voice when she spoke of her career. After a while, Mrs. Landry asked whether Paul had called her.

Marie hesitated, and when she replied, her tone of voice was distant, "Yes, we went to dinner together." Her mother would never hear the entire truth about that night, just the aftermath.

"A few days after that dinner," Marie said, "he mailed me divorce papers which I signed and returned."

This news didn't surprise her mom, but hearing it disappointed her tremendously. *God only knew what demons Paul had to deal with, losing a child and a wife.* She said, "I'm sorry to hear that, Marie. He's about the nicest young man you'll ever find. I wish you and your daddy hadn't written him off."

Before daybreak on Wednesday, December 23rd, Marie drove her mother to the hospital for surgery. She was resigned and ready, also looking forward to walking with her friends again after a quick recovery. Marie stayed with her through pre-op holding, where she met Dr. Blanchard, the orthopedic surgeon.

Arriving for the 7:30 am surgery, Marie held her mother's hand the entire time the nurses readied her to move into the operating room. Just before taking her to the O.R., they left mother and daughter alone briefly.

Her mother looked intently into her daughter's eyes as if studying what she saw.

Marie began to feel uneasy. "Mom? Why are you looking at me like that?"

"I swear, Marie Landry, it sure looks to me like you are pregnant! I can read it all over your face!"

Stunned, Marie touched her face with her hand, trying to feel the invisible thing that only a mother could see.

The nurses returned suddenly and unlocked the wheels of her bed. "Time for goodbyes, you two!" Looking at Marie, the nurse said, "We'll find you in the waiting room and let you know as soon as the doctor gives the word!"

As they wheeled her mom away, Marie only had time to say, "I love you, Mom. I'll be here waiting for you!"

She focused on her mother's loving smile as the bed disappeared around the corner.

❧

They escorted Marie to the surgical waiting room. The cup of coffee she'd had for breakfast was quickly proving to be inadequate. The receptionist gave her a pager so she could go to the cafeteria, but said, "Take your time, the surgery will be a minimum of two hours. It's unlikely the pager will go off before then. When it does, just come on back here, okay?"

Her mother had been in surgery for less than an hour by the time Marie finished her pancakes. She made a silent promise to start eating better as she placed her tray and utensils on the conveyer. As she turned away, her pager went off.

Surely, they aren't done with the surgery this quickly?

A nurse waited for her at the entrance to the waiting room. Marie didn't like the look on her face.

"Marie Landry?" she inquired.

"Yes… is my mama okay?"

"Dr. Blanchard is waiting to speak to you. He is in one of the private rooms. Right this way, please."

The nurse walked briskly toward a door, knocked and then entered, saying, "Here is Mrs. Landry's daughter, sir."

Dr. Blanchard stood and held out his hand to Marie. It was cold and clammy, and his surgical cap had sweat stains over his forehead. They both sat.

"There is no easy way for me to tell you this, Marie. Your mother developed a blood clot that went directly to her lungs. There was nothing we could...."

Marie collapsed to the floor.

❧

Marie opened her eyes from blackness. The overhead lights caused her to turn her eyes away as sounds returned. She was in the postop recovery room, the place she was supposed to meet her mother after surgery. Instead, she was the one on the gurney.

As her eyes adjusted, she could see people surrounding her, one of them, next to her head, was Dr. Blanchard.

"Marie, you had us worried. So worried that I had the nurses draw some blood. How many weeks have you been pregnant?"

"I'm not pregnant, that's impossible."

As the awful nightmare hit, Marie began to cry, "And this is not about *me!* Were you just about to tell me that my mother died during surgery?"

Dr. Blanchard glanced down at her and said, "Yes, Marie. I'm so sorry."

Marie used the handrails to raise herself, as she proclaimed, "*This was elective surgery for her... she was only going to be in this hospital for a few days! Then we would celebrate a late Christmas together. This surgery was her Christmas present to herself!* This can't happen, it's just not fair, now go back in that room and try harder, she's always hard to wake up!"

Dr. Blanchard didn't move. He just kept repeating, "I'm so very sorry, Marie."

As the doctor and nurses did their best to console her, Marie cried herself into a fetal ball. Surrounded by people that she didn't know. She was heartbroken and all alone.

❧

It wasn't easy, but Marie managed to stay in school the spring semester of 1981, juggling her design curriculum, her mother's estate, and a second surprise pregnancy. Despite this, she demanded, of herself, to love and want this child from the beginning. No matter what happened, she could never blame herself again for the loss of a child.

Somehow, she managed to find the time to see a counselor who continued to stress the importance of including Paul in the life of their child. After many sessions, Marie reluctantly agreed to try to contact her former husband. Unbeknownst to the counselor, Marie, as usual, would do things her way. First, she would test the waters with Savannah.

It took a few days to build up the nerve, then one evening, she dialed.

"Savannah Morel," came the response.

"Hi Savannah, it's Marie." There was no response.

For all Marie knew, their phones had disconnected. Then she heard breathing on the other end.

"Savannah? Are you there?"

"Marie… you have a lot of gall calling me. If I were you, I'd make this fast, no matter what cockamamie excuse you have for calling. I've got countless other things I'd rather do than speak to you."

Savannah was no longer the sister Marie had always wanted. They never shared the same blood, and tonight, that was obvious. Marie had just willingly jumped from the frying pan into the fire. Now the silence emanated from her side.

Savannah took advantage of the dead space from Marie's hesitation, "I'll have you know, Ms. Landry, that Paul is in a perfect place right now. He has two law schools already fighting over him: Tulane, and L. S. U. From what my girlfriends tell me, any girl with a brain and great looks has been following him around when they heard YOU were gone!"

Marie could only listen because there was no break in Savannah's tirade for her to say anything.

"He wants to go to L.S.U., but I can tell he is hesitating because YOU are there. You think your career and what YOU want are so important that you can just throw a good man's life away like it's a rotten sack of your daddy's shrimp? I have to admit; this is the first time in my life that I'm mad at God because he's preventing me from jumping right through this phone and ripping your hair out by the roots!"

Savannah stopped talking long enough to catch her breath, then almost yelled through the phone, *"So please tell me, Miss Prima Donna Artist, why you would call now? Does Paul owe you another chunk of his soul? Wasn't his heart enough for you to destroy and devour?"*

All Marie could say was, "I won't be at L.S.U. much longer, I'd hate to keep him from…"

Pouncing on one word only, "You would hate? That won't surprise anyone! All you seem capable of is HATE!"

Realizing the magnitude of her mistake, Marie silently placed her phone back into the cradle and vowed to be long gone from L.S.U., before Paul Morel arrived.

43

FEBRUARY 12, 1999
RHODE ISLAND

It was the Friday before Valentine's Day. In two days, the twentieth anniversary of Marie's marriage to Paul would arrive. Each year since that day in the French Quarter, she had dealt with that day in different ways; always with the intent of diverting her mind. She hoped each year would get easier, but even her counselor had warned her that it might not. Despite her attempts, emotional detachment from her ex-husband had not been easy. Try as she might to move on, a growing guilt lived with her each day in the name of Camille, his daughter that he didn't know existed.

Marie walked out of her office early today. Rare for her, she arranged to leave her last class with one of her aides who eagerly agreed to fill in for her. An early start home would allow her time to stop by the deli on the way home and begin preparation for a surprise dinner for Billy. He was due to return from New York later today. She couldn't wait to see his face when he arrived home to an evening of wine, dinner, and… her. It's what she needed also.

This weekend, she hoped to distance her mind from a lot of things. The most significant obstacle in her way was an increasing demand from Camille to meet her birth father. Marie was unsure where he was or if he was even alive.

She coaxed those thoughts out of her mind as she jumped in her car. Her BMW sped away from the parking lot, almost as if it were coaxing her home. She pulled the visor down to keep the midday sun from her eyes as she relaxed with thoughts of all the good things that had come her way in Providence, Rhode Island. What she achieved was, in no small part, the result of her passion for what she did.

It had taken much time and hard work, but Marie was rewarded for her efforts with tenure at the Rhode Island School of Design. Shortly after arriving, the Dean took her under his wing, allowing her eventually to fly on her own. Now, she and Dr. Maitlin were the best of friends. The move to Providence allowed her to start her life over. She had proven to herself and others that she was not only a talented designer, but a teacher to be respected. Here, she felt fulfilled.

Today, Marie was resigned to try and bury one memory by creating a new one. It seemed like yesterday since she, her child, and Billy had moved to his home of Providence. The move had occurred immediately following her graduation. She couldn't wait to leave Louisiana.

Driving the beautiful route home, she reminisced about many good things that had happened since she left L.S.U. She convinced herself that life hadn't started until she moved away. Her daughter, Camille, had grown into a beautiful, well-adjusted teen, and their lives together, although anything but traditional, provided them with comforts, achieved in no small part, by hard work and determination. Marie took great pride in having reached the professional goal set for herself, one she fiercely committed to when she was Camille's age.

Reflecting on her past, she was a mere child when they arrived in Providence, a planted seed given a chance to sprout and bloom. Try as she might initially to distance herself from guilt and pain that haunted her, she realized now that it had been the fertile soil needed for inner growth. And, with counseling, she had grown into a good place.

Today, as she drove, new angst washed over her. The pending anniversary from so long ago was affecting her more than she realized. She'd never made any effort to allow Camille to meet her father, and her daughter's insistence was growing by the day. Long-buried thoughts of what happened so many years ago now played before her eyes like it was yesterday.

Marie pulled into the deli parking lot just as emotions overwhelmed her. Now, she could see the trail of unpaid debt that followed her. It was her job, as Camille's parent, to pay that forward. She needed to make sure that Camille could meet her father. It had been so many years, and she didn't have any idea where to find him. She only hoped she hadn't waited too long.

She cried for Camille for several minutes before drying her eyes. In retrospect, her teenage daughter had been the mature one, patiently enduring one excuse after another from her mother. It felt odd to enter the store with her sunglasses on, but her plan required her to keep moving.

Her daughter, the light of her life, was almost eighteen. Camille knew little of the pain her mother felt, but how could she? *I shut her off every time she asked questions,* Marie lamented.

Providence was the only town Camille had ever known. Camille Landry was born by elective C-section on July 15, 1981, in Baton Rouge, Louisiana. Dr. Fran Lenoux, a high-risk obstetrics specialist, obtained Marie's records from New Orleans, and when the day arrived, carefully and expertly brought the miracle of Camille into this world. A planned hysterectomy prevented massive bleeding, and none of the typed and cross-matched blood set aside was needed. Camille would never meet, much less get to know her Grandmother Landry. Marie spoke of her often.

It was interesting that Camille never asked about her other grandparents. That, although a relief for Marie, was also a shame. They were good people, and Camille was related by blood to them. Marie wondered if she hadn't asked because she knew doing so would hurt her mother.

Considering all the emotional pain from Louisiana, she recalled how easy it had been to move far away with her infant daughter after graduation. She had plenty of money from her parent's estate to cover grad school, and even if she didn't, Billy's family was very wealthy.

Everything had come together here. It was easy to fall in love with the school, the change of seasons, and the coastline of Providence. Billy took more effort. Tonight, she would try again.

Billy had one redeeming character. He'd willingly stepped in to become a decent surrogate father to Camille. After Marie exited the deli, she sat in her parked car for a minute, allowing an intimate thought to spread a smile across her face. She recalled the first time she and Billy spent the night together. Infinitely more experienced, he showed her that lovemaking was an art to enjoy for hours. She needed to feel that again tonight.

Pushing those thoughts aside, she focused again on her daughter. The time was fast arriving that she would need to tell her more about her father. Until now, all Camille knew was that she and her father divorced before she was born. Only of late had Camille inquired more about him. Marie was having increased difficulty diverting her attention away from that topic.

There was a huge unknown that worried Marie about Camille meeting Paul. Surely, he was married and very likely had other children. Finding by surprise that she had hidden his teenage daughter from him for almost eighteen years would probably upset him tremendously. She thought about her last call to Paul's sister, Savannah. It was right after finding that she was pregnant again. The entire reason to call her had been to get a feel for whether she could or should call Paul with the news. Between the last words from him outside the student union, and Savannah's tirade, speaking with Paul again *for any reason* seemed unthinkable. But for Camille, that needed to change.

Tonight, she needed answers. Where, if anywhere, was her relationship with Billy going. She wanted to feel a spark from him, not from sex alone, but that feeling that only a woman knows when a man truly loves and wants them. She needed to discover if he wanted her and only her. Marie had felt that once before in her life. At the time, she was too young to understand how rare and elusive it was. Only from Camille's father, had she felt that way. Marie had matured enough to know that a spark from only one couldn't sustain a relationship. It took two.

She drove slowly, obeying the posted speed limits, as she compared her life of flying literally under the radar, to Billy who always lived on the edge. He lived to travel fast and get noticed. It was his audacity that would take New York by storm when his concepts were picked, despite stiff competition, for several major high-rise additions close to the World Trade Center. At first, he feigned the notoriety, stating he was "honored," but Marie noticed that Billy could never be honored enough. He was spending significantly more time away from home, like his trip today to New York.

The closer to home she drove, the more she reflected about their lives together. The years of teaching, writing, and production seemed worth it… most of the time. Either a person was cut out for academia, or they weren't. It seemed to be her path, and his. She knew with certainty that Billy Trieger was born to teach, he was in his element in front of a class or "audience" as he would say.

Billy achieved tenure in the School of Architecture after just seven years. Marie often wondered how much his father's sizeable contributions to the college helped along the way. To his credit, Billy was a charismatic, take-charge kind of guy, a trait that many admired. But the irony of returning home on this day to the congenial yet unfaithful man she had cohabitated with for well over a decade, gave her pause as she slowly drove on.

Neither wanted marriage, and from what she'd heard through friends and associates, Billy had taken great liberties with the monogamous promise they had initially made to each other. She didn't consider herself squeaky clean, not from having an affair, but because both of their careers meant more to them than they did to each other. For a while, this loose arrangement was what she wanted, but now the lack of real commitment seemed vacant and obtuse.

Being the mother of a high school senior was never easy—the worry for her safety, concerns about her future, and judgments she would make in life. But Camille had been the ideal daughter. Billy often reminded her that her daughter didn't have the flighty impetuousness that her artsy mother seemed to have. She was level-headed and grounded in ways that were unlike Marie. *Paul,* she thought…

Camille would spend the night with a friend tonight. Billy was due home around 6 pm from New York, and Marie hoped to surprise him with an early Valentine's dinner. He would have to fly back out to New York on Sunday, the actual day. Driving past the outskirts of Providence after work, she was anxious to slip off her shoes, grab a glass of wine, and cook a delicious dinner for Billy and her.

Billy was very easy on the eyes. Standing six-foot-two, wavy black hair with gray streaks, as he aged, he just got better looking.

She glanced at her aging hands on the steering wheel and wondered if Billy looked past what nature was doing to his once beautiful girl. The gray streaks in her blonde hair didn't add anything distinguished. As she drove along, the houses grew further apart, ironically mimicking their relationship. She was almost home.

After the death of her mother and her talk with Savannah, Marie had needed to leave Louisiana. It didn't take much for Billy to win her over after she came to that realization. When he'd asked her where her change in heart had come from, her response had been brutally honest, "I hoped you'd be my tour guide to lead me away from Louisiana." Billy had been the vehicle for her change, but not the catalyst.

She turned into the driveway, still trying to shut out thoughts of the past and enjoy this moment. Turning the car off, she grabbed the bag of groceries from the deli and mounted the stone steps to the front door. At the landing, she turned around to admire the wooded field across the road. It was beautiful here. She found herself whispering a prayer for an early spring as she pulled out her keys. To her surprise, she discovered that the door was already unlocked. *Billy, home already?*

As she stepped through the door, a shiver ran through her whole body. Directly ahead at the top of the stairs, stood Heather, one of her design interns. Completely naked, she was dumbfounded at the sight of Marie. Billy approached her from the upstairs hallway, also naked, and pressed himself against her, asking, "Why are you just standing here, baby, I was waiting for you?" Heather didn't answer him and only stared in the direction of the downstairs foyer. Billy looked down to see what Heather had.

This time, he'd gone too far.

44

FEBRUARY 14, 1999

SAVANNAH

Most women love Valentine's Day. For too many years, Savannah dreaded it. For years she had woken on this day with palpitations and feelings of ill-will. Not even the good that always came her way on this special day could displace her other feelings of angst and anticipation.

Unable to sleep, she quietly slipped from the bedroom, seeking the solitude of the early morning and a strong cup of coffee. While it perked, she sat on the patio, viewing the sun as it rose through the woods behind their comfortable home, outside Baton Rouge. *Someday,* she thought, *Valentine's Day might become special again.*

Savannah felt blessed with a tremendously loving and affectionate husband. He was not her problem with this special day. She knew, with certainty, that he would present her with roses and chocolate, along with a beautiful and thoughtful card. Her husband was the epitome of a great spouse and a wonderful father to their children.

Her problem on this day was her brother, Paul. He hadn't been so lucky, and after seventeen years, he still couldn't accept the loss of his wife, Marie. There was no doubt he would call again today because this was the twentieth anniversary of the day he and Marie had married. From the day she left him, and despite her affection for her brother, Savannah had been unsympathetic to his pain. Every year she woke early to begin a personal pep rally, hoping to change her tune and be kinder to Paul when he called. *Where is superhuman strength when you need it?*

Savannah typically loved the early mornings. Today she looked out her windows seeking solitude and could only visualize the trouble she would have holding her tongue when he called. She had never told her brother about her last phone conversation with Marie, the wife he refused to divorce. All these years, he remained married to a woman no one had seen or heard from in seventeen years. Paul didn't even know if she was alive. Savannah was willing to admit that the tone of voice she used during that last call, one that some might refer to as "screaming," may have had something to do with Marie leaving for good. Savannah was no dummy. She knew that Marie's call was just testing the waters before going back with Paul. *Over my dead body! Good riddance,* she thought.

All Savannah knew was that her brother epitomized the phrase, "Love is Blind". And now, another year had passed, and his anniversary threatened her sanity again.

When she woke this morning, she knew it wasn't a matter of *if*, but *when* he would call. The two of them remained best friends since childhood, and, at least in her mind, it was because of her that he also decided to pursue the profession of Law. *Her* degree carried more "sway", she'd told him. "Not just anyone is accepted to Tulane Law."

The truth was, Paul received nods from two schools; Tulane and L.S.U. After finishing Tulane undergrad, he chose to attend law school in Baton Rouge at L.S.U.

She was proud of her little brother. He chose a more noble path than the bread and butter, pay the bills type of law she and her husband practiced. Paul was selected to intern with the Governor's office while in school, writing briefs and appearing before the State Supreme Court, helping to overhaul antiquated Civil Rights Laws. Then, Tulane courted him back, hiring him as a Professor of Civil Law.

Although he would always be her little brother, he impressed her and the entire family with his ethics and love of teaching. Savannah recalled visiting one of Paul's lectures in the past, hearing him passionately impress on his students that, "Words, written in a legal document, can never take the place of helping those less fortunate around you with your own hands and heart. The fundamental meaning of civil rights is quite simple, *all people have the right to be treated civilly, and this right has no color or gender."*

She had seen it firsthand; he taught his students to be stewards of the law they create. He spoke to his students passionately, "Legally decreeing that a person has rights means nothing unless that person can feel the truth of it in their daily lives. We have a dual role in this world around us. We have the ability to change people's lives through the justice system, and we have the obligation in our personal lives to live what we profess."

Paul lived his life according to his own words. He took personal pride in helping his friends and neighbors, spreading not only the sweat equity of new paint but the warmth of goodwill. "Real civility happens one exchange at a time," she'd heard him say.

So, sipping on her coffee this morning, she prepared herself to eschew the civility that Paul demanded of himself when he called. Her problem was, for seventeen years, she'd been unable to speak calmly or politely with her brother in regards to Marie. She was still too angry.

Sometime today, the phone would ring, and her potential for real civility would very likely evaporate like many good intentions. The time would be the exact time that Paul and Marie were declared legally married, at 4:18 pm, February 14th. She could set her watch by it. Savannah knew what her proper response *should* be but also knew herself well enough to realize what would happen *again*. Like before, she would pick up the phone and listen while biting her tongue. When he came up for a breath, she knew she would be unable to hold back from repeating, "When are you going to move on with your life and file the divorce papers, brother?"

The coffee had just finished perking, and as she reached for a cup, the phone rang…

45

1,485 MILES – TWENTY YEARS

Shit, Savannah thought, *nobody calls this early on Sunday morning.*

Checking the caller I.D., *he's calling early today. At least I can get this over soon.*

She no longer looked forward to Valentine's Day for just this reason. Paul always called her on this day. And today was what would have been his twentieth anniversary.

Grabbing the portable phone cradled in her lap before it woke her family, Savannah said, "Hello? Paul?"

"Hi, Sis, I guess you know what day it is."

"What day, what planet, YES! But do you, brother? And pardon me for asking, but you've never called this early on your anniversary. Are you okay?"

There was no response.

Civility didn't even have a chance this morning. Savannah went straight for her brother's jugular, "Have you located that envelope yet? You've only had it for what, SEVENTEEN YEARS?"

"I'm sure it's around here somewhere, but I guess this is just my annual call to say that I'm not ready to open it. Did you realize this is the twentieth anniversary?"

"Yes. I can't tell you how long I've been dreading this day and your call. Hell, I just worry about *you*, Paul. Have you been on a date or anything? You're not getting any younger, you know. It's long past time for you to move on with your life!"

"I did go on a date."

Savannah held her breath. She couldn't believe what she'd just heard. This admission was a huge step for him. "I'm all ears, brother!"

"Do you remember Mrs. Morrisey, the nice lady down the street whose husband passed last fall?"

Savannah, having been reeled in, shook her head on the other end of the line and said nothing. Especially this morning, she regretted the inability to reach through the phone and strangle her little brother.

"Well," he said, "she and I went out for burgers and fries at the Walgreens down the street. She likes peach milkshakes almost as much as me!"

"Okay, enough of that dump truck load of crap. Twenty years of celibacy is an admirable milestone for monks, not for thirty-eight-year-old law professors! You need to put your hands on that packet and act! My kids are going to be in college before they ever have any cousins!"

"I still love her, Sis. I'm just not ready."

"I love you too, but one of these years, *if I have to continue to answer these painful calls*, I'm gonna finally figure a way to jump through this phone and rip one of your lungs out. You drive me crazy!"

They both laughed.

Speaking for only a short time this morning, Savannah admitted, "I need to change my attitude about your anniversary."

"That would be nice," he replied.

"Yep. I should look at this day differently, not as a day to dread, but to celebrate! This day marks another year of her being gone!"

"I love you too, Sis. Please tell everyone I miss them."

Savannah heard a dial tone.

The previous Friday, 1,485 miles away in Providence, Marie exited the house in shock immediately after finding Billy naked with a coed. The surprise caused her to drop the bag of groceries on the foyer floor, but that too was his mess to clean. Billie didn't follow her out. Even his audience obsession didn't allow him to be seen in public, naked.

She was happy to find her good friend, Dr. Maitlin, working hard in his office, and more than willing to console his best professor. Like a father, he listened, and when she finally calmed enough to listen, he recommended a plan. "Marie, you've mentioned before that you wanted to spend time with Camille, visiting colleges on a road trip together. I'm willing to bet that her school would agree to a few weeks off for her to check out some campuses. You have no worries here. I think it would be best for you should take a sabbatical. Take as much time as both of you need. We will be here for you when you return."

Marie thanked him as he walked with her to her car. On arrival, they hugged, and Dr. Maitlin added, "You might need another place to stay tonight." He dangled a key toward her in his outstretched fingers. "This key will open the visiting faculty suite here on campus. It's yours as long as you need it, Marie."

Dr. Maitlin was a gem. As he walked away, she got into her car and searched for her phone to see if Camille had tried to call. She still wasn't sure about this new texting thing but saw advantages tonight because a text wouldn't give away her shaky voice. There were seven text messages from Billy. She ignored them and began a text message to Camille, letting her know that she was working late at school and would be staying there overnight in the suite. It ended with, "Hope you're having a blast. I'm getting the urge to go on a college road trip with you soon, think it over, and let's make it happen! Love, Mom." Now all she needed was a toothbrush, soap, and Pinot Grigio. Just not in that order.

By the next night, Camille knew there was more to this than met the eye. The simple fact that her mother refused to go home spoke volumes. Marie went back to the house after Billy left on Sunday for clothes and necessary things, but refused to respond to his text messages or calls.

❧

Fifteen years ago, most of Paul's family stopped pressing him about the divorce. The packet, returned from Marie promptly, still sat under some clothes on the top shelf of his closet untouched.

Savannah was the lone holdout urging her brother to proceed legally. "It's not too late, Paul!" she'd say. She had been happily married for the last twelve years and had two children, Vanessa aged ten, and Robert, aka Junior, seven years old. She and her husband, Robert Perry, Sr., lived and practiced law together in Baton Rouge.

Paul loved being an uncle. He'd always loved kids. It was painful for Savannah to see him continue as a single man, having so much to offer a wife and children of his own.

But after Marie left, he'd not been the same. Not only did he refuse to move out of the home on Plum Street, but he ignored all his sister's recommendations about "brightening up" his space. Paul had said, "Those paintings still bring me such joy. I'm just not ready." Year after year, that remained his answer.

He rented the house to a tenant for the three years while he was in Baton Rouge, attending law school. The stipulation for the renter was to leave the paintings where they were.

Now, he'd been back for over ten years and had become an esteemed member of the Tulane Law Faculty. Speculation by co-workers swirled around him silently, concerning a wife identified only by a wedding band on his finger. For Paul, it was none of their business.

The twentieth anniversary of his marriage found him alone at home, as usual. Watching the afternoon sun fade over the fence in his back yard, he took the last sip of his beer at the kitchen table and decided to heed his sister's pleas finally and render a disposition to the unopened divorce papers. The sad thing was, he had no idea what possible good could come from opening that envelope.

As he stood to throw the bottle in the trash, he thought of the time Marie had made her mother's famous roasted chicken. The memory of that huge hen in the trash can caused him to burst out laughing. Looking back, even that had been a good time.

He'd done his best to stay busy over the years for at least one reason. It helped prevent self-pity. Tonight, he was due. He'd held up his end of the marriage, faithfully, and he had no idea where Marie was, much less who she was with now.

Paul found himself standing in front of his closet. The folder, barely visible under a pile of old clothes unmoved for years, slid into his hand with resistance. He sat on the bed and stared at his younger, more easily read handwriting, showing his address as the sender and the receiver.

Wow, he thought, *postage had really gone up over the years...*

The flap, barely sealed in place, quickly allowed his finger to slide underneath and reveal the pages inside. He pulled them out slowly. There, in the designated areas on both documents, was her signature. True to form, it surprised him that she'd signed it in another way also. Both pages were spotted and crinkled from long ago tears, sealed within. Looking closer, underneath her name on the divorce paper, she had written, "I want my other paintings back!"

Paul chuckled to himself, *After twenty years, she should know that possession is nine-tenths of the law.*

Holding onto the signed papers, he ceremoniously upended the envelope in the trashcan close to the bed. As he did, he heard a metallic clang at the bottom of the can. Looking in, he pulled the papers out of the trash, revealing a gold band with attached amethyst at the bottom, cast away by neglect, and now abandoned into the garbage, no different than Marie had done to their marriage.

It had been burdensome, holding on for so long to a memory. He remained emotionally starved every day. Life was passing him by, and holding on had grown harder by the day.

He reached in and picked the ring up. *Perhaps Royal Antiques would repurchase it.* He'd have to check that out the next time he was in the French Quarter.

46

A PAINTING COMES TO LIFE

The busy two-week trip south along the east coast left mother and daughter only four more days. Marie was feeling a time crunch to return Camille to school in Rhode Island.

Camille wasn't surprised to hear that Billy was history. Her mother was finally able to tell her that she wouldn't be going back to him when they returned. Camille acknowledged that although they never yelled or screamed at each other, they also didn't seem to be in love. She didn't know all the details but knew her mother wasn't happy with him.

Neither had been impressed with any of the schools they had seen so far. Yesterday, they had arrived in Tuscaloosa to visit the University of Alabama and returned to their hotel today after drawing another blank. Back in their hotel room, her mother discussed their need to return to Rhode Island. It would take two days to drive home from here, and neither was ready. Camille hadn't found a school she really liked, and her mother had no desire to face Billy.

Marie, suddenly resolute, made the call, "Sweetie, we need to get up early in the morning and start home. We both need to get back."

Anticipating an early start in the morning, they were in bed with the lights out by 9 pm. But sleep had other ideas. While talking through the darkness that separated their beds for the last hour, Camille had been trying to find the opportune moment to say what had really been on her mind. Then, her mother said, "Goodnight, baby, we'll talk more on the way home."

Marie knew that her daughter was wide awake, and like her, unready to return to Providence. Marie didn't know what was keeping Camille awake tonight, or that the real conversation was about to begin.

The darkness provided courage for Camille to broach a long-overdue conversation. "Mom? There's something else we need to talk about tonight."

"Okay, honey, what's up?"

Darkness amplified the silence until Camille gained the courage to begin. She realized the weight of the words she was about to unload. Despite how many times she had practiced them, they flowed from her lips with a life all their own. "*Mom, you need to listen to me now*. You are a wonderful mother and have been there for me every step of my life, *except one.*"

Camille had Marie's full attention. The moment she had feared was finally upon them as she took advantage of the seconds it took for Camille to take a deep breath. Responding with words that compounded her denial, "What are you trying to say, Camille?"

"Well, you must have tried so hard to find such a stellar man as Billy to be my replacement father! Is it true that in your generation, they put plastic trinkets in boxes of cereal? Is that where you found him? For seventeen years, you and he have tried to play grownup together. Well, I'm here to say, it's not enough! I deserve a mother who will be honest with me. I'm no longer a baby! I have a right to know the circumstances of how I came into this world!

"Surely this person that you barely even acknowledge as a sperm donor had a name! Maybe you should change your name to 'Mary?' You know, the second one in history to experience immaculate conception? Mom, I've tried to be patient because I know you have been going to counseling for as long as I can remember, and I've wondered if it had something to do with my dad. I'm old enough to know and understand that there is something you're not telling me, and I'm old enough for the truth *now*."

Dead silence surrounded them. Marie knew this day would come. Her counselor had encouraged her to talk to Camille long before now, and she should never have waited this long. There was never going to be a perfect time to inform Camille of moments she had tried so hard to forget; moments of guilt, pain, and heartache. Marie began to sob.

Camille spoke again, somewhat surprised that her passionate plea hadn't chipped a hole in the emotional barrier her mother guarded. "I know more than you realize, Mom. One day, I was looking for something in the garage, and I came across a cardboard tube with a painting in it. It was a painting of you when you were younger, standing with a handsome man in front of a run-down looking place called Talulah's. Was that in New Orleans?"

"Yes, it was."

"Well, I wondered if that good-looking man in your painting *might* be my Dad?"

Camille allowed no time for a response before she fired another volley, "The librarian in school helped me do an online search in the library. I was able to find my birth certificate. Everything on it was as I expected, except for one thing. In the place that listed the name of my father, it said 'Father Unknown'. It made me angry to see that. Why would you have told them that?"

Marie sat up and turned on the light between their beds. She leaned against the headboard with her eyes closed and arms folded, remaining resolutely silent as if meditating.

Camille began to cry now as she yelled, *"No, Mom. You can't do this to me! I have a right to know who my father is! You should have told me before now. I'm not going anywhere else with you until you tell me the truth!"*

The only response heard from her mother was whimpering.

After a few minutes, Camille, now dry-eyed, turned out the light between them and rolled over, away from her mother.

In a few moments, Camille felt the edge of the bed next to her move. Her mother had gotten out of bed and moved to hers, sitting as close to her as she could. A monotone voice said, "Dr. Sechler warned me not to put this day off for so long. 'It isn't fair to your daughter,' she'd said. But of all the things that she helped me to learn about myself, the hardest to face was the reality of who I was at the time I found out I was pregnant with you. I'm not that person anymore, Camille, but that is the person who will be judged the day I introduce you to your father. I was a selfish young girl who put her career ahead of not only my husband but your best interests."

Camille rolled back to face her mother, pleading, "But Mom, everyone changes! If my father is a good person, he'll understand!"

"I'm not so sure. There is much more to my guilt, Camille. You know the dragonfly necklace that I wear every day, and the dragonfly logo I sign my paintings with?"

"Yes."

"You had an older brother. I adopted the dragonfly as my signature because one hovered close to your brother one day."

"*What?* Where is he? I need to meet him too… *what do you mean… 'had'?*"

"His name was Ernie, and he was a miracle baby. He survived a premature birth, and during his delivery, I almost bled to death. That's something we need to talk about more another time, something that might be a concern for you someday too."

"Okay…" Camille said softly.

"When I found out I was pregnant, I was resentful from that moment. I resented your father, Paul, the baby Ernie, and especially the future that I wanted, forced to be placed on hold, *indefinitely*. My pregnancy was unplanned, and your father and I were not yet married. Joyous events that I had envisioned happening at the right time and in the right way, played out in terrible ways I never imagined. I was too immature, emotionally, and completely unprepared for Ernie, your father, or marriage."

Camille waited patiently as her mother hesitated.

Tonight, the truth became impossible to restrain as she and Camille arrived at this intersection of raw emotions. *Now, my lips must cooperate,* Marie thought. Her heart felt lighter from the mere thought of her next words that began to flow as she looked her adolescent daughter in the eyes, "At two months of age, Ernie, your brother, died in his crib from Sudden Infant Death Syndrome. After all these years, I still grieve his loss. Closure for me was almost impossible because, for many years, I blamed myself for his death. I never wanted to run away from your father. I was trying to run away from my own guilt."

Marie was emotionally spent. She had finally released her tsunami of pain, but now worried for the person in its path. Silence flooded the room, and each passing moment intensified her fear that her storm would seek more destruction. She glanced over and Camille's face was turned away and unresponsive.

More needed to be released, holding back was impossible now. Into the silence, Marie continued, "For many years, I blamed myself. Even worse, I used his death as my excuse to move on with my life and obtain the coveted career that seemed so precious to me. I made the choice to leave your father, Camille. That is *all* on me. He is a good, kind man, and I have done him, and you, a grave injustice by running away. I made a conscious decision to keep your father out of your life, to remove all reminders of what happened. I know now that keeping you from your father was a tremendously selfish move, made by a woman whose emotional growth died the day your brother died. I am so sorry for what I have done."

Camille looked horrified and angrier than before.

Her mother couldn't stop now, saying, "Through lots of counseling and discussion with medical experts, I've been able to release most of the guilt about Ernie's death. The part that has been even harder was coming to terms with my selfishness concerning your birth. Your father's name is Paul Morel. I've not spoken to him or his family since before you were born. I tried to hide this information from you intentionally, thinking I would never again have to face your father or my shame. Your father probably won't even speak to me now, after what I've done. I'm hoping that someday, at least you will forgive me."

Camille held her hand over her mouth in shock as her eyes flooded with tears. Mother and daughter cried separately.

Barely able to speak, she said, *"Mama, how could you?"*

Her daughter had just asked the one question that Marie could never justify. Dr. Sechler had told her that the only way was to forgive herself first.

Marie needed to finish this now. With a distant voice, displaced by time, she looked blankly at the wall and continued, "Shortly after Ernie died, I left your father. I didn't even tell him I was leaving. *I just left.* I didn't care at all about his feelings, and wouldn't for the longest time."

"So where in the world did I come from?" Camille asked.

"The doctor that saved my life when Ernie was born told us that it was improbable I could ever become pregnant again. After I left your father and transferred to L.S.U., I agreed to a visit requested by him. He had called stating he wanted to see me and take me to dinner, and we both agreed to a platonic visit. He didn't pressure me in any way, and I repressed my feelings that knew he wanted me back. From the moment he picked me up, your father was a perfect gentleman. It was me that kept ordering more beer at dinner, and one thing led to another. What happened that night was not something either of us intended. It was me that sent out mixed signals. When I woke the next morning in his motel room, I was so upset with myself that I lashed out at him.

"The thing I regret the most is that I blamed what happened on your father, but it wasn't his fault at all. It was cruel for me to give your father false hopes, then rip them away again. He didn't deserve that. We both said things, hurtful things, and I vowed never to go back, even after learning I was pregnant. Billy allowed me the opportunity to move far away."

Accusingly, Camille blurted, "Are you telling me you never made *any* effort to contact my father?"

Marie stood and went to the sink in the bathroom to get a glass of water. When she returned, she sat in a chair close to the bed.

"Dr. Sechler and I spent many sessions working through this. She helped me to understand that I really *did* try. I just tried the wrong way. The doctor helped me to see that my effort was with the wrong person. You see, I was afraid to contact your father, so I contacted his fiercely loyal sister, Savannah."

"Jeez, Mom! Is that where my beautiful middle name came from? Some crazy aunt who kept me from ever meeting my own father?"

"Everything Savannah said to me, I deserved. And it was exactly that passionate devotion to your father that made me want to give you her name. I hope someday you can meet her. I'm not sure she will ever speak to me again."

Camille remained silent, finally appearing more contemplative than upset. Marie could only imagine how overwhelming this was for her to hear tonight. Turning to face her mother again, Camille asked, "Do you even know where my father is?"

"No, honey. I'm sorry to say I don't. He had wanted to go to law school, but I have no idea where he would have gone after I left. I hope you can meet him someday, but please understand that when you do, he is probably married and could have other children."

"I know, Mom." Trying to sound upbeat, she added, "We are so close to New Orleans, and I'd hoped we'd have time to see Tulane University. From what you've said before, it was always your favorite school."

Marie stood and walked over to Camille's bed. She placed her cupped hands on the sides of Camille's face, pulling her close to kiss her forehead. "Honey," she said, "we just don't have enough time left to go there. We need to get back. I need to find us a new place to live, and you need to finish your school year." Marie sat her glass on the credenza and slipped back under the sheets of her bed.

Confidently, Camille moved to her mother's bed and said, "I think we can make this work! Let's drive to New Orleans tomorrow, and on Sunday, I can fly home, and you can take your time driving back to Rhode Island. Felicity is my best friend, and her family could pick me up at the airport in Providence, and I could just stay with them!"

Marie thought for a moment. *Dr. Maitlin's granddaughter, Felicity, also attends Camille's high school, and Camille could probably stay with them. It might work...*

"Get some sleep, my princess, we're heading in one of two directions in the morning after I make some phone calls. Okay? No promises..."

"That sounds great, Mom. Thank you. And thank you too for finally being honest with me. I know that wasn't easy for you, either."

"I love you with all my heart, sweetie. Thank you for being my daughter. We'll do our best to find your dad together. Please try to bear with me a little longer. This won't be easy for me, but if I could, I'd move the world for you."

47
TULANE

The next morning, everything worked. Dr. Maitlin's son, Phil, said they'd be happy to pick her up at the airport and provide a place to stay.

Marie called and made the plane reservations for Camille, and shortly after 3 pm, they approached the offramp to St. Charles Avenue.

The further they went on St. Charles, the more excited Camille became. "Mama! This is the most beautiful place!" Camille was in awe as they drove past streetcars and stately homes covered in ivy.

"Maybe we could ride a streetcar later today or tomorrow," Marie said. "Before we go to the campus, I'd like to take you to a special place that was a refuge for us, not far away."

They passed the university and turned into Audubon Park. Camille was speechless at the beauty that resided within an easy walk from campus. As they slowly drove along, Marie glanced without comment at the tree she and Paul had called their own.

Camille exclaimed, "There is even a zoo? This place is incredible, Mom!"

Marie was unprepared for the flood of emotion that attempted to overwhelm her. Memories, long suppressed, flooded her mind as the nearly unchanged scenes before them reminded her of the man who shared them with her. She was happy that her daughter's eyes were so preoccupied; she knew her face showed her emotions like a beacon on a moonless night.

Later, as they toured the campus, Marie pointed out her dorm room window in passing, but did not comment except to say that "the rooms are comfortable and quiet, most of the time."

Without a formal declaration, it was evident that Tulane excited Camille like no other school had. She felt a good vibe from the university and friendly students she met.

It had been a long day, and they were both getting hungry. When they arrived at their car, Marie said, "It's a long shot, but if this bakery shop is still in business, and hasn't sold all its goods yet today, we might be able to get something sweet to take back to the hotel."

"This wouldn't be that bakery in your painting, would it?"

"Sure is. Talulah's Pie. The best baked pies I have ever had."

There was a feeling of anonymity Marie felt from the passage of so many years. *If Talulah's is even still there, surely it has changed hands,* she thought. There was little concern about meeting anyone from Marie's past as they pulled away from campus. Those people were probably as long gone from here as she was. Part of her hoped that the bakery closed for good. That would allow complete closure of that chapter.

Marie drove down St. Charles to where it met South Carrollton, then exited left toward River Road. After a few blocks, she turned her car into the gravel lot she knew so well from the past. Abruptly, she slid to a stop as the sight before her eyes took her breath away.

"Mama, are you okay?" Camille asked.

Without a comment, Marie opened her door, exited, and stood gawking at the house in front of her.

"It's so beautiful..." Marie said. "Camille, you wouldn't believe how much this bakery has changed. It's incredible. It looks just the way I'd imagined it."

Camille had absolutely no idea what she was talking about. She was also out of the car now and standing next to her mother. They both gazed at the bright yellow shop in front of them. It stood out like a diamond in the rough. Marie told her how years ago, this shotgun house had been vacant of any vegetation. Now, they both saw beautiful flowers sprouting all around it.

Marie started to sniffle, and Camille asked her what was wrong.

"It's nothing, honey. Your Dad and I came here regularly for a while. This place was not nearly as nice looking all those years ago. Someone has really fixed it up. In fact, it looks exactly..." Marie hesitated, saying, "It looks incredibly nice, now."

"You're right; it is much prettier now than that painting I saw in the garage back home!"

Marie couldn't believe her eyes. It looked *exactly* like the painting she had done for Paul. The one in which she imagined how Talulah's could look if given the proper T.L.C.

Still, in awe, Marie continued, "Well, anyway, a sweet lady named Talulah, owns it or used to, and she baked the most wonderful pies."

Marie looked around in all directions, then back at the door. "It looks like they're closed, I'm afraid we've gotten here too late. I'm sorry, Camille. Guess we better get going."

As they returned to the car, they were startled by the sound of the latch from the upper door. Marie turned around and couldn't believe her eyes. It was Talulah, looking out over the door, casting a suspicious eye toward her parking lot.

Talulah's previously jet-black hair was gray now, her face appearing even rounder than before. Behind her stood a younger woman looking over her shoulder.

Then came a familiar voice, "You peoples be sightseeing in the wrong place, and your car messin' up my gravel! This ain't no place for cars anyhow! Now go ahead on where you come from, Talulah be closed till tomorrow."

She had a chance to leave and maintain anonymity, but something inside her wouldn't allow it. Marie, standing by her car door, called back, "Talulah... it really is you... it's so nice to see you again, I..."

Then Marie received a second chance as she heard, "Lady, I don't know who you is..." Talulah glanced briefly at their Rhode Island license plate before adding, "but we is closed, and it been another *long* day, so we say, goodnight. If you wants pie, leave your car somewhere else and get in line like the other peoples after 3 pm any day but the Sabbath! Now, y'all have a good night."

And with that, Talulah shut the door, a door that Marie knew better than to interfere. "Maybe we could come back tomorrow," she said to Camille as they walked toward their car. "The pie here is outstanding!"

"Did you know that woman, Mom?"

"Yes, but she must not have recognized me. It was probably best that she didn't."

Marie was so surprised to see Talulah when she opened the door that she had almost blown her anonymity. A trip down memory lane was no comparison with the chocolate pie, which she could practically taste. "We'll do our best to try again tomorrow," she said as they pulled out of the lot.

In about thirty minutes, they arrived at the Riverside Hilton, which connected to a long indoor walking mall along the Mississippi River. From there, they browsed in shops and ate a dinner of delicious crab cakes while looking at the river traffic through huge glass windows. There, they discussed their plans for the next day.

Baton Rouge was a day trip away, so they decided to wake early in the morning for the seventy-mile drive to see one more college. Marie wanted Camille to visit the L.S.U. Campus before returning home. With the early start, they hoped to return to Talulah's by 3 pm.

The next day, they saw as much of the sprawling campus as they could, including Mike the Tiger, L.S.U.'s famous mascot. Camille was impressed with what she saw, and again found delightful students eager to answer questions.

On the walk back to the car, Camille mentioned that she preferred the smaller campus at Tulane. Her mother wasn't surprised because it was that same thing that attracted her to Tulane years before. Camille was impressed with L.S.U., but Tulane was still her favorite.

The traffic was light, allowing a speedy trip back to New Orleans. They drove directly to the exit at South Carrolton, which would lead them to Talulah's. They would arrive right on time for what Marie called "the possibility of pie".

Camille's response to the second day of *possibility* was incredulous. "What do you mean, 'possibility'? Are you telling me that we might go there again and still not get a pie? Who could run a business like that?"

"All I can say is that Miss Talulah does something to her pie that, to my knowledge, has never been duplicated. It's like tasting a piece of heaven. As soon as it touches your tongue, the goodness melts into your soul. Wait until you taste one, then you'll understand."

"You mean *if* I taste one?" Camille chirped, as they both laughed.

Marie parked a few blocks away in a residential area, only to find an already formed line at Talulah's. She scanned the people ahead of them, curious to see if Bea was here. She was an older woman when they'd met, years ago, but as determined to get pie as she was old. Bea remained a beautiful memory.

Stepping into line, they both took a deep breath. They hadn't stopped moving since before daybreak, and both were relieved to be in this gravel lot.

"Mama, what flavor is your favorite?" Camille asked as she peered around the people ahead, trying to see the menu.

Her mother replied, "The chocolate is to die for! I can't even remember trying another flavor. So that's the direction I'm headed!"

Camille turned toward her mother and said, "Flavor alert, Mom, I believe you're going to have to broaden your horizon today. I don't see chocolate on the board!"

With a flare of panic, Marie focused on the menu ahead of them and, sure enough, found no chocolate. But that wasn't the only change. The list seemed to be serving a hefty dose of revenge. Not only was chocolate missing from the bottom, but in a prominent spot at the top of the menu was Paul's favorite, *Peach.*

Suddenly, the top door opened as Talulah began to sing her trademark song, her lyrics just as beautiful as the very first night:

"Come and see Talulah,
In the evening every night!
Come and see Talulah,

You can't only take one bite!
Oh, come and get a warm pie,
Till your belly says, 'No more!'
Oh, come and see Talulah,
As my pies, come cross, the door!"

Camille was like a child in Disney World; her eyes were so full. "Mama," she said, "Her voice is as beautiful as you'd said!"

Clearly, they heard Talulah bellow, "NEXT!"

It wasn't long until they stood at the front of the line. Talulah glanced at Marie only briefly as she applied powdered sugar to more pies. She placed the shaker down and looked back with a more skeptical eye at the previous night's parking lot culprit. Her eyes weren't as good as they used to be, but there was something very familiar about this woman. With her usual haste, she blurted, "Glad you found another place to park, 'Rhode Island'. What pie you want?"

Marie's false-hope took over, as she replied, "Well, Miss Talulah, I really would like one of your chocolate…"

From the back of the line, somewhere, they heard, "Talulah ain't got no chocolate, lady, *it ain't on the sign!"*

"Child, I ain't had no chocolate 'round here for years. You best pick somthin' else a'fore these peoples behind you gets upset!"

Marie couldn't look at Talulah. She stared at the porch floor and, with hesitation, said, "Peach then. I'd like to try your peach, please."

Talulah turned and asked, "How 'bout you, Missy?"

Camille looked at Talulah with her usual sweet smile and said, "Strawberry, Miss Talulah, I'd like a Strawberry for here and one to go."

Those words, and the way she spoke them, caused Talulah to stop, dead still, as she studied Camille. It was like she'd seen a ghost. She was frozen. It was then that Talulah knew who 'Rhode Island' was. She had also seen Paul's kind eyes in the face of his child.

What was happening was uncomfortable enough for Camille, but not near as much as for her mother.

Slowly, Talulah turned toward Marie, leaned across the door, and said firmly, "Paul ain't tell me 'bout no daughter, Marie. He don't know, do he?"

Marie was on the verge of tears once again. Miraculously, she held them back to say, "We can wait around for a little while, maybe until you finish serving. We could talk more then."

Talulah turned to her side behind the door and said, "Delilah, takes the lady's money." Then she focused out into the line and yelled, "NEXT!"

Delilah stepped up to the door. She was beautiful. Handing Marie the bag, she said, "That'll be five dollars, please."

Marie handed her the money, as she said, "Haven't you grown into a gorgeous woman! It's been so long; I hope you've been well!"

"Yes, ma'am, I'm married now and have two children. I work full time with my momma, and ever since I got my GED, I work at the hospital some too."

"Oh," Marie said, "you got your GED! That's great, Delilah. Congratulations!"

"I couldn't have done it without Mr. Paul's help, ma'am. And even better, Mr. Paul is tutoring Mama, and she's just about a year away from getting hers!" Delilah looked at Camille and said, *"You're a lucky girl to have a father like Mr. Paul."*

It was too much for Marie. As the years of running away suddenly smacked her squarely in the face, she allowed embarrassment to surface. Her smile evaporated, and curtly she said, "Thanks, Delilah, tell your mother we'll try to stick around for a little while. Come on, Camille, we're just in the way up here."

Marie was sweating. She didn't know what to do now. All the guilt built up for two decades assaulted her as she walked away from Talulah's door.

They stopped at the edge of the lot close to River Road. Trying to avoid the present and the past, Marie fumbled in the bag to find that Camille's pies were on top. She handed one to Camille, who was being way too quiet. The peach pie pulled from the bottom of the bag bore a pinky finger crust edge, obviously stolen from chocolate. Not only did

Talulah remove chocolate from her menu, but she gave its crust to peach. Marie was personally insulted.

They both took a bite. Camille remained quiet as she devoured her pie.

It didn't take Marie long to figure out why Paul liked the peach pie. It melted in her mouth.

As good as the pie was, it fell into a stomach that had turned into a knot the moment Talulah confronted her about Camille. With every passing second, Marie became more intimidated while waiting for Talulah.

Shortly after finishing her pie, she looked at Camille and said, "I'm tired, sweetie, unless they finish soon, let's just go back to the hotel, okay?"

Camille, incredulous, said, "*Oh no, you don't.* You can't do that now. It's time, Mom. It's *past time* for me to meet my real father. He sounds delightful whenever anyone speaks about him."

A few moments passed, and from behind, they heard an out-of-breath voice…

"I've always wanted a daughter."

48
THE LOST EGG

Delilah had immediately called Paul. He was sitting at his kitchen table, prepping for his classes for the coming week.

As her name appeared on the caller I.D., Paul didn't hesitate to pick up. He had worried about Talulah for a while. She had suffered what the doctors called a "small" heart attack earlier this year, but she hadn't allowed it to slow her down. He hoped she was okay and answered his phone quickly.

"Hello, Paul?" inquired a frantic sounding Delilah, "you need to come to the bakery right away."

"Is it your mother? Is she okay?"

"No, Paul, Mama is fine. I'm calling you about Marie."

"WHO?"

"It's Marie, Paul. She's here... *now*... in the gravel parking lot by the road. You've got to come right away!"

There was silence from Paul's end. Then, Delilah heard a shuffling noise in the background before the call went dead. She continued to speak into the silence out of frustration, "Did you hear me? You need to come right away. I'm not sure how long she... or the person that's with her will be here."

He hadn't heard the part about the other person. Paul was already in his car speeding down South Carrollton Avenue, ignoring posted limits and blaring his horn at every vehicle in an intersection that might pull out in his way.

In a few short minutes, he pulled over a block away from Talulah's and ran the distance to her parking lot.

He scanned the lot quickly to find Marie talking to a young girl. Approaching from behind, he overheard their conversation as he approached. He had not yet heard the girl's name, but did listen to her call Marie "*Mom.*"

How is that possible?

He also overheard that this young girl sought her *father.* His head spun from the death-defying drive here, and shortness of breath from running. So many unpleasant surprises had happened with Marie that Paul had no expectations of what was or what could be.

Words, filled with new hope, spilled from his lips like an arrow from the bow of a starving hunter as he responded to what the young girl had said. With his confession from behind them, he still wondered, *Could this be my daughter?*

Marie turned toward his voice and began to ball like a baby. He felt his arms involuntarily encircle his long-lost wife.

Is this just a dream?

Marie spoke as quickly as her raw emotions would allow. Paul heard words that only minutes before he could not have imagined.

"Paul, I'd like to introduce you to Camille Savannah Landry. She is your daughter."

Each held the other as they turned to face Camille, who, already in tears, dove to embrace her father.

They stood together as their eyes baptized the resurrection of three hearts. When they slowly parted, still holding each other's hands, who did they see but Talulah and Delilah, standing close and waiting patiently. Holding out their hands toward them, the new family included them in their circle as Talulah and Delilah started to sing, "I Know the Lord Will Make A Way."

Others standing by in the gravel lot began to sing this beautiful old gospel song. Talulah's voice was strong and confident, as she and the others sang:

"I know the Lord will make a way,
Yes, He will!
He'll make a way for you,
He will lead you safely through,
I know the Lord will make a way…"

When they finished, Talulah approached Marie and said, "Welcome back, Miss Marie. Won't you please stop by jus' a bit more often? Y'all have a beautiful girl."

She and Delilah turned to walk back to the Dutch door, which was fully open, top, and bottom. Others commented that this was the first time anyone could remember the bottom door open. Talulah and her daughter disappeared inside to close the shop for the night.

It's not possible to flip a switch after twenty years. Time doesn't stand still, and we can never return to any lost minute. Each new day has possibilities, as Paul found out tonight. He wouldn't let time lost keep him from relishing every new moment. The three remained in the parking lot for over an hour talking, long after others were gone. Mostly, the focus was on Camille tonight, and Paul showed genuine interest in her search for a college. It delighted him to hear of the possibility that she would attend Tulane. In time, he hoped to hear more about Marie's accomplishments in Design.

Before parting, Camille invited Paul to be present with them the next day to see her off at Louis Armstrong International Airport.

"If it's okay with your mother, I'd love to go with you."

"Sure!" Marie said, "That sounds like a great idea; we can pick you up. All we need is your address."

He couldn't believe his good fortune. Smiling at Marie, he said, "Have you forgotten where we used to live?"

"No way, Paul. You still live in our… I mean *the* house on Plum Street?"

"Sure do!"

"Wow. That makes finding you easier than I thought. We'll honk the horn at 9 am."

"Wonderful," he said.

As Marie watched Paul and Camille interacting, she was in awe of the benevolence of this man after everything she'd put him through. He seemed to hold no grudge and genuinely appreciated their presence. It was as though they had always been there with him. As if Marie and his daughter had left for just a day, shopping, or to a movie. None of them could deny the extraordinary thing that happened tonight, unforeseen, yet cherished.

They parted with hugs and tears.

❧

The next morning, mother and daughter picked him up on time. Arriving at the gate, Marie hugged Camille goodbye first. Then she watched her daughter hesitate even longer in the arms of her father, and overheard as they each promised to see each other soon. Camille walked into the jetway with a full heart.

Walking back to the car, Marie wondered if the boom would drop now that Camille wasn't present. She knew she deserved the worst that Paul might summon. What happened instead was another surprise. She quickly realized that this kind, mature man refused to allow the past to ruin even a minute of his future. For the first time in her adult life, Marie recognized how much he still loved her. And it was then that she noticed something that surprised her even more. *She had never loved anyone as much as him*. There was no better feeling she could imagine.

Paul had no idea what was running through Marie's mind and had no plans to press her in any way. He was happy for today and didn't ask any personal questions.

As they drove down Interstate 10 into town, Marie looked over at Paul's left hand, resting on his thigh, and said, "When I first saw that band on your finger, I thought you had remarried. But that is the ring from our marriage, isn't it?"

He looked at her and smiled. "Yes, it is."

"What kept you from remarrying after our divorce?" she asked.

Smiling even broader, "A married man can't remarry, Marie. It's not legal. I never divorced you."

"But the papers, Paul… I signed them and sent them back to you as you requested…"

"I never opened the envelope until our recent anniversary, Marie. I hope I don't upset or offend you by saying that I never gave up hope."

Marie was stunned. A car beside her honked as she absent-mindedly drifted into the adjacent lane.

"Want me to drive, Marie?"

Ignoring him, her curiosity took over, "Surely you've dated then… don't try to tell me there's not some young, attractive, *opposite of me* out there somewhere?"

"Nope. Married men don't date others."

Speechless now, Marie drove on in silence. As they pulled up in front of the house, Marie shut the engine off as they sat quietly. She still had no idea what to say.

Soon, Paul asked, "When are you heading north?"

"Probably in the morning."

"Why don't you come back later for dinner? I can check and see if Talulah and Delilah would like to come?"

A voice in Marie's head was screaming at her, *Say yes, you fool! Do it now!*

"That sounds wonderful, Paul, and thank you, but I'm going to get an early start."

"Well at least come in for a minute, you can leave whenever you want. Just two old married friends, hanging out for a little while? I promise you, I don't have more than two beers in the fridge. What do you say?"

Paul had stirred Marie's emotions thoroughly, causing an instantaneous cascade of guilt-filled reflection. In a heartbeat, just behind her lips, two answers waged a fierce battle with one another.

Fearing the outcome, she hesitated, hoping the victor would represent her sincere wish. The last day had been unbelievable. This man, whose life she had devastated, never gave up on her. He never gave up on love. She still didn't know whether she could start over; whether *they* could start over.

A wonderfully warm shiver expanded throughout her body, as her answer became obvious. Love is the most powerful emotion. "Okay," she said, "just for a few minutes."

"Great," he said. Paul exited the car, ran around, and opened Marie's door. She took a deep breath at the front door and found it was easier to walk in than she expected.

Standing in the living room, Marie transported back 20 years as she gazed at her artwork, still on the walls where she had left it. The vacant spot remained where she had removed the one painting. Without a comment about that, she walked over to the impressionistic painting she had done of Talulah's bakery, showing the bright yellow paint, beautiful flowers and plants.

"This one…" she pointed at the painting, "did Talulah use this as a reference for painting the real shop?"

"No. She didn't, but I did. I got some of the local businesses like the Camellia Grill, and others to chip in some money for paint and materials a few years ago, and Clarence and I did the work. Not bad, don't you think?"

"I was floored when I saw it. It is beautiful now." Marie continued to look at him, her eyes filled with unanswered questions.

"Is there something else you want to ask?" Paul inquired.

"I sure do. Something has really been gnawing at me. I'd also like to know whose idea it was to get rid of chocolate pie? Oh… and to add peach?"

"I seem to recall that you had more to do with that change than I did. Talulah was pretty upset with you. If you need more clarification, I'm sure she'd be happy to fill you in." As he started to walk away, he said, "I'm going to the kitchen for a beer, would you like one?"

"Yes, thank you."

"Okay, then. Why don't you come out to the kitchen and we'll sit? I have something to show you."

As they entered the kitchen, Paul pulled out a chair for her and said, "Sit here; it's the best seat for the show."

He went over to the fridge and pulled out two bottles of Dixie beer, opened them, and sat down opposite her.

"Cheers!" Paul held his beer out for a toast, "Here's to a chance visit I never expected!"

Marie clanged her bottle against his and said, "Was that just a line, or is there really a show visible from this seat?"

"Look out the window… see that nest in the crotch of that branch about ten feet up?"

Paul pointed at a conifer nearby in the back yard as Marie leaned toward him to see.

"Yes, I see it. Is that a baby's head sticking up?"

Paul took a swig of beer, then said, "Yep. In all the years I've lived here, I've never seen a Purple Finch. That's their nest. They are beautiful birds, and they'll come into view soon. Several weekends ago, I sat here and watched the female build that tightly weaved nest. Her mate brought her supplies, but she did it all herself. They mate for life, Marie."

"Wow, Paul. Is there just the one baby?"

"There were two. Not long after they finished the nest, I saw the mother begin to sit in it. I watched for a while and noticed that she would leave for a little while now and then. So, I positioned a ladder close by, and one time when she flew off, I peeked. There were two eggs in the nest. A few days later, I looked out while I was eating breakfast, and she was sitting on her nest as usual, but something caught my eye in the grass beneath her. When I walked out, I saw that there was a broken egg on the ground under the nest. She had lost one, and only God knows why."

Easing back in her chair, she took a sip of beer, then looked through the window again to say, "For Ernie, we didn't even have our nest ready. We were both just baby birds ourselves."

Paul could no longer hold back. He reached out for her hand to say,

"Maybe you and I can still be like these Purple Finches anyway? It's said, Marie, that sightings of a Purple Finch symbolize brighter days ahead. And, like them, we still have a baby in our nest to care for."

Neither had any other place at this moment that they would rather be. Their beers were long gone as they continued to discuss the positive things that happened in their lives since they last saw each other. Marie's passion for art had blossomed in the field of design, and she too loved to teach. She showed Paul pictures from her phone of some of her personal creations, and awards from her peers.

Paul spoke of his own passions. "I learned that one should never underestimate the effect of the ripples."

Marie remembered that word. "Ripples," she said, "wasn't that another Talulah-ism? I remember you telling me about that after you visited Delilah when she was in Charity Hospital."

"Yes," Paul said, "That was one of many wise things I learned from Talulah. Everything we say or do can have a ripple effect on those around us. Good or bad.

"Talulah taught me far more than I ever could have taught her," Paul recalled. "If you and I hadn't ignored stereotypes and kept an open mind, we never could have come to the place we are now. Talulah may not have had the benefit of formal education, but she has been one of the most positive influences in my life. She generated so many good ripples around me as I watched how she dealt with significant hurdles, one step at a time. She overcame so much with so little. Those lessons took hold in my life and helped me to transform the lives of many others. Whenever I teach my lectures on civil rights, I send out ripples of my own, and have watched as my graduates left to spread more."

"It appears that you've turned many things around, Paul. Talulah's shop is beautiful now, and that is spreading out in all directions in her neighborhood."

"Her pies symbolize much more than sweet goodness, Marie. Each one is a nugget of 'Community.' She fills her pies with little pieces of her heart, each bite capable of bringing a smile to people's faces. She also shares beautiful music that livens their souls."

Marie nodded her agreement. "You mean just like she and Delilah did that day at Ernie's funeral."

"Yes," he said. "There is something we can all learn from one another if we only listen. Have you ever noticed the difference between the faces of children and many adults? Children are amazed at what they see every time they open their eyes, and it shows on their faces. Think of the adults you meet each day, and how weary some look. Where did their enthusiasm go? So many adults go through their days with a mask of hurt. If we let it, life will quickly take away our joy. I've made my choice. I like to smile."

Paul looked out the window. The Purple Martin father was on the nest, feeding the chick. He looked at Marie, who was smiling as she also watched.

He said, "She gave me a wonderful Talulah-ism one day after you left. I was in such a bad place, with that, and Ernie's death. She said, "There is nothing that God will put in your path that you can't handle, Paul Morel. All you must do is try to put one foot ahead of the other, and you'll get where you want to go. So, Marie Landry, I've waited for you to return, one day at a time."

These words from Paul carried such an emotional charge that Marie couldn't respond.

They continued to sit quietly a while longer. The avian parents intermittently returned to their ever-hungry offspring. Paul wrote his cellphone number on a pad and pushed it across the table to Marie.

After this exchange, it was time for Marie to leave. Paul walked her to the door, where they shared a long embrace.

Marie whispered in his ear, "I'm just so sorry, Paul. When I've thought of the things I needed to say to you if we ever met again… I…"

"Hold on, Marie. If you're going to bring up the past, then I've got something to chip in."

A large part of Marie still waited for the boom to drop. Guilt is hard to shake. She held her breath.

He released her so he could reach into the pocket of his shirt. Grasping something tightly, he said, "Hold out your hand, please."

Marie held out a nervous palm.

Into it, Paul placed a small object. Curling her fingers over it, he continued to hold her hand with his and said, "The miner of the metal in your hand found a gift from the earth that made him smile. What he found could have been thousands or even millions of years in the making. With what he found, the miner made enough money to feed his family, as did the jeweler that turned it into what you hold. A series of events, impossible to predict, led us to this ring before and now. What you hold in your hand has the greatest potential it has ever had. What you do with it is yours and yours alone to decide."

Marie opened her hand to find her wedding band. She leaned forward and kissed his lips.

49

FILLING THE VOID

As she drove away, he felt the uncertainty return, as fear and doubt began to cloud his thoughts. If there was anything Paul had learned in law school, it was that sometimes, after making the best argument for his case that he could imagine, a verdict in his favor was not guaranteed.

As he watched Marie drive away from Plum Street, he imagined that she had a lot of thinking to do. Little did he realize that a block away from his house, she pulled over to see if the ring still fit. It did, and it felt so right on her finger, she did not attempt to remove it. As tears of joy fell from her eyes, she laughed out loud at the irony. Before this trip south, she hadn't been able to put her finger on the one thing missing in her otherwise successful life, and now she had. She knew that from this day forward, the ring would stay on her finger: forever. She could never make up for the lost years, but with his help, she would find that it wasn't necessary. The past is in the past, and only today and tomorrow matter.

She called Paul every evening on her way home, and they often spoke from the suite that Dr. Maitlin continued to allow her and Camille to use.

A few weeks after she left New Orleans, Paul received a long, carefully sealed tube in the mail. Inside, was a new painting and letter, which read:

"Dear Paul,

I will eventually return the painting of us that I took when I left Plum Street so many years ago. Seeing the spot on the wall where it was missing made me sadder than words can express. But until I can return it in person, I'd like you to put this new painting temporarily in its place to fill the void left by the other one. It won't be in proper chronological order like the others, but I hope we can soon change that too. This new painting is another impression of mine, a new hope for us, my vision of what our new house uptown might look like when we give our old house to Camille. But that's about a year or so away. So, no rush… just food for thought!

I love you,
Marie"

As he unrolled the painting, a small photo appeared. It was a picture of Marie and Camille holding each other's hand outstretched toward the photographer. He saw Marie's wedding band on her finger. The painting she sent was a depiction of Marie and him, sitting next to each other in Adirondack style chairs, on a beautiful stone porch with an ivy filled trellis. Young children were laughing and in motion as if chasing one another. *Grandchildren?* he wondered.

He looked for her signature in the usual place on the bottom right, but instead, found a tiny dragonfly. *It was the dragonfly from the day of Ernie's burial, which had become her logo.*

He hung the painting right away, snapping a photo with his phone to send to her.

Later that evening, Paul sat at the kitchen table with his notebook filled with Talulah-isms. Opening it, he turned to one of the few blank pages and titled it: Paul-ism. There he wrote, "*If we only open our eyes while we dream, the possibilities before us can become real.*"

EPILOGUE - VALENTINE'S DAY, 2000

The year before, when Marie returned to Rhode Island, friends and associates immediately began to comment about her "new look". She knew she felt differently, but didn't realize how much it showed. Every day someone would say, "I've never seen you this happy!"

Dr. Maitlin was the first to learn she would be moving away. Although he would miss her tremendously as a colleague and a friend, he was thrilled for her and made plans to visit Louisiana for the renewal of her wedding vows in New Roads.

Marie's experience and references quickly landed her a job with a prestigious Design firm in New Orleans. She planned to start part-time at first to allow time to refocus on their marriage and their new home together.

Paul would soon learn that Camille and Marie had legally changed their last names. They informed him immediately before entering the church in New Roads together on Valentine's Day. Camille was now Camille Morel, and Marie was Marie Landy-Morel.

Life for Paul just kept getting better. He never asked for or expected them to change their names. It was like icing on a beignet… that much sweeter.

So, twenty-one years to the day since Marie and Paul were married in the French Quarter, Father Patrick, a recently ordained and highly respected priest in his hometown, renewed the marital vows between Marie and Paul after Monday morning mass. Camille joined them as they walked down the aisle hand in hand. Everyone was happy for this couple who had lost one another in darkness, only to find the light of love still shining brightly between them. Their reunion brought joy to all.

A reception of celebration followed on the grounds around Pelican's Retreat, the family's home. The reunited couple was surrounded by many family and friends, including Talulah, Delilah, her husband Reginald, and their two young daughters, Faith and Bea. Talulah's friend, Beatrice, had lived just long enough to meet her namesake.

Just days before, everyone had attended Talulah's graduation ceremony in New Orleans. She was not only the oldest person that day to receive a GED diploma, but her smile had provided proof that she was the proudest.

Marie regretted that Paul's paternal grandparents were no longer with them to witness these events. She was comforted to know that they, too, had never given up hope for the couple.

Savannah and her parents were very happy for them both. Marie and Savannah rekindled their relationship from where it first started and would remain best friends for life.

Tables overflowed with food and drink, and even the weather cooperated on this seasonably warm day in February. It didn't take much coaxing from Paul for Talulah and her family to begin a thoughtful and beautiful a cappella rendition of the gospel song, "I Believe". She couldn't have found a more perfect song as the words rang out soft and true:

"I believe for every drop of rain that falls,
A flower grows.
I believe that somewhere in the darkest night,
A candle glows..."

There wasn't a dry eye when they finished this song. Talulah's choice had been perfect. In her usual flare, Talulah picked up the pace with a lively selection of hymns that had everyone clapping under the live oaks. The music ushered up to them and heaven above, moved everyone.

Camille felt at home from the beginning with her newfound family. She was in her second semester at Tulane, and like her father and her aunt Savannah, she was interested in law.

Savannah gave encouraging words to Camille, saying, "Honey, I'm so happy another smart lady like you is going into law! We've got our work cut out for us, trying to straighten up what these men have left undone!" Little did they realize then that someday, Camille would join her aunt and uncle's firm in Baton Rouge.

For now, Camille looked forward to moving into the house on Plum Street. This transition was planned for next semester when she became a sophomore. Her parents would live there until they finished minor renovations on their new home. A dream turned to reality; it was a home in the garden district, which had a porch bearing an uncanny resemblance to her mother's painting.

As the merriment continued into the afternoon, mother, father, and daughter walked together the short distance to the family graveyard. Camille had chosen a picture of Ernie to have affixed to the outside of the crypt. The frame holding the image was picked with her mother and displayed a delicate dragonfly on the corner. Their steps slowed as they approached the well-kept Morel family plot containing several above-ground tombs.

Paul approached Ernie's crypt. It was the one in which his grandparents rested. He turned around to the girls to say, "Camille Savannah Landry, I'd like to introduce you to the spot where your brother Ernie rests. But you won't find him or anyone else here, just his memory. If you doubt that, ask Talulah. We believe he and the rest of our departed family are having a grand time together in Heaven, and they are also present here now, circling us with love. One day, we will all meet on the other side again, because *love conquers all."*

Camille kissed the picture before her Dad affixed it to the stone. With joined hands, they walked back to their new life together.

THE END

TO OUR READERS

What would any author be without their readers? Thank *you* for joining us! I have always included a lot about myself in my books, and this time, my wife, Felicia Elise Gros, enmeshed herself and has done an extraordinary job of bringing the characters in *Talulah's Pie,* to life. Together we crafted a true to life love story and hope you have enjoyed it!

Since 2017, with the release of my first book, *Cold Silence of Deception,* I've been busy. Following the genre of action/adventure my next book was one of historical fiction, *Surrogate of Betrayal.* The story, near and dear to me, is about men who returned from the war in Vietnam. It detailed how the war affected them and their families. My third book, *Cut from the Fold,* is a murder mystery released earlier this year. It is packed with twists and turns. If you've not read it, you'll have to find out!

I was so pleased that my wife, Felicia, joined me in the creation of *Talulah's Pie.* Without her advice and comments, this book would never have been what it is. Louisiana is part of us, and we could easily visualize the scenes played out in this book.

Thank you all for your support. *It is an honor that so many take the time to comment and leave reviews on Amazon.* It is all greatly appreciated!

All the best,
Eric Redmon & Felicia Gros
Winchester, Virginia
2020

ALSO BY ERIC REDMON

Eric Redmon is an author of three other novels:

Cut from the Fold

Surrogate of Betrayal

Cold Silence of Deception

For more details and to find your next book, search for
Eric Redmon & Felicia Gros,
on Amazon.

Thank you!
Be well, be happy, and stay safe!

Made in USA - Kendallville, IN
1179764_9780578720395
10.13.2020 1017